T0137558

"Lucy Dillon's latest offering is the perfect Christmas stocking filler—especially for animal lovers. . . . Shut out the world on a cold winter's night with this entertaining and easy-to-read tale." **—*News of the World* (U.K.)**

PRAISE FOR

Lost Dogs and Lonely Hearts

"Fun and romantic. *Marley and Me* fans will love it."
—*Closer* (U.K.)

"This is the perfect read for a cold winter's night."
—*News of the World* (U.K.)

"An easy, tongue-in-cheek romp . . . A contemporary Bridget Jones, but with canines instead of chardonnay." —*Stylist* (U.K.)

"I loved this book! Heartwarming, real, and entertaining."
—Katie Fforde, author of *Love Letters* and *Wedding Season*

"Dillon has a real knack for creating mini-stories within an overall arc, and pulling them together gradually in time for a nice crescendo ending. . . . It's funny and charming . . . a fabulous story that you won't want to put down, guaranteed to warm the heart of even the most devout *non-dog* person." —*The Bookbag*

"In this engaging and stirring novel, Dillon vividly evokes the lives of three women and their unexpectedly connected fates . . . a beautiful and gripping tale of loss, friendship, and starting over that will tug at readers' heartstrings and keep them hooked till the very end." —*Publishers Weekly*

"Only the hardest of hearts could refuse to cheer for this warm, entertaining, uplifting story of dogs and people rescuing each other." —*Booklist*

Berkley titles by Lucy Dillon

Walking Back to Happiness
Lost Dogs and Lonely Hearts

Walking Back to Happiness

LUCY DILLON

BERKLEY BOOKS, NEW YORK

THE BERKLEY PUBLISHING GROUP
Published by the Penguin Group
Penguin Group (USA) Inc.
375 Hudson Street, New York, New York 10014, USA
Penguin Group (Canada), 90 Eglinton Avenue East, Suite 700, Toronto, Ontario M4P 2Y3, Canada
(a division of Pearson Penguin Canada Inc.)
Penguin Books Ltd., 80 Strand, London WC2R 0RL, England
Penguin Group Ireland, 25 St. Stephen's Green, Dublin 2, Ireland (a division of Penguin Books Ltd.)
Penguin Group (Australia), 250 Camberwell Road, Camberwell, Victoria 3124, Australia
(a division of Pearson Australia Group Pty. Ltd.)
Penguin Books India Pvt. Ltd., 11 Community Centre, Panchsheel Park, New Delhi—110 017, India
Penguin Group (NZ), 67 Apollo Drive, Rosedale, Auckland 0632, New Zealand
(a division of Pearson New Zealand Ltd.)
Penguin Books (South Africa) (Pty.) Ltd., 24 Sturdee Avenue, Rosebank, Johannesburg 2196,
South Africa

Penguin Books Ltd., Registered Offices: 80 Strand, London WC2R 0RL, England

This book is an original publication of The Berkley Publishing Group.

Cover photograph by Janie Airy / Getty Images. Cover design by Rita Frangie.
Interior text design by Laura K. Corless.

PRINTING HISTORY
Berkley trade paperback edition / December 2011

Library of Congress Cataloging-in-Publication Data

Dillon, Lucy, 1974–
Walking back to happiness / Lucy Dillon.—Berkley trade paperback ed.
p. cm.
ISBN 978-0-425-24479-1
1. Single women—Fiction. 2. Dogs—Fiction. 3. Human-animal relationships—Fiction. 4. Self-realization in women—Fiction. I. Title.
PR6104.I43W35 2011
823'.92—dc23

2011023463

146122990

Chapter 1

Ben and Juliet Falconer's Jack Russell–ish terrier was called Minton because on the way to the rescue center to choose their new puppy, Ben heard a terrible joke on the radio about a dog called Minton who'd swallowed a shuttlecock. He'd been a bad dog. *Bad* Minton.

"Bad Minton!" Ben had yelled gleefully. "That is *the* best name for a dog!"

They'd been driving out of Longhampton, just past the big cherry tree that flooded the crest of the hill with a champagne pop of pink blossom. It was three years ago, on the May bank holiday—the first day Ben had taken off in months. Juliet could remember exactly how he'd looked as he'd turned in his seat, brown eyes crinkling with the rubbishness of the joke. "Bad Minton! Do you get it, Jools? Badminton? Ha-ha, ha-ha-ha!"

That moment stuck in Juliet's mind because of two things that were so typically Ben. One was the giggle that bubbled unexpectedly out of his rugged, outdoorsy frame, an infectious delight that had always made her smile too, from the first time she'd heard it—over an equally terrible joke—at school.

The other was the cherry tree. Ben loved it. He was a landscape gardener and had a geeky passion for trees in general, but that one was his favorite in the whole town. They never drove past it in spring without him making her promise that if he died before her, she'd have a big cherry tree planted so at least she could look at the cascading, ballerina-skirt blossom and be happy, once a year.

Juliet couldn't bear to think about that now. She'd found a different way to drive out of Longhampton because even seeing the tree made her vision blur dangerously at the wheel.

The scruffy little terrier they'd been shown at the rescue center had been called Dodger, but once he and Ben laid eyes on each other, he was Minton. With his eager eyes and wagging stump of a tail, he looked the type of dog who'd eat a shuttlecock just to make his master laugh. He'd run through *sit*, *beg*, and *down* while they were still talking to the rescue manager.

Minton gazed sadly at Juliet from his basket. He was the color of double cream, apart from one brown patch over his left eye. She'd suggested Patch. Or Captain Hook. It had fallen on deaf ears; Minton and Ben were already shaking hands.

Minton was always Ben's dog, despite the fact that Juliet fed him, cleaned up after him, and prized the socks out of his mouth. Ben took him to work, sitting up front in his van's passenger seat, and it was Ben's long stride that Minton scampered happily to keep up with. Minton and Juliet were best friends now, though. Sometimes she wondered who was looking after whom.

"Juliet, you look tired. Are you eating?"

She nodded at him.

"Juliet!"

Juliet squinted. She could have sworn Minton had rolled his eyes at her.

Reluctantly, she tore her gaze away from him and directed it toward her mother. Diane was sitting on the sheet-covered chair, her knees clamped together. Her kind face was taut with worry—and the effort of not showing it. Ben had always said she wasn't so much a "the glass is half full" sort as a "the glass is half empty and made of *glass*" natural worrier.

"You're *not* eating," she went on. "I've just had a look in your fridge. All that food I sent over last week is still in there. All out of date now. And it was nice stuff too," she added, with a touch of resentment. "Ready meals. So you wouldn't have to cook."

"Mum, I'm fine. Do I look like I'm fading away?"

Diane squinted at her daughter. "Yes," she said. "Actually, you do."

Juliet knew for a fact that she didn't. Ten years as a professional caterer, specializing in cupcakes for weddings and gourmet biscuits, meant she'd laid down a fair store of emergency flab rations that she was nowhere near depleting yet. Granted, she didn't feel much like plowing through a steak and kidney pie, even a luxury one with organic pastry, but it was amazing how well Kit Kats still went down. She could eat a whole packet. Sometimes she did. There was no one there to tell her not to.

Juliet looked down at her hands, which *were* now looking older, and thinner. There were fine lines around her gold wedding band. Proper widow's hands. It gave her a morbid sense of satisfaction, something she could thrust at all those people whose faces said, "But you're too young to be a widow!"—as if losing the one person who held her entire life in his heart were somehow less devastating, less *real*, because she was only thirty-one.

"You need to get some fresh air." Diane left a cunning pause.

"Minton needs more exercise. You're letting him down, keeping him cooped up in here with you."

Any hint of neglect toward Ben's dog always nipped Juliet into a response. "I *am* walking him!" she protested.

"When?"

"When I go to Tesc—" She stopped, and looked up.

Diane met her eyes, and her expression was woebegone. Juliet knew she knew. There was no point denying it, and something in her mother's face—confusion, not just pity—made her jut out her chin and finish.

"When I go to Tesco," she said. "I walk him then."

"And *when* are you going to Tesco?" persisted Diane.

Juliet didn't answer.

"Kathy Gibbon saw you," Diane said. "She was coming back off her shift at the hospital. She saw you in the car park. Oh, Juliet! What sort of person does their shopping at *four in the morning*?"

"The sort of person who likes to go to the supermarket when it's nice and quiet. When it's not full of people asking me how I'm coping." Juliet patted her knee and Minton leaped up to her side, leaning into her with his firm body. "Minton doesn't mind. He's got one of those balls with a light in it. It's fun. Isn't it?" she added, to him.

Minton closed his eyes with pleasure as she scratched behind his ears. Making Minton happy was simple.

"But I *worry* about you, wandering around in the middle of the night on your own." Diane's voice wavered, her head clearly thronging with the full range of horrors that could befall a woman and a small dog in Longhampton's retail park in the wee small hours. "Anything could happen!"

It nearly made Juliet laugh, in an ironic sort of way. Being mugged would take her mind off everything else.

"Mum," she said, very reasonably, "what's the worst thing that could happen to me? My husband died eight months ago, I'm a cook who can't work because I can't taste anything, and our so-called forever house is going to have to be forever, with the property market like this. Being mugged doesn't worry me. I could use the compensation to pay for the new bathroom."

Diane's pale eyes widened in cartoon shock behind her glasses and Juliet missed Ben for the fifth time that day, this time for his cheerfully black sense of humor. They'd been the only ones in the family with *any* sense of humor, come to that.

It's the little things I miss you for most, she thought, bracing herself against the melancholy that washed over her whole body, even now. *I just can't get used to moments like these, when I feel worse than on my own, because you'd have laughed, and it'd have become one of those in-jokes.*

She flinched at the thought of the long strands of in-jokes they'd stored up over fifteen years, gone in a blink.

"Have there been attacks?" Diane demanded. "In the retail park?"

"No, it's perfectly safe, Mum." Juliet could have kicked herself: That would be going on Diane and Louise's list of "Places That Were Too Dangerous to Take Toby." The soft-play area where someone's toddler had eaten a marble, the coffee shop on the High Street that allows dogs inside, now the retail park.

Minton hadn't settled. He was still turning round and round on Juliet's knee, unable to find a comfy spot. He'd always been sociable, but now he seemed to share Juliet's resentment at having their solitude interrupted.

"Poor little fella." Diane sighed. "Is he still sleeping by Ben's—"

"Yes," said Juliet shortly. "Shall I make us a cup of tea?" She got up, glad of the chance to move.

Diane and Minton trailed after her into the kitchen, which still had no cupboards or countertops or proper floor. Or tiles. She and Ben had been brainstorming ideas for their ideal kitchen the day before he died, blithely ripping out the old MDF units, thinking they'd be replaced soon enough. Magazine pages were still Sellotaped to the bare plaster, creased and tatty now.

Juliet could sense her mother looking around at the mess, assessing the exposed wires and sharp edges. Her sister, Louise, had been over a few times with Toby, her son, but she kept him firmly in the sitting room, or strapped in his buggy, if she could get away with it.

"You know, I could ask your dad to come round and sort out the plastering," said Diane, as if it had just occurred to her. "He's quite handy with the Polyfilla."

"That's very kind, but it's okay." Juliet unplugged the toaster from the adapter and plugged the kettle in. Her dad, Eric, was already "popping in" to tidy up the garden for her once a week. That was fine; it was a family joke that Juliet had whatever the opposite of a green thumb was, and besides, Dad liked gardening. He said it was because he couldn't bear to see Ben's efforts go to seed, but Juliet suspected he didn't trust her with sharp implements. She was so spacey these days that she'd probably take her own foot off if she had to mow the lawn.

The decorating was something else entirely, though, and she didn't want any interference from her family, however well-meaning. She and Ben had had grand ideas for the kitchen, the heart of their forever house. They were going to buy an Aga (cream, reconditioned), with a whistling kettle and clothes-drying rack. Minton would curl up against it in winter, and she'd make jam and drop scones on it. If she closed her eyes, Juliet could still hear Ben telling her about renovating the original Victorian tiles, and custom-building shelves, and how he was going to make a baker's paradise.

They were the plans. For the time being, Juliet was still using the toaster and the travel kettle she'd had at college.

"It's better that it's all left as it is," she said stubbornly, feeling her mother's despairing glances at the chaos.

"But you've got to live here, darling," said Diane. "Life goes on." The last word was swallowed up in a guilty gulp. Juliet knew without turning round that her mother had her hand to her mouth; she could see her stricken reflection in the mirror opposite. "Sorry, I didn't mean . . ."

Juliet got out a cloth and wiped the toast crumbs from her breakfast off the counter. "I'm going to get builders in. They'll want to see it as it is. Give them a better sense of what needs doing."

"You've been saying that for weeks. I know it's hard, but Ben wouldn't want you to be living in a house with no proper shower." Diane was trying to be firm, but her voice cracked. "Let me call Keith. He did a lovely job on our conservatory. You'll barely know he's there. If it's money, your dad and I can tide you over. Just a couple of rooms. Just so I know you're not living in a building site."

Something tightened inside Juliet, like cling film wrapping round her heart, suffocating her. *I don't want anything to be changed in here,* she thought. She'd got over that initial paralysis, where even experiencing a birthday without Ben seemed like a betrayal, but she couldn't bring herself to call the builders. This had been *their* project. Their forever house. She didn't want to turn it into a forever house Ben would never share.

The kettle boiled and Juliet reached out for it, but Diane stopped her.

"Juliet," she said, "I can't sleep for worrying about you. Your dad can't sleep for worrying about both of us. Please. Let us pay for you to get a decent shower put in."

"*Please* don't worry about me." Juliet gently freed her hand and reached for the mugs. Wedding presents. Pink Emma Bridgewater hearts. "I'm actually . . ."

The banging set up again from next door, drowning out her words.

"You're what?" Diane yelled over the racket.

"I'm fine, honestly!"

Juliet guessed that the Kelly children were playing their human Mouse Trap game—or that was what she pictured going on from the clattering, yelling, and general muffled noise of small feet jumping over stuff. They did it a couple of times an afternoon, starting from the top of the house, running along the landing, then down the stairs, along the hallway and into the garden, accompanied by whatever selection of animals they were currently looking after for their school.

It never took them long to reach the garden. It wasn't a huge house, the semidetached mirror image of Juliet's. They were Laburnum Villa; she was Myrtle Villa. They were squat houses with elegant double fronts, two stories plus attic, long gardens with raspberry canes, a compost heap, and a shared apple tree, red front doors. They both had wooden floorboards.

Juliet knew all about the wooden floorboards. One of the Kelly girls had got tap shoes for some birthday or other and practiced a lot.

Diane flinched as feet bumped down the bare stairs. "What the hell is going on next door?"

"Don't worry, they'll stop at half past five. That's when tea gets dished out."

"But I thought your next-door neighbor was that nice old body who ran the mobile library. Wendy, wasn't it?"

"She moved . . ." Juliet had to raise her voice as a particularly loud bang ricocheted off the wall behind them. "Wendy moved a while back and the Kellys bought it. They've got four kids. He works away. Not sure what she does. I think they've a lodger."

The cacophony moved into the back garden, drifting through the kitchen windows. A girl's voice was shouting something about "clearing the VIP area," and there was a frenzied shrieking. Minton slunk over to his basket and curled up, paws tucked beneath him. He hadn't been formally introduced to next door. He wasn't exactly clamoring to make the acquaintance of the cat Juliet had spotted lurking in her rosebushes.

There was another paint-cracking bang. Diane winced, and Juliet smiled wanly and passed her a mug of coffee.

"How do you put up with that all day?" she asked. "I'd have back-to-back migraines."

"Oh, I suppose I tune it out. At least they're not playing computer games." Juliet had no idea why she was defending the Kellys. She didn't even know what all their names were. There were two girls, two boys, she knew that much, and they all had red hair, and one of the boys had asthma attacks. At regular intervals, someone would yell, "Quick, where's Spike's inhaler?" and there would be more stampeding.

"Is anyone in charge of them?" Diane went over to the window and peered out over what would have been Juliet's vegetable patch, trying to get a glimpse through the ragged box hedge that separated the two long gardens. "Dear God, they've got a trampoline. They've got a *cat* on the trampoline!"

"Their mum's around somewhere. Kit Kat?" Juliet helped herself and dunked one finger in the hot coffee.

"Thank you but I won't," said Diane. "Dr. Dryden's told me to watch my sugars. Juliet, love, don't take this the wrong way, but if you're not going to sort out builders, what about getting a cleaner in? Once a week, just to run a duster over the place."

"I'm fine, Mum."

"I'd pay for it. It would be a swap." Diane hesitated. "A favor for a favor, if you like."

Juliet eyed her mother with some suspicion. "Favors" were usually thinly veiled attempts to prize her out of her house in the name of social rehabilitation. Diane and Louise had let a decent amount of time pass after the funeral, but then they'd started to come up with these "favors"—most recently, a plea to do Diane's Saturday morning dog-walking stint at the rescue center on the hill. Three walks in five hours and as many bacon sandwiches as she could eat.

Juliet had declined. She had her own dog to walk, thank you.

Diane looked more guilty than anxious, though, and Juliet caved in.

"You don't need to bribe me to do you a favor," she said. "I don't need a cleaner. What do you want me to do?"

"Look after Coco for me. Just two or three days during the week."

Juliet frowned..That wasn't what she'd been expecting; if anything, her mum had been taking Minton for the odd walk, along with Coco, their elderly chocolate Lab. Coco was twelve and, apart from mild flatulence caused by Dad slipping her sausages against the vet's strict instructions, had absolutely no faults whatsoever.

"Why?"

"Because I'm going to be looking after Toby at mine."

"So? Coco'll just take herself off to her bed and watch telly in the kitchen, won't she? That's what she does normally." Juliet looked down at her mug and realized she'd nearly finished her coffee. It was amazing how fast she could drink coffee these days. It barely touched the sides; somehow the heat didn't register the way it used to. Another weird side effect of Ben's death. All her senses felt dulled. Planed down smooth, like the floorboards they'd started to strip down in the sitting room. Sometimes she wondered if she'd ever feel sharp-edged emotions again, and if not, whether that was necessarily a bad thing.

Juliet got up to put the kettle back on. Moving stopped the thoughts.

"Anyway, can't Dad take her out for a walk?" she added, over her shoulder.

"Well, no. He'll be out at his Welsh class."

"His *what*?"

"It's just a summer school, not a full course." Since taking early retirement Eric had racked up nearly all the Foundation courses at the local college. As he liked to tell people, he could complain about the food in most European countries. "I'll be on my own."

"So? What difference does that make?"

"Louise is a bit bothered about Coco being around toddlers. She says—and she's quite right to have her concerns, Juliet; you see it in the papers all the time—she says that dogs that aren't used to children can never be trusted one hundred percent. She thinks it'd be nicer for Coco to be somewhere else entirely, rather than shut out in the garden . . ."

"That's big of her."

". . . and I thought, since you weren't back at work yet, it wouldn't be much of a hardship for Coco to come round here." Diane didn't draw breath, which made Juliet wonder just how long she'd been rehearsing this on her way over. "You could take them both out for a walk. It'd do Minton good to get some daylight. Vitamin D."

Juliet made fresh coffee without speaking and then put her mug down on an old copy of *Ideal Home* from August 2009. There'd been a time when she'd bought them all, every month. It seemed a bit ridiculous now. A Belfast sink was a Belfast sink, and anyway, she didn't have the money.

"Say something, Juliet." Diane fidgeted with her scarf. "You know I hate it when you go silent on me."

"I'm not being silent. I'm just . . ." Not used to talking to people in real time. Answering machines and e-mails had allowed Juliet to keep everything at a safe distance, giving her time to fashion a response that wouldn't make her sound mad, as she so often did these days.

She felt a twist of irritation at being put on the spot, especially on account of her sister's ridiculous Precious First Born–itis. "Poor Coco. Booted out of her own house just because she has paws. What's she going to do? Fart on him? You shouldn't encourage Louise when she's like this, you know, Mum. Since she had Toby she acts as if every room's a death trap."

Diane winced at the word *death*.

"Don't. If anyone's allowed to say that, I am." Juliet's pulse surged with recklessness. She really could say whatever she wanted for the first time in her life: No one seemed to hold anything against her. "Coco's not going to savage Toby. Or has Louise decided that since she can't wet-wipe a Labrador, they're banned?"

"There's no need for sarcasm," said Diane. "She's entitled to her opinion. You see things differently when you're a mum."

Juliet's fizzing mood flattened in an instant, and she pushed the tip of her tongue against her teeth. This was the single emotion that cut through the general ache: bitter regret for the future she'd lost too. It kept leaping on her when she looked at Toby and saw Peter, Louise's husband, in his worried eyebrows, and realized she'd never see Ben's cheeky grin in a chubby baby face now. His genes were gone, and she had only herself to blame.

Diane was still talking. "It's only fair that I support Louise, the way I've been there for you," she went on. "Not that I begrudge a single second, and I thank God that we're practically on the doorstep, but Louise needs a hand now, and I think it's about time you got yourself out and about."

Juliet opened her mouth to say something about her sister's need for any help from anyone, but something stopped her. Ben's gentle hand on her back. He'd defused so many bickering family moments before they sparked into a row.

Juliet had one sister, Louise, who had been perfect from an early age, and one less perfect but equally ambitious brother, Ian, who had emigrated to Australia and married a personal trainer called Vanda, with whom he had two little girls. Louise had the legal career, the two cars, and the designer house; Juliet had the happy marriage to her childhood sweetheart, just like Mum and Dad; Ian had the freedom to do whatever he wanted without fear of interference, and a deep tan.

Until Ben had died, and Juliet had gone back to being the youngest child everyone had to help and talk to as if she were nine. Particularly Louise, who wasn't nearly as grateful as she should be to have Peter, a man who . . .

Deep breath, she thought. That was what Ben had said whenever she'd paused to scream silently into the hall mirror during a phone call. *Take one slow, deep breath and imagine you're a tree with long roots in the cool ground.*

"What's Louise doing that she needs you to babysit?" she asked, instead.

"Going back to work," said Diane. Her expression struggled between pride and concern and finally settled on pride. "She's finally negotiated flexible hours. Don't look so surprised! She's been trying for ages. They don't get many Crown Prosecution solicitors of her caliber round here." She nodded toward the local paper she'd brought, still unopened on the counter. "And goodness knows we need them. Did you *see* what was on the front of the *Longhampton Gazette* this week? That business about the vandalism?"

"I don't think Louise personally stops crimes happening," said Juliet.

"I do," said Diane. "They don't get off when she's prosecuting. They know that."

"But didn't she say she wanted to be a full-time mum when Toby was born?" Juliet forced herself not to do a sarcastic impression of the smug lectures they'd suffered about the importance of a Play-Doh-wielding mother figure in a child's formative years. "I thought Peter was fine about her staying at home while he went out and played computer games for a living?"

"He doesn't play computer games. He *designs* them. As well you know. Anyway, it's not about that," said Diane. "She's spent a lot of time working her way up. She shouldn't throw it away."

That was such a 180-degree swivel from her previous position that Diane blushed while Juliet's jaw dropped open. Luckily for both of them, the yelling started up in the garden with new ferocity.

As Diane made a cat's-bum face at the racket, it occurred to Juliet that the alternative to sitting Coco might be sitting Toby while her mother looked after Minton. That she definitely wasn't up for, for any number of reasons.

"Whatever," she said, raising her voice above the cacophony. "Bring Coco round."

"Thanks, love," said Diane. "Tuesday, Wednesday, alternate Thursdays. Now then," she added, the serious business dispensed with, "I might just spoil myself with a Kit Kat . . ."

As she dipped into the biscuit barrel, something clattered against the kitchen window and a shriek went up. Something about Spike's inhaler.

Chapter 2

Louise had made a list the night before of all the things she needed to do before leaving for her first day back at work, but it hadn't calmed her down. If anything, it made her panic that she'd forgotten something really important, and wouldn't realize until she was back in her office.

Eighteen months she'd been off, with Toby. It felt like a lot longer. It felt like starting again as a trainee, with the butterflies in her stomach.

She slugged back a mouthful of lukewarm coffee and blinked at the neat column of tasks, bullet-pointed in order of importance.

Pack Toby's day bag. She was doing that now.

Defrost Toby's lunch/pack in cool bag.

Remind Peter re nursery direct debit. Even part-time, it was stretching them. Peter had kept his gym membership, but hers had gone. Thank God for her mother.

Check Juliet up/awake.

She grimaced, then picked up the kitchen phone and pressed

the speed-dial button for her sister. It was impossible to predict what mood you'd get with Juliet. Spacey and miserable was the best option. Openly hostile and/or crying was the worst. Louise hated hearing her cry, but she wasn't good at vague comfort, like her mother was, and she'd run out of helpful, practical things to say. Juliet had never been the easiest person to help.

It rang several times, and then Juliet answered, with a sleepy yawn.

Louise glanced at the clock. Ten to eight. This didn't bode well for her schedule.

"Morning," she said brightly, tapping her nail against the marble counter. Pale pink speed-dry varnish. Slapped on last night in an attempt to bolster her confidence. "Up and about?"

"Yes," said Juliet.

"All set to drive over to Mum's? To get Coco?"

"There's no need to remind me, I am aware of the orders." Juliet's voice sounded teenage on the phone. Cross and resentful—and deliberately pushing it. "Remind me again why we all have to go to Mum's? You're nearer."

"Mum doesn't have the right kind of car seat for Toby."

"What? She's got some sort of seat in the back of her car, hasn't she?"

Louise removed the spoon from Toby's fat little hands and wiped his face. He looked cross, about as cross as Juliet sounded, and Louise flinched. He *knew* she was planning to abandon him. He had Peter's eyes: trusting and blinky.

"It's not the right one. Don't say anything—she went to a lot of bother. I'm going to swap it."

Juliet made a noise. "How did she get the wrong one? I thought you had a nursery list. I mean, there was only one suitable baby sling, wasn't there? And one bouncer?"

Louise ignored the tone in Juliet's voice, the same way she tuned out the defense solicitor's insinuating tones in court. Just the facts.

"I'm dealing with it. But in the meantime, it's easier if I drop Toby off and you go round to get Coco. Before eight fifteen, ideally." She wiped the side of the high chair as she spoke, then dropped the wipe into the bin.

"And what if I don't have the right sort of car for the dog?"

Oh, stop it, Juliet, thought Louise. *We're all tired. We're all stressed.*

"You do," she said patiently. "Ben took Minton to work every day in the exact van that's parked outside your house. Coco will be fine in the back."

There was a pause. Louise didn't like doing this to Juliet, forcing her out of her shell like a reluctant crab, but it was the only way. Sometimes it was better when there was only one way. That was her current mantra: forward, forward, forward, and don't look back.

She turned to put Toby's empty breakfast bowl in the dishwasher and her eye snagged on the long, framed photo of her wedding day, hanging in pride of place over the kitchen table. The brand-new Mr. and Mrs. Davies, caught in the three different stages of their first dance: in a romantic ballroom hold, then Peter's arm slung round her waist as she tipped trustingly backward, then the *Dirty Dancing* lift they'd practiced for weeks, way before it was fashionable to have big, showstopping, choreographed numbers.

All two hundred guests were gazing openmouthed in their direction, clearly wowed by geeky Peter and cool Louise transformed into slick dancers, but she and Peter were locked in each other's eyes, as if there were no one else there.

They looked familiar, but that wasn't her. It certainly wasn't Peter. Not just because they were thinner and polished; something else was different. They looked like a couple. And, Louise realized with a guilty start, that six years on, the first thing she noticed about the photo was how elegant the table settings looked.

She pulled herself up. She was *lucky* to have her husband. Reliable, cheerful Peter, who'd turned his passion for computers into a profitable software company. Peter, who joked that he'd never leave her, because that would mean dismantling their wireless setup. Even talking to Juliet made her feel pathetically grateful that it wasn't her sitting in a half-decorated dump, smelling of dogs and only eating Kit Kats.

Louise forced a cheerful note into her voice. Juliet responded very badly to pity.

"I'm setting off now, so if you leave in the next five minutes, we'll dovetail perfectly. You don't even have to get dressed. Put a coat on over your pajamas if you want—it's what most of the school-run mums do."

"I get dressed in the mornings," said Juliet huffily. "I'm a widow, not an invalid."

"Good. I'm glad to hear it!"

The bathroom door opened upstairs and then three seconds later, Peter's feet trotted down the stairs, the same perky one-two-three, one-two-three gallop she heard every morning. He swept past her, smelling of mouthwash and aftershave, heading for the kitchen to pick up the apple for his lunchbox. She knew, from the detailed explanation over last night's dinner, that his small company was doing some kind of communal health kick.

"Morning," he called out as he passed. "Hello, my big boy!" he went on, in much more enthusiastic tones, seeing Toby in his high chair. Toby clapped his hands with delight, and Louise suppressed a twinge of irritation. Fed, dressed, and washed was Toby's natural state as far as Peter was concerned, never mind the hour it had taken to get him to that stage while Peter was getting ready for work.

"Was that Peter? He sounds cheerful," observed Juliet. "I thought Toby was teething?"

"Peter has the luxury of earplugs." Louise followed him into the kitchen, trying not to catch her own haggard reflection in the hall mirror. "I'll be there in twenty minutes, okay? Please don't be late. It's my first day back and I know they'll all be waiting for me to turn up late covered in sick."

"Isn't it normally your clients who turn up covered in sick?"

"Very funny. Come on, we need to leave."

"What time can I bring Coco back to Mum's?"

"Five-ish? I should be back by five." Louise ignored the whine in Juliet's voice and began to gather the various color-coded bags together: Toby's toys, his food, a change of clothes. All prepared the night before while Peter was upstairs "researching" some online game. "I appreciate this."

"It's not a problem. I'd never forgive myself if Toby got some dog hair in his yogurt."

"No one's—"

"Dogs aren't all slavering killers, you know."

"I'm not saying they are," said Louise. She didn't have the time or the inclination to let Juliet get on her doggy soapbox, but she could feel herself being drawn into one of their routine squabbles. "But Mum can't be everywhere at once. She'd never forgive herself if Toby shoved a pencil up Coco's nose or something. Look, why are you taking this so personally? It's not personal."

"I'm not."

"Is it because I didn't ask you to babysit?"

"No!" Juliet sounded horrified. "I just . . ."

There was a pause at the end of the line that Louise might have listened to more carefully if she hadn't been trying to juggle the phone and extract Toby from his chair, while indicating to Peter that the washing machine needed emptying before he left the house. "Fine," she said instead. "I'll see you at Mum's. Fifteen minutes."

Juliet's Victorian villa was in a suburb of Longhampton called Rosehill, a pub-and-church village that had been swallowed up as the town sprawled outward in the prosperous years before the war when Longhampton had temporarily been the jam-and-preserve capital of the Midlands.

Her parents lived on the other side of town in an executive new-build estate that had what her dad called "decent-sized garages." Getting over there meant tackling Longhampton's complicated one-way system, something Juliet enjoyed doing only at night. At night, she could sweep around the empty lanes, letting the signs dictate her route round the ornate redbrick town hall and the park with its stiff-necked tulips that Ben had always laughed at. At rush hour, however, it was clogged with angry, impatient traffic.

Juliet was only at the first of five roundabouts and hadn't moved for ten minutes. The tension headache that had started as she left the security of her house intensified as the radio kept reminding her that she was going to be late, then later, and her knuckles whitened on the steering wheel.

The van was heating up, and it seemed to release traces of Ben's familiar smell. Soap. Earth. Sweat. But there was nowhere to pull over and cry, like she could at night, so Juliet swallowed and turned up the radio, forcing herself to sing so she wouldn't think.

It wasn't great, but it was an improvement on the weeks when she couldn't even open the van door, and her dad had had to run it round the block for her to keep the battery charged.

She struggled through the traffic, keeping her cool for Minton's safety's sake, and finally parked outside her mum's house, where Louise's Citroën Picasso was already outside. Coco was sitting on the doorstep, an anxious expression on her elderly face. If she'd had a label and a little suitcase, she couldn't have looked more tragic, thought Juliet.

"At last!" Diane came rushing out. She had an apron tied over her navy slacks, a cloth in one hand and Dettol spray in the other. "Are you okay?"

"I'm fine," said Juliet. She opened her door, leaving Minton sticking his nose out of the gap in the passenger window.

"We were starting to get worried." Diane was peering at her, checking for signs of widowly meltdown. "We thought you . . . Well, you're here now. Come on in, Louise is just getting Toby settled."

Juliet wanted to point out that Louise was only going back to work, not going into space. It was just another step in her perfect life plan. *She* was the one who no longer had a life plan.

"Oh, finally," said Louise when she entered the kitchen.

It was spotless. Diane's standards had ramped right up with the arrival of Toby. She'd even bought a steam cleaner to meet Louise's exacting criteria on hygiene, and the kitchen smelled pine fresh. Juliet noted that she was the only person wearing shoes, including her dad, who was keeping well out of it in the sitting room, studying a *Guide to Wales* with his beige-socked feet up on a stool and his reading glasses perched on his bald head.

"Hello, Dad!" she called through.

"Bore da, Juliet cariad! Shw mae?" he said, then added, "Don't ask me anything else, it's as far as we've got."

Louise rolled her eyes and unpacked some home-frozen food from the cool bag. "Any excuse to get out of the house," she muttered.

"Just because I'm old doesn't mean my brain's gone," said Eric. "Or my hearing."

"*Bore da*, Toby," said Juliet.

Toby gazed solemnly back at her from the table with Peter's round brown eyes, topped with Louise's blond hair. Though she'd never actually said it out loud, Juliet was always reminded of penguins when she saw Toby. Fluffy, serious penguin chicks, regarding the world from under Louise's protective feet.

"Well done, you, for driving over here in the traffic." Diane appeared from the hall, closed the door behind her to keep Coco at bay, and grabbed Juliet's hands. She squeezed them, as she would a small child. "That's another hurdle you're over, eh? The roundabouts in rush hour!"

Juliet smiled wanly.

"Now, I've made a list." Diane dug in her bag and handed her a piece of paper. "It's very important that you take Coco out before eleven. She always needs to do a"—she dropped her voice—"a *solid toilet* after breakfast but before her main walk. I usually take her out at lunchtime, once round the park, and up to the woods alternate days. Today's a woods day. She likes to be on the lead going up, but not coming back—it makes her feel more grown up. I haven't fed her because going in the car makes her gassy, so here's a bag with her kibble. Try her on half a cup before—"

Louise and Juliet both stared at their mother.

"Mum, I do have a dog," said Juliet.

"And dogs don't need to feel *grown up*," said Louise. "That's the most ridiculous thing I've ever heard. I need to get a move on—I'm late already." She grabbed a purple file marked *Toby: Routine* from the breakfast bar. "There's everything you need in here, plus all the phone numbers if there are any problems."

As she handed the thick file to Diane, Juliet wondered if children came with operating instructions after all. It certainly looked as if Toby's full warranty were in there.

"There won't be any *problems*," trilled her mother. "Toby's going to have a lovely day with Granny, isn't he?"

Toby said nothing. He just stared back at Mummy, Auntie Jools, and Granny, and blinked.

Diane hadn't been lying about one thing: Coco was a gassy traveler, breakfast or not. Juliet had only got halfway to the roundabout when the first wafts of nervous Labrador came drifting back from the depths of the van. She pressed on regardless: Her one aim now was to get home, close the door, and put the kettle on, so she could sink into another day of soothing, day-filling television, with Minton curled up on her knee. Coco too, if she felt like it.

Diane's list lay accusingly on the dashboard, in the nonslip tray where Ben used to put his phone and job notes. Juliet glanced over at it while the lights by the town hall were on red; it was a timetable.

Her mother had actually written out a *timetable* for the dog.

Well, she can forget that, thought Juliet. *I'm doing her a favor here. It's not like Coco's fitted with an odometer. She's not going to know if we've spent the day watching* Homes Under the Hammer *or scaling Longhampton Ridge.* Maybe Coco would prefer a day's relaxation.

"How about it, Coco?" she called back. "Feet up? Face pack?"

Coco didn't respond, but a fruity waft of something drifted forward. Juliet opened Minton's window and, safe in his harness, he stuck his nose out, letting his ears flap in the breeze.

Chapter 3

Louise sucked in her stomach and inched the waistband of her work skirt down until the hem covered her knees. It was, she had to admit, a bit on the tight side.

She'd had plenty of time in the last three weeks to try on her old court suits before her first day back at work and, if necessary, buy some new ones, but that was one item on her to-do list she'd ignored. Not just because she couldn't face the unforgiving changing-room lights after two years of the same three pairs of stretchy Lycra yoga pants, but because she didn't actually *want* new clothes.

Louise just wanted everything to be back exactly where it was when she'd gone on maternity leave. Right down to her navy Margaret Howell suits and the takeaway coffee she'd picked up from the café that was still, thankfully, run by the same people she remembered.

She paused in front of the brass plaque outside the CPS office building next to the Magistrates' Court and ruffled her newly cut hair, trying to get the lift the hairstylist had got into it. There was a fine line between choppy and mumsy, and she wasn't sure which side she'd fallen on.

She frowned and peered nearer; was it the brass, or had she overdone it on her blusher? *Maybe I should nip back to the café and check*, thought Louise, then got a firm grip on herself.

You're being stupid, she told herself.

Up until one minute ago, she couldn't get inside the building fast enough. From the moment she had picked up the phone to call her old boss, Douglas, and asked him, on the quiet, whether the flexible position they'd tried to tempt her back with last year was still on offer, Louise had been counting down the days until she was at her desk again.

Now, though, her heart was racing with nerves and she wasn't sure her famous poker face was good enough to cover it up.

Was it all going to come back? Had things moved on? More importantly, was she still the same person she'd been when she left, clutching the generous envelope of Mothercare vouchers and the smart stilettos she'd kept under her desk for court like a trophy? Louise had spent days rereading her case notes, battling her mind back into fighting shape, shaking out the legal jargon from under the fuzzy heaps of pregnancy trivia. Her brain had never let her down. The one thing she wasn't sure about was herself.

Bulletproof. That was what a good CPS solicitor was. Totally bulletproof. Predictable, with unquestionable integrity.

Can I still say that's me, though? she asked her reflection, distorted by the engraved details of the building's opening ceremony. *With what I know now about myself?*

"Louise? Louise!"

She felt a big hand clap down on her shoulder and turned to see Douglas Shelwick beaming all over his round, red face. Same tie, same glasses, slightly less hair, but otherwise, just as she'd left him.

"Might have known you'd beat me into the office," he went on, dispensing a polite kiss in the direction of her right cheek. "Great to see you back. You're looking very well!"

"It's just bronzer," said Louise, then added, with a flash of her old bantering confidence, "and a burning desire to get back to cleaning up the mean streets of Longhampton!"

If Douglas spotted the effort in that, he didn't show it. Instead his grin broadened, and he opened the door for her, gesturing for her to go in. "How's the lad? Sleeping through?"

"Like clockwork," lied Louise. Not a good start, but if she said it often enough, it might come true. "Has done from the beginning." She took a surreptitious sniff of the foyer: same public-service building smell of cleaning fluids and the coffee machine. Comfortingly familiar too.

"Takes after his mum, then. One hundred percent reliable." Douglas laughed, and Louise's growing relaxation cramped in her chest.

"Now, as you might have heard, we've had a reshuffle since you left, so I can't give you your old office back," he went on, leading her through to the Senior Prosecutors' department, where several new staff were already at their desks. Louise didn't recognize them, but they were probably trainees. Young, and keen. Not important enough for Douglas to introduce her yet, anyway.

"The window's quite a bit smaller, and you'll have to share an assistant for a few months, but I'll have a quiet word and see if maybe there might be something better coming up."

Louise recognized the door he was opening: It belonged to Deidre Jackson, the office manager. Her office still reeked of Elnett hair spray and had a view onto the pigeon-poo-spattered air-conditioning units. Two years ago she'd have roared at Douglas until she got a view of the side street at least, but now she just wanted to get on.

"This is fine," she said, putting her briefcase down on the

plastic chair opposite the desk, which was bare apart from a computer and an overflowing in-tray of case files. "Nice and quiet. So where've you put Deidre?" she joked. "In the stationery cupboard? I hope I haven't bumped her out into the *main office*."

Douglas's avuncular face froze. "No. Didn't you hear? Deidre's left."

"Really?"

He seemed surprised at *her* surprise. "Well, I say *left* . . . Turned out she'd been fiddling expenses for one of the senior prosecutors. It all came out when the council audit team came in and shook us down."

Louise was mortified. She'd assured Douglas she'd kept a close eye on the news from the office. Which she had, sort of. She'd read the local paper now and again. "I knew there'd been rationalizations, but I didn't realize . . . ?"

"Yup, it's a tight ship now, with the budget cuts. No room for dead wood." Douglas pulled on a faintly fake-looking smile. Louise guessed his long lunches had gone in the budget cuts too. "Anyway! Onwards and upward. We have a general team roundup at nine thirty, before court, so if you want to make your way over to the meeting room, I'll ask one of the IT guys to get your computer set up. We can do all the meet-and-greets then."

"Great," said Louise.

When he was gone—shouting, "Hey, hey, Jim! What time d'you call this?" across the office—she took a framed photograph of Toby in his lion costume out of her briefcase and put it on the desk in front of her. He looked like a somber lamb in lion's clothing: utterly adorable.

She hesitated, remembering how she'd mercilessly taken the mick out of colleagues who'd displayed family photos like mawkish trophies—"proof that they were human," she'd laughed in the office kitchen. Was that what they'd be saying about her?

She made to move it onto the filing cabinet but stopped and put it back next to the computer, where she could see it. Toby was the reason she was there. His future happiness was the whole reason she was leaving him at home with her mum.

Briefly, Louise closed her eyes and said a small prayer to whoever was listening. *Help me to be me again*, she thought, *so I can be the mum Toby deserves, and the wife Peter married.*

There was silence, apart from the clatter of pigeons outside. Louise wasn't surprised. After Ben's shocking, unexpected death, she didn't really believe you got answers from anywhere other than your own subconscious anymore. The trouble was, her own inner voice, usually so definite and reassuring, had gone very quiet of late.

I've made a start, she told herself. *Here I am.*

Then she took a deep breath and lifted the first case file off the pile—a long-running tale of neighborly warfare, featuring names she remembered from the last time round—and set her well-trained legal brain into search-and-fillet mode.

By the time Louise was making her first official phone call of the day, on the other side of town, Juliet was finally picking up the phone, after it had rung four times in a row, interrupting *Escape to the Country.*

"Sorry to bother you, love," said Diane, as if Juliet had picked up the first time, "but I was just wondering—how was Coco's poo?"

"What?" Juliet muted the couple thinking of buying a house in St. Leonard's or possibly Brighton. Or possibly Southampton.

"Was it . . . like Play-Doh? Or more Mr. Whippy?"

Juliet switched off the television irritably. She hadn't really been rooting for the couple, if she was being honest; she operated on a scale of deserving, based on somewhat shady criteria like how much they appreciated period fittings and whether they wore matching fleeces. These two were showing signs of ingratitude and didn't, Juliet had decided, deserve a pantry.

"I don't know. I didn't look."

"Well, can you? Only she's had a bit of a funny tummy and I'm changing her food. I want to make sure it's agreeing with her."

Juliet looked over to the other sofa, where Coco was lying with her big brown head on a cushion. Her eyes were rolled back, and she was wearing the delirious expression of a dog who normally wasn't allowed anywhere near a sofa.

"She looks fine to me, Mum."

"Really?" There was a wistful pause. "Not missing me?"

Coco huffed snoozily, her graying muzzle wrinkling in pursuit of a dream rabbit. One big paw twitched, but not enough to disturb Minton, who was using her haunch as a pillow.

"Maybe a little," said Juliet.

"She'll be lost without her mummy, poor Coco. I was thinking . . ." Diane went on, in a bright tone. "Maybe we could meet up for our walk? I've got a buggy here for Toby—we could have a nice stroll through the park together. Say in half an hour or so? Give you a chance to put your shoes on."

Juliet felt the tightening around her chest that came whenever anyone suggested doing anything she hadn't had time to think about.

"What about Coco? Isn't that the point—that she and Toby have to be kept apart . . . ?"

"Oh, she's on her lead. We could talk about Keith," Diane went on.

"Keith?"

"Keith the builder we're going to get in to quote for your work. Like we were talking about the other day. It's a good time to crack on, with the summer sales starting. Your dad's having a word with Keith this afternoon. We'll pay half if you're—"

"Mum! Stop it!" Juliet's voice came out too loud, and Minton jerked awake. Coco didn't stir, but Minton slid off the sofa and sat by her feet, waiting.

She swallowed and rubbed her own neck. "Sorry. I just . . . don't know if I'm ready."

"Don't make it sound like I'm forcing you," said Diane, hurt. "Didn't your counselor suggest that starting work on the house might help with coming to terms with losing Ben?"

"Amongst other things. It sounds very quiet back there," said Juliet, changing the subject. "Is Toby asleep?"

"No, he's painting. He's just lovely and quiet for his granny, aren't you, Toby? Juliet, this is as good a moment as any to talk about how we can help you get your life back on—"

"Well, I was just about to take Coco out to the woods for her walk," blurted Juliet.

Even as the word was leaving her mouth, she knew she'd made a schoolgirl error: Coco's ears twitched and her eyes opened. Before Juliet had time to backtrack, Coco had joined Minton at her feet, both with *Walk me* written all over their eager faces.

Juliet tried to convey silently that they weren't really going for a walk, that it was just a human figure of speech. It didn't seem to get through.

Meanwhile, Diane was making more noises about "hopping into the car," and in desperation, Juliet headed her off at the pass.

"Mum, we'll talk later," she said. "I don't want to get behind on Coco's schedule."

It had been a while since Juliet had taken Minton on a formal walk around the delights of Longhampton. Running around Ben's clients' gardens all day had worn him out so much that by the time he got home he was happy to snore between them on the sofa, chasing rabbits in his sleep.

Diane had included a helpful sketch map of the route she normally took with Coco, and Juliet set off on it. It involved a short drive into town for her, then went along the canal path toward the middle of town and then round the formal gardens of the municipal park, now dazzling with splashy crimson geraniums and purple wallflowers circling the old bandstand. From there, it headed up into Coneygreen Woods, the Forestry Commission copse where Ben liked to test Juliet on her trees and Minton liked to chase squirrels.

Coco ambled along by Juliet's side, and Minton scampered back and forward on his extending lead, sniffing and cocking his leg every now and again like a teenager tagging a wall. There were more people around than Juliet had expected to see on a Tuesday midmorning, some elderly, some mothers pushing buggies in twos and threes, most of them walking a dog, like her. And whereas the mothers and the shoppers were happy to leave her alone, all the people with dogs seemed determined to chat. Not about normal human things, though—just about the dogs.

"Oh, she's a nice old girl. How old?"

"Don't tell me—Patch, is it?"

"Ah, I bet you get through some food, don't you?"

Each friendly attempt at conversation made Juliet more and more tense. The June sun was warm, and a peaceful English-morning calm hung over the park, but her heart was pounding. There was a reason she walked Minton at night: She didn't *want* to talk to people. With everyone who approached her, she felt herself shrink back into her shell, fists clenched with the effort of not running away.

The worst thing was, they all seemed to know Minton and Coco.

"Minton!" she protested as he barreled up to one old dear with a fluffy white West Highland terrier sporting a tartan jacket despite the warm sunshine. "Sorry," she said, "he's very—"

"Oh, we're old friends with Minton." The old lady bent down to ruffle his ears. "Clever boy, you never forget a face, do you?" She straightened up, and beamed at Juliet. "It's Mrs. Hinchley. I've been meaning to get in touch with Ben—he did such a lovely job of my patio. I was wondering if he's got time to take a look at my daughter's garden."

Juliet's head pounded, and the self-defense explanation mechanism kicked in.

"I'm afraid he's dead," she said. The story rattled out of her in one go, with no gaps for questions. "He had a heart attack, last October. They don't know why—he was very fit. It's not as uncommon as you'd think. Yes, it was a horrible shock. I miss him horribly. Minton was with him when it happened, so at least he wasn't on his own at the end. That's a small comfort, but I worry about Minton sometimes."

The old lady's smile froze as the pieces fell into place. "Oh, I'm so sorry, my dear . . ."

"No, it's fine," said Juliet, automatically. For a second, she thought Mrs. Hinchley was going to hug her, and she moved a step back. She hated to seem rude, but the helpful things people said had the power to undo everything. She wasn't "brave," she wasn't "still very young," and she honestly didn't think "time is a great healer." After eight months without Ben she felt numb, which was an improvement on flayed alive, but still barely felt like living.

"No, it isn't," said Mrs. Hinchley. "It's not fine. But it will be one day."

Juliet forced a smile through her watery eyes, and privately doubted it.

The self-help bereavement books that had arrived from people who didn't send her flowers suggested that it took a year to start getting over the death of your loved one. Juliet had a wall calendar in the kitchen, and each night, after she'd filled up the day with television, she crossed off another box. There were still four pages until October 13, but the date loomed ahead of her like a finishing tape, a day she simultaneously dreaded and looked forward to.

Hopefully, on October 13, this heavy coat of sadness would lift off her shoulders and she'd start to feel like she could breathe again. It didn't feel possible now, but Juliet wanted to believe the books.

Mrs. Hinchley patted her arm. "He was a wonderful gardener, your Ben. If he looked after you as carefully as he looked after my roses, you must have felt like the most important girl in the world."

Juliet bit her lip. That was exactly how Ben had made her feel: tended, and special, grown from a seedling of a girl into the woman she was now. And now she was nobody, and nobody's. Spinning, like one of those satellites that gets blown off course in space.

Come on, she thought. *You should be past this by now.*

"Sorry," she said, wiping her nose. "I'm walking my mother's dog. We need to get home."

"Good for you, getting out and about," said the old lady. "Fresh air's a great healer."

That was a new one, thought Juliet.

She tugged Coco's lead and forced a quick smile on her face. They set off walking faster than Coco was used to, and she panted to keep up.

"You're more sociable than me, Minton," said Juliet, once they were out of earshot. "Did Daddy make a nice patio? Did Mrs. Hinchley have anything she wanted to bury underneath it? Should we be asking questions about the bell-ringing group?"

Talking to Minton kept Juliet from going mad. He let her natter on endlessly about Ben without making the sad face everyone else pulled—the one that always seemed to turn the conversation to how wonderful he'd been, what a perfect marriage they'd had. But there were times when that made her feel even worse. Only Minton let her whimper about how selfish he'd been to die and leave her all on her own, with an unfinished house and a wrecked future.

Coco started to pull to one side with more enthusiasm, and Juliet looked to see where she was going.

A round figure in a red fleece vest and practical navy slacks was heading past the ornate bandstand toward them, pushing a buggy containing a small, fuzzy-headed boy in dungarees. She waved enthusiastically.

"It's Granny Di," said Juliet. "I don't believe it. She's checking up on us."

Louise had known a whole new world of weariness in the first year of Toby's life, but the weariness she felt now that she was back at work, when she collected him from her mother's and finally collapsed on her huge squashy sofa at home, was like nothing else.

Her brain hurt. Her eyes were ready to shut. Her feet were killing her in the new heels she'd bought online the previous week, thinking that at least her feet wouldn't have put on weight. Wrong! In the olden days, she'd have worn them in, or rubbed the heels with Vaseline, but there'd been no time. There never was.

Everything was done in a rush these days. Peter got back in from work at six and rushed to bathe Toby while she got some supper together and dealt with the laundry, the post, the hoovering. She didn't stop rushing from the moment she got up to the moment she rushed to get into bed before Peter. There were no pauses in her day anymore.

Her favorite part of the day had always been that first crisp, cool sip of white wine as she eased off her shoes. Now it was the first delighted, baby-powdered cuddle from Toby when she picked him up from her mother's house, or from the nursery. The feeling of his hot starfish hands on her face made her heart explode with love, as if the day had just gone into color from black and white.

She sat hypnotized with love now, as Toby babbled away at her, pressing parts of her face with his hands. *I could stay here all day*, thought Louise, drunk on infatuation and exhaustion.

Chores, said a voice in her head, and somehow she dragged herself off the sofa, put Toby on her hip, and took them both upstairs to get changed.

"Did you have a lovely time with Granny?" she asked, as she changed out of her work suit and into her forgiving yoga trousers. He gazed into her eyes, tugging at the invisible thread that bound them together. "Did you? Did you miss Mummy? Mummy missed you."

She picked him up again and padded downstairs in her bare feet, setting up a to-do list in her head for the next hour, before Peter got in. Food, play, bath, food for adults . . .

"Shall we do our chores first?" she asked Toby. "Good idea. Let's start with the thing we mustn't forget. Can you pick up your watering can? You can? Good boy!"

They went through the conservatory and down the garden path toward the greenhouse the previous owners had put in. Louise's garden was huge, big enough for a proper lawn and a rose garden and a vegetable plot, and space for a trampoline and/or cricket square when the need arose.

Ben hadn't been their gardener—they'd agreed it would have been a bit too awkward, paying your brother-in-law—but he'd advised them a lot on the apple trees and had had some good suggestions for easy vegetables Louise could grow while she'd been on maternity leave. He'd noticed how restless she'd been, her brain spinning without the daily challenge of cases, and without asking had suggested just what she needed—a project, something she could see growing. Something that wasn't Toby.

Louise stopped, Toby on her hip, and surveyed the garden. She missed Ben and his straightforward attitude to life. She'd known him since she was a teenager, and it was hard to see the garden without imagining him in it, showing her something she'd never noticed before. She'd seen him kneeling to smell these flowers, or yank out a weed, so many times; she'd often imagined what he and Juliet would look like when they were celebrating their golden wedding anniversary. Much the same: Ben with gray hair, Juliet with three kids and their mother's glasses. It still surprised her to think she'd never see him again.

Louise sighed, pushed open the door to the greenhouse, and made her way over to the far end. It was empty—only Ben had used it, as an overflow for his own cuttings—apart from five small pots, containing a single sapling each.

About a month before Ben died, in September, he'd brought her the five cuttings, which he said he'd taken from the big cherry tree at the top of the hill heading out toward Rosehill.

"They were trimming it back, so I grabbed some cuttings while I could," he said, beaming with delight at having snapped up something precious. "It's our favorite tree—thought I'd see if I could grow a little one of our own, to put in the garden so Jools can see the blossom every year when she wakes up. Don't tell her, though—I want it to be a surprise. An anniversary present, if they take."

Louise had been touched that he'd wanted to include her in his secret, and even more touched by the characteristic sweetness of his gesture. That was Ben all over—Peter would take her out for dinner, or give her some money to treat herself to a spa day, but Juliet and Ben lavished their own time on their gifts. Juliet knew what Ben's favorite cakes were; Ben took seedlings and cuttings for her.

She hadn't had the heart to tell Juliet about the saplings after Ben died. All five had taken—he'd planted them meticulously and given her instructions about feeding and covering them up—and now they were growing into young plants. If things hadn't been so strained between her and Juliet, Louise might have told her about them now; Juliet seemed on the road to recovery, even if she wasn't very far down it.

Toby waved his watering can at the shoots like a conjurer trying to turn them into trees. "Tree!" he said.

"Yes, trees," said Louise, checking the notes for how much feed to give them. They looked strong, but she hated the thought of giving them to Juliet only for them to fail. It would seem so horribly symbolic. And Juliet could wipe out the most sturdy houseplant within hours.

I'll know when the time's right, thought Louise, pressing the soil with her fingertips. She liked to think of the moment her sister would discover the little legacy her husband had left, and cry happy tears for his thoughtfulness and love, in among the sad ones. Till then it was comforting to watch the cherry trees keep on growing, sprouting new shoots, driving their roots farther and farther into the soil. It made her feel better about her sister, about poor lost Ben, to think she was helping them, without the words that seemed to get in the way more and more these days.

Chapter 4

Juliet's favorite place in the house was in her big armchair by the sitting-room window, where she could look out over the long, narrow garden Ben had started to overhaul and doze off.

They hadn't been able to afford a lot of furniture, but this armchair was the first "investment" piece: a squashy velvet antique that they'd bought at the local auction and dragged home in the back of their van. Juliet had bid way over the odds, but she'd fallen in love, not just with the chair, but with the room she was going to build around its soft red depths.

She'd already decided on deep-mulberry walls and a refurbished fireplace for a wood-burning stove that they could drink tea next to in the winter, with a space for Minton's basket. The front room was light and airy, with a view onto the street and wisteria tickling the window edges, but the back room looked out over the garden, and she'd angled the chair now so it faced the bank of roses and fruit bushes Ben had put in for her.

Juliet assembled her equipment on the broad arm: mug of tea,

CD remote control, CD player loaded with the music that reminded her of him, photograph album of their honeymoon in New York, big white hankies. Her dad always had a proper hanky, and he always gave it to her when she cried, so now she had quite a collection. He never asked for them back.

This was her designated Grief Hour, as recommended by the counselor Diane had dragged her to see a few months ago. It was a "recovery-stage" tactic, designed to focus all her flailing emotions into one exhausting torrent of tears, rather than let them spread through her day, tangling her up like a net. Jabbing herself with all the worst reminders of Ben and their lost life was supposed to lessen the impact of each photo and song, old shirt, or scribbled postcard, until normal life became more "real" than the old life she was trying to wish back. Juliet wasn't sure it really worked like that.

The prompts she'd collected weren't slowly losing their capacity to reduce her to tears at all. She'd found one green shirt that still smelled of him, but bringing it out to cry over had started to make it smell of her, so she'd hidden it in her wardrobe for safekeeping, like a holy relic. The music especially still tore at her chest like claws, starting at her throat and raking slowly down her chest with each breath, but now she felt as if she were betraying Ben by trying to ration her grief into manageable chunks for her own convenience.

She pressed play on the CD player and the opening bars of Coldplay's *X&Y* album seeped into the room like the processional in a church. Carefully, she opened the album and moved the first sheet of old-fashioned tissue paper back to the photograph of Ben standing outside JFK Airport, with the *Just Married* stickers on his battered rucksack. It was the first time in America for both of them. An adventure. They'd promised to go back for their silver wedding anniversary, and stay in the posh hotel they'd only been able to afford one drink in.

A fat tear rolled down her chin, and she caught it quickly before it splashed onto the page. Ben had laughed when she'd gone to Boots with the memory stick from his digital camera, but that was exactly what bothered Juliet—something so small and losable couldn't be responsible for holding her precious memories. She wanted printed-out evidence, in old-fashioned photo corners and tissue leaves, because their love was the old-fashioned for-life sort.

"But it's all in our heads," Ben had insisted. It was. But Ben had gone, and with it, the other half of her honeymoon.

The counselor was wrong, anyway, she thought, forcing herself to turn the page. Looking at how happy they'd been was getting harder, because now, after eight months, she'd finally accepted that he wasn't coming back. It had come to her one wakeful night, as if her brain had been waiting to spring it on her. As if she were hovering over her own body, Juliet had seen her future stretched out like a flat, gray sea: no land to aim for, no points to navigate round, just the sense that she was being swept further and further away from the happiness and solidity of her old life.

Juliet closed her eyes and let the music wash through her.

It's like I've died too, she thought, curling her hand around Minton's hot ear, as the opening bars of "Fix You" sent shock waves of longing through her. *Nothing new is coming into my life, and all the old stuff is slipping out of my head. No one can fix me.*

X&Y had been "their" summer album. It reminded her of lying on the balcony of their old house, slipping in and out of dozy, sun-drenched sleep as the bees buzzed round the flowerpots. They hardly ever went on holiday—summer was the busiest time for Ben's gardens and the weddings Juliet catered. They'd made a holiday at home instead, sleeping out on the balcony under mosquito nets, going to bed in the afternoon, getting woozily drunk on homemade sangria.

That was the happiest moment in my life, she thought, as the sudden memory of Ben's warm body pressed against hers hit her with an unexpected force. She'd woken in the early morning to find his bare arm draped around her, his nose nuzzled into her neck. He'd looked like a slumbering god, and she'd lain there for ages, just looking at him, almost scared by how much she loved him, amazed that the perfect man for her had been born in her hometown, not on the other side of the world.

Why *did he die?* she asked for the millionth time, as hot tears leaked between her lashes. Why hadn't she had any warning, so she could have pinned that last day in her head properly? Not just the last day—the last month, the last year? So she could have said some of the things she'd meant to. And so she could have bitten her tongue on some of the things he really *didn't* need to hear her say.

Like, "How can we ever have a child, if you're determined to be a teenager forever?"

It had seemed such a brilliant line at the time. But then her last words to Ben had been the tail end of a stupid, petty row.

Juliet flinched with shame. Ben's cross face replaced the lovely image of his golden shoulders, and she flicked the CD on to something less painful. There were no specific memories attached to Athlete, other than a rather average gig they'd been to in Birmingham.

Minton stirred on her lap, picking up her distress vibrations in his sleep. He loved the armchair too; he burrowed into the tiny space she had left. Juliet could feel his little body heating up through his thin coat, and it was comforting as she gazed sightlessly into the long grass outside.

Ben had had big plans for the garden. Juliet still had the actual big plans: bright colored-pencil sketches of masses of perennials, a cherry tree, and a vegetable plot-herb garden affair, all labeled in his haphazard handwriting. He'd let her buy armfuls of interior décor magazines each month, so long as she didn't try to interfere with his banks of crocuses and the arches of honeysuckle he wanted to grow, so the garden would smell as magical at night as it did during the day.

They were going to have a hammock, between the trees. And a swing, and an area for a sandbox for any future baby Falconers . . .

Juliet gulped for air as the pain swamped her chest again. The distant screams and giggles from next door's garden were going through her like knives. She turned up the CD player in an effort to drown them out and pressed the hot mug of tea to her lips.

Then suddenly the lights went off and the music stopped. The whole house was plunged into silence.

For a second, Juliet felt intense relief, as if she'd finally managed to turn off the rest of the world. Minton didn't move. She closed her eyes and sank into the velvety peace.

Then the yelling started up from next door. There were thuds coming from inside now too. Annoying rhythmic thuds.

I could go to bed now, Juliet thought, from behind her eyelids. *I don't need lights, or electricity. I can leave this until the morning; if it's a power cut, it'll be back on by then.*

And if it's not a power cut? demanded a voice in her head. Her dad's voice. *What if something's gone wrong in the house? Where's the fuse box? What if it's a gas leak or something?*

Juliet pushed the voice away. Her capacity to ignore whatever she didn't want to acknowledge had grown amazingly over the last few months.

I can eat cereal. Minton doesn't have hot food. I can go to Mum's for a bath.

And if the house blows up? Are you covered? Did you renew the insurance? Are you just going to sit there?

Yes, she thought. *I am. Because I'm on my own now.*

There was another thud behind the wall, then a howl of protest, then the sound of rock music.

Juliet's eyes snapped open.

Bloody hell. It was bad enough having her Grief Hour disturbed by their racket, but now she couldn't ignore the fact that it wasn't a general power cut; it was a problem with her house.

An irrational surge of anger rose up in her, and Juliet pushed herself out of her chair so abruptly that Minton had to scramble in midair to land the right way up.

Juliet marched through her darkened house down the front path and shoved open the Kellys' gate. She had to step over a couple of pink bicycles on the way up their path, but it didn't dissipate the hot energy coursing through her. She stood on the step and banged on the front door, but there was such a racket going on inside that she couldn't hear if the bell was working. She could barely even hear her own knocking.

Someone, deep inside the house, seemed to be playing the riff from "Whole Lotta Love" on a bass guitar. Over and over again, with one note wrong each time, while everyone else bellowed "Dur dur dur dur DUH!" in encouragement.

Juliet wrapped her cardigan tighter round herself, though it wasn't cold. If she'd thought about it, she'd have put her shoes on, instead of her sheepskin slippers. They weren't very stampy, and she felt like stamping her feet.

Now that she was here, the Kelly chaos had shifted its impact: It wasn't irritating; it felt personal. They were noisy and annoying, but they were having a really, really good time. The whole family was joining in, and she was going to look like the bitter old widow next door, spoiling their fun.

Loneliness and anger swept through her. What had she done to end up here? She and Ben should have been expecting a baby by now. In a few months' time they might have been apologizing to the *Kellys* for the noise. When had Fate decided that no, she wasn't going to have a family, but these stupid, selfish people were going to have *four*?

Juliet clenched her fists and was on the point of pounding again when the door swung open.

A man she didn't recognize appeared, holding a can of beer. Blue jeans, plaid shirt over a Thin Lizzy T-shirt, curly black hair. Looked like a builder. Maybe he was a builder. That would explain some of the banging, she thought.

He lifted a hand to ward off her wrath, then gave her a disarmingly wide smile. "Before you say a word, I'm sorry about the noise, but it's Salvador's birthday," he said, in a strong Irish accent. "Alec's back from the Philosophy tour, just for tonight, but he's bought the kid a bass guitar—thinks he's got to get him started early if he's going to play Glastonbury before his old man's *too* old to go and watch him."

"It's so loud I can . . ." Juliet started, but all she could see was the proud dad, standing by the side of the stage while a little boy grappled with the huge guitar. It was ridiculous—she didn't even know these people, and anyway, this Salvador wasn't going to be headlining Glastonbury for at least another ten years, if ever, going by his inability to grasp a five-note riff—but something snapped inside her, and her eyes filled with hot tears.

"Jeez." The man looked horrified. "Don't tell me—you're a Zep fan? I'll tell him to try something else if it's . . ."

"No, no. It's my electricity," she said, wiping her eyes. "I thought it might be a power cut, but obviously you're fine here."

He seemed relieved. "It's probably just a fuse. You need to reset your trip switch."

Trip switch? What the hell was that?

"I don't know where it is!" Juliet wailed. "I don't even know where the fuse box is. My husband dealt with all that."

As she said it, she knew that made her sound like a spoiled housewife, but it wasn't quite what she meant. She and Ben had a running joke about dividing the household chores into "your hassle" and "my hassle" when they married. They even had a whiteboard list that they were allowed to add to: She had to deal with family birthdays and Minton's vet trips, while he changed fuses and cleaned the oven. It was a deal—for every hassle you passed on, you had to pick one up.

But how could you explain that to a stranger? It just reminded her that that list and the little acts of love it represented had evaporated when Ben died, and now her fuse box was very much her hassle—and would be forever.

"I . . ." she began, and then stopped, fighting to control herself.

"Hey, hey." The man reached out and patted her arm awkwardly.

"Lorcan! Who is it?" yelled a woman's voice from the kitchen.

"Lorrrrcaaaan! Loorrrrrcaaan!" parroted the kids. "Come back, Looorcaaaan!"

"I'm Lorcan Hennessey," he said, holding out his hand with mock seriousness. "Hello."

"Juliet," she managed. "Falconer."

"Right, well, now I'm not a stranger, do you want me to come next door and check out your fuses?" He winked. "So you can plug your own stereo back in to drown out Sal?"

"If you don't mind." It occurred to her that she hadn't actually told Lorcan that she lived next door. Had the Kellys been talking about the miserable woman next door who might kick off about the noise?

"No problem. Hang on, let me grab a torch. Stay there. Emer? Emer, where's the torch in this godforsaken kip?"

Juliet couldn't resist peering into the hallway. She'd only ever been in as far as the porch when Wendy lived there, and hadn't been in since. The black-and-white Victorian floor tiles were the same as hers, but they were almost hidden by a collection of stuff that oozed out from baskets, bags, and shoe racks, creeping over the floor space. Trainers, books, wellies, footballs, magazines, supermarket Bags for Life—the flotsam and jetsam of family life.

Worryingly, there were a couple of empty cages there too. Hamster-sized, with abandoned wheels.

Juliet could smell curry, and hot bread. Her stomach rumbled and she remembered she'd fed Minton but not herself again.

"Right, I'm with you." Lorcan reappeared, bearing an enormous torch. He gestured to the door. "Lead on!"

Feeling self-conscious, Juliet walked back down the overgrown path and through her own front door. Suddenly the stack of boxes still unpacked in the front sitting room seemed more obvious.

"Just moved in?" Lorcan asked, heading straight for the stairs. "Or are you having work done?"

"We've been here a year. I mean, I've been here a year. Haven't got round to starting the renovation," she said.

"Makes sense. No point unpacking only to pack up again. Right, now, your fuses are most likely under the stairs. It's where Emer's are."

He worked the torch beam up and down the paneled area, looking for the access to the understairs. Minton padded in from the kitchen, his claws making clicking noises on the tiles, and when he sensed a strange man, he set up a chilling growl, a furious noise Juliet had never heard him make before.

"Sorry, he's quite protective," she said.

"Steady on, fella." Lorcan crouched down to let Minton sniff his hands. "There's a good lad. Keeping an eye out for Mum, eh? Nothing to worry about here." He tickled him round the ear and Minton stopped growling. He didn't roll over, though.

Juliet watched him. She didn't get any weirdo vibes from Lorcan—quite the opposite—but Minton seemed wary. Minton was her barometer these days, now that her own judgment about people was haywire, and she trusted him.

Lorcan straightened up and found the hidden catch to the stair cupboard. As he flashed the torch around in the depths, the rest of the hall was plunged into darkness, apart from the faint moonlight coming through the landing window.

"So, be honest with me, what was it?" His voice was muffled. "Dodgy hair straighteners? Plug you'd wired up yourself?"

"I don't know," said Juliet. "Everything just went off."

Lorcan's curly head emerged from the darkness. "Sure you do! Don't have to tell me, though. You'd tripped it out," he explained. "Come and look, so you can do it yourself next time."

Juliet stepped toward the cupboard, aware that her mother would be white-knuckled with panic at the thought of getting into a confined space with a complete stranger armed with a massive torch, in an empty house, with only a small terrier for protection.

"You won't get electrocuted," said Lorcan, mistaking her reluctance for DIY squeamishness. "Promise." He held up his hands and grinned, that wide smile again.

He looks as if he should be in a band, thought Juliet, randomly. His hands were broad and he wore some kind of Celtic ring on one finger and a bandage on another.

If he were going to attack me, he'd have done it by now, she thought. And Minton hadn't gone for him.

She smiled quickly and crouched down where he was indicating.

"See this switch is down? It should be up." He flicked it, and the lights came back on. "First place you check. Anything more complicated, call your electrician."

Juliet nodded. Lorcan had a definitely male smell. Not unpleasant, just not . . . something she was used to smelling.

He straightened up and brushed the dust off his jeans. He was about to speak when her stomach let out an embarrassing gurgle, and he laughed.

"I take it you've not eaten," he said. "Want to come next door for a bite to eat? Emer's about to dish up a curry. She does a mean curry. Sal's allowed to request what he wants, since it's his special day, and he's overordered."

"Um, no, it's okay," said Juliet, automatically. She didn't feel up to joining a birthday dinner table, let alone one that would be as boisterous as the Kellys'. She guessed Emer was the mother, and assumed Alec was their father, but there were so many of them she didn't know, plus whatever guests they had. Hundreds, by the sound of it.

"It's no bother," insisted Lorcan. "She always makes too much. She forgets how many she's cooking for most of the time, and everyone's home. Alec flew back this morning." He winked. "Some dad he is. He's skipping out on Sal's actual party. Off-their-heads metalers, no problem; ten eleven-year-olds at the bowling alley, he's outta there."

"What does Alec do?" Juliet asked, curious.

"He runs a road crew for rock bands. Used to be a roadie himself, but now he's management. Gets flown all over the place. You didn't know?"

"I haven't really . . . been around," she admitted. "Famous bands?"

"Pretty famous." Lorcan grinned at her. "Come next door, have a chat. Let him tell you some stories—God knows Emer's heard them enough times. He'll be glad of some fresh ears."

Juliet was tempted for a second, but something stopped her.

"I . . ." she began, but Lorcan seemed to know what she was about to say.

He rolled his eyes and nodded toward the thumping bass,

which had started up again through the walls. "No need to bother with a polite excuse. I love the kids to death, but you've got to build up your tolerance when it comes to the noise. Listen, what about if I nip back and get us a takeaway? To be honest, I wouldn't mind an excuse to eat my tarka dhal without Florrie bending my ear about hamsters or what have you." Lorcan winked. "I can say your fuses are bollixed. You'd be doing me a favor."

"Um, it's a bit of a mess here," said Juliet. She struggled to pinpoint the swirl of contradictory thoughts jamming her head; part of her wanted to hurry him out, so she could get back to her private misery, but a smaller part quite fancied hearing more about her rock star neighbors. Not to mention the curry. The smell of it had triggered a rare bout of appetite.

She glanced down at Minton, who was glaring at Lorcan. His feelings seemed pretty clear.

Lorcan's smile broadened, reaching his blue eyes. They twinkled flirtatiously. "Mess? It doesn't bother me. I'm used to it. When you're on your own, who cares what the sink's like? There are silver linings to every breakup, right? If you get us a bottle of wine opened and . . ."

Juliet froze. It was a throwaway remark but it felt like a slap. *When you're on your own?* How did he know that? Had Emer next door told him Ben had *walked out*?

Her skin went cold as another thought struck her. Was Lorcan coming on to her? Was that what Minton had picked up? Someone moving in on Ben's patch?

God, how lost was she?

"No," she said. "Maybe it's not a good idea." Her voice sounded stiff and uptight, more like Louise than her normal easy tone.

Lorcan seemed confused. "Sorry, did I say something wrong?"

"I haven't had a breakup." Juliet hugged herself. "My husband died. I'm a widow. My husband was called Ben. We were together for fifteen years. I wish I *had* been dumped, then there'd be some chance of getting him back."

"Oh, man, I didn't . . ."

Juliet didn't bother to see what was going across Lorcan's face. She made straight for the door and held it open for him.

"Thanks for sorting out the fuses," she said, her eyes fixed on the crisply tessellating tiles. They were box-fresh Victorian, preserved by years of manky carpeting; one of the few parts of the house that didn't make her heart sink.

Lorcan stepped outside, then turned back on the step. "Emer didn't know," he apologized. "She just assumed . . ."

"That I was too young? Or not sad enough?" Juliet knew it was unfair to lash him with her bitterness when he'd been kind, but she couldn't stop herself. She was churning inside with emotions she hadn't sifted through yet.

"Well, we know now," said Lorcan simply. "I'm very sorry for your loss." He started down the path, then turned and added, "You know you're welcome to drop in anytime. For a chat or tea, or whatever. I know Emer'd be glad of some grown-up company."

"I will," said Juliet, but she had no intention of doing it.

Chapter 5

Louise was aware that she got her thirst for qualifications from her father, but she hoped she hadn't inherited her mother's interfering genes.

Diane had called her on her mobile while she was on her way to knock out a morning's worth of public-disorder charges, fussing about Juliet's still-unfinished bathroom.

"We need to find Juliet a shower," she'd said. "It's keeping me awake, thinking of her with just a bath. Anything can happen in a bath. Call me when you get in. We need to make a plan."

Which was why, at ten to seven, Louise was sitting at her laptop, Toby on her knee, surfing the Net for bathroom fittings while Diane worried in her ear about Juliet's sanitation.

"Ben mentioned that they were looking for something Victorian to fit in with the house," said Louise, clicking through some beautiful brass showerheads with chunky enameled taps. "When he was here before . . . well, you know."

"But will it work? I don't want her living in some kind of tatty antique shop where nothing works, just because it looks right."

"No, Mum, it's all reproduction these days. Like our shower—it looks Art Deco but it's got a thermostatic temperature gauge." Louise stopped at a shower that was perfect for Juliet's house; in fact, she had a feeling it was one of the ones Ben had pointed at when she'd shown him the brochure for their bathroom. "Ah! I think I've got it. Blimey. It's not cheap."

There was a muted exchange on the other end, and her father abruptly came on the phone.

"Hello, love," said Eric. He didn't have a lot of time for Diane's machinations. Louise could almost hear him whipping his reading glasses off and rubbing his eyes with frustration after listening to the other side of their conversation for so long. "About this shower. Just get the right one and we'll pay for it. Doesn't matter what it costs."

"But Juliet won't let you buy it for her. She's really proud about things like that." Louise hesitated, remembering the last time she'd tried to help out, offering their old sofa. "She won't like the idea of us sticking our noses in."

"I've a big enough nose to deal with that," said Eric, and recited his credit card number.

An hour's conversation dealt with in under a minute; Louise had to hand it to her dad, he knew how to get things done.

The kitchen had been a bomb site when Louise had dashed upstairs, but when she came down from putting Toby to bed, it was spotless. Three candles were flickering on the kitchen table and the good wineglasses were out.

She looked at them stupidly, trying to work out why Peter hadn't just used the recycled ones that went into the machine. And why he'd put linen napkins on the plates. They never used napkins—they hadn't used napkins even when they didn't have the machine on seven hours a day cleaning up after Toby, the human laundry maker.

Louise picked up the one on her plate. It still had the wedding-list crease in it. From Auntie Cathy, who'd actually said, "Well done, Louise, you'll never be poor with a computer boffin!" in the receiving line.

"Is everything okay?" she called into the utility room. She could hear the fridge opening and shutting.

"That was quick." Peter reappeared, looking flustered. He was wearing the stripy barbecue apron over his suit, with his shirt-sleeves rolled up underneath. In one hand was a bottle of wine; in the other was a chiller bucket. He smiled, showing his small white teeth, and waved at the table. "Sit down. Let me get you a drink—white wine okay?"

Louise pulled out a chair. She knew she should be bowled over by this display of attention, especially since Peter had been at some big software conference all day too, but an unwelcome knot of tension had begun to turn in the base of her stomach.

"Should I go back upstairs and get changed?" she joked uncomfortably. "I feel a bit underdressed."

"No, you're fine," said Peter, but there was a second's hesitation, and she knew he was taking in the saggy knees of her yoga pants. Louise had pulled on her old mummy uniform of black Lycra separates as soon as she'd got in; there was only really one office skirt that fitted, and she didn't dare risk any accidents.

"I'll get changed," she said. It was silly, but she didn't feel relaxed, him in his suit, her with VPL, probably. A bit of her died inside. She hadn't given VPL a moment's thought until today. That was what being back in a pencil skirt did. "Give me a moment, I'll nip upstairs and get—"

"No, just sit down!" Peter's frustrated tone was too forceful, but he heard it and smiled, quickly, softening his voice. "No, there's no need. You look great as you are. Just sit down and relax. Tell me how today went."

"Um, it went pretty well," she said, editing out her skipped lunch and undignified dash to pick up Toby. "I've been in court most of the day, waiting for witnesses. Some of them really milk it, turning up in shades and everything. You'd think they were on *The X Factor*, the way they keep us waiting. Douglas has given me a really boring set of cases to start off with, probably checking my brain's still where I left it."

"Course it is." He poured a glass of wine and handed it to her.

Louise eyed him tetchily. Was Peter actually listening? Didn't he realize how genuinely worried she was, that she might not be able to pick it up again, especially with budget cuts?

"How was your day?" she asked politely, and Peter launched into a story about some approach from an ad agency in America who wanted them to write some viral game software for "a top-secret client," but who his co-director Jason had heard might be some other company she hadn't heard of either.

Louise tried to listen and keep her face alert and engaged, but it was tough. She was tired. And Peter never focused on the interesting bits, like what the viral game might be. Or how long after Techmate's first big-league deal ex-stoner Jason had stopped wearing trainers to work and started buying handmade Italian shoes.

It had been exactly the same when Louise was at home: Peter would ask a few questions about Toby—the *last* thing she wanted to talk about after a whole day of child-rearing—and then ramble on about work. He didn't even sympathize with how knackered she was. He, on the other hand, was positively chirpy, as befitted someone who'd slept through Toby's nocturnal operatics.

Louise let him talk. It was easier. While he explained about the new engine Jason was developing, he served up a Waitrose

Dine at Home chicken supreme with some salad, which Louise ate instead of the potatoes, mindful of her skirt. Peter was still rhapsodizing about the commercial possibilities when he brought out a pair of crème brûlées.

Louise let herself eat half, then pushed hers over to Peter. He tucked into it happily. He had the metabolism of a racehorse. It had been one of the things she'd fancied about him when they first met: his lanky arms sticking out of the hooded college sweatshirt. The archetypal cute geek.

"Is there any reason for this?" she asked, unable to stop herself as he topped up her wineglass. "I mean, the lovely meal and candlelight treatment?"

Peter raised his eyebrows. "I know you spend a lot of time with devious people, but does there have to be a reason to make my wife supper?"

"No," said Louise. "It's just . . . you've gone to so much trouble."

"Well, I know we can't go out without a big military operation, so I thought I'd bring the date home." He topped up his own glass and raised it in a toast. "Saves on the taxi. And babysitter."

"So this is a date?" Louise's mouth twitched.

"Of course. Table for two at Chez Peter, couple of glasses of Chardonnay, Classic FM—limited menu, I'll grant you, but the service is better than at La Galette." He smiled across the table, and the candlelight caught the romantic look in his eye. "And no one's going to hurry us out after dessert." Peter stretched out his hand and slid his fingers between hers. "Or object if we get a bit amorous at the table. Or under it, even."

Louise squeezed his hand, then pointed her spoon over the crème brûlée she'd pushed over to him. "Or make me feel bad about helping myself to this last bit of pudding! Mmm!"

She was starting to sense where this was going, and she felt as if she were in a little boat heading toward Niagara Falls, paddling hopelessly against the current. Her foot curled itself round the leg of her chair, just as Peter's foot sought hers and missed.

"That sort of thing," said Peter, and Louise thought she detected a faint note of flatness in his voice.

Guilt flooded her. She should be grateful to have a husband who not only tried to seduce her over dinner, but actually made the dinner himself. *Come on, Louise,* she scolded herself. *Get over this.*

"Well, it's lovely. Really lovely. If I'd known, I'd have dressed up," she gabbled, wanting to tell him what he wanted to hear.

"You don't need to. You're gorgeous as you are."

"I'm not, I'm all . . ." Louise started, but Peter reached out and put a finger on her lips. She wondered if he expected her to bite it saucily.

Because if he did, he was going to be disappointed.

"I just wanted you to know that I'm really proud of you for going back to work," he said. "Very proud. You're a great solicitor, as well as a great mum. But—let me say this, okay?—there's no pressure from me to stick it out if it's too much stress. If you decided that, actually, no, you'd rather be at home with Toby, then I'd be fine with that."

"I'm not—"

"No, hear me out, Lou. I'm not trying to undermine you. I just want you to know that you don't have to prove anything. We can work the money out. If you're there a few months and it's just too much . . . I'm not going to say I told you so."

Louise looked up into Peter's face. He was still a cute geek, she thought, but she didn't get that shiver deep inside that she used to. His eyes were deep brown and he suited his ironically nerdy glasses. His cheekbones were sharp, and Anka, their cleaner, always blushed and fanned herself if he came in after a run. He ran a lot more often since Ben died. But just lately . . . it was an observation, not an instinct.

"I want to contribute to our family," she said, falling back on her best reason.

"You do! You contribute more than I do just by bringing Toby up," Peter replied, almost hurt. "That's the most important job anyone can have." He ran a hand through his dark hair and pushed his chair away from the table. "Let's go next door."

He picked up the wine bottle in the cooler. "Another advantage of Chez Peter—don't need to get a cab to a late-night bar. Remember that? Chasing around London, trying to find somewhere that was open after one?"

"And always ending up in that terrible place that you thought was a transvestite bar but wasn't?" Louise knew she was playing for time at the table.

"No danger of that here." Peter pretended to think. "As far as I know. Come on, come next door. Into the Lounge of Lurve."

Slowly, Louise took the glass and got up, blowing out the candles on the table.

In the sitting room, Peter dimmed the lights on his fancy remote control, setting the bottle and the baby monitor on the coffee table. The music had moved on to some Ella Fitzgerald collection—grown-up, world-weary songs.

He kicked off his shoes and settled himself on the big love seat they'd bought in the Heal's sale two years before Toby. It was cream suede, shaped like a waltzer, gloriously impractical.

That seems like someone else's life, thought Louise with a pang. *The days before I even considered whether something wiped clean or not.*

Peter patted the space next to him.

"C'm'ere, Lulu," he said, and a voice in her head told her that her husband looked devilishly handsome in the low light, his hair tousled like a film star's, his eyes clearly admiring her, even in these manky old yoga pants.

Louise walked over, clutching her glass. When she sat down, Peter caught her bare feet and swung them over his lap, so she was in his arms. Gently, he removed the glass from her hand and tipped her back so they were snuggled against each other.

"How long has it been since we had an evening to ourselves on the sofa?" he asked, nuzzling into her neck. "We should do this more often."

"Mmm," said Louise. She could feel her body tensing up even as her mind was telling her to relax, that if she just went with this, the feelings would come.

"You know, the other thing I wanted you to know was that if you decided that it'd be easier to take some more time off now and focus on the family, then go back full time in a few years, I'd be right behind you."

Focus on the family? What exactly did he mean by that?

Louise said nothing, but Peter carried on, his voice slurring a little with the wine. He'd polished off most of the bottle while she'd sipped nervously at hers.

"You're so amazing with Toby. And he's amazing too. I never thought I'd be one of those men who go all gooey about children, but he's the best thing that's ever happened to me. I know I wasn't as keen as you in the beginning, but . . ." He curled his finger softly under Louise's chin so she had to look up into his eyes and see how serious he was.

Then he said the words she'd been dreading.

"I'd really like us to have another baby, Lulu."

Louise's heart sank, but she made herself smile. "Would you?"

"I know we said there should be a gap, so you could get back to work, but to be honest, I just wasn't sure how we'd cope. I think we're coping pretty well, though, aren't we?" He leaned forward and traced a line of kisses from the curve of her ear down her neck. "I don't think another baby would be that much more work."

The kisses made Louise shiver, but not in the way Peter hoped.

He *would* say that, she fumed inside. He wasn't the one waking up to deal with stinking nappies at three in the morning, or easing cracked nipples into a bra that felt like it was made of sandpaper. Peter's vision of parenthood was based entirely on her own desperate efficiency.

She bit her lip so as not to let that out.

"I can't," she said. "Don't you think they'd go mad at the CPS if I came back from work and immediately buggered off on maternity leave again? It's hardly professional, when Douglas had to pull strings to get me back."

"Let them sue you. There are rules about letting intelligent, gorgeous women have as many babies as they possibly can. Or there should be." He lingered in the hollow of her neck, his warm breath making a hot spot on her skin. "Anyway, it might not happen at once. It might take months. Which is why we need to get practicing . . ."

"Mmm," said Louise, because she felt that was the least she could do. Peter's arm was round her now; he was stroking her waist, his long fingers inching under her T-shirt. "Peter," she murmured, pushing his hand down.

"What?"

"I don't know if it's the right time. I mean, Juliet . . ."

"What about Juliet?"

"She's still grieving. Mum says she gets really tearful about the kids she'll never have with Ben. I know . . . I mean, I think she was thinking about starting a family. And now she'll never be able to."

Peter sat up, frustrated. "Well, I understand that, but we can't put our family on hold in case Juliet gets upset. Surely she's already upset about Toby if that's the case?"

That hadn't escaped Louise's notice. "Maybe she is. I've seen her with Minton. He's like her substitute child. The way she talks to him, plans her days around him. It makes me sad, thinking she might never have a baby of her own."

"She will! She's only thirty. Plenty of time to meet someone and have as many as she wants."

"Thirty-one. And they won't be Ben's. That's the problem."

Peter gazed at her, stroking the hair out of her eyes. "You know, you're the kindest woman I've ever met."

"I'm not . . ." Louise winced.

"You are. You're so thoughtful about other people. It's just one of the many things I love about you. And that's why I feel it's my *duty*, as your *husband*"—he punctuated each word with a nuzzle—"to make sure you're *wined* and *dined*, and kept very, very happy at home . . ."

He hadn't listened to anything she'd just said, thought Louise despairingly, as Peter went in for a proper, passionate kiss, holding her tightly in his arms so she couldn't move. After a second's resistance, Louise made herself relax and let it all happen to her, registering in her head that Peter was doing every single thing that used to turn her insides to water—from the angle of his kiss to the way his hand was caressing the curve of her waist, the one part of herself that she was completely happy about.

She let her hands roam on autopilot too, finding the soft spot behind his ear, half stroking, half scratching his head. From the muffled noises he was making into her throat, it was working for him, even if she was just going through the motions.

Louise felt as if she were floating above herself, watching the scene like one of the police forensics team. *I've changed*, she thought. *But when?*

At what moment did I go from someone who spends thousands on "an investment sofa" to someone who spends thousands on baby clothes that last days? At what moment did my desire for this very desirable man drain away, leaving just the shell of the loving wife he still sees? Was it sudden, or slow?

Louise knew from the pages and pages of Internet advice she'd consumed over the last few months that experts would point to the moment that Toby was born, when suddenly there was a new love in her life, an irrational, fierce one that would barge all other distractions out of the way.

Deep down, though, she knew it wasn't that. The love she felt for Toby had been the same love she felt for Peter, but magnified. It was a good excuse, the postbaby world realignment, but it wasn't the truth. Louise's legal mind could pinpoint the exact moment when her whole world had tilted and begun the awful slide into secrets and doubts. Lies and behavior that she couldn't believe were hers.

It was the day her sister phoned her and told her that Ben, tanned, cider-drinking, life-loving Ben, two years below her at school, had dropped dead of a heart attack. That had been the catalyst for all this.

"Louise," murmured Peter, quite urgently. "Unfold your arms."

She realized her left arm was clamped tightly against her side, stopping him from lifting her T-shirt above her head. She didn't want Peter to touch her. She didn't want his hands on her skin, in case something in her body gave her away and suddenly he saw that she was a very different person.

Louise's stomach churned. This mental floundering scared her, after a lifetime of knowing her own mind with analytic precision. A new baby might bring them together; it would be company for Toby; it would be a fresh start; they were lucky enough to afford a bigger family. It might even be a little girl. On the other hand, it would mean time off work again, it would mean stepping backward, and Louise's eyes were fixed firmly forward now. There was no going back.

"Louise," Peter repeated, and she could feel the mood draining away for him.

Come on, she told herself. *You just need to get into it. Fake it till you make it. You can't let this turn into a pattern.*

She moved her arm, allowing him to stroke her back, and there was a crackle, then a distinct gurgle on the baby monitor, a noise that she knew was about to turn into a full-blown howl of outrage. Louise was ashamed at the relief that washed through her system.

"Sorry," she said, pulling her T-shirt down with a rueful smile. "Must have sensed that coming. Knew it was too good to last."

Peter sighed and threw himself back on the sofa. "How do you think he'll feel about sleepovers? Too young?"

"Too young, yes," she said. "I'll sort it out. Do you want to watch a DVD or something? Pick it out; I'll be back down in a minute."

"Fine," he said flatly, and reached for the wine bottle.

Louise bit her lip. It could wait for now. But not for long.

Chapter 6

"If it's a bad time, I can call back later," said Ruth.

Ben's mother always said that before one of her long calls; she never meant it. The one time Juliet had tried, gently, to ask her to call back later because her own mother was there, Ruth had burst into hacking tears that were so loud that even Minton had heard them, and he'd gone running into the garden with fear. It had taken every last ounce of Juliet's own strength to persuade her that she really did want to talk.

She had no idea where the strength had come from for the subsequent hour-long list of Ben's wonderful skills, and funny sayings, and all the other memories Ruth felt she had to share, to keep something of her son alive.

The trouble was, Juliet didn't like talking about Ben. She much preferred to *think* about him. Talking about him just reminded her that he was gone and wasn't coming back. All those past tenses, and the occasional present tense thrown in to wrong-foot them both.

"No, it's not a bad time, Ruth," said Juliet, muting the television but keeping her eyes firmly glued to the couple in the blue fleeces smugly assuming their vintage soda siphon was going to make more than the fifty gullible quid they paid for it.

Don't deserve to win. Should have listened to the expert, she thought, then shook herself.

Focus on Ruth. In need of support, just like me. Ben's dad, Raymond, wasn't a talker. He'd taken to working longer hours since Ben's death—Ruth said to take his mind off his loss, but Juliet suspected it was to escape Ruth's bewildered, furious grief.

Fifteen minutes. That was all it would take. Up until a month ago, Ruth had rung every single day; now at least she had three days of news to ask about.

"So, how are you feeling?" she asked, absently stroking Minton's warm ears.

"Oh, I'm coping." The usual *No, I'm not* sigh. "I don't think we'll ever get over it, not properly. Not when it's your only child. I can't believe how people forget! Can you believe this morning, the silly woman in the post office asked me if I was going on holiday anywhere nice! Going on holiday! I can barely get myself together to go shopping . . ."

Minton slid off the seat and stood by the door, his ears pricked. Juliet patted the seat next to her, but he wouldn't come back up. "People don't understand," she said. "You can't expect them to, until they've been there. Any news on the bench?"

The memorial bench was the only thing that kept Ruth going. She'd already been in wrangles with the council Parks Department about exactly where it was to be sited, what sort of wood was permissible, and so on. Juliet wasn't entirely convinced that the bench was the best memorial for Ben; he hated benches in the park, much preferring to lounge on the grass. But it was Ruth's project, and if it gave her some practical focus for her grief, Juliet wasn't going to argue.

"I've been talking to some artisan craftsmen," said Ruth, "but I don't want to rush it. I want it to be exactly how Ben would have wanted."

Juliet looked around the room at the unplastered walls and the lumpy section of wallpaper that Ben hadn't quite got round to steaming off before the steamer went back to Wickes. The Rugby World Cup had got in the way.

"How do you mean?" she joked. "Finished by the year 2019 and still not varnished?"

There was a haughty pause on the other end. "Ben was a very reliable worker," huffed Ruth. "As all those clients who came to the funeral were happy to confirm. He wouldn't have had the client list he did if he was unreliable, would he?"

"I'm not saying that." Juliet closed her eyes. *Oh, Ben, jokes are now banned,* she thought, into the ether. "It's just, you know . . . our house never really got beyond the preparation stage. Probably because he was out doing extra work for his clients."

And hadn't *that* been a topic of discussion.

"Ben worked hard to provide—" Ruth began.

Juliet fell back onto apologies. "I'm sorry, that came out wrong. My brain's all over the place. I'm not sleeping much."

"Have you been to the doctor? You need to keep asking, but mine's given me some very good pills that aren't exactly tranquilizers . . ."

Juliet gazed blankly at the bargaineers while Ruth's doctor speech washed over her. Like the bench dramas, it was familiar: their failure to understand, their refusal to hand out as many pills as Ruth felt she needed. Juliet didn't want tranquilizers or antidepressants. She didn't want to feel normal.

". . . said exercise was as good as a course of treatment, but I can't, with my knees, so I said, no, I've heard that there's a new Xanax that you can take . . ."

Minton was staring at the door, even though there had been no knock or ring of the bell. Juliet clicked her tongue and patted the seat, but he wouldn't come.

She hoped this wasn't the Greyfriars Bobby thing starting again. For months Minton had lain, awake, with his head on his paws by Ben's work boots, still where he'd left them in the porch. Juliet hadn't had the heart to move them, and Minton's forlorn but hopeful loyalty had the power to reduce her to tears.

He looked round at the sound of her tutting, then looked back at the door. Juliet felt a shiver run across her skin, despite the warmth. What was he looking at?

Was it Ben? Coming back?

She got up from the chair, with Ruth still rambling on about what she'd told the doctor about their prescription charges. There was a cloakroom porch between the sitting room and the actual front door—marked up where Ben had planned to knock through, eventually—and when Juliet reached Minton at the back-room door, she felt a cold draft, as if she'd stepped into a cold spot. Just like they always said on psychic programs.

Minton thrashed his tail in warning and Juliet's pulse thudded in her throat.

Are you here, Ben? she thought, with an irrational longing. *Can you feel how much I miss you? Have I pulled you back with my wishing?*

". . . Juliet? Juliet, did you hear what I just said?"

"Ruth, there's someone at the door," said Juliet. "I'm really sorry—I'll call you back as soon as I can."

She pressed the button on the portable phone and closed her

eyes, breathing in all the smell memories she could while she pictured Ben's handsome face, his crooked nose, the fine lines that had started to creep around his brown eyes. A wave of longing hit her as she actually smelled his scent—the mingled traces of sweat and earth and Right Guard deodorant.

And then she heard a man's voice. For a brief second, Juliet felt light-headed with fear and hope and disbelief.

Then she recognized her mother's voice talking back.

Disappointment swelled up in her stomach. Juliet opened the door into the hall and found the front door open. That was the draft, and the smell—fresh air blowing in through the coats and jackets, carrying tiny traces in the invisible stream.

Minton trotted forward, nosing at the door.

Why was the door open? Why hadn't her mother come in? It wasn't her style, not knocking and marching straight in there.

Juliet hugged her cardigan tighter around her and stepped into the porch, not looking sideways at the familiar work jacket hanging near the door. "Mum?" she called.

"Oh, hello, love! I was just having a chat with Lorcan here about your building work."

Diane was standing on the bottom step, nearly on the street. Her cheeks were flushed pink, and her eyes were bright. Juliet noticed she was wearing fresh lipstick, something she never usually bothered with.

The reason for this sparkle was leaning on next door's front gatepost: Lorcan from next door, eating a piece of toast. When he saw Juliet, his casual stance shifted and he straightened up. The confidence dropped off him. "Morning, so!"

Coco was lying down between them, obviously bored with the conversation, but when she saw Minton, her big ears pricked up and she swayed to her feet. Minton scampered out to sniff her.

"Morning," said Juliet awkwardly. Maybe she'd been a bit rude the other night, practically shoving him out of the house.

But he came on to you over the fuses, argued a voice in her head. *What were you meant to say?*

"Your mam says you're looking to start work on your house." Lorcan sounded interested, not as if he were pitching.

"At some point, yes," Juliet started, but Diane leaped in with a smile.

"Juliet doesn't even have a shower, can you believe? Better to get on with it sooner rather than later, while the weather's good, weren't you saying, Lorcan? The survey they had done when they bought this place came back with some recommendations about the roof. And that was well over a year ago, Juliet. We've had a lot of bad weather since then, and you had that leak . . ."

"Mum, it's in hand." Juliet gave her mother a beady look. "And I thought Dad was speaking to Keith?"

"Keith's in Menorca with the family for a few weeks. Anyway, Lorcan's going to come and give you a quote." Diane beamed with pleasure as she delivered her trump card. "Tomorrow."

"Not a quote as such. Just an idea of what needs doing. I've a few days off between jobs," Lorcan explained, as Juliet's jaw clenched in preparation for objecting. "Not saying you have to engage me for the work, like, but it'll put you in the picture. Some of these cowboys'll give you a whole list of nonsense and assume you don't have the first clue."

"Lorcan's been doing some amazing things next door while he's staying with Emer," Diane went on, fluffing her fluffy hair even more. She hadn't looked this animated since the book club re-formed with her at the helm, thought Juliet. "So you can always go round and check out his handiwork! He's been telling me about some lovely floating shelves he built."

"By magic?" inquired Juliet. Fine, she needn't take the come-on personally; he clearly charmed every woman he met as a matter of course.

Lorcan's dark-blue eyes crinkled with amusement. "No, with sunken screws. You can pop in and have a look if you want. Emer won't mind."

"Emer's husband, Alec, knows Mark Knopfler!" said Diane, as if she hobnobbed with rock bands on a daily basis. "And Emer used to be *with the band*!" she added, with some euphemistic air quotes that she must have picked up off Lorcan, because Juliet was pretty sure her mother thought "with the band" meant playing the tambourine at the back.

Juliet made a face at her mother. No wonder there'd been a draft: The front door had clearly been open long enough for her to conduct a full interview. "So I hear."

"Not *just* Mark Knopfler," said Lorcan. "Other elderly rock stars are available. And don't let Emer hear you say she was a groupie. But you get the picture."

"Emer's from Galway," said Diane. "And she and Lorcan know each other from—"

"Mum," said Juliet warningly. "At least wait until the poor man's left before you dish all his secrets."

"I'm just filling you in," said Diane, with a final girlish fluff of the hair. "I'm sorry about my daughter," she added to Lorcan, in her most charming tone, "she's not from the 'cup of sugar' generation. If she'd only introduced herself earlier, she could have had you looking round ages ago!"

Juliet was too shocked to remind her that the Kellys had moved in during the hazy twilight zone between Ben's death and his funeral. The moving van had blocked the road so the men with their funeral cars had had to park in Devonshire Street while they shifted it. Juliet had a vague memory of a big man with a beard apologizing, then reversing into next door's Citroën.

Lorcan seemed to sense her tetchiness. "Anyway," he said, looking quickly between them, "I've got to see a man about some paint. Shall we say ten tomorrow? We can be all done by lunch."

"That'd be fine," said Diane. "Ten it is."

"Grand." Lorcan raised his hand and headed off toward the van parked outside the Kellys' house.

"Ten it is," Juliet repeated in the same vaguely Irish accent Diane had been using. "Begorrah, begorrah."

"What?"

"Copying his accent. Honestly."

"He seems rather charming."

"I know. He's . . . very nice. That doesn't mean you can just hijack someone and demand that they come round to deal with my decorating like I'm some kind of useless case who can't even call a builder."

Diane looked outraged. "I did nothing of the sort. He was popping round himself to check on your fuses, actually."

"Was he?"

"Yes. You didn't tell me your fuses had gone. Why didn't you call your father?" Her face froze. "What else haven't you been telling us about, Juliet? Is this house a death trap? Maybe he shouldn't wait until tomorrow. Maybe this needs sorting right now!"

Diane turned to stop Lorcan getting into his van, but Juliet grabbed her arm. "No! My fuses are fine. I've been watching television. Come in, I'll make you a cup of tea on my perfectly working kettle."

"No," said Diane firmly. "That's why Coco and I are here, to get you away from daytime television and tea. You need to get out and about! Fresh air! With us—isn't that right, Coco?"

They both glanced down at Coco. She didn't look that desperate to hit the park. The gleam in her brown eyes said *Sofa* to Juliet.

"I just wanted to make it up to her," confided Diane. "You

know, not taking her out myself the other day." She fondled Coco's soft head. "I missed our walk as much as she did. Get your coat on. Minton! Can you fetch your lead? Your lead? For a walk?"

She was using the sort of baby voice Juliet never ever used on Minton. She and Ben had an agreement that if they did talk to their dog, it would be in totally adult tones.

"He doesn't do tricks. He's a *terrier*, Mum."

Annoyingly, Minton then grabbed his collar from the hook by the door and proudly began to chew it, and at that point Juliet gave up.

He's a very interesting man, that Lorcan. Did you know he used to be a roadie with Alec? And he and Emer used to play in a folk-rock group in Kilburn?"

"That wouldn't surprise me," said Juliet. "I hope they can play better than Salvador."

"Salvador?"

"Emer's son. He's got a bass guitar and a tin ear."

They were strolling down Longhampton's heritage trail—or the canal towpath, as it had been quite recently—Minton on his long lead, sniffing and scuttling, while Coco ambled between them, more like a third lady than a dog.

"You *are* going to let Lorcan have a look at the house, aren't you?" Diane said. "It would put my mind at rest. Knowing you had at least the kitchen nice and warm before winter."

"Yes, fine," said Juliet.

"You're just saying that to stop me nagging."

"You're absolutely right." Juliet jerked Minton away from a suspicious clump of bushes, then added, "But I will let him look round. Don't want to upset the neighbors."

"Good. I'm pleased." Diane sighed. "Then maybe you can make

a list. Decide what to do first. Prioritize the work. Then you've got options."

"Options?"

"Well . . ." Diane fiddled in her bag for Coco's tennis ball. "You might decide to sell it. Move somewhere smaller and invest the money. Or stay."

Juliet could tell she only said *stay* because she had to supply an extra "option." She'd already ignored a lot of hinting from her dad about how much work the garden would be on her own—hints that were more about her being on her own than the garden.

"I don't want to move." *I don't even want to turn it into a home Ben wouldn't recognize,* she added to herself.

"Well, you can't stay in a house with no proper shower, can you?"

Before Juliet could respond, Diane lobbed the ball, with an encouraging "Coco, go! Coco, go!" Minton hared after it, needing no encouragement, and Coco lumbered after him, to humor Diane.

"I'm glad I met Lorcan today," said Diane. "It makes me feel less worried about you, knowing that you've got someone decent you can call on next door, if there was an emergency. Well, like the other night, in fact. He seems like a very nice man."

Juliet shot a sidelong glance at her mother. She could nip *that* in the bud. "That's what the Yellow Pages are for. Anyway, do you know he's decent? He *flirted* with me—probably only came round as an excuse to chat me up. You might like that oily Irish charm, but I don't. So don't bother trying to set us up, just because he's single and conveniently located."

"Oh! Juliet, I wouldn't do that!"

Juliet clamped her lips together. Recently she'd noticed Diane and Louise, whether they were aware of it or not, auditioning friends and acquaintances for the role of "Man Who Gets Juliet

Back into the World of the Living." She really didn't want one. It was just that she couldn't imagine the idea of loving someone who wasn't Ben; her heart felt as if it had been bulldozed. There was nothing there. Even her memories of loving Ben sometimes felt more like echoes of love, rather than the real, breathing thing.

Anyway, the same counselor who'd told her it would take a year to recover also said that any posttraumatic emotion was just the heart trying to reboot itself, and therefore a recipe for disaster.

"Ooh, look!" said Diane. "It's Hector."

"Hector?" There was a middle-aged woman in a sun visor coming down the towpath toward them, but no man.

"Hello, Hector!" yelled Diane, in a strange tone Juliet hadn't heard before, and immediately a dachshund shot out from under a bush and made straight for Coco, his stubby tail wagging.

Coco whinnied in surprise and shot back to Diane's side, her own tail protectively between her legs. It didn't stop the dachshund from sniffing and leaping around her lady parts.

"Oh, naughty Hector, it's your girlfriend! Hello, Coco!" exclaimed the woman—to Diane, Juliet noticed.

"Now then, Coco," said Diane—again, to the woman. "Be nice."

Be nice? thought Juliet. Be nice? *Allow yourself to be hit on by a grizzly dachshund carrying on like a boozed-up Premiership footballer in a nightclub? Why are they talking through the dogs, like puppets? Why don't they just say, "Hello, Diane! Hello, Pam!?"*

Minton was hovering uncertainly around Coco, unsure of his responsibilities. Hector, unlike Minton, had an impressive pair of hairy testicles and looked the type to know what to do with them.

Juliet flicked her eyebrows at her mother, waiting to be introduced.

Diane looked a little flustered, then said, "Oh, sorry—this is

Hector, Juliet. And this is Minton! Minton's from Four Oaks Dog Rescue, on the hill."

"Really?" said the lady on the other end of Hector's lead. "So's Hector! What a small world. We're almost related!"

Has my mother really just introduced my dog to another dog and not the owner? marveled Juliet.

"I hope you don't mind my asking," Hector's still-nameless owner went on, "but where does Coco go *on holiday*?" She mouthed *on holiday* under her breath as if it were a euphemism, and glanced guiltily at Hector at the same time.

"Sometimes she goes up to Rachel at Four Oaks, but normally Juliet looks after her," said Diane.

"Oh, I was hoping you wouldn't say that." The lady's mac heaved with the force of her sigh. "Rachel's all booked up and I don't like letting him go somewhere he's not been before. It's just for a few days. I tried to get one of those Animal Aunts, you know, the people who pop in and feed them and play with them . . . My sister's in hospital," she added, to Juliet. "Hector doesn't like being left on his own."

"Well, if it's just dog-sitting for a few days, Juliet could probably help you out," said Diane. "That's what she's doing for me—I'm minding my grandson two or three days a week, so Coco's round at Juliet's with Minton."

Juliet opened her mouth, but it was too late. The woman was nearly exploding with gratitude.

"Would you? Really? I'd be happy to pay the same as Four Oaks—it'd only be for a few days. He's such a good boy. If he gets his walk at lunchtime, he's happy to doze the rest of the day in front of the telly."

Hector was now sniffing intimately at Minton, who hardly knew where to look. He turned his eyes to Juliet, pleading with her to help.

"I'm not a registered dog-sitter," she began, but no one was listening.

"Let me give you my phone number, and some dates . . ." The woman was scrabbling in her bag for a pen and paper. "Oh, it would take a weight off my mind. There's only me that can go with Una, and they won't let dogs anywhere near the oncology unit, obviously . . . I'd be back by five."

Juliet's resistance weakened. Oncology unit.

"There!" The woman handed her a piece of paper. On it, she'd written two phone numbers, Hector's name, and also his kennel club name, Grizzlehound Captain Caveman.

Juliet had to ask her what her own name was.

"Me? Oh, Barbara. Barbara Taylor," she replied, with surprise. "Sorry, I want to call you Mrs. Minton, but you're . . . ?"

"Juliet Falconer," said Juliet. "And this is Diane. Diane Summers."

Her mother tried to disguise it, but Juliet could tell this was news to all parties—apart from Coco and Hector.

Juliet waited until Mrs. Taylor and Hector were out of earshot before she turned to her mother and hissed, "What was that about?"

"It'll get you out of the house," said Diane. "And it's a good turn."

"Please don't organize me," said Juliet. "I'm a grown woman. I'm perfectly capable of organizing myself."

Diane said nothing but threw the ball for Coco and Minton in a particularly pleased-with-herself manner that made Juliet wonder if she'd been trying to engineer the meeting for a while.

Chapter 7

Lorcan knocked on her door the next morning as promised, in between *Crimewatch Roadshow* and *Cash in the Attic.*

He was wearing a Black Sabbath tour T-shirt that showed off some scratches on his wiry arms, and a heavy pair of boots over his jeans. There were bits of leaf in his hair and some green smudges, and he seemed to be making an effort to be super polite.

"I'm not interrupting, am I?" he asked, as Minton investigated the muddy leg of his jeans on the doorstep. "I can come back later, if you want—just holler over the fence." He jerked a thumb toward it. "Emer wants her ramblers cut right back before she'll give me any lunch."

"Have you no gardening gloves?" said Juliet, looking at his scratched hands. Ben had skin like a rhino and even he wouldn't go near rambling roses without gauntlets.

Lorcan shook his head and his curls bounced. "Nope. I've got roadies' hands. Like asbestos. Roisin came out with some oven gloves, bless her. I'm nearly done now, though."

"I'll lend you some," said Juliet. "My husband was a gardener and he wouldn't leave the house without his. He once got a thorn under his nail that went septic, and every time he saw someone without gloves on, he . . ."

The pang. The swift, dark pang that bloomed under her ribs whenever she said something that Ben'd never say aloud again. Even the seriously tedious anecdotes she never thought she'd miss.

Quickly, while Lorcan's face was still registering confusion, Juliet opened the door wide and changed the subject. "Um, come on in. Now's as good a time as any."

"Right." Lorcan gave her a brief, searching look, which she hoped wasn't going to turn into some kind of awkward apology.

"Sorry about the other night," he began. "I was—"

"You caught me at a bad moment," said Juliet, quickly. "It was rude of me to assume. Probably not even your type. Let's forget it."

He met her eye and looked about to say something, but Juliet held up a hand. "And that's not an invitation to tell me what your type is. Just tell me about my house."

"Okay," said Lorcan. He rapped on the door frame. It didn't make a great noise. "You know this probably needs to come out? I noticed it before, while I was talking to your mum. And your locks aren't fitted properly."

"Aren't they?" Juliet chewed her lip.

"No, you need a five-bar one. This is wobbly, look."

Ben had mentioned something about locks—they were chalked on the to-do list in the kitchen. Already her chest was tightening with resistance; she didn't *want* someone telling her all the things that needed to change.

"You want to get those fixed sharpish, in case you're not valid. Insurance companies can be bastards like that." He gave the lock a tap. "I can sort that out for you pretty easily, though—won't take long. Put your mind at rest. And your mam's."

Oh *great*. What, *exactly*, had Diane said to Lorcan on the doorstep about her building requirements? She'd probably bribed him to report back on what needed doing, so she could check up.

She'd never hear the end of it if it got back to her parents that Ben hadn't quite got round to fitting proper locks. She heard herself say, "Could you do that, please?"

"No problem," said Lorcan, with a dazzling smile. "I'll do it today." He turned the smile off, self-consciously. "If that's okay?"

Juliet nodded. *Damn*, she thought. *I should be doing my builder poker face.* This was definitely one of "Ben's hassles"—bluffing for workmen. She was probably giving off all the sucker signals, whereas Ben would have been tapping the door frame right back, making up stuff about lintels. And what about the insurance? Was she supposed to have told them Ben was dead? Had she done that? Or had Mum?

Minton stopped sniffing Lorcan's legs and returned to Juliet's side, leaning against her shin. He regarded Lorcan with suspicion but didn't growl.

"I know it's a cheek asking," said Lorcan, "but is there any chance of a cup of tea?"

"Tea?" Juliet was off tea. She'd drunk so much hot sweet tea in the past eight months that her insides were probably the color of a reproduction mahogany sideboard.

Lorcan nodded. "Now Emer's a manager's wife, she's only got this ridiculous coffee machine yoke. Does everything apart from grow the beans. It's so complicated she has to get Sal to turn it on for her. I keep telling her, the lifestyle police aren't going to come round and bust you for having a fecking teapot!"

For some reason, Juliet felt a desperate giggle bubble up through her tears; she had no idea why—it wasn't really funny; she wanted to cry, not laugh. Maybe it was just something about Lorcan's face. The rise and fall of his accent made it sound as if he were on the verge of delivering some wicked punch line, even when he wasn't. And she'd had very little sleep.

"Tea. Okay." She led the way, past the still-packed boxes of books stacked by the stairs into the back kitchen.

"Funny how two houses next door can be so different, eh?" said Lorcan. He leaned against the fridge, as she put the kettle on and got two mugs out of the sink. After what he'd said the other night about being single and not bothering, she wished she'd got round to washing up her breakfast dishes.

"Different in what way?"

"Oh, you know. Someone's knocked through yours, making all this nice light. It feels twice the size." He waved a scratched hand around, assessing the airy space between the kitchen and the back room. "Emer's . . . Well, that old dear'd been in there on her own for years. It's all teeny tiny rooms, and bookshelves, and corners. Looks cluttered even when it's tidy. At least you've got the blank canvas. I'm having to swing the old sledgehammer around."

"It was like this when we moved in, half done. It was one of the reasons we could afford it—the last owner started to renovate from scratch, then had to move for work." Juliet got the teapot out. "But thanks for the vote of confidence. My mum and dad tend to focus more on the unfinished floors and the wires."

"Ah, now, I'm not saying you haven't a lot on your plate, but the basics are done for you. And it's a nice house. Happy feeling."

The kettle boiled. Juliet didn't pick it up. "Do you think so?"

He nodded. "I see all sorts of houses. And this is a happy house." Then, realizing his mistake, his expression changed. The sunniness left his eyes and he covered his whole face with one big hand. "Jesus, I didn't mean . . . I'm so sorry," he mumbled. "That's a stupid thing to say. Again. You idiot."

Calmly, Juliet poured the boiling water into the pink-hearts Emma Bridgewater teapot, the wedding-list gift from her Auntie

Cathy, who had got drunk at the reception and told her mother it was a shame Juliet hadn't aimed higher than a gardener. Unlike high-flying Louise and her Peter, who'd "end up like Bill Gates, mark my words."

"It's fine," she said. *It's fine* came out on autopilot; she'd said it a lot, usually while serving hot sweet tea to well-meaning visitors. "We thought it was a happy house too, when we bought it. It's not the house's fault things have been less happy since then."

Lorcan wiped his hand down his face and peered over the top, contrite. "I'm so sorry. Your mother filled me in on your loss. She didn't say when, though?"

"It was last October. It's not like measles. You don't suddenly look cured."

"No, I didn't mean—"

"Would it be easier if widows wore a black armband?" Juliet went on crossly. "Or a mourning veil, so people can remember?"

"I'm really sorry," pleaded Lorcan, but Juliet was on a roll.

"Maybe one of those little ribbon pins, in black?"

He raised his hands. "Enough! I get it!"

Juliet deflated suddenly. "Ben didn't die here, if that's what you mean. He died in the street round the corner."

She realized she was clutching the biscuit barrel tightly to her chest. At one point she was refilling it daily for all the visitors, throwing chocolate digestives in it like a Roman offering, so people had something to do when they ran out of consoling comments.

Stop it, she thought, and pulled off the lid. "Biscuit?"

"Thanks." Lorcan didn't bother with the *No, I shouldn't* routine; he took three at once. "Had you been married long?"

"Five years." Juliet mashed the tea bags against the side of the pot, too impatient to wait for the tea to brew naturally. Now that she'd had her little outburst, she didn't want to make small talk about her dead husband with this very alive man. Death was awkward;

her strange single-but-not-single situation was awkward. He was making her feel awkward and unspecifically annoyed.

How can I make this quick? she was thinking, when Lorcan coughed and spoke.

"So, kitchen plans?" he asked. "Freestanding units, or fitted?"

Juliet looked up and saw he had a little notebook like a sketch-pad and was methodically scanning the kitchen, his head bobbing like a bird as he took in the details.

"The walls need skimming and painting, and tiles. What did you have in mind for the floor?" Lorcan stopped scribbling and raised an eyebrow.

"I . . ." Juliet paused. "I don't know."

They hadn't talked about the kitchen floor. Ben's plans for the garden were beautifully detailed, but his plans for the house had been vague. "It's all in my head," he'd said, when she'd pressed him for a budget or some details she could start searching eBay for. His head, of course, was no longer accessible.

"You could put tiles down, or do some underfloor heating?" suggested Lorcan. "That's what Emer's after." He grinned. "Nice in the winter for the dog. For the paws, you know."

"Minton wants an Aga," said Juliet. "Apparently he put in a request. He'd also like a towel rail in the bathroom."

"Expensive taste for a ratter, haven't you?" Lorcan said solemnly, and Juliet realized Minton had followed them in and was sitting at the top of the stairs, his back straight in observation. "I suppose you'll have ideas about removing that cat flap in the kitchen?"

She started to smile at Minton's stern supervision, then stopped. A lump had forced its way up her throat. This was what she didn't want—to see the dream house taking shape.

"Maybe you should just quote on the basics," she said, in a voice that sounded high even to her. "One option is to make it salable and just . . ." Juliet made herself say it as if it were her own idea, not her dad's. "Put it back on the market."

"Not a bad idea," said Lorcan, nodding encouragingly. "I've seen a good few houses make money still round here. And if Alec's investing. . . . Is that my tea? Milk, three sugars, if you don't mind."

Juliet poured two cups, spooned masses of sugar into both, and pushed his over the counter, clutching hers in hands that barely registered the scalding heat.

Lorcan took a sip and sighed appreciatively. "Ah, you've had builders before."

"No, gardeners," said Juliet, and he gave her a quick, grateful smile.

Lorcan was being nice, but she could tell he was treading carefully, not wanting to overstep whatever invisible mark she'd laid down by overdoing the charm.

"Do you want to see the rest of the house?" asked Juliet.

They started at the top, on the landing that looked down over the long back garden.

In next door's garden, they could see two red-haired girls bouncing energetically on the trampoline, surrounded by toys and garden furniture. The shrieks seeped through the window frames, which rattled as they walked up the stairs.

"I think the windows need replacing," she said, noticing the peeling white paint on the outside sill. It had got worse over the winter and now curled back, like the tongue of an old shoe, exposing the pale wood beneath. "We were thinking about double glazing too. Keep the . . ." She was about to say, "Keep the noise out," but managed to change it to "Keep the draft out."

Lorcan gave her a knowing look. "Keep Roisin and Florrie out, more like. I'd like to soundproof them myself." He ripped a page out of his notebook and started to fold it into squares. "I think Alec deliberately stands next to speakers before he comes home, deafens himself up a bit. There."

He wedged the paper between the frames. "That should stop it rattling for the time being. I'll put it on the list. You've got, what, four bedrooms up here?"

He stood on the threshold of Juliet and Ben's room and peered in. "Master bedroom?"

Juliet was struck with protectiveness. "Yes, but this room's fine . . ."

No one had ever been in that room apart from her and Ben. Not even her mother. After he died, it had been the one place she'd been able to close the door and be alone with him, when the house was full of other people and their concern.

Lorcan stood at the door and scribbled, and Juliet saw it for the first time through someone else's eyes: the chair draped with the three outfits she wore in rotation, the previous-owner-but-one's salmon-pink walls with tester-pot stripes by the fireplace where she and Ben had argued over sage versus cream, and the short wall covered in framed photographs of the two of them.

Well, it was, under the sheet that she'd pinned over it one sleepless night. Juliet couldn't bear to take down the photographs and see the ghostly spaces left where the wallpaper had faded beneath, but she couldn't bear to look at them either, so she'd covered them up. It looked like a shroud.

"What's under here?" asked Lorcan, lifting one edge of the sheet. "That's one way to ignore cracks in the . . . Oh. Sorry."

"Take it down," said Juliet bravely. "It's got to come off sometime."

"Are you sure?" Lorcan looked at her, checking her reaction. "I feel like I'm coming here in hobnailed boots."

She nodded, and slowly he pulled out the drawing pins she'd hammered in with a book, and the sheet fell away to reveal the jumbled frames, grouped into a haphazard mass of memories, the quick heads-squeezed-together, arm's-length snaps formalized in gilt frames like butterflies. Ben's easygoing smile never changing, though his blond mop of hair went from streaky surfer to cropped to the last, almost grown-up style. Juliet never really looked at herself, but now she saw herself through Lorcan's eyes; she started off as a baby-faced teenager, all apple cheeks and home henna jobs, but by the end her face had sharpened into adulthood, and her mousy curls were more or less tamed.

What didn't change was the connection between her and Ben in every shot, even when they weren't looking at each other. They were always touching—their hands, their foreheads, their shoulders.

"That's a grand wall of photographs," said Lorcan. "They must go back a bit. Is that Glastonbury you're at there?" He pointed to the top one: she and Ben with stupid jester hats and blissed-out expressions.

"Yes, our first holiday away, after our A-levels." First holiday, first camping, first serious bout of cystitis. Trampled grass, Jack Daniel's and supermarket cola, early-morning hangover sex, all leaping out at her from their heavy-lidded eyes.

Juliet ran a hand over her mouth. She'd told the same stories to so many people—how they met, how he'd proposed—that it had stopped meaning very much. But now, in this room, telling them to a stranger who'd only know what she described, she felt weak. How could you sum up a marriage in a few words?

You couldn't, she decided.

"Um, basically, I don't think there's anything wrong in here. It just needs sloshing with new paint."

"Well . . ." Lorcan pulled a face, his wide mouth stretching in apology, and pointed to the wall behind the fireplace.

"What?" She was already turning to show him the main spare room.

"There's that crack?"

Juliet had to step into the room to see what he was talking about, but when she looked, she could see it: a crack running from the side of the fireplace up the flue and across the ceiling. Why hadn't she seen that before? Had it always been there? Had it happened recently?

"Oh . . . shit."

"Might be nothing," said Lorcan. "Old houses are full of cracked plaster. They shift about in cold weather, you know. But you should get it checked out—wouldn't want to find out it's something serious."

"Like?"

He paused. "Well, subsidence? Damp?"

Juliet's heart sank. That was something *else* she didn't need, discovering that the surveyor had missed some mine shaft under the house, or something.

"I'm sure it's just cosmetic," said Lorcan, reassuringly. "Only it's best not to ignore cracks and hope they'll go away. In my experience, at least."

Juliet raised her chin at him. "Still think this is a happy house, or are you changing your mind?"

"Course not," said Lorcan, retreating to the landing. "It's a good family house—look at all this space . . ."

She winced. "Not that I need it now."

"That doesn't change the house," he said evenly.

"Spare room," said Juliet, flicking her hand toward the bedroom opposite. "Spare spare room over there. And . . ." The little room tucked in between the bathroom and the airing cupboard was going to be the nursery, though she and Ben hadn't actually said that aloud. Warm and cozy, more like a nest than a room.

"Dressing room?" offered Lorcan. "You could knock through and make an en suite if you wanted. A wet room? Emer's desperate for a wet room. Although the state Salvador leaves the bathroom in, you'd think she had one already."

"I might think about that," said Juliet. She peered at his notebook, now several pages in, all covered with his neat handwriting and sketches. For some reason she hadn't expected a builder's notes to be so precise. "God, it's mounting up."

"Sure, it's not." Lorcan paused. "Okay, it is. But that's what you get for buying a four-bed Victorian house. It's not an overnighter."

"How long?"

"I've barely looked at the downstairs yet . . ."

"How long? Be honest."

Lorcan gave her a level look, and his eyes weren't flirtatious now. They were serious, as if he understood the vulnerable position she was in. "Six months? That's if you can keep your eye on what's going on, or not. Builders have a habit of taking on a couple of jobs at once and overlapping them."

Juliet's heart sank. That would take until Christmas, if she started it tomorrow. Way beyond the one-year deadline that dominated her thoughts like a finish line.

The thought of having anyone in her house for more than an hour made her feel crotchety. Six months would drive her absolutely insane. For one mad second she fantasized about handing her mum the keys and what was left of Ben's life insurance to pay the builders, then buying one of those round-the-world tickets, but that would mean leaving Ben. And Minton. And *Time Team*. And all the other tiny anchors keeping her from whirling off into the darkness.

"Were you hoping I'd say three weeks?" he inquired. "Because I think you've been watching a bit too much daytime telly."

"Why do you keep going on about daytime telly?" demanded

Juliet defensively. "I don't spend my whole life watching daytime bloody television."

"That's not what your mam says." He was smiling gently, but the words cut Juliet with an unexpected sharpness. "She says you can predict the actual sale prices on *Bargain Hunt* before the auctioneer comes on."

"That was one program. One lucky guess. And my mother has *no idea* what I need to do to get through the . . ." Juliet heard her voice rising, along with the pounding in her chest.

She closed her eyes and tried to find Ben's voice. Deep breath. One thing at a time.

That was what had got her through the funeral, the floating weeks after: fixing on one thing at a time. If everyone was going to be on her case now about the unfinished house, then fine. It could be another handrail to lead her through these weird, empty days until she felt ready to face the world again. She'd just have to do it *exactly* the way Ben would have wanted, right down to the old brass door handles he'd got so excited about.

When she opened her eyes, Lorcan was rubbing his forehead with his long fingers. "I just keep saying the wrong thing to you," he groaned.

Juliet considered playing her widow card and flouncing downstairs, but she felt unexpectedly sorry for him. He'd only repeated what her mother had said, probably thinking it was a family joke. Her mum had been right; the fuses incident aside, he was a nice guy. He hadn't sucked his teeth once, and when his phone had rung, he'd left it in his back pocket.

"Sorry," she said, with a burst of honesty. "Sometimes I think I'm fine, and then I realize I'm not."

"I know," he said, as if he understood. "It's not easy."

Juliet didn't want the conversation to go any further in that direction. The prospect of digging into the house was more than enough to deal with. "Okay, so that's upstairs. Downstairs is a bit more complicated . . ."

Lorcan and Juliet made their way around the ground floor as he talked her through the options she had, and she nodded and concentrated, forcing herself to ask questions at first, but then realizing they were coming of their own accord.

The more Lorcan talked, sweeping his hand around to describe hidden lighting or paint effects, the easier he made it sound, and Juliet was surprised to find herself wishing some of it were done already.

". . . Yeah, sure we can put blinds in here," he was saying, then cocked his head. "Is that your doorbell?"

"I can't hear anything."

Minton could. He'd stopped following them and was staring toward the front door, his white ears cocked.

Then the doorbell rang, a long peal like someone leaning on it.

"Excuse me," said Juliet, and went down the hall.

When she opened the front door, the two little girls from next door stood on the step, grass seeds and dead petals in their tangled mops of copper hair.

It was the first time Juliet had seen the twins up close; she had no idea how old they were—six? Seven? How could you tell if you didn't have kids?—but they looked practically identical, only one had a Led Zeppelin T-shirt over her gypsy skirt, and the other had Bad Company. Both had round blue eyes that blinked from behind gold-rimmed glasses.

"Is Lorcan there, please?" said one in a pretty singsong accent that was half Irish, half London.

"Yes, he's . . ." Juliet found herself in the unfamiliar position of being unsettled by someone who only came up to her waist. "I'll just . . ."

Lorcan appeared behind her. "What do you two holy terrors want now?"

"Mum says can you come home, please—she's a jar she needs opening," said the Led Zeppelin girl.

"Tell her to bang it on the side of the counter," said Lorcan.

"She's done that. She says she fecking nearly broke the counter."

Lorcan turned to Juliet and looked apologetic. "I'm sorry, would you excuse me for—" Then he frowned and turned back to the girls. "Roisin! Don't say *fecking*!"

Roisin's porcelain brow wrinkled. "I could say worse. I could say—"

Lorcan waggled a finger and made a scary face. Roisin didn't seem very scared.

"She could say *bleeding*," said the other.

Roisin looked at her sister, as scandalized as a mother superior, but not as convincing. "Florrie!"

She turned back to Lorcan with a coy look that seemed to have been learned from someone much older. "Aren't you going to introduce us?"

"Juliet, I can only apologize." Lorcan raised his hands. "This is Roisin Kelly, the one with the *language*, and this is Florrie Kelly, with the . . . What is that, Florrie?"

"A mouse." Florrie held up the furry object she'd got out of her skirt pocket and showed its pink nose to Lorcan. "I found him in the garden."

Minton let out a sharp bark and would have jerked forward if Juliet hadn't grabbed onto his collar and lifted him off the ground. Tucked under her arm, he wriggled crossly.

"Put that away," said Lorcan. "Before he gets eaten."

"Will you come and open this fecking jar, Lorcan?" repeated Roisin. "Because we won't get any lunch if you don't. It's pesto."

Juliet checked her watch. Half past twelve. She'd missed everything up to *Bargain Hunt*. The morning had gone by really quickly.

"Do you want to come with me and see Emer's bathroom?" he asked. "I could show you better than I can describe it."

"Lorcan . . ." The little girl tugged his T-shirt.

"No, it's okay," said Juliet. "I've . . . I've got to take Minton out."

It was true, but as she said it, she felt a glimmer of something that she couldn't entirely put her finger on.

It was only when Juliet was halfway round the park that she let herself admit the truth: Actually, despite the noise and the bad start with Lorcan, she wanted to go next door, but for the first time in years she felt shy.

Chapter 8

When Louise and Juliet were teenagers, Juliet used to bounce into Louise's room while she was doing her homework and get her to score her in magazine quizzes—the sort that told you what your Friendship Style was, or which *Sex and the City* character you were most like. Juliet had a sneaky habit of changing her answers midstream, if she thought she was headed in a direction she didn't fancy, and Louise was hardline.

Juliet, being pretty straightforward and guileless, loved being told what she was "really" like, although Louise could have told her without ringing *a*, *b*, or *c*. Juliet was simply the nicest person she'd ever met. A typical Goat, as the magazines would say; the color yellow; a Labradoodle.

Louise, on the other hand, didn't bother with the quizzes because she knew exactly what she thought about everything from nuclear power to adultery, via the euro and reality television, thanks to six years on the school debating team. She'd applied the same (typical Snake; navy blue; horse) analysis to herself and she knew what she was, flaws and all. Methodical, hardworking, predictable, groomed. She'd never be popular or cutely tousled, like Juliet, but Louise was happy with the certainties in her life. Her ambition was to be as happily married as her mum, but with an interesting job, like her dad.

Nothing much changed in the intervening years: She found a career that ticked all her "need for neatness" boxes and a husband who made her melt inside in a surprisingly messy way, but who liked a clean bath as much as she did.

But that was before Toby was born. In the space of two years, things had happened that cracked every assumption she had. The truth slowly dawning on Louise was that, these days, she didn't really know what sort of woman she was at all anymore.

The changes had started as soon as the second blue line appeared on the test, just two months after she and Peter had decided that they'd done all the holidays they wanted and were ready for a baby. Louise had assumed she'd feel serene, but actually she'd felt panicky. While Peter was still hugging her and crying, Louise could feel herself becoming someone new, herself and someone else at the same time, someone vitally important, and yet secondary to the life splitting and re-forming inside her.

She'd tried to explain the strange dislocation to Peter, but he just said, "You'll always be first to me," which wasn't the point.

It didn't help that her pregnancy coincided with Techmate's breakthrough sale to a bigger software company, and Peter had gone from being a designer to a company director overnight and nearly doubled his hours at work. He'd made it to both scans, where he'd spent more time looking at the ultrasound machines than at Toby, but the deal had reached a tricky stage around the time of the delivery, and then in the weeks that followed, Peter's paternity leave was cut so short that he sometimes called her Jason by mistake as he fell into bed, earplugs in.

Louise didn't like to confess that she found one day alone with Toby more stressful and frustrating than a whole week in court. If it hadn't been for the mother-and-baby group, Louise thought she'd have gone mad altogether. They'd stayed in contact after the babies were born, carrying on meeting up mainly as an excuse to get out of the house, and those post-birth lunches had been fun. Apart from Organic Karen, who argued with everyone, including the surgeon performing her C-section, the group turned out to be a really nice, normal bunch of women.

Rachel worked at the rescue center, an ex-Londoner who wore wellies and Chanel nail varnish and still seemed surprised to be a mother. Paula was a physio at the private hospital, whose fourth girl was born the same day as Toby and who had them all doing pelvic-floor exercises; and Susie was a stay-at-home mum with the miracle baby and only half a fallopian tube.

And Michael, that rare thing—the baby group dad. At first he'd been there with his partner, Anna, but increasingly Anna hadn't come. She'd seemed stressed and didn't join in with the groans about stomachs like pizza dough and sleep deprivation. Louise envied Anna at first, for having a man who'd make time to come along, but her eagle eyes spotted the cracks in the body language before their baby was even born; they barely touched when they were there together, and she was always complaining about him when they were apart. That surprised Louise: Michael seemed like a very hands-on dad, always making his little girl laugh. He made Louise laugh too, with his confident, self-deprecating jokes. And most flattering of all, he didn't just talk to her about the baby.

One day, on their way out of the coffee shop, she'd asked casually, "How's Anna? We never see her," and he'd looked strained but had said, "She's fine. But we've split up. We're going to co-parent."

"But you can't leave *us*!" Louise had blurted out, then blushed at the way it had come out. "Sorry, what a selfish reaction! I mean, I'm really sorry . . ."

Michael had looked at her. "I won't be leaving you lot," he'd said. "Where else would I find out where to get the best nipple cream?"

That had been a while ago. They didn't refer to Anna in the group and treated Michael more like one of the mums, albeit taller and better at collapsing a buggy with a single kick.

But Louise didn't think of him like that at all; to her, Michael was a lifeline to the old Louise, who had opinions about Virginia Woolf, not Gina Ford. The conversation they had on the way back through the park after lunch slowly became the highlight of her monotonous week, and she stored up all the funny observations and questions that Peter didn't bother to listen to in the hour or so of sentient non-baby-tending time they shared at the end of the day.

All he ever wanted to talk about when he came home was Toby. Which, much as she adored her beautiful boy, was the only thing Louise *didn't* want to talk about.

It was on one of those walks back from lunch that Louise had told Michael about the cherry tree saplings Ben had dropped off the previous day, and his plan to grow them for Juliet.

"That's such a romantic idea," he'd said at once, without prompting. "And it's like love, isn't it, coming and going. Flowering, then lying dormant, then flowering again."

"I'd rather have an evergreen, if you're going to be metaphorical about it," she'd replied. "Not flashy, but year-round. No dead bits."

Michael had stopped pushing the buggy and looked at her. "Really?" he'd asked, with a different tone in his voice. A new tone that unsettled her. "You don't want that amazing cherry blossom feeling, even if it's just once a year?"

That had been the moment when something had tipped inside Louise, and she'd realized she wasn't quite what she thought she was. And after that, when she watered Ben's sturdy baby trees in her greenhouse, she saw Michael's hands on the buggy handles, his freckled arms under his polo shirt. The flicker of excitement in her stomach, and her horrified fascination at this new, new Louise emerging.

Ben had warned her not to overwater the saplings. Louise had to remind herself of that each time she headed for the greenhouse.

By ten o'clock, Juliet was curled up in her big chair with Minton snoring on her knee, making hot patches on her leg with each breath. The television was off—nighttime schedules didn't have the same comforting predictability as daytime—and she was listening to Coldplay, and crying gently, so as not to wake him. On the thick arms of the chair were photos, one of Ben's work diaries, and his wallet, still with exactly the same money and cards in it.

Juliet didn't feel any worse or better for her tears, just tired.

Minton's ears drew back and he sat up, suddenly alert. Juliet ignored him. Minton could tell if a cat had so much as stepped into their back garden; he took it very personally. She stroked his ear and tried to bring Ben's summer clothes back into her mind. That had been the year he got badly sunburned on an unexpectedly hot day and had had to wear shirts for the rest of . . .

Or was that the previous year? She frowned, with her eyes shut, and her brain was about to ask Ben; then—as happened ten times a day—she realized there was no way she could ever check that again. It was gone. A yawning pain rose in her chest.

There was a noise in the porch, and Minton slipped off her knee to investigate. It sounded like the brass letterbox clattering. Probably pizza leaflets. For six months after Ben died, her dad had had all her mail redirected to his house, so she wouldn't have to be faced with Ben's name every morning. Eric had sorted it carefully, dealing with the financial red tape, and gently redelivered packages of cards and notes each morning, pretending each time that he was "just passing."

The condolence letters had dried up now, as had the phone calls. It was as if everyone had forgotten she was still abandoned. The first junk mail addressed to Ben had sent a chill through her heart, though, and it was only then that Juliet realized what a shield her dad had been.

She heaved herself out of the chair and went through to the porch to see what had come through the letterbox.

It wasn't a pizza leaflet. It was an A4 envelope, addressed to Juliet in a bold print she didn't recognize. Her name was written in purple felt-tip.

She headed back to the kitchen, opening it as she went. Inside was a stapled set of papers, partly typed and partly written over. Intrigued, Juliet flipped on the kettle and the small table lamp that really belonged in the bedroom but was doubling as a kitchen light for the time being.

Juliet, read the postcard on the top. It was a free postcard from a cinema.

> *I've done you a full quotation for the work on your house. One set to show any workmen, so they know you mean business. The other set I've marked up for yourself. It's more realistic. I could probably fit you in if you want me to do the work, but can't do it all at once. Give us a call, anyway. You know where I am.*
>
> *Cheers,*
> *Lorcan*

The list went on for several pages in Lorcan's measured handwriting. Juliet hesitated, before she read on. She still had another thirty minutes of miserable wallowing left; did she have the energy to look at this? Was it cheating to distract herself early?

Minton's claws skittered over the kitchen floor. He ended up underneath the Tupperware box with the Bonios—not begging, just hinting with his shiny eyes. He looked perky. He looked, Juliet thought, quite happy that Grief Hour had ended early and normal nighttime service had been resumed.

Me too, she thought. *There's only so much Coldplay a girl can take.*

With a sigh, she opened the lid and offered him a Bonio, which he took delicately from her hand and carried off to the kitchen sofa to eat in peace, keeping an eye on her at the same time.

Juliet made herself a coffee and started to skim the list, which went on for page after page: *Plaster sitting room, repaint rooms × 8, check windows, refit bathroom suite . . .*

In her mind's eye she could see the house changing around her like a fast-forwarded home improvement show, soft colors climbing the ragged walls like ivy and neutral carpets swooping over bare boards like the tide coming in. Part of her shrank from that. *How will I know if it's what Ben would have liked*, she agonized, *without Ben here to ask?*

Lorcan's notes were frank. *Don't let any cheeky bastards charge you extra for paint*, he'd written. *I've got a contact who can get you trade prices.*

Juliet tried to stand outside her body for a moment. It made sense to use someone she knew. Lorcan had said himself that builders needed supervision; who better to get than the builder who lived next door? She could supervise him from the comfort of her own room, and check out his lunch breaks from her garden.

"God," said Juliet out loud, "that almost sounds like Louise talking."

Minton looked up from the sofa.

"Sorry," she said. "Just trying to think how Auntie Lou would tackle this."

Louise would make a plan, then action it—just as she had with marriage, career, babies. It was almost surprising that Lou hadn't been round to look at the building work herself—she'd had their conservatory built in the same time it had taken Juliet and Ben to choose a bird table.

For some reason, Juliet got a snakes-and-ladders image in her head whenever she thought of Louise: One moment she and Louise had been even, with something in common for the first time in years, and then Louise had shot up a ladder to motherhood, while she'd slid back so many squares, right back to the beginning. No baby. No husband. Nothing. Just a slow climb back and no chance now of a golden wedding anniversary, not unless they invented eternal-life tablets before she was fifty.

Juliet closed her eyes and let the jealousy wash through. It wasn't a nice emotion, but Louise had everything she'd ever wanted. Everything. And she didn't seem to realize how precious it all was, how easily it could all be lost.

She opened her eyes again, this time shying away from the memories that sprang into her mind.

Focus on what you can change, she told herself. *Like this house.*

At the end of the notes was a costing, and it made Juliet feel a bit sick. Lorcan had added, *I could do it for 20 percent less but not in one go, which would spread the cost out.*

She put the list down on the kitchen table and clutched her hot cup between both hands. That was a *lot* more than she'd expected. The romantic plan had been for her and Ben to do up their dream house together, room by room, in their own vision. *Romantic* meaning "no choice"—they'd stretched themselves to get it in the first place, with most of their savings going into the deposit. And "her and Ben" really meant Ben doing the DIY with help from his mates, and her choosing colors and where the plug sockets went.

There was no budget for builders. Most of his life insurance payout had been swallowed up by the mortgage—and that made Juliet's mind turn uncomfortably to the other matter she'd been trying not to think about: her job.

Juliet had worked for her friend Kim's catering company, Kim's Kitchen, since she'd left college. They'd built up a reputation for wedding receptions, mainly because of Juliet's intricate cupcake towers, which had become their signature. Kim had other caterers working for her, but she and Juliet were old friends, and when Ben died, she'd generously given her leave with some pay, even though she didn't have to.

It had been awkward, extending her time off, but she wasn't sure she could work anyway: Juliet's taste buds had completely gone. She didn't want to eat anything, or bake anything, or cook anything, now that Ben wasn't here to taste and enjoy her meals. There didn't seem to be any point. And for someone as keen on food as Juliet, that was a genuinely disorientating sensation.

But Ben's life insurance had only paid for the house, not her bills. She'd have to get some money coming in at some point, now that what little savings she'd had was almost gone. She wasn't eating, but Minton was. Like a king, as she tried to make up for his loss with sell-by-date steak and sausages.

Juliet looked at Lorcan's estimates again. Daytime television wisdom used to say that doing up a house and then selling it could be a worthwhile job in itself, but the experts had gone quite quiet on that front lately.

"No money in dream homes anymore, Minton," she said, then rolled her eyes at herself. When had she started talking non-ironically to him? That was a sign that it was time to turn in. "Bedtime."

Minton leaped happily off the sofa, and they headed upstairs together.

Chapter 9

When the doorbell rang at eight in the morning, it cut through a dream Juliet was having about Ben's funeral. This time, she wasn't just sitting in the front pew like a statue; she was standing up at the lectern, saying all the beautiful, honest things that only occurred to her later, when her brain emerged from the haze of Xanax, and it was too late.

Everyone was crying as she spoke, and when she looked up from the shiny black coffin, covered in flowers from Ben's old clients' gardens, she saw Ben himself at the back of the church, listening, crying, smiling at her, in his favorite old T-shirt. It was the green one.

The doorbell rang again.

She struggled to consciousness and realized Minton was curled up on her chest. When she moved, he jerked to life.

"Who the hell's that?" She checked her watch. "At this hour?"

It was warm under the duvet, and snug. Juliet considered

pretending she wasn't in, but the doorbell rang more impatiently. Then someone knocked, for good measure.

Minton leaped down to investigate, and with a sigh, Juliet threw back the duvet and followed him downstairs.

Outside, she found Diane on the step, plucking deadheads off her climbing rose while Coco watched. Diane looked perky and upbeat in her new Power Granny outfit—nothing dangly, flat Clarks pumps, and dark trousers. All very wipe-clean.

"Hello, love! Oh! Did I wake you? Are you . . . up?" she added, frowning at her pajama bottoms coupled with an outdoor fleece.

"I've been out already this morning." Juliet rubbed her bleary eyes. She'd tossed and turned for hours; then when she'd given up and gone downstairs for some tea, there'd been no milk or biscuits, so she and Minton had driven over to the all-night Tesco, where exhaustion had finally ambushed her at the self-checkout. Her moonlit wanderings round the supermarket weren't so comforting now that she was keeping daylight hours too.

"Not Tesco again?"

"Does it matter?" Not that she was going to tell her mother, but Juliet planned to make up the missing hours on the sofa, with Coco.

Diane pulled a worried face. "We'll talk about it later—I can't stop. I thought I'd bring Coco to you this time. Save you driving over to Louise's." She handed Juliet a Ziploc bag of food, with a separate one of treats. "Make sure she gets her full walk, darling. She's got her weigh-in at the vet's on Monday—she's on their diet plan. We both are. The surgery's in league with the vet."

Diane looked a bit shifty and handed Juliet a plastic clip. "Oh, and . . . would you mind popping this on?"

"What's this?"

"A pedometer. I'm supposed to wear it, then times it by three for Coco."

"But, Mum, that's cheating!" Juliet protested. "You can't—"

"Bye!" And Diane was gone.

Juliet, Coco, and Minton stayed under Juliet's duvet for a soothing hour of antiques and toast. Minton and Coco ate most of the toast.

Sewing boxes were bought, then sold. The TV sun shone. The dogs snored, content, and Coco's warm bulk soothed Juliet in a way that made her pathetically grateful to the big Labrador. There was something comforting about being lain on; it wasn't quite as good as a human cuddle, but it was enough.

The three of them could have stayed like that indefinitely, but they were disturbed at eleven by the sound of drilling from next door. Drilling that the television couldn't drown out. Just when Juliet thought she might be able to cope with earplugs and subtitles, Roisin and Florrie arrived on the doorstep with a slice of sponge cake covered in green icing and coconut.

"Are you not up yet?" demanded Roisin. "Why aren't you up? Grown-ups should be up and dressed before children. It's the law."

"Mum's sent you some cake," said Florrie, proffering the plate.

"Is this to do with that noise?" Juliet asked. She had to raise her voice.

"What noise?" yelled Roisin. "We're not having building work done!"

Juliet narrowed her eyes. That sounded like a practiced response. It made her wonder about building regulations. She was pretty sure this was a conservation area.

"Is this Salvador's birthday cake?" she asked. If it was, it was several days old.

"Yes," said Florrie. "Mum says it's a bribe. But it's nice cake. Roisin ate some of the icing off it, sorry. Hello, doggies!" She shoved the plate at Juliet and bent down to stroke Minton, who'd appeared like Juliet's shadow.

Juliet grabbed him with her spare hand before he could sniff out any pet rodents concealed about Florrie's person. "Mind out for your mice." She scooped him up awkwardly under one arm. "How long's this going on for? This not-building work?"

"Till Lorcan's put up the big plank."

"Right." What was that? Juliet's heart sank. "Are they knocking down walls in there?"

"Do you want the cake?" asked Roisin. "Because I'll have it if you don't."

"I'll have it," she said. "Tell your mum thanks, but I hope this won't be going on all day." Juliet paused. "Tell your uncle Lorcan that too."

The girls eyed her, not suspiciously, but with a curiosity that seemed beyond their years.

"What do you *do*?" Roisin went on. "Why aren't you at work?"

Florrie nudged her. "Rois-*in. Questions.*"

"I'm going out," said Juliet. "With my dogs. And I hope it'll be a bit quieter when I come back."

A quick shower later and Juliet stood by the front door, readying herself for the outside world. She stuffed a bag of kibble, some poo bags, and Ben's whistle into her jacket pockets, then checked her bag for her phone, her purse, her hankies, her mints, her keys, the Rescue Remedy she'd need if she bumped into someone she knew who'd ask her how she was getting on . . .

Don't bother, said a silkily persuasive voice in her head. *There's a St. Trinian's film on at two. Just put Mum's pedometer on Minton and make them run round the garden. Give Roisin and Florrie a quid each to throw balls.*

She closed her eyes and fought to keep the energy going, but when she opened them, Minton was gazing up at her. He was actually trembling with excitement at the prospect of going for a walk, even with his harness on, but even so, he wasn't pawing the door or tugging at the lead.

Even Coco looked quite excited.

"Oh, Minton," she said, feeling bad. His world used to be the whole of Longhampton and all the gardens within twenty miles. Now it was just the house. And the towpath, if he was lucky.

I'll take my iPod, she thought. *If I put that on, I won't have to talk to anyone. I'll be out, but not open for chatting.*

"Step on it," she told the pair of them, over the sound of renewed banging next door. "I want to be back for *Flog It!*"

Juliet parked in the free car park by the library and set off on Diane's prescribed route toward the municipal gardens, then out of the gate at the end of the park and up the hill into the Forestry Commission trail.

The path was quiet, but Juliet put her iPod on, anyway—music blocked out any real thoughts, and sent out a *not for chatting* message to other walkers. She walked briskly, to keep up with Minton's bustling investigations, and let her eyes drift around as they turned down toward the canal. The route was familiar now, but her eye, sharpened by Ben's enthusiastic botany lessons, spotted the difference in the wild hedges: The blackberry bushes and nettles were taller and more lush after a few days' rain, and white flowers had spread out along the hedgerows.

Coco and Minton obviously saw changes everywhere, stopping every hundred meters to sniff furiously at nothing and, in Minton's case, leave a calling card. "Pee-mail," as Diane had put it, indulgently.

Juliet did not want to turn into *that* sort of dog owner. The pun-making kind.

As they got nearer the town center, they passed a few people she recognized by sight—the woman who owned the café in town that let dogs in being towed along by a basset hound, a man with a border collie—and all of them would have stopped to pet Minton, but Juliet smiled politely and kept walking. She didn't mind them smiling at her dogs, but she wasn't ready yet to talk to anyone herself. The outside world, in its unpredictability, was something she wanted to keep at arm's length.

Juliet stopped at the coffee stand by the wrought-iron gates and ordered a cappuccino to drink as she did a lap of the park, to keep herself awake as much as anything. She was juggling leads and bags when she heard someone call her name.

"Juliet!"

Juliet spun round, but she didn't see anyone she knew.

"Your change?"

"Oh. Right, thanks." She turned back to put her purse in her bag, with two leads over one wrist, when a woman in a quilted jacket and knee-length skirt came right up to her.

"Juliet!" She was beaming as if they were old friends.

Juliet tried a cautious smile but felt herself retract, like a crab pulling itself inside its shell. *I don't want to talk to anyone*, she thought. *Isn't it obvious from my face?*

"I'm so glad I saw you. I was hoping you'd be around. Hector! Hector, stop that right now. Oh, you are a one for the pretty girls!"

When Juliet looked down and saw the lascivious dachshund sniffing Coco's ample rear end, the penny dropped. It was . . . She had to cudgel her brains not to think, *Mrs. Hector* . . . Barbara Taylor.

"I just thought, spotting you there, it'd be a good idea for you to take him for a bit of a trial first, before you have him officially. Make sure you two get on. And if you could get him walking a bit more obediently, I'd be ever so grateful."

How was she meant to do that? Juliet wasn't sure what she could say. She wanted to point out that she was no expert, but did Barbara honestly think she was? Was this another of her mother's interferences?

"As it happens, I've got to nip into town now," Barbara went on. "I was going to leave him up at the rescue center for the morning, but since I've bumped into you, maybe you could have him instead? Just for an hour or so, time for a w-a-l-k."

"I'm not—"

"I've got your number, haven't I? I'll give you a ring when I'm done and we can meet up!"

Juliet guessed that Barbara Taylor had a large family. She delivered all these instructions in a manner that sounded like they were only suggestions but actually didn't leave any room for discussion. And somehow, Juliet's fall-back Angry Widow persona wasn't coming through. How annoying—just when she could have used it.

"I don't live in town," she said weakly. "I've just brought the dogs in for a walk, and I wasn't planning to be out long . . ."

"No problem! Whiz him round the dog trail and I'll be back in no time. Be good, Hector! Bye now!"

Juliet found herself standing by the coffee stand with three leads, one cooling coffee, her change, and, now, a pile of poo to clear up.

"Do you need a hand?" asked the coffee girl kindly.

The only advantage Juliet could see in walking three dogs at once was that at least no one was coming anywhere near her with the dog world's answer to Russell Brand on the end of an extendable lead.

It was bad enough trying to find a pace that suited Coco on one hand and Minton and Hector on the other, but finding a way of walking them so Hector wasn't constantly doing the dog equivalent of bottom-pinching at Coco—and any other passing bitch—was harder.

"Get *away* from her," said Juliet, yanking Hector back from a Yorkshire terrier. "She's not your type. I'm sorry," she added to the owner. "Sorry!"

"Hello, Hector," said the owner, and walked on with a sympathetic smile.

"You are showing me up," hissed Juliet. "Get a hold of yourself."

Hector strutted on regardless, his beard bristling with confidence.

They were out of the paint-box flower beds of the municipal gardens now, heading up the path toward the forest behind. Every so often yellow signs steered them between the different trails on offer, and red dog-poo bins gave a not-so-subtle reminder of whom the woods really belonged to.

Minton loved Coneygreen Woods; they were riddled with squirrels and rabbits, and Juliet knew that if she let him off, he'd be gone in a flash. Hector, too, strained at his extending lead, wriggling under bushes on his short legs.

This had been a favorite Sunday walk for her and Ben, a leisurely stroll around Coneygreen, Ben testing her on her tree knowledge and letting Minton dig to his heart's content, then back down into town for sausage sandwiches at the Wild Dog Café, where you could bring your pooch inside while you had brunch.

Juliet's feet had taken the path up the hill automatically, and she hadn't thought about where she'd end up until she was there:

right in front of the viewing point that looked down on the corrugated streets and Victorian chimney clusters of Longhampton. The one nightclub, Majestic, where she and Ben had sneaked in as underage teenagers, next to the self-important arch of the railway station. The half-demolished church bombed in the war that they'd done a project on at school, the old Masonic Hall that was supposedly haunted. The viewing platform was the place where they'd always stopped midwalk and pointed all this familiar stuff out, the same every time.

Juliet looked over the town now, but none of this meant half so much now that Ben wasn't here to say it to. All those memories like cobwebs, so delicate and now so easily lost. If she forgot, who was there to remind her?

She gritted her teeth and made herself look, picking out the details anyway. Tears pricked at her eyes, but she carried on; a couple of months earlier, this would have been completely impossible. She was making tiny steps forward. Maybe the Grief Hour was achieving something.

Then she realized the leads had gone slack in her hand.

Coco sat by her feet, out of either obedience or laziness, but Minton and Hector were nowhere to be seen. In a panic, Juliet pressed the rewind button on Minton's long line and it went tense—which meant somewhere far, far away he was doing a comedy recoil—but Hector's didn't.

Hector's lead spun back, and at the end of it was a collar. He'd broken loose.

"Shit." Juliet looked around for something to tie Coco to, then thought better of it. Losing Coco to Longhampton's first recorded dog thief would just put the tin lid on things.

"Come on," she said, tugging her to her feet. "We've got to look for that stupid sausage dog."

Minton had gone missing in these woods before, and Juliet

remembered the stomach-churning panic that had set in after twenty minutes' fruitless yelling. They were dense woods with plenty of rabbit holes for little dogs to wedge themselves in. In fact, weren't dachshunds designed to go down rabbit holes? Hector looked the type to dive in first without thinking about an exit strategy. Her heart sank.

"Hector? Hector! Minton, come here!"

Juliet was trotting and pulling on Minton's lead at the same time. Several feet away, his white rear end emerged from a thick outcrop of bracken, followed, after a quick wriggle, by his cross face. Leaves were stuck in his harness, like a badly camouflaged soldier.

"Where's Hector?" she demanded, irrationally. "Where's he gone?"

It was at times like these that she wished she'd trained Minton to do something more useful than just bring her the remote control.

"Hector!" she yelled. Blood was pumping in her temples, squeezing her brain, and panic had set in, sharpened by the disproportionate fury that laced many minor situations recently.

How had this happened? *Why* was she now faced with this embarrassing, stressful—

"Get off! Get off!"

Juliet stopped and listened. Someone was yelling up ahead.

And there was yapping too. Two lots of yapping, one the deep yap of an amorous dachshund.

"Off!"

"Oh, bollocks," breathed Juliet, and broke into a run. The path wound round to the right and steepened, with trees on either side, and it wasn't until she turned the corner, breathless, that she saw a man grabbing a black-and-white cocker spaniel and practically holding it above his head, while Hector danced about on his hind legs, pawing the man's trousers.

"Hector! Come here right now!" Juliet sprinted the final few meters and reached out with the collar. As she did, she slipped on some loose leaves and lurched to the ground, knocking the man off balance. He staggered, already weaving under the weight of his own dog, and they both landed in the bracken with a crash.

Minton and Coco, still attached to Juliet's wrist by the leads, followed.

Juliet lay motionless for a couple of seconds, while the barking reverberated around the trees. There had been times in the past eight months when she'd stepped out of her own head, watching her distress as if it were a television drama, and now she wished she could do the same. Only she couldn't. She was definitely feeling every ounce of mortification going, even if her body was still impervious to physical pain.

The man started scrambling to his feet, and she felt obliged to do the same, though she could have lain there a bit longer, working out what to say. Apologies rushed out of her, on autopilot because she didn't feel like apologizing deep down. She felt like roaring and crashing around like a giant, hurling Hector over the trees, followed by Barbara Taylor, for putting her in this position.

"I'm so sorry," she gabbled. "Really sorry. He's not my dog. He must have slipped his collar."

"Why wasn't it on tighter?" the man demanded.

"I don't know. I didn't put it on. I'm just walking him . . . Come here, Hector!" Juliet grabbed the dachshund by the scruff of his neck and clamped him between her knees to get his collar on.

"If you can't control him, then he should be in some kind of harness," the man continued. He was well-spoken but obviously angry. "Did you see what he was trying to do to my dog, for God's sake! That's tantamount to assault."

"Is she in season?" Juliet was struggling to stay polite, even though she knew she was in the wrong. "Should she even be *out*?"

The man straightened up and glared at her. "Damson's spayed. He's wasting his time. Seriously, behavior like that . . . it's going to get him reported. It's outrageous."

Juliet sank back on her heels as the anger abruptly left her. It did that.

She raked a hand through her hair and wished she were somewhere else. "I'm really sorry. I'm going to tell his owner to get him some bromide, or whatever they gave soldiers in the war. Hector, stop wriggling!"

Juliet added an extra shake—not hard, but the same shake Minton administered to his stuffed toys—and gripped his scruff. Hector seemed to respond, turning his dark-brown eyes up at her with new respect.

She looked at the man, who was calming his spaniel down, stroking her feathery ears and making dog-person soothing noises.

At least it was a man and not some nice old dear she'd rugby-tackled into the bushes. Quite a handsome man too, she thought. He reminded her of the younger antiques-expert regular, the one who had all the grannies giggling into their pottery—tall and professional-looking with sandy-blond hair that flopped onto his face, and glasses. Intelligent hazel eyes behind the glasses, and a wry mouth that might smile at some point, but probably not in the next five minutes, going by his expression.

"Have you ripped anything?" she asked.

He looked down, inspecting his jacket and jeans. "No, I'm fine. Could have been worse. Could have landed in the brambles." He nodded toward the spiky bushes a few feet to their left.

"Or in the poo bin." Juliet nodded toward the other side of the path. Actually, now that she inspected the scene, it could have been a *lot* worse.

"Indeed. And are you okay? You took much more of a crash than I did."

When she looked back, the man was staring at her, clearly checking her out for damage. She put a hand to her head, in case she was covered in something embarrassing. "I'm fine."

"And the dogs?"

"Oh, they're fine too." This was getting awkward now. Was this stiff questioning some kind of preliminary to insurance claims? She started attaching the leads to her various dogs. "I'll have a word with Hector's owner. You're right—he needs to see the vet."

Juliet bent down again and stroked the spaniel's soft head. "Sorry, Damson. It won't happen again. You shouldn't have to suffer sex pests on your walk. Even if you are beautiful."

She was expecting a snappy retort from her owner, but the man let out a short laugh. "Well, dogs are dogs. You can't expect them to do dinner and a film. Hector, is it?" The eyes behind the glasses weren't so angry now. They were almost amused.

"Yup. And Coco, and Minton. Minton's mine. I'm just walking the other two."

"We were . . ." He indicated up the hill. "Which way were you going?"

Juliet hesitated. Was he suggesting they walk together, or making sure she didn't take her dogs in the same direction?

"I'm heading back into town," she said. "I think it's time Hector had an early bath."

"Right. Well, then." He pressed his lips together and nodded.

What am I meant to say? wondered Juliet. There was obviously a gap here for something. Compensation for Damson's hurt feelings? A box of Bonios for pain and suffering?

"Sorry again," she said. "Come on, you lot."

It was only when Juliet was halfway down the hill that she realized that in proper dog-walker fashion, she'd introduced her dogs but not herself.

Juliet, Minton, Coco, and a subdued Hector did several uneventful laps of the rose gardens before Barbara Taylor reappeared at the mobile coffee stand, laden down with bags. She'd clearly made the most of her dog-sitting time in Longhampton's main square, particularly M&S.

"Here," she said, before Juliet could start telling her what Hector had been up to. "Is ten pounds okay? It's what I give Rachel up at the rescue center for half a day. I know I was gone a bit longer than I said."

"That's . . ." Juliet didn't have a free hand, so Barbara tucked the note into her jacket pocket.

"We didn't discuss a rate for the days, did we?" she went on. "I'd be happy to pay the same as I give Rachel, plus a little bit more because he'll be getting one-on-one attention." She bent down and chucked Hector's beard. "He's a mummy's boy, aren't you?"

Juliet squinted against the sun. "That's not exactly how I'd describe him. Don't you find him a little bit . . . frisky?"

"Frisky?" Barbara laughed. "He can be a naughty boy, but that's why I love him."

Hector let her ruffle his beard, as if butter wouldn't melt.

Maybe I should give him the benefit of the doubt, thought Juliet. *It was probably my fault for letting him out of my sight.* She flashed him a look that said, *You're on a warning, mate.*

"He might be better on a harness," she said, thinking of some other dogs she'd seen on the way. "Might make him easier to control?"

"Ooh, do you think? I'll look into it," said Barbara, as if Juliet knew what she was talking about. "You've obviously got a knack with dogs! Look at these three."

Minton, Coco, and Hector were sitting in a neat line next to Juliet, not so much as sniffing at the coffee stand.

"Come on, Hector," she said, taking his lead. "Let's get you home. We'll see you soon, Juliet! Bye now! Bye-bye, Minton!"

Juliet started to say, "Bye, Hector!" but she stopped herself, just in time.

Coco and Minton gazed up at her, like two children overwhelmed with relief that the nightmare playmate has gone, but too polite to say so.

"Home," said Juliet. "We're missing *Time Team*."

She'd have to let them both up on the sofa with her to make up for it.

Chapter 10

It was a Monday, and that meant no Coco. And that meant no need to get up.

Juliet hadn't bothered to wake up properly when the alarm went off, and had instead rolled over, trying to get herself back into a nice dream about Ben. But even though she tried to conjure up scenes from their photo album, the images stayed stubbornly static, and when the doorbell rang again, she threw back the covers crossly.

She grabbed her dressing gown from the back of the door and yanked it over her pajamas, stamping down each step as the doorbell carried on ringing.

"What?" she demanded, as she pulled the door open, expecting to see her mother with Coco. "Can't you just leave her with the—Oh."

Lorcan was on the doorstep, in a Bad Company T-shirt that was the adult version of Roisin's, with a couple of big plastic bags on the path next to him. His hair was even more disheveled than hers, as if he'd just rolled out of bed himself.

"I've come to fix your shower."

"I don't have a shower," said Juliet.

"So I hear." Lorcan swept a hand toward the bags. "But you do now."

"Sorry, you've lost me."

"Your mam gave me a call, asked me how things were going with your building work. Don't look so surprised—she took my card. She needs someone to have a look at her gutters."

She does not, thought Juliet. Keith had been Diane's first port of call for anything bigger than a broken lightbulb for twenty years.

She made a mental note to take her mother up on that, but there was no point being rude to Lorcan.

"And while we were chatting," he went on, bending down to tweak Minton's ears, "she asked me if you'd got round to fitting a shower yet, and I said, no, I hadn't seen one in there, and she said she'd stand you a bathroom upgrade." He pointed to the bag. "This one came into my possession, if you know what I mean." Lorcan pulled a *Say no more* face.

"You mean it fell off the back of a lorry?" asked Juliet. She folded her arms, aware that she was standing on her doorstep in her pajamas. She didn't even know what time it was, but Lorcan was showing no sign that there was anything amiss.

"Indeed it did. But very carefully." His blue eyes twinkled, and then he seemed to remember he had to knock off the charm with her. "Luckily for you and your lovely period house, it's a good-quality brass shower system that'd go very nicely with your décor. As I can demonstrate to you. Perhaps over a cup of tea?"

He swept a hand toward the boxes, and Juliet knew this was the point in the conversation where she was supposed to let him in and ask if he'd eaten breakfast yet because she could always put some toast on, et cetera.

But some residual stubbornness kept her hand on the door frame. *What happened to adult boundaries*, she thought, childishly. *Did Mum check with me before she told Lorcan to come round?*

"Um, I hadn't really made any decisions about the bathroom. I was still thinking about what order to do all that work," she said. "It was quite a lot to take in. Thanks, by the way. Do I . . . owe you anything for your time?"

"Oh, no." Lorcan flapped his hand and she noticed the friendship bracelet on his wrist; it looked like something one of the girls had made. "Do some babysitting for Emer or something. Feed their cat when they're away."

"They go away?"

"Not often." Lorcan caught the note of hopefulness in her voice and grinned. "Come on, now, this is a good shower. And your mam's paying. I'd snatch her hand off meself."

"I don't—"

"Juliet, you've got long hair," he pointed out. "How are you washing it, if you don't have a shower?"

"Shower attachments," she said, without thinking. "On the bath taps." Which didn't mix properly. And dribbled. She didn't add that, though.

"Shower attachments?" Lorcan looked askance. "Are we in 1981? Come on. Everyone needs a good shower; it's a human right. I can have this in before you can say *Head and Shoulders*." He glanced at his watch. "Before teatime, anyway."

Juliet had nothing to do, and there was no reason not to throw the door open and make Lorcan a cup of tea to get things moving, but she felt the barriers going up. And not just because she wasn't dressed. "I'm about to go out for a walk," she said. "Well, I mean, not now, but soon. It's not a good time. I'm not . . . ready to start with the shower. There's other stuff needs doing first."

"Sheez, I can work around mess," said Lorcan. "You've seen next door."

Juliet hugged herself. It seemed like such a small thing, a shower, but it wasn't. Not to her. Showers were the only concrete aspect of the house that she and Ben had actually talked about properly; he wanted a proper Victorian shower, the size of a dinner plate. One they could stand under together.

Was there any point getting a big one now? Would getting a big one be a sign to Ben that she planned to shower with someone else in his place?

"I'm not . . ." she said, and her voice cracked. "I don't mean to be rude, but it's the first step. Probably doesn't seem like a lot, but it's . . . you know."

Lorcan's cheeriness crumpled. "Fair enough. I just had a free morning and thought, after we'd talked about your bathroom the other day, you seemed okay about . . . Look, when would be a good time? I can leave the stuff here and pop round some other day. Or get someone else. Or not do it at all."

"I'm really sorry." She gulped. "I'm not . . . It just comes and goes. I was fine when we went round the house! Honestly, I was fine. I am fine now."

"You're not. It's okay to be in bits. I understand." He was fiddling with the tape measure.

Come on, Juliet, she urged herself.

Think of the lovely shower.

That I'll never share.

"Why don't you leave it here," she said quickly. "I'll call round and talk about when's a good time to fit it later. We can discuss the quote too. Talk about . . . whatever it is you talk about with building work."

The words tumbled out of her, and she hardly knew what she was saying, but the worry lines around Lorcan's eyes relaxed and some of the confidence returned.

"Grand," he said, shifting the bags into her porch. "I'm in and out—you've got my number."

"I have." Juliet started to close the door. "Thanks."

"Have a good walk." Lorcan winked and then sauntered off down the path, hands in the pockets of his battered jeans.

Juliet closed the door as quietly as she could, so he wouldn't think she was slamming it on him, but wanting it shut all the same. Her heart was hammering, and she felt agitated, as if she'd just defended the house from attack.

Minton came over and sniffed at the boxes as she sank back against the tiles of the porch wall. His eager nose moved the bag aside and she got a glimpse of the shower fitting.

It was a beautiful brass Victorian raincloud one. The exact same one she'd picked out of the interiors magazine.

Even though Coco didn't need walking, Minton still went to the door at their usual time, and Juliet didn't have the heart to tell him no.

She didn't feel up to the park and the gardens, where people were bound to stop and talk to Minton, if not her. She didn't feel up to running into Spaniel Man again either and having to make some off-the-cuff, dog-owners-together quip about horny Hector.

Instead she headed for the far end of Longhampton's footpath network, which snaked behind the 1930s Bishops Meadow estate and the pond that had probably once hosted a fairly active ducking stool but was now mainly weed. There was no one around, but to be on the safe side, she plugged in her iPod and strode purposefully down the gentle hill, listening to an audiobook of *Emma* and engaging with Jane Austen in a way she'd never managed at school.

After a while, her breathing got into a rhythm and her brain zoned out, and all that filled her mind was the blue sky above her; the fresh, green-smelling summer air in her nose; and the words in her head. Minton skittered along happily next to her, keeping pace, and to Juliet's surprise, the sun on her face made her heart lift in an innocent way.

But the sight of a friendly-looking elderly couple with three yapping Yorkshire terriers made her divert at the bottom. The road curved toward an old-fashioned parade of small shops, and Juliet knew she could loop round on herself and rejoin her original route. They were already smiling, doing that too-far-to-speak-now-but-we're-getting-to-you! eyebrow jiggling.

Juliet didn't want to be rude; she just really didn't want to chat.

"Come on, Minton," she said, tugging him away from a lamppost. "Let's see what's new on South Parade."

When Juliet was little, South Parade had had frumpy ladies-outfitters-type boutiques with warped cellophane in the bay windows. In the last few years, however, yummy mummies had colonized the big family houses nearby, and now the haberdasheries and wool shops had been made over into blackboarded delicatessens and pottery cafés. Diane had frequented Angela's Hair for years; now it was rebranded as Angel Hair.

Juliet gazed at the sleek new exterior and tried to imagine that she'd once played with Velcro rollers and setting lotion on the floor of this—she peered at the sign—*authorized Aveda spa experience.*

I have to tell Ben that Angela's doing hot stones, she thought. *He could cut her a deal on really big pebbles . . .*

A lump bulged in her throat.

Juliet looked for something to distract herself, and her eye fell on the new price list. Lorcan's comment about her hair had made her realize she hadn't had a haircut for nearly a year. Her hair certainly hadn't been tumbling then; it had been a neat, if curly bob.

Maybe it's time to get it cut, she thought, *now that I'm past the* shave it all off, I don't care *stage*. The same book that had told her she'd feel better in a year also warned against any sudden beauty decisions—radical haircuts, memorial tattoos, and so on.

Juliet widened her eyes at the prices—the towels weren't the only thing to have gone upmarket—but as she peered inside to see if there was any evidence of gold-plated hair dryers being used, she spotted her mother. Diane was paying at the cash register, and as she turned to pretend to consider the shampoo and conditioner being sold quite fiercely to her, she in turn spotted Juliet through the window.

Their eyes met.

Damn, thought Juliet. There was no sneaking off.

Juliet frowned and raised her eyebrows, racking her brains for something she needed to be getting back home for. She wasn't even walking someone else's dog. *Maybe I could be going to collect Hector*, she thought.

Diane flapped her hands, said something to the receptionist, then dashed out.

"What are you doing here?" She looked quite flustered.

"Walking Minton. Is that big news?"

"No, I just . . ." Diane plastered a smile on her face. "It's just nice to see you two out and about. Hello, Minton!"

Now that she was out of the salon, Juliet could see her mother's hair properly, and she was genuinely taken aback.

It was the first time in twenty years that she'd seen Diane with a style other than her usual mum cut. This was freshly layered and shimmering with expensive highlights, and cut in a style that made her look like one of the attractive "older models" in the M&S catalog.

"Mum, have you had highlights?" she asked.

"Yes." Diane patted her blow-dry self-consciously. "Some honey lights, Angela said."

"And proper layers?" Juliet knew she was staring. "It takes *years* off you."

"Does it? You could find a nicer way of putting that, Juliet, but . . . thank you. Sometimes it's good to make . . . a few changes. Now, coffee? We can sit outside. And don't pretend you've got something to be doing." Diane wagged a finger playfully. "Unless you're going to tell me you've escaped from some building work?"

"I want to talk to you about that," said Juliet grimly.

"Well, let's do it over a coffee." Her mother dropped her voice. "Angela's had one of those new machines put in. I didn't like to say, but . . ." She pulled a face. "Watery. We can walk Minton up to that place you like on the High Street, the one that lets you bring dogs in. What about that?"

This was quite a concession, Juliet knew; Louise and Diane weren't convinced about the hygiene in the Wild Dog Café, despite its spotless surfaces and perfect cappuccinos. Juliet loved it, but she hadn't been in for a while; it reminded her too much of taking Minton there with Ben.

"Let's just go to whatever the Coffee Pot's calling itself now," she said, nodding toward the end of the shops.

Juliet allowed her mother to steer her down to the café at the end, which had once served lukewarm Crusha milkshakes and now served 327 variations on a cappuccino and called itself the Pantry. Minton curled up under the table and tried not to be noticed.

"Mum, why did you buy me a shower and then send Lorcan round with it?" said Juliet when the coffees had arrived, in huge cups with too-small handles.

"You make it sound so bossy! I just called him to see how he'd got on with your estimates, because your father wanted to know, and he mentioned he had a shower going begging. I said, 'What a good idea. We'll take that off your hands,' and there you have it."

That sounded rehearsed to Juliet. "He just happened to have exactly the shower that Ben and I were looking at?"

"Is it?" Diane seemed surprised. "Well, then. It's meant to be."

"Mum, I really appreciate you doing this, but—"

"You can do what you want with the rest of the house," said Diane, "but no daughter of mine is going to live without proper shower facilities, and that's that." She paused, and her voice changed. "Please. Just let him install it. It'd make me feel better."

Juliet dipped her biscuit into the froth. Even she could see that it was churlish to argue; it was the shower they'd have put in anyway. Or rather the shower they'd have bought and then left lying around for eight months, while she nagged Ben to install it.

She frowned at herself. That was mean. He'd have put it in by now.

"Okay, Mum," she said. "It's very kind of you. I'll see when Lorcan can come and install it."

"Good!" Diane reached over and patted her hand. "Good. He's a nice chap, Lorcan. Reminds me of Ben."

"Mum, why does everyone have to look like someone else?" demanded Juliet, pulling her hand back as if it were hot. "Can't you let people be themselves?"

"I don't know what you—"

"You do! Peter's 'got a look of Tom Cruise.' Dad's the dead spit of Paul Newman. If he lost all his hair." Juliet paused sardonically. "Ruth still hasn't forgiven you for telling her she reminded you of Carol Vorderman. Ben is *nothing* like Lorcan. I mean, Lorcan's nothing . . ." She swallowed and started again. "Lorcan's dark-haired. Ben was blond. Lorcan's too thick to wear gloves to tackle roses. His eyes are a different color. He's shorter than Ben . . . Do you want me to go on?"

"I didn't mean *physically*," said Diane, patting her lips with a paper napkin. She was wearing lipstick again, Juliet noted. "There's just something about him that reminds me. He seems . . . capable. Kind."

"Well, I don't see it," said Juliet, stubbornly.

Diane seemed to realize she'd said the wrong thing. "I'm sorry. Anyway," she went on, changing the subject as delicately as an oil tanker, "I saw Kim today in the supermarket. Have you told her when you're going back to work?"

"Sort of. She said I should ring her when I felt up to it. She doesn't want a repeat of the cupcakes."

In an attempt to ease Juliet back into work a few months ago, Kim had asked her to make a hundred cupcakes for a wedding reception. Juliet was used to knocking out two hundred in a morning, but these had been sad and flat and awful. Louise and Diane had ended up baking them through the night for her.

"But how's she managing without you?" Diane persisted. "It's your busiest time of year."

"I *know*, Mum."

Wedding season hovered in the air between them.

Juliet stirred her coffee. The honest truth was, she didn't like people at the moment. Happy, living, married people. That was why Minton and Coco were infinitely preferable. They were highly unlikely to get married on her, or tell her she just needed to get back in the saddle, or something equally unhelpful.

"You might find it helps," Diane went on. "My friend Jean went straight back to the library when Philip died. She said thinking about something else took her mind off it."

"Mum, I don't want to let Kim down by being useless. That does neither of us any favors. Maybe in the autumn."

After the year's up. After my life gets rebooted.

Diane wasn't giving in. "Louise says Peter's looking for extra staff at Techmate now this new project's got the green light."

Juliet made a noise.

"Or there's volunteer work. I was talking to Rachel at book group and she was saying the rescue's desperately short of volunteer walkers over the summer months, when everyone's on holiday. And you're so good with dogs. In fact . . ." Diane pulled her handbag up onto the table and started searching through it. "I did tell Mrs. Cox you'd give her a call."

Juliet racked her brains. Diane's book group had a large cast and usually spent the discussion part discussing the people who hadn't made it, rather than the novel. "Mrs. Cox . . . my old piano teacher?"

"Yes, she comes along most months. She's amazing for over eighty. She's the only one who's read the book, and doesn't mind giving us what for. It's like being back in school again!"

God, it was unfair, thought Juliet, momentarily distracted from her annoyance at Diane's nagging. How come piano teachers could make it past eighty, while fit, outdoorsy gardeners only got thirty-one years?

"But she doesn't have dogs," she pointed out. "Hasn't she got cats? Those big, white Persian cats—the ones who ate cream from the good tea service, while you lot got horrible old chipped mugs the time you did *The Kite Runner*?"

"They're the ones! They are a bit . . . special. Anyway, Mrs. Cox is going on one of those Scandinavian cruises and would rather they didn't go into a cattery. They cry, poor things. I said you'd give her a ring and see about popping in to feed them while she's off."

"Mum!" Juliet felt hemmed in. "Why did you say I'd do that?"

"Oh, don't be like that, Juliet. She's only a few doors down from you in Rosehill. You could do it on your way back from walking Minton and Coco. Here, this is her number. Go on."

Diane pushed the paper at Juliet. "It's not care in the community," she added. "She'd pay you. And it's good for you to get out."

That, Juliet realized, was the point of all this. Getting her *out*.

"I'm out now, aren't I?" Juliet glared mutinously over the coffees.

It wasn't so much the act of feeding Mrs. Cox's cats—she didn't mind that—it was being shoved into someone else's routine. Making their routine hers, when she'd spent the last few months protecting herself from people and their demands and questions. Juliet could feel her carefully constructed wall of programs and naps being interrupted, and it unsettled her.

"Think of the cats," said Diane. "All alone in the cattery, with no home comforts. They hate it. I bet Minton would hate it too. You'd be doing them a favor as much as Mrs. Cox. Half an hour twice a day. Come on."

Juliet took the piece of paper. There didn't seem to be much point in refusing; she could always ring Mrs. Cox and find a good reason to let her down gently. And, she had to admit, the image of the lonely cats did strike a chord. Even if part of that chord was one of fear that she was headed for a life of spoiled pets who needed babysitting while she took herself on singles cruises.

"Why don't you call her now?" said Diane firmly. It wasn't a request.

Juliet tried to resist, but her energy had gone again. "Fine," she said.

Mrs. Cox sounded delighted to hear from her, which made Juliet suspect that Diane had prebrokered the deal, and invited her to drop in the following afternoon, "to meet my furry dictators." Minton, she assured Juliet, wouldn't be a problem, if she wanted to bring him too.

"They saw off a Labrador at the vet's last week," she chuckled indulgently. "They're no shrinking violets."

Juliet glanced down at Minton as she finished the call. He was lying by her feet, muzzle on his paws. "Poor Mints," she said. "No one's asked you if you mind sharing, have they?"

"He's a good boy," said Diane, and slipped him a bit of croissant under the table.

"And *that's* why Coco's on a diet," said Juliet, before she could stop herself.

Back in Rosehill, Juliet let Minton scuttle inside ahead of her to check for intruders or mice, as he always did, as the new man of the house.

It was promisingly quiet. So quiet she could hear the tick of the clock in the front sitting room. She slipped off her shoes and hunted for her comforting sheepskin slippers, already feeling herself sinking into the downward slope of the day, toward evening and bed, and another day ticked off.

There was a black-and-white film on Channel 4 that she'd ringed in her *Radio Times* for this afternoon; it had already started, but it was easy to pick up: some lovely doomed romance between two impeccably enunciated British actors, set during the war with plenty of uniforms and thin mustaches.

Trevor Howard had barely got his stiff upper lip out, however, when the peace of the house was shattered by the sound of two people playing recorders—in more of a competition than a duet.

Juliet closed her eyes. Could she ignore that? With the sound turned up loud on the telly?

No. They were playing at the very edge of her tolerance. And her tolerance was already five points lower than normal, thanks to the Mrs. Cox thing.

"Stay there," she called out to Minton. "Quick trip next door. Then teatime."

The recorders got louder as she strode up the path, squeaking with tantrumy fury.

No wonder Alec's never here, thought Juliet, clenching her fists. *He's probably not even on tour. He's probably just lying in blissful, solitary silence in the Watford Travelodge.*

She banged on the door, louder than she meant to. Then, when no one appeared to hear her, she banged again so hard the panes of glass rattled.

Where does this come from? she wondered, distracted by her own strength. Superwidow. Punching holes through concrete one minute, lying exhausted in front of the telly the next.

There was the sound of footsteps, and then Lorcan swung the door open. "Hello there," he said. "And I'm very, *very* sorry."

"You don't know what I'm here to say yet," said Juliet.

"I don't," he agreed, "but I find it's safer to apologize for them first. Saves time, with four of them on the loose. Frankly I'd rather not know what they've been up to."

There was something about his bewildered expression that made it impossible for Juliet to deliver the killer lines about aural torture that she'd thought up between her front door and his. Also, he had bits of plaster stuck in his curls and didn't seem to realize it.

"It's the recorders," she began, and as if for illustration, the playing started up again, this time a solo effort, like a banshee wailing at the top of the house.

"Roisin," said Lorcan. "She thinks she's the gift. She's tied a scarf to the end and she's tootling away like she's in a band." He mimed Roisin's closed-eye swaying. "Very Stevie Nicks."

"Well, can you get her to stop?" Juliet asked. "I'd hate to have to snap a recorder over my knee, but I'm willing to give it a go."

"I will." Lorcan leaned backward and roared, "Roisin! Stop your racket!" up the stairs.

The noise stopped at once.

"It's my fault," he went on, rubbing his face. "I'm supposed to be supervising music practice. Emer's had to rush off to the clinic with Spike, and Salvador's at his football night."

"Oh, no!" Juliet felt bad for making a fuss. "Is Spike okay?"

"Spike? Yeah, he's fine. Whatever it is'll come out the other end soon enough, apparently. Hey, will you come in for a cup of coffee?" Lorcan opened the door wider. "We were about to make some tea, just me and the girls," he went on, somehow divining her reluctance to deal with a lot of faces. "And if you're talking, Roisin and Florrie can't be playing their recorders, right?"

"Um, I won't," she said. "I've . . . I've left Minton. He doesn't like being on his own. He gets worried that I'm not coming back."

That was a bit of a lie, one she'd used a lot over the last year. Minton was fine on his own for a while; it was when she fell asleep during the day and was wakened by him desperately trying to lick her face back to life that her heart broke.

"Fair play," said Lorcan. "We'll keep it down, anyway. Must be driving Minton batty."

"Actually, there was something," Juliet began, then stopped.

This was a big step, but it was so easy just to ask.

Go on, she told herself. *Do it*.

"It's about the shower." Juliet swallowed. "When's a good time to fit it?"

"Fan—" He was about to say, "Fantastic," but he stopped before the whole word came out. Maybe he sensed that it was more than just a bathroom fitting. "I can do it this week," he said. "No time like the present. Now, listen, will you be wanting someone in to tile the wall behind it too? I'll be making a bit of a mess of it, cutting into the tiles. I know some good quick lads who could sort that out."

"Oh. Is tiling expensive?" Juliet asked. "And . . . is it hard?"

"It's a bit fiddly. Why? Are you thinking of doing it yourself?"

"No, it's just that . . ." She glanced down at the cluttered porch, with its bags of recycling, then looked back up at Lorcan. He was studying her with his friendly blue eyes, and the honest response spilled out of her. "It's just that *one*, I don't have a big budget, especially if the rest of the house needs fixing, and *two*, I was meant to be doing this with my husband. We were going to do it together . . ." She trailed off. How did you tell the builder you'd asked to do some work that actually you didn't want random builders; you wanted someone to transform your house *with*? Someone to learn with?

"I don't want to rush into a major financial commitment just yet," she said. "I only need a shower."

"I hear you," said Lorcan. "Well, why don't you start with the shower and see how it goes? What time are you up and about in the mornings? I keep forgetting what's normal when I'm here." He rolled his eyes backward in the general direction of the Kellys. "And I've been on a tour with Alec where we actually got *ahead* of the jet lag."

Juliet thought that sounded cool, even if she didn't quite understand how it was possible. It was mainly Lorcan's accent. It could make going to the shops sound pretty rock-'n'-roll.

"I'm usually up about half past seven. Depending on whether I'm walking my mom's dog or not."

"That's fine with me. Give me a radio, and lots of tea, and I'm away. I'm not one of these philosopher builders who like to talk . . . Oh, look who it is. Longhampton's first rock recorderist."

One of the red-haired twins had appeared behind Lorcan, with the cat following at her heels.

"Hello, Roisin," guessed Juliet. Fifty-fifty.

"*I'm* not Roisin," she said reprovingly. "I'm Florrie."

"You can tell by the cat," Lorcan pointed out. "Florrie has familiars, but Smokey's very scared of Roisin, isn't she?"

"Loorrrrcan," said Florrie, clinging to Lorcan's leg but keeping her unsettling blue eyes fixed on Juliet. "Lorcan, are you making some chocolate brownies for tea? We always have brownies when you're here."

"I've got a *great* recipe for brownies," said Juliet.

"Have you indeed?" said Lorcan. "It's the only thing I make."

"Very domestic goddess."

"Well." He looked sheepish. "I'm better at the ones with added extras. If you know what I mean."

"Lorcan lets us clean out the bowl. Mum doesn't," said Florrie. "Dad doesn't even let us have brownies."

Juliet itched to ask what the setup was with Lorcan and the Kellys. She knew he was a roadie with Alec and had played in a band with Emer, but why was he living with them now? Was he minding the children? It was clearly something complicated and rock-'n'-roll, and although she was curious, she also felt shy, as if asking would be intruding, displaying her ignorance.

"Sure you won't come in?" he asked again, but as he spoke, a taxi pulled up outside and Emer tumbled out, with Spike in tow. Her tortoiseshell hair was in wild corkscrews, and she was wearing a denim waistcoat over her maxi-dress. It would have looked embarrassingly unfashionable on anyone else, but somehow looked fine on Emer.

Spike was wearing a knight's helmet, with an *I was brave at the hospital!* sticker on his T-shirt. His glasses glinted through the eye slits.

"He," she said, pointing to Spike, "has got to stop eating random things! You"—she pointed to Florrie—"have got to stop telling him to. Hi, Juliet. Jayzus, is that kettle on? I'm gagging for a cup of coffee."

She rushed past Juliet in a cloud of perfume, not in an unfriendly way. Spike followed, staring at the huge bandage on his thumb through his helmet. He bumped into the side of the door, straightened himself up, then carried on.

"Come on in," said Lorcan. "You can clean out the bowl."

"Muuuuum!" Juliet heard the thunder of feet on the stairs—Roisin, she guessed. In the kitchen, the radio was turned on full blast, and Emer started singing along.

The whole house was exploding into life like a speeded-up flower opening.

This is what Lorcan meant when he said mine was a family house, thought Juliet. *Only I've got nothing to fill it.* Sadness swallowed her in a big gulp, and she needed to get away back to Minton, her wet-nosed, loyal, but silent family.

"It's okay. Things to do. I'll see you in the morning," she said hurriedly.

"Will do." Lorcan seemed on the verge of saying something else, but changed his mind and grinned. "And if you feel like making some of those brownies, I'd be happy to taste-test them compared to mine . . ."

"I'll see," said Juliet.

As she turned to walk down the path, she caught Lorcan yanking Florrie's plait from behind, then feigning ignorance when she spun round and yelped.

"It's the ghhhhoooooossssst!" he hooted, and she sprinted down the hall, screeching deliriously for Roisin.

Nothing like Ben, thought Juliet. Mum was losing her marbles.

Chapter 11

Louise wished she had a job where lunches were an actual, scheduled part of the business day—a literary agent, maybe, or something in local government—where you could take your work out to meet a nice tricolor salad, and ideally have someone else pay for it.

She knew such lunches went on, because she saw them happening through the window of Ferrari's, Longhampton's power-lunching restaurant, on her sprint to the sandwich shop to get the baguette she was supposed to eat without getting marks on the papers she didn't have time to stop reading if she wanted to leave on the dot of four to get Toby from whoever was looking after him for the day.

Louise joined the queue snaking onto the High Street outside Daily Bread and felt a pang of nostalgia for something that already seemed like a different world. Lunch at home with Toby had been a leisurely affair, with much chatting about airplanes and trains going into tunnels, and whether Mummy's homemade meals were a cut above the supermarket options.

Even better were the lunches she'd had out with the NCT crowd. Unashamed carb fests, where they'd confessed all their parenting faux pas and *Where does this go?* moments, and cackled darkly until their stitches ached about the stupid things they thought they'd do with their perfect, easy-sleeping cherubs before they actually arrived.

It wasn't all rose-tinted, she reminded herself. Feeding Toby involved a frustrating amount of wiping up and begging. He only seemed to buck up his table manners for suppertime when Peter got home in time to feed him and quiz her on the day's activities, as if he could catch up on parenting by debrief, while Toby sat there glowing like a Pampers advert.

Was it really any wonder she'd ended up needing to turn herself into someone . . .

Stop right there, thought Louise. *Stop it. Do not think about it. Get back on track. Back in the line for baguettes, back in Douglas's good books with overtime. The old Louise Davies is* back.

Her mobile rang in her pocket and she grabbed it, her mind racing between her mum, Toby, the nursery, work . . .

Another side effect of Ben's death: No phone call now came without a frisson of possible disaster.

"Lulu? Can you talk?"

It was Peter. Her heart sank a little bit.

"Hi," she said, inching forward in the queue. "I'm just getting lunch."

"Can't talk for long," he said, as he always did when he called during the day. "I just wanted to see if you were available on Friday night—for a date?"

"Who with?" Louise hated the *ha-ha!* tone in her voice. It felt forced, but then so did asking your wife if she was free for a date.

"With me! I've managed to squeeze us into a *very* small wine-tasting supper that they're running at the White Hart." Peter paused, waiting for her gasp of delight. "You know, the one that was in the paper at the weekend. In Guidley."

"I know where you mean." It was an old pub that had very expensive linens and a chef who'd escaped from the River Café with his own pasta machine. "It sounded amazing."

"Should be! Thought I'd let you know early so you could get the babysitting sorted out."

Babysitting being something only *she* could sort out, of course, thought Louise, grumpily. Either from her piled-high desk in the CPS building or from the queue of a deli.

"Fine," she said. "I'll make some calls and get back to you."

Louise realized a microsecond too late that she sounded like her own assistant, but by then Peter was in the process of ringing off himself and probably hadn't noticed that they'd just conducted a whole conversation using the voices of bad local rep actors.

She sighed and put the phone back in her bag.

"Hi? Next? What can I get you?" called the number four sandwich maker.

Louise stared at the chalkboard and realized she wasn't actually hungry, but she ordered a Greek salad baguette, because that was what she'd always had for lunch before she'd had Toby, and somehow just seeing it being prepared in the same old way brought a little bit of smoothness back to her chest.

Before Toby, Louise had been the office cheerleader for the why-should-we-cover-for-the-mums? brigade, and so she tried to make her babysitting pleas while she walked back to the court for the afternoon session. She didn't want anyone listening in and reminding her of her old smug idiocy.

Diane was her first port of call.

"Hello, darling." Diane's voice was hushed. "Is everything okay? I can't really talk now."

"Can't you?" Louise checked her watch. "Where are you? In the library?"

"No. Um, what's up? Is it Toby?"

"Sort of." Louise was a bit thrown by Diane's evasiveness. Juliet had mentioned that she'd been acting a bit odd when she'd run into her the other day. There was the new haircut, for a start. And talk of laser eye surgery. "I don't suppose you could have Toby for the evening on Friday, could you? Peter's taking me out for a wine-tasting dinner at the White Hart."

"Oh lovely! Like a date!" whispered Diane.

"That's the idea."

"Oh, I'm *so* pleased you two are getting some time together. It's really important when you're in the early years to remember you're not just Mummy and Daddy. If your father and I hadn't bought the caravan after Ian was born, we—"

"Mmm, so can you?" Louise didn't want her mum venturing any further down that road; there had already been several pointed conversations about "not waiting too late" and the sixteen-month age gap between her and Juliet. She hoped Diane wasn't making similar comments about aging ovaries to poor Juliet.

She flinched, remembering some pretty tactless things *she'd* said to Juliet, before Ben died. Things she wished she could explain, if only she and Juliet were on their old easy terms. There was a lot that Louise wished she could go back and undo, but falling out with her sister, at the worst possible time in her whole life, was at the top of the list.

Diane was making apologetic noises. "Did you say Friday? I can't do Friday. I'm helping Beryl with the supper for the book group. *Thursday's* fine . . ."

"No, it's got to be Friday." Louise felt a guilty frisson of relief. Maybe they wouldn't be able to go. Maybe there'd be a reprieve—from the date and from the romantic overtures that were bound to follow.

No, come on, she told herself. *It's like going to the gym; you enjoy it once you get there. And you* love *Italian food.*

"Why don't you phone Juliet?" her mother suggested. "She'll be in. She can pop over for a few hours. If you put Toby to bed before you go out, she won't even have to worry about settling him."

"What about Minton? She'd have to leave him at her house."

"Oh, he'll be fine on his own for one evening," said Diane. "Or she could leave him next door with Lorcan."

"Lorcan?" Louise felt painfully out of the loop. It was months since Juliet had told her anything more personal than . . . She racked her brains. Juliet hadn't even discussed how she'd felt after the funeral. That was how bad things were.

"Yes, the builder who lives next door with the Kellys. Very nice chap. Bit unshaven but reliable. Bit of a flirt, but that never hurt anyone!"

"She never mentioned anything like that to me," said Louise.

"Didn't she?" Diane sounded surprised. "I thought . . . Well. I'm sure she will, if you two get a chance to chat properly over a bottle of wine. Like you used to."

"We're both pretty busy," said Louise, defensively. "I barely get time to wash my hair since I've gone back to work. And I don't want to *force* Jools into seeing me."

There was a pause from Diane's end.

"What, Mum?" she asked, more briskly than she meant to. "Go on, whatever you're thinking."

"Have you two fallen out and not told me?"

Louise stopped walking and stepped into the doorway of

Boots. She'd been waiting months for her mother to come out and ask that exact question, but now that it was out there, hanging between them, she wasn't sure what she should say.

Yes, she and Juliet had fallen out, but not in that hair-pulling, Jeremy-Kyle-fishwife, slanging-match way. It was worse than that. It had been a really simple conversation that had started well but gone down an unexpected track, like an out-of-control toboggan, and left them both startled at how little they actually knew about each other.

It had been a night "away from the boys," just the two of them round at hers with a bottle of wine. But after just one glass, Juliet had let slip something about her and Ben that had stunned Louise into temporary silence, and, because she wasn't sure what advice to offer, that had led her to confess something equally awful to Juliet. But the expression on her sister's face had stopped her, just before the biggest confession.

Even here, outside Boots on the High Street, she could still see Juliet's eyes, usually so forgiving, hardening like coal. And then she'd grabbed her coat and left, without waiting for the explanation, and Louise had been left to polish off the rest of the wine, plus half another bottle, and then it had been too late to phone her up and say the words that would have fixed things between friends. Juliet wasn't a friend, though, she was her sister.

It would have been bad enough facing Juliet the next morning, once the hangover had worn off, but just twenty-four hours later, Ben was lying dead in Longhampton Hospital, and grief and confusion had flooded the whole family. Not washing the bad feelings away like sand, but somehow solidifying them, like the bodies at Pompeii. It was all still there—the secrets, the unasked questions—but hidden.

Louise rested her head against the marble of the shop front and wondered how much, if any, of this her mother needed to know. Maybe a better question was, how much did she already know?

"Why do you say that?" she hedged.

Diane didn't have Louise's court skills. She might be a schemer, but under questioning, she was open like Juliet, confessing everything.

"Because there's an *atmosphere* when you two are together. I noticed it the other day, when I picked up Toby. She was behaving very odd. Be honest—is it that she's jealous of you having him? I didn't think she and Ben were trying for children. But then would she tell me? Did she say anything to you?"

Louise felt bad, grabbing the nearest excuse, but she did. "I think they were thinking about it. That's why I don't want to force babysitting on her. Don't want to rub it in."

"Oh, but she loves Toby," said Diane immediately. "Juliet's *young*, plenty of time for her to have her own family yet. I mean, I know it wouldn't be Ben's, and I know he was the love of her life, but . . . Oh dear. It's so hard knowing what to do for the best. I think it would help, though, being part of your family. She needs her big sister."

Louise saw Juliet's angry face in her mind's eye. If she thought of that conversation every time she thought of Juliet, she assumed Juliet felt the same. It made her shrink inside, out of cowardice. Presumably Juliet felt the same.

"And she needs Toby," Diane went on. "She needs someone to love right now. Someone other than Minton. Bless him, but he won't ever be able to tell her he loves her back, will he? Be the bigger girl, Louise. Build the bridges."

"Fine, I'll ask her," she said.

"Oh, that makes me feel better," said Diane, and Louise couldn't help wondering if her mother would be quite so bothered if she knew what *she* did about poor, tragic Juliet, and why her two girls—so similar in some ways, so different in others—weren't really talking.

Ironically, Juliet was only a few hundred meters from Louise when she rang, doing her round of the park with Coco, Minton, and Hector.

It was amazing, the difference in Hector's manners, now that he had a harness and a walker who gave him instructions, instead of letting him haul her around. He also seemed to have resolved his issues with Minton, and the two of them barreled along matily ahead of Juliet and Coco, sometimes giving each other a shoulder barge like a couple of lads out on the town.

Juliet was pleased Minton had a friend. Even if he was a friend who might lead her innocent boy into terrible ways, it took some of the pressure off her when it came to amusing him. She didn't think his current life was anywhere near as entertaining and varied as the one he'd lived at Ben's side.

Coco plodded away, and Juliet, with Diane's pedometer, plodded next to her in her lovely protective bubble of chapter seventeen of Jane Austen's *Emma*, which she was still listening to on her iPod. The polite nods of recognition she received from other walkers weren't unlike the formal relationships going on in her ears. Blond Wild Dog Café Owner with Red-and-White Basset Hound Called Bertie now beamed in a familiar manner, even if she didn't know her name, as did Retired Man in Flat Cap with Surprisingly Butch Scottie Called Churchill, who actually touched the brim of his cap as he passed.

Life was much more civilized when people had to leave calling cards, thought Juliet, heading out of the park and up the hill toward Coneygreen Woods. It was much easier to be a widow then too. Widows had a timetable, right down to what clothes they wore to let people know which stage they'd reached in their grieving. And people knew what to say and didn't come out with stupid, upsetting things like "Time is a great healer" or "He had a good innings."

She stopped as the narrator was suspended, midwitticism, and the sound of a ringtone cut in. When she wrestled the phone out of her bag and saw it was Louise, not her mother, Juliet's heart sank a bit, but she answered it anyway.

"Jools, it's me." Louise sounded bright—and a bit fake. "How are *you*?"

"I'm fine."

"What are you up to? Everything okay?"

Juliet rolled her eyes at Hector. She could do without this quiz every time her mother and sister rang. If she was contemplating a razor blade and a bottle of gin, she'd hardly tell them. "I'm walking the dogs."

"Oh, you're out! Wonderful! Listen, are you around on Friday night?"

"No, I'm going to Paris for the night," said Juliet. "Of course I'm in."

Already, she could guess where this was headed. Was this another of Louise's invitations to dinner . . . "to meet some new faces"? How many unattached computer nerds could there be in one small town?

"Would you like to come and spend some time with Toby?" asked Louise. "Peter's taking me out for dinner."

The no-date-thanks objections scrolling through Juliet's mind like screen credits—*I'm not ready; I have nothing to talk about; I'd be betraying Ben*—froze.

Toby? Louise had never asked her to look after Toby before.

And more to the point, *Peter was taking Lou out for dinner?*

"Do you mean, would I like to babysit Toby?" She tugged Minton back from his eager inspection of a crumpled KFC bag.

There was a pause, and Juliet knew Louise was kicking herself for revealing her hand. Obviously not back in full court form yet, she thought, triumphantly.

"Well, yes. But he'd love to have his auntie look after him. You can come over earlier and help me bathe him and put him down, if you want. I mean," Louise added, backtracking over the usual eggshells, but too late, "that'd be nice, but you don't have to."

Juliet didn't answer immediately, and not just because she wanted to make her sister uncomfortable. She liked Toby, and he was hardly on the Kelly scale of feral, but she wasn't totally confident about her toddler-minding capabilities. How much damage could he do to himself?

You could always take him round to Emer's, pointed out a voice in her head.

Emer and Juliet were on tentative "dropping in" terms, after Emer had invited herself in for coffee a few days ago with a box of biscuits she wasn't "meant to be eating." She had ended up staying three hours, telling her about washing blouses for various Britpop legends until Roisin came round to get her. Minton had curled up by her bare, green-polished toes; always a good sign.

Maybe it was the date part. The last time she and Louise had talked, before Ben died, Peter's lack of dating behavior had been, well . . . a real problem. Had something changed?

Well, *yes,* she reminded herself. Ben's death had probably revitalized their marriage at the same time as it had destroyed hers. Just one of the many outrageous side effects of the unfairness she had to live with and everyone else seemed to use as a helpful carpe diem lesson.

"I'm supposed to be going round to feed Mrs. Cox's cats at six," she began.

"Come after that," said Louise. "How will the cats know if it's six? Do they have watches?"

"They have a routine," said Juliet. She squinted at a tree that had burst into flower since the last time she'd passed; amazing how impatient nature could be. *I must ask Ben what kind of—*

"Can't you ask Peter's mum?" she blurted out, to fill the space in her head where that thought was going.

"I could, but I'd like you to do it," said Louise, unexpectedly, and the weariness in her voice cut through Juliet's barriers.

"Fine, okay. How long for?"

"It won't be late. We're both shattered—I bet we leave before pudding. If we don't fall asleep in it! To be honest, I'd rather someone took Toby out for dinner and we got to go to bed at seven!"

Juliet noted that Louise was doing her condescending voice—the overcheerful one she put on while trying to pretend that the fantastic thing she had was actually a bit of a trial, so she wouldn't feel jealous. Baby, job, car that needed expensive servicing. Boo-hoo, not. It was actually more irritating than plain boasting.

Louise sounded more strained than normal. Maybe it wasn't just put on, though. It almost sounded as if she were trying to convince herself.

"It's nice that you're going on a date," said Juliet. "Romantic table for two, is it?"

"Yes. We're . . . Peter's making a bit more effort."

"Isn't it a bit late for that?"

As soon as she said it, Juliet knew it was a low blow, and she felt bad, but it was too late to take it back, and Louise wasn't helping by being so dignified.

Awkward.

Someone was waving at her from the top of the hill, where the paths forked off on the different nature trails.

Juliet squinted. The sun had finally come out from behind the gray clouds and was streaming through the lacy treetops. It was a man, a man with a spaniel.

She recognized the spaniel immediately—it was Damson. Her owner had obviously identified her too by the three dogs dragging her along, because he was waving.

Juliet swapped Coco's lead into her other hand, tucked the phone under her ear, and waved back. Louise had got herself back on track by nattering on about feeding times and other stuff, and the man was walking toward her, covering the ground quite fast.

This time, Juliet reckoned she'd have recognized him without the spaniel clue; his ruffled hair was familiar, as were his glasses and his Barbour jacket with the Ziploc bag of treats poking out. Telltale dog-owner sign. He was smiling too, in preparation for saying hi.

The thought of on-the-spot conversation gave her the usual frisson of panic. Juliet calculated she had about two minutes to get off the phone, put her headphones in, and appear absorbed in her audiobook of *Emma*, if she didn't want to look rude.

". . . about six?" Louise finished up.

"Yeah, fine," said Juliet, fingering her earphones. Should she? Shouldn't she?

He was nearer now. The man pointed at Damson, then at the coffee stand, made a drinky-drinky gesture.

"Great," said Louise. "Toby's looking forward to it already! Is there anything you'd like me to leave in the fridge for your supper?"

"Whatever. I don't mind. I don't eat much." Louise was ticking off precious seconds of thinking time with her stupid questions about whether Juliet was getting enough vitamins, and then, before she could gather her excuses, Louise had rung off and Damson and Mark (it was Mark, wasn't it? thought Juliet, racking her brains. Or Luke? He looked like a Mark) were near enough for Hector to start barking whatever the dog equivalent of *Hello, darlin', nice legs* was at Damson.

"Stop it," she hissed. "You are dragging me into—"

Too late. He was right there.

"Hello," she said. "Sorry about him. I haven't walked the attitude out of him yet today."

"Oh, he's just being friendly," said Mark. "What a gorgeous day, eh? I shouldn't have come out in this"—he flicked at his jacket—"but it's got all the bits and pieces in it, and I couldn't be bothered unloading it all."

"You should do what I do and just have black plastic bags in every single coat," said Juliet. "I even found one in my pocket at . . ."

She was about to say, *at my husband's funeral*. God, that had nearly finished her off. She'd held it together quite well up till then, but when she'd pulled the stray poo bag out along with the gloves she needed for the freezing churchyard, all Juliet had been able to think of was Minton's paws clicking away on the floorboards at night, searching the house for his master when he thought she was asleep.

". . . at my nephew's christening," she finished. Because that was true too. "Came in handy for getting rid of some pukey baby wipes."

"A hundred and one uses! Do you fancy a coffee?" he asked. "I was hoping to see you, actually—there's something I wanted to ask."

He smiled hopefully as he spoke, and Juliet let herself be steered toward the stand.

Just do it, she told herself. Just have the coffee and talk for five minutes and it's another five minutes over, and another conversation done, and another step nearer to normality.

After some lead juggling, they were soon holding too-hot cappuccinos and waiting a little awkwardly for change. Mark grinned nervously at her while the coffee girl counted his change from a twenty-pound note.

"Am I right in thinking you're a dog walker?" he asked, as they set off slowly around the flower bed paths.

"Well, not *professionally*," Juliet began, then heard Louise's voice in the back of her mind. *Don't be so negative.* How else was she going to afford to eat, if she was still avoiding Kim's calls and pleading unreliability?

"I'm just starting up," she said, in a different, more Louise tone. "I've just got two dogs at the moment, and some cats."

"So you might have time to walk Damson?"

"Don't you walk her enough yourself?" She didn't add, *I see you most days*, in case that made her look a bit . . . stalkery.

"I do. I mean, I did." Mark sipped his coffee and made a face. "My job's changed and I'm in the office three days a week now. My ex has decided she doesn't want custody of Damson anymore—too much stress, apparently with . . . everything else—so we're in a bit of a fix, aren't we, Dam?"

He glanced down at Damson, walking close to Coco's substantial side for sisterly support. "My next-door neighbor's been popping in to let her out at lunchtime, but she doesn't want to make it a regular thing. I can't blame her. I don't want to put Damson in kennels for the day when she just needs a run at lunchtime. She'll happily sleep the rest of the day if she's tired, and she gets on with your lot, so . . ."

He raised his blond eyebrows, just like the antiques man on telly did when he was trying to persuade a couple to take a risk on a vase. "I'm happy to pay the going rate. Whatever that is."

"Of course," said Juliet, as if she already knew what that was. "Which days?"

"Tuesday, Wednesday, Thursday?"

"That might work," said Juliet. "I'd have to check the diary."

Mark seemed relieved. "Great! What's the routine? Do I drop her off?"

"Well," said Juliet, feeling she ought to sound semi-organized, "Hector's owner gives me a set of keys and I pick him up, walk him, then take him back, check he's got some water, and leave him to nap. But she's not far from me. Don't worry," she added, "I've got one of those secure key cupboards, with proper locks." Ben had had one, for his clients' house keys. "Where do you live?"

"Down by the canal. Riverside Walk."

Ooh, thought Juliet. *The nice new-build houses. Executive.*

"Okay," she said, thinking on her feet. "Give me your number and I'll give you a call."

It occurred to Juliet, as he was writing down his details, that it'd be a good time to clear up the name thing.

But as usual, like all owners, he'd written *Damson*, his number, and his address.

And as usual, she just smiled, embarrassed, and said, "Great!"

Chapter 12

It was amazing, thought Juliet, the things you could find out about a person just from feeding their pets.

For a start, Mrs. Cox was a widow, with a near-biblical horde of grandchildren and great-grandchildren, and a massively sweet tooth if the catering-size boxes of Thorntons toffee in her pantry were anything to go by. She had three entire shelves of tinned sardines, one of pilchards, and a separate washing machine for the cats. And she kept all the supermarkets' special-offer vouchers clipped to clothes pegs along her kitchen window to remind her to use them.

It was almost like being on a daytime television program, Juliet thought, going round the geranium baskets in the sitting room with a watering can, as requested by Mrs. Cox in her note. All the fun of looking at someone else's house, but without the actual "having to talk to them" bit or paying £4.80 for an interiors magazine. Perfect.

Well, she had to talk to the cats. They seemed to expect a bit of conversation from the regal way they were staring at her.

"Are you okay?" she asked Bianca, through a mouthful of treacle toffee ("Help yourself to tea, coffee, et cetera!"). "You seem a bit down. Are you missing your mum?"

Boris definitely seemed sadder than the last time she'd seen him. There was a droop to his eyes that hadn't been there before, and his tail looked . . . less powder-puffy. Juliet wasn't an expert on cats, but he looked almost deflated.

"What's up, chaps?" she asked, concerned. "You haven't even touched your salmon."

She put down the watering can and jiggled the Wedgwood saucers on the side, piled with freshly mashed red salmon (proper John West, not store brand), but neither cat showed so much as a flicker of interest.

"Is it the wrong temperature?" inquired Juliet. "Did I get the wrong bowls? Maybe you'd prefer it on the floor?"

No response.

Juliet frowned and pulled the new red file out of her satchel. No doubt tipped off by Diane, the pet-sitting pimp, Louise had dropped round a load of office stationery: clear plastic wallets for instructions, different-colored pens and receipt books and labels. Everything but poo bags, basically.

"You've got to get organized," she'd bossed, in classic Louise style. "It'll instill confidence in your clients."

"Clients? I'm not exactly—"

"You've got to show you're taking it seriously." Louise had looked quite fierce, especially dressed in her court suit. "When you're caring for someone else's loved one, whether it's a cat or a baby, they want to feel they're in safe hands."

There'd been a short pause, and Juliet had wondered if she was supposed to speak, but Louise suddenly added, "You're doing something really useful here, Juliet. You're making a difference to people's lives. Go, you!"

Juliet couldn't stop herself. *"Go, you?"* she'd repeated incredulously. "How long have you been back at work?"

Louise had grimaced at herself. "Okay, maybe that doesn't work out of the office, but we're proud of you. Me and Mum. You're, you know, getting out."

She didn't actually say, *Moving on*, but Juliet knew that was a prelude to the usual lecture-in-disguise about having the rest of her life ahead of her, and frankly she hadn't had the energy for it, after an afternoon encounter between Hector and someone's sexually ambiguous Old English sheepdog.

If she'd had more energy, she'd have done something about this weird tension between them, but it was too big to deal, and she wasn't sure where to start.

Luckily Louise had dashed off to collect Toby from the nursery, and that had been that.

Juliet flipped through the Daily Routines file until she came to Mrs. Cox's printed directions for the care of Bianca and Boris. It wasn't a big file—so far only Hector, the cats, and Coco had pages—but the way Diane was giving out her details, it would soon be full. Scraps of paper with details of summer holidays and addresses flopped about in the empty sleeves, waiting for Juliet to follow them up.

" 'Bianca likes Radio Four,' " Juliet read aloud. " 'Boris prefers silence, so make sure two rooms have the radio on and two don't.' "

She looked up. Boris had wandered off, and Bianca was sniffing at the salmon as if Juliet had laced it with antifreeze.

"Are you lonely?" she asked. "Are you bored? Am I supposed to eat at the same time?"

Bianca turned her flat face away from the saucer, like a prima ballerina doing the Dying Swan.

"I'm really sorry," said Juliet, feeling she was failing badly in quite a simple task. "I've never had a cat. I'm more of a dog person. I want to help, but . . ."

She gazed around the kitchen, hoping for a clue. Months of house programs and antiques searches had led her to think that a person's soft furnishings held the secret solution to most problems. Mrs. Cox had a whole set of Moorcroft pottery dishes on her dresser, and framed photographs of family everywhere Juliet looked. Children, teenagers, young people with babies, all extending the Cox line. Again, Juliet felt the pang of her own snapped-off family tree and squeezed her eyes shut against the sudden clutch in her stomach.

Down by her feet, Bianca mewed piteously. The imperious air had fallen away. She just looked sad. Abandoned.

"You'd rather be with your mum, wouldn't you? On a cruise. I can see you on a cruise, Bianca." Juliet picked her up and immediately she began to purr, her little body vibrating. Underneath the fluff there was barely any cat at all.

"Poor Bianca," she murmured, as the elderly cat rubbed her silky head against her neck. "You just want a cuddle, don't you? There was nothing about that in the notes. Silly Mummy, forgetting the most important part."

But why would there be? Affection and the odd kind word was just something you did with your pets—with *anyone* you loved. It was so instinctive it wasn't even part of the contract.

And you didn't even notice it until it wasn't there anymore. That was what Juliet missed: the offer of a coffee when someone made one for himself, the unexpected hug when she was washing up. The contact and thoughts that stopped each day from feeling like solitary confinement.

The falling sensation rushed up at her, accompanied by that darkness, the rest of her life stretching out, alone. Minton wouldn't be around forever, and . . .

More pitiful mewling broke through Juliet's thoughts, and she looked down to see Boris scratching at himself on the floor, his white fur polluted with hideous black lumps like leeches. One giant blob was stuck to his face and he was batting it hopelessly with a paw.

"Boris!" Juliet dumped Bianca unceremoniously on the kitchen table and grabbed her brother. "What have you got on your—"

Treacle toffee. Lots of it. All stuck on his long, white fur.

"Oh . . . no," said Juliet.

Back in the front seat of the van, Minton wasn't thrilled to see Juliet come out of the house armed with a big wicker cat basket, and Bianca and Boris weren't delighted to see Minton, despite what Mrs. Cox had said about them fending off a Labrador at the vet's, but Juliet didn't think any of them had a choice.

It wasn't even as though she had any bright ideas about how she was going to get the toffees out of Boris's fur, but she didn't want to do her panicking in Mrs. Cox's house, just in case a neighbor heard the squalling and popped round to check that Juliet wasn't torturing the cats. And she had to be round at Louise's to babysit by half past six, which didn't leave a lot of time for emergency feline hairdressing.

But when she turned the key in her own front door, she realized her house wasn't audience-free either: The strains of something loud by Guns N' Roses drifted down her stairs, accompanied by singing and hammering.

Lorcan was in, doing something in the bathroom.

Oh *great*, she thought. This was the first time since Ben died that she could remember coming in to find music on, someone moving around in her house—which was disturbing enough on its own—but now she'd have an audience for her unprofessional cat panic.

Minton's tail was beating against the door like a drum. He wasn't hiding his delight at hearing that Lorcan was in, the fickle creature.

"Lorcan?" she yelled up the stairs, then wondered why she was announcing herself in her own house.

"Juliet?" The music was switched off and Lorcan's feet came pounding down the stairs. "Guess what?"

"What?" She put Boris and Bianca's basket down on the sofa, and their flat heads appeared against the wire front, checking out the sitting room.

Lorcan appeared in the doorway, his broad face wreathed in smiles, his black curls flattened slightly with sweat. "I hope either Minton or yourself has come back from that dog walking all covered in mud, because the new shower is . . . Oh." He stopped, seeing the cat basket and her distraught face. "Have you been crying?"

"No. The shower's in?" said Juliet.

"Yeah. Well, nearly. I was hoping to get it done before you got back, but . . . Is that a cat?"

"Two." Juliet clutched her forehead, as Boris began mewling again, desperate to get out.

"Can I . . . help?" he tried.

"I don't know. Do you know how to get toffee out of fur? Any clever tricks with turps?" she asked desperately.

"No," said Lorcan. "I once singed my hair on a lighting rig. Had to shave the lot. Looked like a matchstick for weeks!"

"Oh God," she groaned, sinking onto the sofa next to the cats. "That's it, then. My career as a pet-sitter, over."

"But I know someone who will know," Lorcan went on.

"Who?"

"Emer." He nodded next door. "You don't want to know the things that Roisin's had stuck in her hair. And she won't let anyone cut it out—show her a pair of scissors and she's like a vampire with garlic."

Faint hope flickered in Juliet's chest. "Will Emer be able to do it on a cat, though? In about half an hour?"

Lorcan gave her an amused glance. "Let me tell you, whatever you've got in that basket's going to scratch a lot less than Roisin."

Lorcan didn't bother to knock but yelled, "Emer?" and went straight on into the hall, Juliet following at a polite distance with the wicker carrier.

Immediately the twins appeared—not silently, but with a fanfare of pounding feet on the bare floorboards.

"Loorrrccaan!" they yelled, throwing themselves at his legs as if he'd been away at sea for months, instead of next door for half a day.

"Calm down," he said, detaching their hands without embarrassment. "No autographs, no pictures."

Was he *really* just a family friend? Juliet wondered. They seemed much closer than that, almost like an uncle. The more she thought about it, the more weird it was that someone like Lorcan didn't live with a girlfriend of his own.

Lorcan caught her confused expression and grinned. "They've seen too many tour videos," he said. "They think this is the way you're meant to greet people."

"Florrie! Look! It's a cat! Juliet's got a *cat!*"

Juliet was flattered that Roisin had remembered her name, but her ears buzzed at the shriekiness of her voice. She wasn't used to so much noise, so close, and neither were Bianca and Boris. They shrank back inside the carrier as Roisin's sticky fingers probed the wire and Florrie kneeled and cooed.

Emer appeared at the back of the hall, drying her hands on a tea towel. Today she was wearing a striped cook's apron over a patchwork dress, and her hair was piled up on her head, but she still exuded a warm sexiness, like a rock-'n'-roll Nigella Lawson.

"Jeez, would you dial it down a notch, Roisin?" she bellowed, only slightly less loudly. "Hello, Juliet! Oh my God, please don't tell me you've brought us more pets. Florrie, don't even look at them," she instructed as Florrie flung herself at the basket. "Don't. Even. Look."

"Florrie's forever filling this place with furry randoms," Lorcan explained over the sound of Florrie's cat-soothing mews. "Anything with one leg, or no ears, or traumatized by the schoolkids. Then they come here and get traumatized properly by Roisin. Emer, Juliet was hoping you could help her with a little problem."

"I'm looking after these Persian cats for someone and . . ." Juliet was conscious of Emer taking her in, noting her jeans, her hair, her voice, her amused half smile never changing. "I don't suppose you know how to get toffee out of fur, do you? Without cutting it?"

"Now, what made you think I might have experience in sticky, messy, toffee-related dramas?" she asked.

"Lorcan thought . . ." Juliet stammered, unsure whether the outrage on Emer's face was serious.

"Like the time Roisin got bubblegum stuck in my hair and you had to put peanut butter on it," suggested Florrie. "Or when Smokey walked in the toffee for the toffee apples you were making and we had to go to the vet's and the vet said that Smokey would have to have an operation and Lorcan put oil on Smokey's paws and you said if it didn't work, we could make mittens out of—"

Emer reached forward and placed her hand over Florrie's mouth. "Smokey is not big enough for mittens. And we love her." She winked at Juliet. "You could say we have some experience of confectionery accidents and long hair, yes. Bring it through. Let's have a look."

Juliet let out a relieved breath. "Thanks."

"If you cat experts don't need me, I'll just . . . nip upstairs and freshen up," said Lorcan. "I'm a bit . . ." He pulled at his T-shirt and Juliet realized it was damp in patches. "Hard work, fitting showers," he added, seeing her face, and she looked away, embarrassed, in case he thought she was checking him out.

"Right, then!" commanded Roisin. "Bring the cat to the operating table!"

Juliet followed Emer down the dark-green hall to the kitchen, bookended by Roisin and Florrie. They had a friendly curiosity that made Juliet feel as if she were the child and they were the grown-ups. She didn't remember being so open with strangers at their age, but then her dad had been a quantity surveyor for Longhampton Council, not a tour manager.

"Excuse the chaos," said Emer, sweeping a stack of paintings off the kitchen table. The room was a jumble of activity. Huge framed tour posters filled the walls, and two large pans of peeled potatoes were standing on the side, with some sort of school science project on the counter and a basket of unironed laundry by the door.

As they all came in, Smokey leaped out of the laundry basket and vanished into the garden, leaving the cat flap clattering in her wake.

"Can I get him out?" asked Florrie, as Juliet put the carrier on the table. "I'll be really careful."

"We all have to be very careful," said Emer. "Remember what happened to Hammy, Roisin."

"Yes, Mum," whined Roisin. "But Hammy wriggled . . ."

"He's gorgeous," cooed Florrie. "What's he called?"

"Boris. Um, can we leave Bianca where she is?"

Bianca stayed firmly on her side of the divider, while Boris emerged blinking into the bright light, his toffee leeches even more grotesque than they had been at Mrs. Cox's.

"That's a *witch's* cat," breathed Roisin. "Like in Harry Potter."

"We've been here before." Emer inspected Boris briskly, pulling the toffees to see how stuck they were. "No problem. We can sort this. I just need to get my magic tools. Now, you stay here," she said to the girls. "Offer Juliet a drink."

"Would you like a drink?" asked Florrie politely, as Emer vanished back up the stairs.

Was she going into the bathroom? wondered Juliet. Where Lorcan was showering? The pipes were clanking, just as hers did when the hot water was running. Maybe there were two showers. Or an en suite.

Both girls were staring at her with their spooky blue eyes. "Oh, er. Thank you, yes," she stammered.

Roisin went over to the huge American fridge and pulled it open. Unlike Juliet's, it was crammed to the gunnels with food and Tupperware containers, and all different kinds of milk.

"What would you like?" She began rhyming off the options, starting with Diet Coke, Coke, and Cherry Coke and heading toward rum and Coke.

While she was listing away, Juliet could hear voices upstairs—Lorcan's and Emer's. In the bathroom?

Stop it, she told herself. *This isn't daytime telly, where you can be nosy.*

"I'll have a Diet Coke. Please."

"Ice and a slice?" inquired Roisin. "Or straight up?"

"On the rocks. Thank you."

As Roisin reached up to get the glasses, Florrie stroked Boris and regarded Juliet with a clear look that Juliet found far more unsettling than Roisin's ghost outfit.

"What's Lorcan doing in your house?" she asked.

"He's fixing my shower."

"Don't you have a man to fix it?"

"No." Juliet swallowed. "My man . . . My husband died."

"Like a ghost?"

"No," said Juliet. "Not like a ghost."

Since they were obviously fine with questions, she thought she might as well try one of her own. "Does Lorcan live here all the time?"

"Not all the time," said Florrie. "Only when Daddy's away."

"Really?"

"Lorcan's Mum's bodyguard," explained Roisin, pushing her very full glass over the table at her. "Like in the films."

"Right . . ." Juliet wasn't sure what to make of that.

"Lorcan looks after Mummy. And fixes the house. And does the thing with the bins where you tie up the bags. She can't do that on her own."

"Well, neither can I," admitted Juliet. Ben had had a knack, a way of spinning the bag that she could never master. He used to laugh about the way she always ended up with yogurt somewhere. It had slipped her mind till now, and of course now she couldn't forget it.

"And Lorcan *loves* Mummy," Roisin went on.

"Roisin!" Florrie turned red.

"Yes, he *does*," said Roisin. "I heard him saying that to her once, in the kitchen." She widened her eyes. "He gave her a hug. She was crying, and he told her that he *loved* her, and . . ."

"Roisin! You were listening! You know what Mummy says about listening!" Florrie mimed something pinching off her nose, then, after a second's thought, reached over and pinched Roisin's nose for her.

Roisin howled in amplified agony and lashed out at Florrie with a surprisingly swift punch.

"Hey, hey!" Juliet stepped between them. "That's enough!"

She felt like Supernanny for about two seconds, until she absorbed Florrie's retaliatory punch right in the side of the hip.

"Ow!" she groaned. "Florrie, you're meant to be the nice one . . ."

"What's going on here? Fight Club's Sunday, right?"

Lorcan appeared in the doorway, his hair wet from the shower and a crumpled T-shirt pulled over his head.

He did look very much at home. Roisin wasn't the most reliable source of info, but even taken with a pinch of salt, it didn't take a lot of imagining. Those weird arrangements rock-music-type people had. Why wouldn't you turn a blind eye to some mate looking after your woman while you weren't at home?

And he was so good with the kids. Were some of them . . . his?

"I was telling Juliet about how you love Mummy," said Roisin shamelessly. "And then Florrie pinched me."

"I did not!"

"Hey." Lorcan put one hand on each girl's head. "Course I love Mummy. And you two. And Spike. And Sal. But not when he's playing his guitar." He looked over them to Juliet and rolled his eyes. "We all love everyone, right? We're all one big, happy, human family."

Juliet felt awkward again, and very suburban.

"Florrie, why don't you go and get Smokey's brush," he said, "and then we can start combing the bits that aren't covered in gunk."

Florrie scuttled off, with Roisin in hot pursuit.

Lorcan glanced down at Boris, now sniffing the fruit bowl curiously, and ruffled his own damp hair.

"They weren't . . . asking questions about your husband, were they?"

She shook her head, embarrassed that actually she'd asked, not them. "No. Well, not really."

"You've got to tell me if they were," he said. "It's a phase they're going through, especially Roisin. She'd make a great journalist—no sense *whatsoever* of the inappropriate. Emer explained that he'd died, but they don't really do angels in heaven with harps in this family. They're a bit more forensic. I hope they didn't upset you?"

"It's okay," said Juliet quickly. Roisin *had* put her finger on her most sensitive spot—the bins, the shower, all the things Ben had done that she'd now have to do on her own. But that wasn't Roisin's fault.

"Shower looks good," Lorcan said, changing the subject, but not as much as he thought he was. "Did you have a think about the tiling?"

"Yes. I've been thinking about all the building work." Juliet took a deep breath and made a leap. "I would like you to do it, but . . . this is going to sound a bit odd."

"Odd?" Lorcan did a double take. "To someone who lives in *this* madhouse? Try me. You want it all papered in zebra stripes? Or you want mirrors on all the ceilings?"

Juliet blushed and half laughed. "No, I'd like to help."

"Ah, now that is weird," said Lorcan, puffing out his cheeks. "Most clients want to get as far away as possible when there's building work on."

"I don't. I want to be part of it. Ben and I . . ." Juliet stroked Boris and didn't meet Lorcan's eye. "We'd planned to do it ourselves, really get to know the house ourselves. I'd like to honor that, a little bit. Anyway, I suppose if I'm going to be on my own, I need to know how to do basic DIY. Nothing complicated, like extensions or anything . . ."

"But you don't mind swinging that sledgehammer they always seem to get out on the telly, right?" Lorcan mimed the reckless lurch of the would-be property developer.

Juliet looked horrified. "No sledgehammers."

"Fair enough. And are you planning on paying me more or less if you're volunteering to help and I'm volunteering to teach plastering for beginners?" he asked, helping himself to the big plastic box of biscuits on the table.

"Oh. Um . . . the same? Unless you think . . ."

"Get out of here." Lorcan laughed. "I'd be happy to have an extra pair of hands. But it's like I said on the note, I've got various jobs booked in, so I can't do it all at once and there's some specialist stuff I'd need to get some mates in to do, like the glazing . . . Tell you what, why don't we start with the bathroom and see how that goes? I'll finish the shower, refit your suite. Then we can paint it, tile it, see how we get on."

"Good idea," said Juliet. That was a manageable project. She was all about manageable projects and the neat spaces they filled up in her calendar. Doing the bathroom should take her up to—what?—the end of September? And that left just a few weeks until the anniversary.

It would be something, to have the bathroom of their dreams completed, at least. Something to share with Ben. Then after that, maybe it would easier. Maybe once she'd got the year under her belt.

Lorcan pointed a bourbon biscuit at her. "Don't forget you've got your pet-sitting, as well as learning DIY. That's keeping you pretty busy, isn't it? You've barely been around this week."

"Well . . ." Juliet screwed up her face and tickled Boris's sticky ears. "If word gets out about Boris's little accident, I might have more time on my hands."

"Ah, come on. What's the worst that can happen? Eh? So we have to shave the poor bugger. How hard is it to find a fluffy white cat? How can you tell the difference, underneath? Florrie can keep the baldy shaved one. Or you can glue some cotton wool on Smokey."

Lorcan grinned his easy grin, and Juliet felt a real smile tickle the corner of her mouth for the first time in ages. A proper dark-edged smile.

"Here!" Emer burst back into the kitchen, followed by Roisin and Florrie bearing various cat-cleaning implements. "We'll start with the peanut butter, and if that fails, we've got some special stuff that Alec got in the States for his motorbikes." She checked the label. "I don't think it's poisonous to cats. It sorted out Spike's last lot of tar in the hair, anyway."

"And if that fails, it's into the freezer for Boris for seven hours," said Lorcan, deadpan, "and out with the iron."

"Nooooo!" howled Roisin and Florrie, so shrilly that Bianca's face vanished from the wire front.

It was actually louder than the recorders. Juliet covered her ears without thinking, but as she did, Lorcan caught her eye and winked.

Chapter 13

What time's Juliet getting here?" asked Peter over his shoulder. "I had a word with the manager at the White Hart and he said if we got there in good time, he might be able to give us the kitchen table, so we can watch them doing the *actual cooking.*"

He was standing in front of the bedroom mirror, fiddling with his best cuff links, the heavy silver knots Louise had given him as a wedding present. He paused, watching her walk in from the en suite, fresh from her cursory shower, and gave her an appreciative smile.

"Are you up for that? Not as romantic as the main dining room, but maybe we can pick up some tips? And I don't know, there's something a bit sexy about a busy kitchen. All that steam and hot air and rushing about."

Louise felt her first pang of guilt for the evening. It was pretty clear that she hadn't made as much effort as he had—the back of Peter's neck was pink where he'd had his hair cut that afternoon, and he was wearing a new shirt, a pale lemony yellow. For years,

Peter had gone to work in his jeans and T-shirt, while she'd trussed herself up in a suit. Now that *he* had to wear a suit more often than not, he made a point of leaving his hair a bit too long and picking nonwhite shirts.

Louise had shaved her legs, but that was it. Not even a bikini wax, because that would give him the impression that she was keen to throw herself back into the baby making, and although she was ashamed of her avoidance tactics, she didn't think it was fair, in some strange fair-play rules, to send out those signals.

She sometimes wondered if Ashleigh at the beauty salon speculated about why her once-quite-adventurous bikini waxing had fallen off lately. Whether the therapists could tell the temperature of their clients' love lives according to their attendance at the hot-wax pot. *They must know all sorts*, she thought, *not just what we tell them*.

She bundled those thoughts away, just in case they were showing on her face.

"Um, Juliet should be here soon," she said. "She's got to feed some cats up the road."

"She's branching out into cats now? Very enterprising. Well, the taxi's booked for seven," Peter went on, checking his hair, then his watch. "Which is . . . twenty minutes."

"You booked a taxi? I'd've driven," said Louise lightly.

"What? To a wine-tasting dinner?" Peter laughed. "I don't want you to miss out on the booze, Lou. It's meant to be a treat, after all the months you couldn't because of Toby. Not that you should go mad . . ." He winked at her, framed in the mirror. "I remember all those rules—no coffee, no tight pants, all that malarkey. But since Toby was conceived after Barry Scott's leaving do, I think we can relax the no-drinking one a bit."

"So we're trying for another baby now, are we?" she asked, before she could stop herself.

Peter looked surprised, then rather awkward. "I thought we weren't trying *not* to?"

Come on, Louise told herself. *A couple of glasses of wine, it'll be good for you. You just need to relax. Stop thinking so much. Look at Peter in his suit, as if you're on a date. Look how handsome he is. How hard he's trying to make this special. You are a lucky woman.*

"Sorry," she said. "That came out wrong. I just . . . It's been a tricky week at work. I don't want to piss Douglas off by dropping him in it again with another maternity leave. Knowing my luck, it'd take one night this time, not eighteen months."

"It's only dinner," said Peter mildly. "I'm not promising anything after."

Louse turned back to the wardrobe and pulled out her stretchy silk dress, the one that always made her feel curvy and confident. It looked smaller than when she'd last had it out.

"Shame Juliet couldn't have come a bit earlier," he said, turning back to his tie. "She could have helped with Toby's bath. Highlight of my day, that is."

"Really?" said Louise, lightly. "Not the late-night feeds? Or the daily *What's up Toby's nose?* ritual? Today it was an acorn. Who knew toddlers' nostrils were so stretchy?"

Peter gave her a look. "Are you being sarcastic?"

"A bit."

Louise knew she was being a cow, and she hated herself. It didn't help that she'd just spent four hundred pounds on beautiful porcelain tiles for Juliet's bathroom, to be delivered to Lorcan, who could pretend he'd got them for fifty quid. The way her mother cooed over Lorcan's tiling abilities made her wonder whether she ought to schedule a surprise visit round there herself.

Peter wandered over to where she was standing, by the chest of drawers with all her underwear neatly stowed in honeycomb segments. "Don't be," he said. "I want to be there to do all the yucky stuff. It's just work is mad right now. I'm going to try to get some time off, so you can go away on your own for a bit. Toby and I will manage."

You won't, thought Louise. *You have no idea.* That had been the great thing about Michael; he didn't need to ask for nightly updates on Toby's food intake, or tell her what she *should* have given him, according to the Internet. Michael knew. He was actually doing it.

Louise felt Peter's arms go around her, and she stiffened.

"Are you going out in this?" he inquired, tugging at her towel.

She clamped her arms against her sides. "No, I was going to wear that wrap dress. Listen, Toby's asleep in his chair, but he's bound to wake up any minute, so can you—"

"He's fine. I've got the baby monitor right here. And we've got twenty minutes." Peter's mouth was against the side of her throat, breathing hot air into the hollow that used to make her turn to pure hot liquid inside. "Which isn't long, but long enough for what I've got in mind, which is a sort of starter . . ."

Now it just tickled. Her head was full of tiles and Toby's sleep patterns. Louise jerked her ear down to her shoulder to stop him. "No," she said. "Jools might come any minute. And I need to get dressed."

"You don't have to." Peter kissed round to the back of her neck, under her hairline. His hands roamed up and down her waist. "At least let me pick your underwear."

"I've already picked," she said, yanking out some industrial flesh-colored Spanx. "I need these."

"Those?" The roaming stopped abruptly. "Absolutely not. Where's that really nice stuff? Let me have a look . . ."

He moved her aside, firmly, and began searching through her underwear drawer.

"What nice stuff?" she asked, thinking he meant a silk set he'd given her for Christmas a few years back. "This?"

"No, the cream ones. With the lace and the . . . you know . . . whatever you call those big ties."

Louise's blood went cold. "I don't know which ones you mean."

Except she did. She knew exactly the underwear he meant; they revealed more than they covered, but they made her feel like a sex goddess even with her wobbly post-Toby tummy. She'd never actually worn them out and about, just bought them and thought about where she might wear them, who might see them. Even buying them had made her feel hot inside. If she hadn't come to her senses when she did, though, she had no doubt that they would have been worn and . . .

"You do. They're not in here; they're in the airing cupboard. I'll go and get them." Peter went out, toward the landing. "Why're they in there anyway?"

"Um, they're hand-wash only." Louise winced. That was not the right response.

"I thought you didn't know the ones I meant?" Peter's voice drifted back, but he sounded amused. "It's okay, Lou, I don't mind you spending money on fancy knickers. So long as I get to see them."

He returned holding the wisps of ludicrously expensive Agent Provocateur satin and lace. Louise felt faintly sick. No, *actually* sick, to see them in Peter's hands.

"When did you wear these?" he asked. "I can't believe I missed them!"

"Oh, I haven't even had them on," she lied hastily, taking the knickers from him with hands that were more steady than her voice.

Little tremors from the one afternoon trying-on session they'd had still flickered in the pit of her stomach, hot flames of guilt and excitement licking away at her, as she remembered how she'd imagined him seeing her, watching her pull the ribbons undone, totally unlike the buttoned-up Louise, or the sick-smelling Mummy Lou. How had she forgotten they were stuffed in the airing cupboard? Why hadn't she just thrown them out?

"So why were they in the airing cupboard?" Peter asked, more curious than suspicious. "Are you turning into your mum, hiding her sale bargains all over the house in case your dad finds them?"

"No! No, I always wash lingerie before I wear it. You never know who's had them on in the shop before you," she said, off the top of her head. It depressed her a bit that he didn't even question that; obviously, that sort of hygiene lunacy was so like her.

"Wear those." Peter's eyes were bright with excitement. "Please."

"They're not really the right kind of knickers, though. I need something smooth under this dress."

Peter made a *Do I care about VPL?* face, and Louise knew she'd fed him the wrong line. He was watching her, now waiting for her to do just that—try them on in front of him.

It was what a good wife set on revitalizing her comatose marriage would do: She'd drop her towel and slowly pull on the gossamer knickers, keeping her eyes locked on her now wildly aroused husband, and then they'd fall on the bed and have frantic, urgent, honeymoon sex in the minutes before Juliet arrived.

The only problem was that Louise didn't even want Peter to see her naked. She was too guilty and ashamed and confused, and above all, the sight of those knickers in particular inflamed every single one of those emotions to unbearable levels.

"Let's leave it as a surprise," she said.

Peter looked at her, trying to work out what she was up to. Then he grinned, manfully, and nodded.

"Go and see that Toby's okay," Louise went on, clinging to her towel. "I'll be down in two minutes."

"Two minutes," he said. "Or I'm coming up to get you, knickers or not."

There was a pause for them both to hear *Preferably not*, and then he trotted down the stairs. One-two-three. One-two-three.

Louise kept the smile on her face until he'd left the room and then, quietly, she closed the door and ripped a hole in the panties until they were unwearable.

She looked at the rash little purchase in her hands, her breath too painful in her chest to breathe.

A lifetime of knowing right from wrong, being meticulous about details—how had she made so much mess in just a few weeks?

But what really scared Louise was the way her plan wasn't working the way she'd intended. She was looking forward, but things from the past kept springing back up in front of her.

Juliet wondered why she felt so discombobulated on her way to Louise's, but couldn't put her finger on it till she was walking up the path and knocking on the shiny green door with the "subtle" security camera thing that they had had fitted the week before Toby was born.

She didn't have Minton with her.

It felt stranger than when she'd taken her wedding ring off for the first time. His small, white, watchful presence by her heel, or in the corner of her eye, was a constant she hadn't thought she could get used to, like the heavy gold band on her finger. When it wasn't there, she couldn't stop fidgeting.

She'd left him curled up on the sofa in the kitchen, with QVC on for soothingly upbeat company. Lorcan had promised to let him out for a wee if she wasn't back by eleven, or if he heard any barking.

"Or if he starts buying any high-value Diamonique items," he'd added, deadpan.

I should have brought him, she fretted. *He could have stayed in the kitchen. What if something happens at home? What if he has a fit? Or a fire starts? Or—*

"Hi!" Louise flung the door open, with Toby in her arms.

She looked slim in a paisley-patterned silk dress, her hair shiny and freshly blow-dried. Toby was cozy and sleepy in an all-in-one with a Jack Russell on the front. Together, Juliet thought with a twinge of envy, they made a perfect *Red* magazine photo spread of a working mum with an active social life and a go-anywhere haircut.

"Look who it is!" Louise went on, pointing rather unnecessarily. "Auntie Juliet!"

"Hi, Toby!" said Juliet, in the same high, baby-addressing tone. She never meant to talk to him like that, but she couldn't help it. "All ready for bed?"

"In the jim-jams you gave him," Louise carried on. "With the doggy. Who's this, Toby?" she asked, squishing the appliqué dog on his fat little tummy.

"Minton," said Toby solemnly, and Juliet's heart melted, despite herself.

"Ah! Here, have a cuddle." Louise dumped her son into Juliet's arms and ushered her through to the kitchen. "We need to rush—the taxi's nearly here."

"Evening, Juliet." Peter was leaning against the counter, flipping through the business pages of the paper. He stopped when she came in and politely directed all his attention to her.

Juliet's brain emptied. She never knew what to say to Peter; he didn't have the usual bloke hobbies. They usually ended up talking about his iPhone.

"Thanks for giving up your Friday night," Peter went on. "We both really appreciate it, and I know Toby's happy to see his Auntie Jools. Aren't you?"

"No problem," said Juliet, shifting a compliant Toby farther up her hip. Peter was looking very magazine spread too, in his suit and . . . blimey, *yellow* shirt. House looked like *Elle Decoration.* Mum and baby looked like *Red.* Husband was like cover star of *Men's Health*, but without the surf shorts. "I hear it's date night?"

She looked over at Louise, but she was busy putting emergency milk bottles together on the side and didn't react.

Peter laughed his quick, controlled laugh. "I don't remember dates taking this much organizing in the old days. Still, I think it'll be worth it. The wine's meant to be excellent. Maybe we should do it again, and you can come too?" He glanced between his wife and her sister. "Hey, how about you two girls go one evening? I'll pick up the tab. Call it an early Christmas present?"

Louise turned round, and this time Juliet thought she caught an expression of constipated horror on her face.

Either Louise hates Peter saying, Hey, *too, or she's appalled at the idea of a night out with me,* she thought, and was surprised by the hurt that needled her chest.

Well, she wasn't thrilled by the idea either. What would they talk about? Louise's guilty secret or hers? Great night out.

"Mmm," she said. "So, what do I need to know?"

Peter pointed to Louise. "Over to you, Lou. Don't you have one of your famous lists?"

"Oh, it's not a list," said Louise hurriedly. "It's just . . . well, it is a list, but it's more for me than for you, so I don't miss anything off. Some numbers—you've got our mobiles, of course, but this is where we are, and that's Peter's mum's number, in case you need her . . ."

"Would you like me to water any plants?" asked Juliet. "Check any vegetables? Move post?"

Louise's expression was blank.

"It's what I do for pet-sitting," explained Juliet. "It was a joke."

God, it was depressing, having to explain jokes the whole time. It really made her think twice about bothering. If it weren't for her mother and Louise worrying about her "mood," she wouldn't.

"Oh! Ha-ha! No, it's fine," said Louise, although she looked a bit askance, probably at having Toby put on the same care schedule as Bianca and Boris Cox. "But feel free to eat whatever you like out of the fridge, and make long-distance calls to your boyfriend." She stopped, and added, anxiously, "Joke. It's what we used to do when we babysat the McGregors. Sorry, it's not a joke at all, now that I think about it."

"It's okay. You stick to the lists." Juliet gave Toby a heave up her hip. He was heavy, and getting heavier by the second as he started to go to sleep. It was nice, but she was bothered that one of her runaway emotions—broodiness, or regret—might ambush her before Louise and Peter had a chance to leave, and it'd get back to their mother. "Should we get him into bed? His batteries seem to have run flat."

"Yes." Louise reached out her arms and Juliet gratefully handed him back, just as a car sounded its horn outside.

"Perfect timing! That'll be our taxi," said Peter. "I'll nip out and grab him, before he decides to take off."

"Great," said Louise. "I'll be three minutes!"

Was there something a bit off about the pair of them tonight? wondered Juliet. Too many exclamation marks, too many shiny smiles? Or was she just accustomed to the silent, non-exclamation-marked company of pets?

Probably that, she thought, following Louise upstairs.

Toby went down obediently, and Juliet and Louise crept out of the blacked-out nursery.

"I'll call you, let you know how it's going," whispered Louise as she shrugged her cropped jacket on. It matched the dress. It had probably been bought all at the same time in an "outfit." Louise always bought in outfits, and she always looked coordinated, even when she was on maternity leave, living in her Sweaty Betty yoga separates.

"No need. We'll be fine. Have a nice time." Juliet found something nice to say. "It's good to see you guys spending time together."

Louise paused at the door, keys in her hand, and suddenly her face was vulnerable beneath the perfect makeup. "We're not . . ." she whispered, then stopped. "I mean, Peter's calling it a date, but we're . . ."

"You're allowed to have a nice night out," said Juliet, firmly. "Life goes on, as Mum likes to say, when she forgets she's not supposed to say it anymore."

That wasn't quite what Louise had meant, and she knew it, but it wasn't the time to get into that.

Louise chewed her lip. "We won't be late."

"Go," said Juliet, pushing her out as the taxi honked.

Babysitting was actually less stressful than pet-sitting, as it turned out.

Juliet settled herself on Louise's huge leather sofa, with the television remote and a stack of Diet Cokes, a pile of glossy magazines, and the baby monitor parked in her sight line. She didn't even have to talk to Toby, as she did with Hector or the Cox cats. She just had to listen in now and again to check that he was breathing.

Peter and Louise had the full Sky package, and Juliet enjoyed flicking through it for half an hour or so, before realizing that she'd seen most of it already on terrestrial TV. She didn't really mind.

As ever, just being in someone else's house was entertainment enough. Only this felt weirder than usual, because she was in the framed family photos that filled the wall around the phone table. The old version of her, where she was half of a pair.

Juliet heaved herself off the sofa, to give it a closer, house-investigator inspection. Unlike the jumbled wall in her bedroom, Louise had clearly arranged hers with the help of a spirit level, and the frames were an artful selection, rather than a mishmash.

There she was with Mum and Dad at Louise's wedding, in the "bride's side" photo, with Ben standing by her, arm slung round her shoulders, beaming with pride.

Ben had been an usher, but he hadn't hired a dove-gray morning suit, like all Peter's university mates. He'd gone in a suit she'd bought for him, a pale-blue linen one that had matched her own simple sunshine-yellow bridesmaid's dress much better. He'd worn it again, just a few months later, for their own spur-of-the-moment wedding.

Well, not exactly spur-of-the-moment. Not after so many years. But after the enormous complicated shenanigans of Louise and Peter's big day, Juliet had decided that she couldn't put her parents through that again, not for a ceremony that wasn't really her anyway, and so she and Ben had practically eloped. The thing that she remembered most about their wedding day was the ramshackle bunch of cuttings he'd brought her in the morning, each one meaning something symbolic.

Ben wasn't the most academic man in the world, but he knew the language of flowers better than anyone.

"Rosemary, so you'll remember all the happy times we've had. Heliotrope, for lifelong love. Eucalyptus, because I'll always protect you . . ."

Juliet closed her eyes in Louise's sitting room, hearing Ben's voice in her mind, as he held each stem between his thick fingers to show her, his suntanned face full of love, and her thumbnail went automatically to her third finger, where her wedding ring had been, until seeing it every day had hurt too much, and she'd taken it off.

Everyone freaked out, but she couldn't stand to be reminded that she was still there, the ring was still there, but the other warm, breathing part of her marriage was gone. *Maybe on the anniversary*, she thought, *I'll be strong enough to put it back on. On a chain round my neck, maybe.*

There was a crackle on the baby monitor and Juliet sprang back to attention, her ears twisting for a cry.

Nothing. *Better check*, she thought, slipping off her shoes to creep upstairs as quietly as possible.

There was more photographic evidence to inspect and enjoy on the way up: Louise's university netball team, debating team, all gilded and lettered. Peter's too. Peter had been in Bridge Club, Badminton Club, Orienteering Society, all the nerdy kids' teams, crouched in awkward poses around various Oxford courtyards.

At the top were Louise's BAGA gymnastics certificates from school, lavishly framed as a Christmas gift from her and Diane, to go with the rest of the hall of fame. Neither Louise nor Peter did irony, so the gilt frames had been a bit wasted. They'd just thanked them, bemused, and hung the frames with the rest of their certificates.

Juliet felt uncomfortable now, looking at the collection. It was meant to be an affectionate joke, but maybe Louise had thought they were being sarcastic? Cruel, even? It was tempting to take it down, now that she was here on her own. It would be even better if she could say to Louise, "You do know we love your high-achieving, box-ticking ways, don't you?" but since their big row, she felt as if Louise was reading double and triple meanings into everything she said, and the gulf between them was growing every day, as a result.

The sad thing was that their falling-out had come at the end of a few months when they'd been closer than they'd ever been, on the back of their weddings, and Louise having Toby, and her and Ben talking about starting their own family. Maternity leave had suited Louise; she'd loosened up a bit, let herself eat bread and watch daytime telly. When she and Ben had gone through a hard patch, it seemed very natural to open up to her big sister, but then Louise had taken a slug of wine and come out with her own bombshell.

Juliet frowned. Louise had admitted that she had a crush, and that it was getting out of hand. That in itself was bizarre enough, coming from Judgey McJudgeson, but she'd been so cagey about who it was, where they'd met, and so on that Juliet had started to think that maybe the object of Louise's crush was someone she knew.

Louise claimed to be agonized, but the feverish gleam in her eyes had given away a very different Louise from the calm, sensible wife and mother Juliet knew, and it had rattled her. She'd been the one who'd gone over *there*, worried about these cracks appearing in her so-called perfect marriage, but hearing Louise, who was supposed to advise her, say that sent her into fresh panic. What if all marriages self-destructed at a certain point, and the raggedness she felt really was the beginning of the end?

If she hadn't been distracted by the wine and her own problems, she might have been able to listen properly to what Louise was saying. Juliet wasn't proud of her hormonal flouncing out, on reflection. Compared with the devastation that followed, what was a little crush?

There was a grumble from the nursery, which turned into a whine. Juliet held her breath and pushed the door open, letting in a shaft of soft light as she peered round.

Toby was sitting up in his cot, staring out through the bars like a caged penguin. His hair, blond like Peter's, was spiky above his pale face.

Juliet smiled, then hesitated, not sure what she should do. Was it better to leave him or pick him up? Would he sense her inexperience and bawl the house down if she tried to soothe him back to sleep?

She couldn't get past it, because Louise was so lucky, she thought, a fierce sense of injustice piercing her chest. She had *everything* Juliet had lost—and she still thought she could gamble with it. It felt worse now than it had when Louise had told her, because she didn't even know whether Louise was still seeing this man who made her face glow like a teenager. Maybe she had that too.

Toby gazed at her through the bars, expecting some affection and attention.

Juliet went over to the cot and picked him out, feeling his sleepy weight against her chest. He nuzzled into her and she felt her heart contract.

What were you meant to say to babies? The same as you said to cats and dogs, presumably—anything that didn't require a response. Juliet had plenty of that sort of conversation.

"Hello," she murmured into his downy head. "Hello, Toby."

That seemed to go down okay.

Juliet paused, feeling a bit stupid, then went on, "Do you know what Ben and I wanted to call your cousin, if one had come along? Hmm? Lily, if she was a little girl. Isn't that a pretty name? Lily Iris Falconer. Or Arthur Quentin for a boy. Don't laugh at the Quentin; it was Ben's granddad's name. We thought *Q* would be a cool nickname. You're the only person who knows that. . . ." She stopped. It felt strange saying it aloud; worse for hearing it, better for getting it out of her head and into the light.

"That we thought we might have had a baby. It didn't work out, though. Not that time. Then we didn't really get our act together." She swallowed. Juliet had wept so bitterly in those bare winter months after Ben died, that thanks to their stupid arguing, she didn't have a trace of him left after he'd gone. "We argued over the silliest things that didn't matter in the end . . . Your mummy is very lucky."

Toby said nothing. She didn't know what he'd wanted her to do; he didn't seem damp in the nappy area, or sick. So Juliet held him, stroking his head as she did with the cats and dogs, until his eyes drooped shut.

Then she laid him back in his warm cot and sat by his small white chest of drawers clutching the huge Peter Rabbit she and Ben had given him, thinking about how different her life might be if she hadn't put off conversations, or measured herself against other people, or waited for Ben to make a decision. But she only knew how pointless all those things were now, when it was too late, and it *still* didn't stop her from avoiding the big problems that swirled around her even now.

Juliet closed her eyes and listened to Toby's snuffly breathing. It wasn't too late for Louise to get herself together. She hoped with all her heart that Louise at least had managed to learn something from all this mess, even if she hadn't.

It was something she was definitely going to teach Toby. Life was just a big game of musical chairs.

Chapter 14

"So how did it go with your old woman with the cats? She didn't cop on about Boris's shampoo and set?"

"No." Juliet stuck the little plastic spacers next to her tile, trying to match Lorcan's neat lines. "In fact, she asked me if I'd taken them to the groomer's, they were looking so great."

"Ah. That means she did."

Of course it meant she did. Mrs. Cox had sent Juliet straight back to her piano lesson days when she'd dropped round to pay her. "They look so delightfully glossy," she'd said. "Have you been giving them vitamins?"

It was the same as the *How long did you practice?* question. It almost made Juliet confess on the spot. But Mrs. Cox's gimlet eye had had a twinkle in it that wasn't entirely down to her luxury cruise, and Juliet had spent half the fee on a really good bottle of wine for Emer. She *owed* her.

"I'm telling myself she didn't," said Juliet. She glanced sideways to the other end of the bath, where Lorcan had already done three tiles. Two white, one glassy green. "Anyway, she's off again in a few weeks' time, so she's asked me if I can repeat my excellent service."

"Off again?"

"Again, yes. I had no idea retired people round here had such busy social lives. It's a whole different world, let me tell you." Juliet was starting to revise her preconceptions about widows and cats. The cats were more likely to die alone than the owners, if this lot were anything to go by. "I've got another cat, opposite Mum's, that I've got to nip in to see this weekend while its owner's sunning herself in Nice. We used to call it the Witch's House when we were little. I've always wanted to see inside, and now I can. Which is nice."

"Isn't it putting a bit of a downer on your own social life, all this pet-sitting?" Lorcan glanced across the bath. "While the cat's away . . . Juliet's looking after it?"

"Doesn't bother me. It's not like I go anywhere on weekends."

Juliet focused on getting the next tile, a "feature" green one, dead straight against the doweling Lorcan had hammered in as a guide.

She liked the green tiles; they weren't what she'd necessarily have chosen herself, but actually they were perfect. Under the glass was a fine layer of metallic paper, which shimmered like fish scales as the light caught it. And according to Lorcan, she'd have paid twice the price if she'd got them in a shop, instead of from his mate, who just happened to have them surplus.

"You never go out ever?"

"Ever."

There was a pause, and Juliet knew she should have made something up. That was the thing about Lorcan; she always forgot to make things up in the flow of talking to him, but he was the only person who made her feel that maybe her life of cats and dogs and Grief Hour and *Bargain Hunt* wasn't normal.

It was because the *Kellys'* life wasn't normal, she reminded herself. Most people didn't schedule their summer holidays around European stadium tours and/or oyster festivals, or whatever Emer had had to get back to Galway for this weekend, leaving Lorcan in charge.

"Well, if you ever want to come down to the pub with us . . ." he offered.

"You're okay," she said, not wanting to intrude. She and Emer saw each other most days for coffee and a dose of gossip (Emer's was better; Juliet's was mostly about who was using budget dog food), but she still felt a bit shy about crashing their social life. Knowing Emer's enthusiastic approach to noise and drink, she wasn't sure she was ready for it yet. "I'm not into shillelaghs. And . . . and . . . green beer."

"Irish people don't *just* go to Irish pubs," he said, huffily. "And eat potatoes and drink Guinness and fight each other."

"Joke."

"Oh. Sorry. I missed it there, in amongst the casual racism. You're still welcome. You don't have to Riverdance."

"No? Shame. Honestly, you're okay." Juliet squashed her tile into the adhesive. Lorcan was making an effort to be friendly, she knew. She just hoped he didn't think there was anything else in it. "I'd rather be here, stripping wallpaper. Didn't you say the walls needed preparing for painting?"

"Fair enough."

There was another pause, filled by De Dannan. In a concession to the relatively early hour, Lorcan had brought a selection of folkier rock music to play while they tiled, instead of his usual long-haired metal rock. It wasn't anything Juliet had heard before, and she wasn't even sure if they were singing in English, but she rather liked it.

"Did you go out much on weekends when Ben was around?"

Lorcan asked. "Were you music fans? Foodies? Theatergoers? Actually, scratch that."

He didn't use the hushed tone most people did when they asked about Ben, if indeed they ever did.

"It depended," said Juliet, pleased to talk about him. "Saturdays were sometimes a bit tricky, if Kim and I had a wedding to cater in the evening, but we always went out on Sunday. Long walk with Minton, pub lunch in the countryside, or brunch in town, snooze. We were writing our own guide to local places you could take your dog to."

"Cool. You should get it published." Lorcan slid a couple of spacers in next to his tile with a practiced hand.

Juliet smiled and reached for another tile. "Maybe I should," she said, but inside she didn't even want to open the notebook and see Ben's haphazard writing, his firm-but-fair marks out of ten, and her own appalled corrections.

"Sounds like you both worked pretty hard," Lorcan went on. "Did you do much traveling in your time off?"

Juliet wanted to say yes, so they didn't sound boring, but again she couldn't. "It's hard when you're self-employed. We were supposed to be going on a long trip to Australia this year, to stay with my brother, Ian, and his wife." She paused, feeling the sharp edges of the glass along the tile. It felt strange, telling Lorcan about something that *was* meant to happen but now couldn't. It was in the future and in the past at the same time, like so much of her life.

Juliet plowed on. "We'd started saving up for the tickets. Ben wanted us to go club class, so he was doing extra gardening to pay for it. It was going to be a second-honeymoon kind of holiday. Our actual honeymoon was in New York," she added.

"Cool place. But that's sad about Australia. Did you get the tickets booked?"

"No. We'd only just started saving up. And to be honest, we

made the plans to go while Ian was over on a holiday here with his kids, and we were all feeling the family love. He offered to have us stay with them to save money, because we only really had enough for flights, so we'd have been kipping on his floor." She paused, remembering the dinner. And the wine. And the slightly drunken offer of Ian's summer house. "I mean, Ian's great in small doses, but he's a bit of a fitness freak these days. And Ben was never very tidy. It might have been awful."

"You're right," said Lorcan. "It might. And the plane might have crashed, and you might all have got food poisoning on the way over and then been eaten by koalas."

"What?"

"You're funny, Juliet. It's like you'd rather it'd been crap. Why don't you just go now?"

"On my own?" she replied.

"Duh. Why not? You're a big girl. Go. You'll never get this time off again. It'd do you good. Fresh start. New experiences."

Juliet stared at Lorcan, standing there with a green tile balanced in one long hand, the extra-strong adhesive dangling from his other as if it weren't about to glue his finger permanently to his leg. It was easy for him to say. He'd traveled all over the place. He'd been with rock bands. He didn't feel like he'd suddenly been reborn, a nervous teenager in a thirty-year-old body.

"I need the money for my house," she said instead. "These tiles aren't going to pay for themselves. Even if they are a bargain."

"That depends on how you look at it," said Lorcan, and turned back to his adhesive.

At half past twelve, Juliet stood up and stepped back from the bath to admire her handiwork. The pattern was emerging now that they'd done four rows, and the sunlight flooding in from the open window made the glass tiles ripple like a swimming pool. It looked beautiful, and worked with the brass shower's stately curve above it. The bathroom was coming back to life.

"That looks really great, doesn't it?" she said, pleased. "Not like a complete beginner slapped it up."

"It looks grand," said Lorcan. "I'll give you ten out of ten. 'Course, you need your grouting, but that's another day." He sat back on his long skinny legs and let out a parched sigh. "Any chance of a cup of tea, now that you're on your feet?"

"I'll put the kettle on," she said. "But I've got to get down to town by one, so you might have to make it yourself. I'm walking a new spaniel. Don't want to be late for my new client."

"One?" Lorcan checked his watch. "You've loads of time!"

"I'm going to walk. I was looking on the map for new places to take the dogs, and I've found this old footpath that goes all the way from behind the church right down into town. It should take me about half an hour and saves on parking."

It had surprised her, seeing the red line pop out of the map like that—the perfect link between her house and the park, via some fields and a small wood. *How come I've never seen that before?* she'd wondered.

Well, probably for the same reason she didn't know where the fuse box was, or how to clip Minton's claws. Because she never had to know, until now.

"No tea?" whined Lorcan. "Don't make me go next door for my tea. Emer's having one of her cleaning fits because there's nits at the school and everything's got bleach in it. It's Russian coffee-mug roulette. It's like being back on the road with The Bends. Don't worry," he added, "you're not meant to have heard of them. Even their mothers can't pick out the bass player. Tea? Please?"

Juliet softened. It wasn't like Damson would be there with a stopwatch, checking up on her. And Lorcan had worked pretty hard this morning.

"Well, okay. Quickly," she said, and his broad smile lit up the bathroom.

Outside in the fields behind her house, Juliet stopped by a stile, lifted her face up, and took a deep breath that ended in an unexpected gulp of regret. June had slipped into July and it was exactly the kind of summer day she and Ben had loved. Warm, but not dry-hot, with a china-blue sky and drifting white clouds, and the smell of cut grass and greenness in the air. A perfect day. She wanted to stop for a second and share it with him in her head.

Ben and Juliet weren't a hot-weather couple, though everyone always assumed they were, from their jobs. Juliet had delicate skin that burned red, and she hated cooking in heat waves. Ben dreaded hosepipe bans and scorched lawns if it got above twenty-eight degrees. Even Minton preferred it cooler—the previous summer had been so blistering he'd had to lie panting in the shade until late afternoon.

Today, the air was soft and buzzing with bumblebees hunting along the hedgerow that marked the old footpath's winding progress down to town. Somewhere in the distance, a tractor was chugging along a cornfield, and red admirals fluttered in and out of her way. Today was the day that, if Ben were here with her, he'd have rung to say, "*This* is the high point of summer, Jools. Stick the cider in the fridge." And they'd have lain in the garden drinking it and looking up at the stars in the clear navy sky.

"Do you fancy a cider in the garden later, Minton?" she said aloud.

His tongue was dangling from one side of his mouth, and there were twigs in his harness from where he'd dived into the hedge in search of rabbits. He looked as if he were laughing.

"Yes," Juliet replied to herself. "I'll put it in the fridge."

Melancholy swept her as she set off again, knowing there would never be another cider with Ben by her side, tickling her feet with the crinkled bottle top, but she forced herself to watch the red-and-black butterflies and feel the sun warming her hair and enjoy it for both of them.

It didn't balance things out, but at least she could hear his voice, noting the blackberry blossom in the hedgerow, and reminding her to go back with a plastic bag for berries in a few weeks' time, without wanting to cry. It just made her sad.

Ben was bossy about free hedgerow fruits, she thought, even from the other side.

Mark's house was at the end of the loop of new townhouses built down by the canal. The estate agent who'd sold the Falconers their renovation project had first tried to show them round a "prime location" on Riverside Walk—until they'd admitted their budget and he'd whipped the details back across the desk as if they were state secrets.

Juliet could hear Damson barking as soon as she turned the corner. Her anxious yapping was setting off other dogs in the neighborhood, like a car alarm echoing round the estate. A woman came out of a house opposite with a bag of recycling, glared in the direction of Mark's house, glared at Juliet, then dumped the bottles in the wheelie bin and slammed back inside.

Juliet picked up her pace, in case Environmental Health was now being summoned. From the look on the neighbor's face, the barking wasn't a new development.

As she got nearer, the barking fluctuated like an old police siren, as if Damson were running up and down toward the door. Then she saw Damson's black-and-white head bounce up by the window, her fluffy paws on the back of the sofa. Her ears were all over the place, and her frantic eyes were white-rimmed as she yapped through the glass at the intruder.

God, thought Juliet, panicking. *Is she sick? Has something happened? Is there a gas leak?*

"Calm down," she said, putting her hands on the glass. "Calm down. It's just me."

Damson's tail started wagging, but she didn't stop barking.

"Hang on, I need to find the key round the back." Juliet made a round-the-back gesture to Damson, who promptly vanished off the sofa, as if she'd understood.

Feeling a bit self-conscious, she walked round the side of the beautifully kept lawn and hunted around in the dead hanging basket (very original hiding place) for the spare key.

She opened the door into Mark's utility room, and Damson flung herself at Juliet's knees like a furry cannonball, nearly knocking her over with licks and yaps. Juliet managed to shut the door behind her and leaned against it, trying to ignore Damson until she was calmer like the training books said, but it was easier said than done. The spaniel was so thrilled that her abandonment was over, she was practically climbing into Juliet's arms.

Minton hung back. Damson was bigger than him.

"Shh, shh," soothed Juliet, checking her over to see if she'd hurt herself. Damson seemed fine, but her heart was racing and she was licking Juliet's hands in pathetic thanks.

Juliet could guess what the problem was, because she'd seen it before herself. Minton had had separation anxiety when they'd first rehomed him, and Rachel at the shelter had told her not to make a fuss when she came in. "Act normal, ignore him till you've got the kettle on, and he'll get the message that going out and coming back isn't such a big deal."

It was so hard, though. Minton had been abandoned once already; Juliet had hated ignoring him. Damson was beside herself with relief to see a human face.

She forced herself to stand up and moved away from the door. She'd made eighty-three cups of coffee (and cried into twenty of them) until Minton had got the message.

"Come on in, Minton," she said, ignoring Damson completely. "How about a drink of water? Splash of ice and lemon, or straight? Straight, no problem. Now, where's the water bowl?"

She looked around Mark's whitewashed utility room. Washing machine, tumble dryer, overflowing basket of ironing, wine rack . . . Damson's plastic feeding area.

Damson had a plastic dog mat with two metal bowls on it. One, her food bowl, was untouched; the other, a water bowl, had barely a millimeter of water left in it.

"No water?" Juliet exclaimed. "On a summer day? That's not great, now, is it?"

Damson had quieted and was sniffing around Minton in a sociable manner. Minton was letting her, but keeping a wary eye on Juliet all the same.

"Where's the sink?" The door to the rest of the house was ajar, from Damson's frantic dashing about, so she didn't think Mark would mind her going in to fill it up.

She pushed open the door and the dogs skittered in after her as she swept it with a professional gaze. Like all the houses she'd been in lately, it smelled of someone else, and that seemed to sharpen her eyes for telling details.

Her first impression was that the kitchen definitely matched the owner. It was stylish and new, with the full complement of foodie implements (espresso machine, Magimix, et cetera), although whether Mark used them, she couldn't tell. All the surfaces were clean, though not quite up to Louise's laboratory standards; she guessed he had a cleaner. There was a large screen print of Paris on one wall, and proper wineglasses in the cabinet. A grown-up kitchen. Very different from the travel kettle and bare walls of her own ramshackle home.

But what about Mark? What clues were there about him? Juliet felt curiosity overtake her as she scanned the room.

Apart from a copy of the Longhampton local paper and a car magazine on the table, there wasn't much to go on. No Moorcroft pottery to price up for auction, no shopping lists on chalkboards to psychoanalyze, and no photos to peer at, except one of him crouching next to Damson on a mountain, stuck to the fridge with a single round magnet.

Mark seemed to be battling to stay upright, his hair blowing into his face, in a polar fleece hat and thick jumper. Damson looked deliriously happy, her ears at a forty-five-degree angle to her downy head.

Maybe the ex had taken the other photos. Or maybe he couldn't bear to see them. *Ooh, I'm getting good*, thought Juliet; I can interpret *absences* now.

She realized Damson was waiting for her water and hurriedly filled up the bowl at the big stainless steel sink. (L'Occitane handwash and lotion set; probably a Christmas gift.) "There now. Don't make a mess, please."

Damson plunged her nose into the water and drank greedily, her long ears trailing in the bowl. Minton waited politely behind her.

Juliet felt a bit strange being alone in Mark's kitchen, on this half-friendly, half-formal basis. It was one thing grouping Mrs. Cox's many grandchildren into family units and calculating how old Barbara Taylor's tea towels were, but this was different. Mark was a single man who'd asked her to pet-sit, but only after they'd chatted in the park, in a kind of flirty way.

She grimaced. *Had* he flirted? She knew she'd overreacted with Lorcan, but her flirt antennae were rubbish—Ben had been at her side all her life, and she'd never fancied anyone else. Chatting with new people was bad enough at the best of times, but men, possible-date men . . . Mark had a polish to him that Ben hadn't had; it made it easy to talk to him, but quite hard, at the same time, to know exactly what was going on.

Juliet knew she'd have to learn to chat with strangers before they could become anything more than just passing faces in the park. At the very least, she needed some new friends, and Mark seemed like a nice guy. If he had any serial-killer tendencies, surely now was the time to snoop around and find them?

Juliet felt an unsettling turn in her stomach that might have been excitement, might have been fear, and she turned her attention back to Damson, who was still lapping messily away.

Poor Damson. That wasn't so nice of Mark. Had he forgotten to top up the water before he went to work, or had she drunk it all because she'd been barking all morning? And if she'd been too upset to finish her breakfast, how long had she been going mad in the house?

Juliet bit her lip, trying to give Mark the benefit of the doubt. He didn't seem like the neglectful sort—he was, after all, paying her to come in and fuss with his dog because he couldn't. But he did seem busy, and preoccupied. Maybe he didn't even know how bad Damson's separation anxiety was. Maybe he didn't *want* to know, what with all the other guilt going on around his separation.

Rachel had said some of the most neurotic rescue dogs they had came from divorcing homes. First the rows, then one half of the human family vanishing, then perhaps the other, then the poor dog passing between the two owners, not knowing whom to love more. No wonder Damson didn't know where her next pat was coming from.

Damson finally stopped drinking, and Juliet bent down and caressed her soggy ears.

"Are you ready for a walk, then? Let's have a nice long walk and you can sleep until Daddy gets home."

The little spaniel wagged her tail so hard Juliet's heart broke a bit.

Juliet gave Damson and Minton a good long walk, all round the park gardens, up through the woods, and into a field, where they raced madly after Minton's ball until both their tongues were flopping happily.

Back home, Damson curled up in her basket under the kitchen table and allowed Minton to take up a corner. Juliet felt better about leaving her now that she was thoroughly worn out, but even so, she knew she had to say something to Mark about the state she'd found her in.

But what? She wasn't a vet, or the dog police. And this wasn't just about the dog; it was about Mark's home life, his relationship. Was it fair to make it sound like it was his fault? At least he was trying.

Juliet got her notebook out of her bag. She'd got into the habit of carrying one—not so much to leave bossy notes for owners, but to answer the worried queries they left her about poo consistency or amount of breakfast eaten.

She chewed her pen for a moment, then wrote:

Dear Daddy,

Can you leave the television on for me next time, please? It drowns out the sound of next door's stupid dog and the woman over the road's baby. It'd help me sleep better and means I don't have to worry about them. QVC would be good, or BBC News 24, ta.

If you could stick a Kong in my basket, that'd be good too.

Oh, and maybe if you could get used to walking around the house in your going-out clothes, jangling your keys, I won't worry so much when you do go out. I just need to know you're coming home because I miss you. A lot.

Love from,
Damson

Juliet thought about drawing a little paw print but decided that would be too much.

She folded the note and propped it up on the table, then looked around for a radio. It took her a while to find the sleek iPod-speaker thing in the corner, but when she turned it on, it was already tuned to a classical station, so she left it.

Damson snored in her basket as soothing waves of Strauss filled the kitchen. Juliet checked that her water bowl was full, then whispered, "Minton?"

At once Minton's head popped up, and he carefully removed himself from the basket, trotting to her side.

Juliet closed the door as quietly as she could and locked it, depositing the keys back in the hanging basket. She kept her ears pricked for the sounds of barking as she walked away but didn't hear a squeak from Mark's house.

The sun came out as she and Minton turned off the pavement onto the footpath that led through the fields back up to Rosehill, and Juliet felt an answering sun come out in her own chest.

She'd made a difference to Damson's little doggy life today. Next time maybe she could do some coming-and-going practice with her too. Maybe she could take one of Minton's spare Kongs.

It was only as they were cresting the hill and the midafternoon butterflies were flying crazily through the corn that Juliet realized that she hadn't actually collected any money.

Chapter 15

If we carry on exercising like this, I'm going to have to get new jeans," said Juliet to Minton as they walked up the road from the vicarage toward the park on Friday afternoon.

She'd felt the difference in her clothes recently; everything was a bit looser, especially round the hips. Her dog-walking jeans—once her gardening jeans—were almost baggy. Baggy jeans had never been a feature of her wardrobe before.

"I suppose it's down to going off Kit Kats at last. And not being able to bake anymore," she went on. She'd had a couple of covert attempts at some biscuits that week, but her touch was still deserting her. They'd been rock hard, or burned, or soggy. Not even Coco fancied them, and Juliet had tipped them into the bin, crestfallen. "As well as schlepping round town with you and your mates. And misery, of course. That helps."

He wagged his tail, pleased to be talked to.

It was nice to be on her own with Minton, thought Juliet, instead of having to steer other dogs around him, and he seemed happy to have her to himself too. They passed a couple of familiar faces by the coffee stand—Wild Dog Café Owner with Bertie, and Man Who Looks Like Bill Nighy with Border Collie—and Juliet found herself saying hello, because she didn't have her iPod earphones in.

For once, she didn't feel herself curling away inside. Juliet even managed a "Gorgeous day" to the Café Owner, and found out, painlessly, that the mobile coffee stand she visited so often was owned by the same café, and that Bertie was four. If Bertie hadn't been pulling like a train toward the woods, a conversation might even have broken out.

The coffee stand was doubling as a mobile ice cream parlor during the summer holidays. Juliet never used to eat ice cream—it was one thing she deliberately let herself get a taste for, like hot chocolate in winter, which she used as a sop to keep her weight under a metric ton. But now, walking over twenty thousand paces a day according to her mother's pedometer, a Magnum seemed like the least she owed herself in such warm weather.

She was tucking into an almond one when she heard someone shouting her name from the other side of the rose beds.

"Juliet!"

Minton looked up from the water bowl next to the freezer, ears twitching.

She turned round. The park was quite full, of shoppers and children on scooters, and older people enjoying the sun. Juliet wasn't sure now that she wanted to be found; this was a private ice cream moment. Was it too late for the earphones?

Yes, it was. A man was rushing up to her, linen jacket flapping as he ran, a satchel bouncing at his side. Also, a spaniel.

It was Mark, with Damson.

"I'm glad I caught you." Mark panted a couple of times, then straightened up, embarrassed by his flushed cheeks. "Sorry! You can tell I'm not walking Damson so much anymore. You haven't taken your money for the week."

"You didn't leave it," said Juliet, hastily wiping chocolate off her chin. "I was going to say something . . ."

"It was in the hall. On the side by the keys. Oooch." Mark was trying to talk and not show how hard he was panting at the same time. "Hang on." He turned round, took a couple of deep breaths, and then turned back.

Was that for my benefit? wondered Juliet. Quite flattering if it was.

"It's this hot weather," she said. "I have to stop halfway up the hill for a breather. And I never go into the hall." She paused. "You leave the back-door key. I don't go traipsing through people's houses."

"Traipse all you like. I don't mind. I can't believe you left that sweet note from Damson and didn't add, 'Where's my effing money?' at the bottom of it!" he said.

"I wouldn't do that." Juliet blushed. "And I hope you didn't mind the note, but I think she needs some help. She's not used to being on her own."

"I know." Mark looked guilty. "My neighbors have said she's been barking all day. I guess I was hoping she'd just . . . I don't know, learn I was coming back?" he ended hopefully.

"Well, yeah. If you could tell them stuff, it would be much easier." She glanced down at Minton. Damson was licking the water off his chin in a maternal fashion; he was enduring it with a stoic politeness that melted Juliet's heart. "He still waits for Ben. I'd give anything to be able to speak dog for five minutes."

"What would you tell him?"

Juliet opened her mouth, then shut it ruefully. "Probably the clichéd stuff people tell me, about heaven being full of everyone you love, plus celebs, and time being a healer."

"And that he needs to get out and meet new people?"

"Now come on, he's been doing that already!" She blinked in the sunshine, unable to read Mark's face properly in the light.

"Can I get you another of those?" he asked, nodding at the ice cream freezer.

"I'm fine with this one, thanks." Juliet angled her head and pretended to look serious. "Where you going to take it out of my walking money?"

"No! Let me give that to you now, before I forget." He took out his wallet immediately and rifled through the notes. He had more cards than Juliet did, and a photograph of a baby tucked in the side.

It took her by surprise; it hadn't even occurred to her that Mark might be a dad. There was no sign of any baby stuff in the house, not like at Louise's. Juliet felt a strange flutter at the thought of him with a child in tow. Then she kicked herself. How addled was her brain, falling for the worst daddy-with-buggy clichés? Fatherhood hadn't made Peter any sexier.

Anyway, it might be a niece or nephew. He might be a doting uncle, like she was a doting aunt.

"Here." Mark handed her some cash. "For this week and next. And can I get a mint Magnum, please?" he said, turning to the girl at the stand.

Juliet liked his tone. Friendly, educated. Polite.

They walked up the rose-garden side of the park together, Juliet trying to finish the tricky last part of her ice cream without getting it all over herself and Mark eating his, in quick neat bites, no messing. The scent drifted off the spread-eagled flowers, and Juliet found herself noting the difference since the last time she'd been there, when the yellow buds were tightly wrapped. Three days of sun had changed everything so quickly.

"You know you were saying you were a Longhampton girl?"

Mark dropped his stick into a litter bin. "Would you mind sharing your expertise with me one night next month? I know it's a way off yet—in August—but I'm assuming your diary's going to be pretty full round then."

"For what?" Juliet didn't say no straight away—some progress—but she was still wary of committing. There was a lot of good telly coming up.

"A mate of mine's organizing an exhibition of photography, all taken round here. He's invited me to the private view, opening, whatever you call it, and I said I'd go, but I've only been here a couple of years, so the lovely moody shots of the precinct are going to be wasted on me." He glanced over and looked conspiratorial. "I need someone to slip me some good lines about the way the photographer's captured the true spirit of the recreation ground."

"Blimey," said Juliet. "Has he got one of the cars on fire they have down there? It's nearly an annual occurrence, just after the schools break up."

Mark feigned horror. "I think it's more *Moonlight on Coneygreen Woods*. He didn't mention war reporting."

They walked on a few steps, and the question hung in the air. Juliet felt he was waiting for her to say yes or no. Well, not no. She could hardly say no; she'd have to come up with some convincing excuse. The trouble was, she couldn't think of one that didn't involve television or staying in to tile the bathroom with her builder, both of which sounded faintly insulting.

And a tiny little flattered voice in her head was pointing out that it might be quite nice.

"Which day is it?" she asked.

"Fifteenth of August. A Thursday. It's a school night, so it won't be late. And I know Chris is convinced no one will come, so even if you just pop along for half an hour, he'll appreciate it. And did

I mention the free wine?" Mark looked cross with himself. "I might be overselling this."

"It sounds fun," said Juliet.

Fun? Where had that come from?

From the relieved expression on his face as soon as she said it, she guessed. Mark was like Damson: eager to please.

"Fantastic! It kicks off seven-ish, in the Memorial Hall. I can meet you there, and if it's really awful, I'll take you for pizza or something to apologize."

"Okay," said Juliet. It was a few weeks away, which gave her time to drop out if she couldn't face it. That was the joy of pet-sitting. You could always invent an emergency dachshund.

"Great." Mark pushed his glasses up his nose, with a smile. "It's a . . . Um, I'll see you there! Well, I'll see you before, probably, won't I? Either around, or at home, or . . ."

"Yes! Yes, of course . . ."

They were both a bit flustered now. Mark hadn't said it, but they'd both heard the word *date* ringing out.

Juliet had read the chapter about new relationships in all her bereavement guides with a sense of detachment, because she couldn't actively imagine starting a new relationship. It was like seeing St. Paul's Cathedral flattened in front of you and then being handed the plans to rebuild it. Technically doable, yes, but what was the point? You'd never get it as good as Christopher Wren, and it'd never be over three hundred years old. Not in your lifetime, anyway.

But even in her still-numb state, she felt a small tingle of excitement that someone was asking her out. Excitement and nerves and a nostalgic fear that she hadn't felt since she was a teenager, although Mark was no teenager—he was an adult, with complicated domestic arrangements, and an air of attractive competence that she couldn't help warming to.

Then, as now, Juliet hadn't known how to handle the awkward seconds after the date-asking, and she had to fight not to blurt out some stupid reason to back out.

Luckily, the universe intervened and her phone started ringing in her bag.

"Ah! Are you late to collect another canine client?" asked Mark.

"If I am, I'm really late." Juliet scrabbled in her bag. "I didn't think I had one . . . Hello?"

"Juliet? It's Emer." She sounded flustered.

"Hello, Emer."

"Lorcan says you're a chef."

"I'm a caterer," said Juliet.

"What's the difference?"

"I make large quantities of edible food and I don't ponce around in a jacket with my name embroidered on it." That was her usual defense of her job, against Louise's glittering career; if Louise had been in catering, she'd have clawed her way up to qualified cordon bleu levels.

Juliet realized that maybe Emer needed her to cook something. The prospect of being summoned to cater a dinner party for rock chick Emer on her current form made her feel sick. "But actually, Emer, I'm not—"

"Brilliant!" There was a lot of noise going on in the background, and Emer sounded distracted. It was Salvador's bass guitar backed with some louder yelling. "Do you do kids' parties?"

"Not as a rule, no." Juliet made an apologetic face at Mark, who waved it away. "And I'm not—"

"Can you do one? I'm . . . Oh, hang on, Lorcan wants a word."

The phone was passed over and Lorcan's familiar voice came on. "Juliet, it's chaos here. We've a situation unfolding."

"There's always a situation unfolding at yours."

"This one's Defcon One. Crap Dad One, actually. Alec was

supposed to be flying in today for Spike's birthday. Special occasion, lots of kids coming, caterers booked. Only he's flown in and passed out, and we can't find the caterer's details, and to be honest, I don't think there ever was one, the useless fecker, because he texted me this morning to ask where you could get a birthday cake near Heathrow Airport."

Lorcan's voice got progressively less jolly and more Irish as he went on, and Juliet suspected he'd walked away from wherever Emer was so he could give full vent to his annoyance.

"Can you help us out?" he asked. "I'll give you all the money in Alec's wallet, which is a lot, believe me."

Juliet shrank inside. The noise was bad enough down the phone; she had no concept of how loud it would be in real life. And emergency cooking in someone else's kitchen? She *hated* that. "Wouldn't it be easier to just get a load of stuff in from M&S?"

"It would, but to be honest with you, Emer's in no state to leave the house, and I can't leave the kids. She's mad at Alec, and she's had a glass of wine on top of her hay fever tablet, *she says*, and . . ." Lorcan sounded worried. "I need someone who knows what they're doing. And you are that woman. Please. I've poisoned entire bands with my quiches. *Please.* My next phone call's to the police. To have myself arrested for the night, so I can get out of here."

Juliet glanced across at Mark, who was crouching down, stroking Minton while Damson hovered next to him. The contrast between the calm of invite-only private views on this end of the phone and near-feral hysteria at the other was almost surreal.

It's kids' food. How hard is that? It's sandwiches and Swiss rolls, she thought. *I suppose I could cook it in my own kitchen. And if they're fed, they'll be quieter. And I do owe Emer for the Boris-washing . . .*

"Fine," she sighed. "But only for you, Lorcan. As a thank-you for the shower and the tiles."

"Good girl. Are you in town? Twenty boys arriving in two hours. He wants a cake like a spaceship and green sausages." Lorcan's tone turned super efficient.

"Two hours? I can't do green sausages in two hours."

Mark looked up, surprised. She rolled her eyes.

"Any sausages will be fine, Emer says."

"Better get a move on, then," she said. "I'll be by the big Sainsbury's."

Thirty minutes later, Lorcan and Juliet staggered into the kitchen under the weight of twenty-one carrier bags of party food.

"Alec's passed out? With this going on?" she yelled over the sound of bass guitar and trumpet. It sounded like a trumpet, anyway.

"He could sleep through a Metallica gig. And he has." Lorcan pulled the sitting-room door shut with his foot, and the noise dropped by half a decibel. "I think the eejit took an Ambien to sleep in the car on the way back and it's knocked him out cold."

"He was driving?"

"Nooo." Lorcan looked amused at her naivety. "He had a car from the airport. The band paid for him to come back for tonight. It's in his contract—he gets to fly back for his children's birthdays. He didn't ask for that," he went on, barging through to the kitchen. "Emer did. She refuses to face them alone. Hi, we're back!"

Juliet thought there was a heap of washing on the kitchen table, but it raised its head and revealed itself to be Emer, bleary-eyed and disheveled, with turquoise kohl halfway down her cheeks. She looked as if one of the twins had scribbled on her and the other had tried to rub it out.

"This time it's divorce," she said incoherently. "The selfish, ignorant—"

"Juliet's going to help with the food," said Lorcan. "Did you do the party games?"

Emer slumped back into her arms and pointed at the pile of newspaper on the table. Juliet didn't want to think what might be contained in the parcel. Visions of Louise preparing the court files for the resulting police case swam before her.

"Emer," she said, addressing Lorcan to save time, "why don't you go and have a lie-down?" Her plan to cook next door wasn't going to work if Emer was out cold too. She'd have to do it here.

Lorcan didn't get a chance to answer before Emer waved him aside.

"I'll be fine," she said. "I'll just sit here. And watch." She reached into the fruit bowl and withdrew a huge pair of shades, which she put on after a couple of attempts. The effect was unsettling, like having a giant fly staring beadily over the table.

"Are you sure you wouldn't be better upstairs?"

Emer waved her hand regally. "Watching and learning," she slurred. "I could do with a Domestic Goddess lesson. God sent me a *miracle* when he moved us next door to you, Juliet."

"Thanks," said Juliet, unpacking the cocktail sausages. "I could say the same."

"Makes up for fecking Alex . . . Hey! Lorcan. Don't just stand there, we need a sound system set up. You can start by unplugging Sal. Cut off his plug if needs be. Ow, my head . . ." And she sank her forehead into her arms.

Lorcan flashed Juliet a *What can you do?* look and disappeared to do the tiny Fly Queen's bidding.

Juliet whizzed round Emer's messy kitchen as fast as she could. She'd had a good few coffees in there now, so she knew where most of the things were kept, but even so she was surprised by the headphones in the bread bin and a small dagger where Juliet would have stored potatoes.

Lorcan reappeared just as she had slung the first baking tray of honey-glazed cocktail sausages into the oven and was looking for a pan to boil eggs in. He had Roisin and Florrie in tow. Their eyes were round, and also ringed in turquoise kohl. They looked like glam-rock cherubs.

"I have a couple of sous chefs for you," he said. "So long as there are no knives involved. We're on our last warning at the emergency room."

Juliet didn't have time to feel her usual nerves in front of the twins. Time was marching on, and the sooner she covered that table in food, the sooner she could be out of there before the mighty hordes of kids arrived and she was roped into refereeing.

"Pan," she said, pointing at Roisin. "For eggs. Big dish," she added, pointing at Florrie.

"Say, 'Yes, Chef!' " said Lorcan. He pushed them toward the cupboards.

"Yes, Chef!" said Florrie at the same time as Roisin said, "Why?"

"Thank you, Florrie!" Juliet dumped the first of many packets of crisps into the dish and started sifting icing sugar into a bowl of Emer's glittery KitchenAid. "Lorcan's going to do the cake."

"What? No, don't be stupid. I can't bake cakes . . ."

"We've already got the cake," she said, pointing at the slab of plain iced sponge. "You're going to ice it." She squinted at the proto-spaceship, trying to work out how much icing she'd need. "Stand back."

Roisin squealed with delight as a cloud of icing sugar filled the kitchen.

"Seriously, Juliet," said Lorcan, over the sound of the mixer.

"Make his cake nice. Poor little guy. He doesn't deserve a botched-up horror."

"Think of it like plastering," said Juliet, handing him a flat knife. "Now, Florrie, ice cream cones?"

After barking semicoherent instructions from beneath her shades, Emer eventually retreated upstairs and made a surprise appearance with a rejuvenated Alec three minutes before three o'clock, when Spike's little guests were due to arrive. They stood in the kitchen doorway like visiting royalty, surveying the mess with a tranquil sort of acceptance. Juliet couldn't believe it was the same woman: Emer's face was now perfectly made up, and she was wearing a fabulous designer tunic thing over her skinny jeans, and some expensive jewelry that looked like an apology made out of diamonds.

She was also intrigued to see Alec. After all of Emer and Lorcan's stories, she'd been expecting some Viking warrior, but instead, she was faced with a tall, bearded geography teacher with very narrow trousers. The only rock-'n'-roll giveaway was the tattoo peeping out of his collar. Juliet thought it probably said *Emer*.

There was a pregnant pause, and then Emer stepped over the discarded bags and Spike, who was playing with a potato ricer. She grabbed Juliet's hands and said, "Thank you," with the sort of heartfelt emotion normally seen at major award ceremonies. "You're amazing."

"Yes, thank you," said Alec. He was Scottish. "I don't know how we can possibly—"

"I've paid her already," said Lorcan, shortly.

"I'll expense it." He grinned nervously. "Double whatever Lorcan gave you."

Juliet didn't miss the chilly look that Lorcan shot at him.

"Do you two . . . feel up to running a party?" she asked tactfully.

"Us? Oh, we're *fine*," said Emer.

Juliet looked over at Lorcan, and he nodded, shortly. "Not sure what we're going to do without the entertainer, but I'm sure we'll come up with something."

"If all else fails, we have an extensive dressing-up box," said Emer, sweeping a grand hand toward upstairs. "Capes, masks, glitter . . . It can change a small boy's life up there."

"Did you like the trumpet?!" said Alec, as if he hadn't been passed out cold hours before. "Surprise gift."

Juliet privately thought that a trumpet wasn't the best choice of instrument for an asthmatic child who kept eating random things, but she said nothing and unwound her apron while she had the chance. "I'll leave you to it," she said. "I've got a Labrador to check up on."

Diane's house was far enough away, surely. Not even Salvador's amplifier could reach that far.

"Ah, don't go yet!" said Emer, suddenly more like her everyday self. "Stay for one drink. I won't make you play pass the parcel, I promise."

"I don't really do kids' parties." Juliet glanced between Emer and Lorcan. Lorcan shrugged, as if he didn't want to force her to stay but wouldn't mind if she hung on for a bit, for moral support. "Maybe one drink," she conceded. "Not alcoholic, though . . ."

Emer clicked her fingers and called, "Bar girls?"

Roisin and Florrie appeared, still sparkly, to take Juliet's complicated drink order.

As Spike's guests began to arrive, Juliet and Lorcan retreated to the kitchen and let Emer and Alec take over the welcoming. To Juliet's surprise, they were easy, natural hosts—charming to the parents, and the right kind of cool to the kids. To her even bigger surprise, when she glanced at her watch again she found an hour had slipped past while she sipped elderflower fizzy cocktails and enjoyed the infectious energy of the party, albeit at a safe distance.

"I've got to go," she yelled over the racket to Lorcan. "I need to take Minton for a walk. He'll be next door under the bed thinking war's broken out."

She caught Emer's eye across the room, where she was painting Kiss faces onto a queue of eager boys, and gestured to the door. Emer made another *Thanks!* gesture, clasping her hands to her bosom. Something warmed inside Juliet. It was stupid to feel so excited about a new friendship at her age, but the Kellys' bonhomie made her feel giddy, and lucky to be swept up in it with such affection. It was nice too, in a guilty way, not to have to worry that she was enjoying herself too much. The inevitable *How are you getting on?* question never came up.

Juliet was picking her way through the debris of presents in the hall when Emer caught her arm.

"Just wanted to say thanks again," she said. "Not just for me, but for Lorcan too. He really appreciates it—I know you did this favor for him, not us."

"No," Juliet started, but Emer cut her off.

"He's a lovely, lovely man," she said, meaningfully.

"Emer, please don't go down that road." She felt awkward for the first time that day, cross that everything was about to be spoiled. It had occurred to Juliet that this conversation might arise, that maybe single Lorcan was as much a victim of the passive setup as she was, but now wasn't the time to have it, not with Abba being pumped out of professional speakers fifteen feet away.

Emer's eyes glittered under her makeup. "I hear you. But we should talk about him sometime. There are things you should know."

"What things?" said Juliet, but Alec appeared behind her, waving a bottle of expensive champagne.

"For later," he said, pushing it into her hand as the trumpet started up, this time played by someone with more lung power than Spike. "You might need it."

"Thanks," said Juliet, and made her escape.

Chapter 16

Now that the summer holidays had well and truly started, Juliet wasn't spending much time in her velvet chair with Minton—or in the house at all. The days on her calendar were ticking by at the same rate, but her old schedule of antiques and home improvement was being replaced by a different routine that made her eyes droop by eleven o'clock and sometimes even made her sleep through the whole night.

In the same way that they'd once "persuaded" everyone to throw parties catered by Kim's Kitchen, Diane and Louise had taken it upon themselves to spread the word about Juliet's pet-walking services, mainly, Juliet suspected, so she couldn't back out of her new "out and about" routine. Louise dropped off small-business guidance leaflets from the council offices and got her some liability insurance, and Diane gave her all of Coco's spare leads and water bowls.

Her phone, once silent for days on end, kept ringing with people asking if she wouldn't mind adding them to her waiting list. It seemed there were a lot of time-squeezed owners in Longhampton, all willing to pay to have their dog whizzed round the park a couple of extra times a week. Juliet could just catch *Homes Under the Hammer* with Minton between opening the door to Coco at eight and going to collect Hector at ten, then walking all three before lunch.

It was at lunchtime that things got really busy—and the boundaries between vicarious telly-based house viewing and the real thing started to blur.

On Mondays and Fridays, they had to detour via Mrs. Rogers, another book-group lady, to collect Spider, a frantic collie cross who needed his ball thrown so often Juliet's right arm felt twice the size when she came back. Diane usually came back from book group grinding her teeth about Mrs. Rogers, and her twee insistence on repeating all the views of "the lovely Mr. Rogers," as well as her own. Juliet decided not to let on that there was a pile of stickers by the hall table to send mail to Mr. C. Y. Rogers to an address in Hunterton, and not one pair of men's boots in the neat shoe rack by the door.

On Tuesday and Thursday afternoons, she let herself in to Louise's colleague Mina Garnett's ultramodern garden flat by the police station, and played with their beagle puppy, Pickle, for an hour. Mina's elegant flat was like something out of her home décor magazines, and Juliet couldn't resist taking camera-phone pics of her shower curtain for inspiration. She also felt like Sherlock Holmes, deducing that Mina and her boyfriend, Ed, did a lot of transatlantic travel, going by the huge bowl of Virgin Atlantic toiletries Pickle nearly upended while Juliet was snapping away.

Juliet wasn't sure how it happened, but somehow, during the summer, it seemed more and more natural to drop in to the Kellys' ever-clattering house of chaos. Maybe it was because the doors were always open in the heat, but she often wandered round there in between walks. Or to find Lorcan. Getting a screwdriver for Lorcan. Seeing if Emer had any handy hints for getting mud off cats. Showing Roisin how to make meringue mice. Letting Florrie practice her vet skills on a patient Minton. A hundred different, very natural reasons to be sitting at Emer's battered kitchen table, instead of her temporary fold-up own.

The main reason, though, was that for the first time in months, Juliet needed to talk to someone about something other than Ben. And it wasn't something she really wanted to share with her mother, or her sister.

Mark was taking up more of her time than any of her other clients, and not because she walked Damson for a good half hour longer than the others: Juliet also seemed to spend another half an hour after the walk pummeling her brains about what to write on the note he now always left in a very prominent place.

It had to be witty, and offhand, like she'd just scribbled it down in passing. It had to be flirty but not flirtatious. It usually had to be in the voice of Damson and/or Minton. The trouble was, all the crypticness was starting to get in the way, and she wasn't well practiced in the art of flirting to begin with.

Juliet knew she was probably wandering into a minefield, but at the same time, tingles ran up and down her arms when she opened the door and saw Mark's folded note waiting for her. It was always funny, and clever, and sounded like him—everything she wished her own notes were. Maybe she was letting herself be influenced by the elegant back-and-forth courtliness in the Jane Austen novels she was working her way through as she walked round the town, but Juliet could feel herself developing the first shivers of a real crush.

So much about Mark seemed like Fate. She told him that he reminded her of the antiques expert on television, as a shy sort of compliment, and he laughed and said that was because he *was*:

he worked for a big local auctioneer, valuing land and farm estates, mostly, but he had done some general sales too. Minton and Damson went to the same vet; Mark had been to some parties she and Kim had catered. He was incredibly easy to talk to and made her feel interesting, drawing out things that she'd never bothered to tell anyone else.

The hot August days went by and the exhibition got nearer, and Juliet still wasn't sure if it was actually a date or not. Or even if she wanted it to be. All the websites and books told her this was probably a disaster waiting to happen, but they were websites. What she wanted was some real advice, from someone who wouldn't look horrified at the way she was letting Ben's memory down.

Emer, luckily, didn't wait for her to raise the topic, but waded straight in one afternoon when Minton and Juliet arrived back from the afternoon's walks, shiny-faced and covered in burs, in search of a cold drink.

Roisin solicitously provided Juliet with Diet Coke on the rocks with a side order of pretzels, having first let her into the VIP area of the kitchen, via a velvet rope across the door. (It was Studio 54 week, chez Kelly, Emer explained.)

"Now then," said Emer, leaning forward conspiratorially once she'd sent the girls packing to the garden to supervise Spike. "Who's your man with the spaniel?"

"What?"

"Your good-looking fella with the spaniel. I saw you having a coffee in the park with him the other day. I almost didn't think it was you, you looked so cheerful, but then I saw Minton and Coco, so I knew it was you."

"When was that?" Juliet hadn't seen Emer, but then she wouldn't have been totally surprised to hear that Emer had been monitoring her from the crystal ball in her bedroom.

"God, I don't know. Friday? What's he called?"

"It's a she. Damson," said Juliet. "She's a working cocker."

"No!" Emer looked appalled. "Not the dog. The man! What's his name?"

"Oh! Mark. I think," Juliet added. She'd almost forgotten that detail; they never actually used names, just *J* and *M* on the notes.

"You *think*?"

"Yes, well, you don't really do human names with dog walkers," said Juliet. "It's just one of those things. You use the dog's name much more, and you never remember what the owner's called."

"I think I'd remember what a hot man like that was called."

Juliet blushed. "I do know. It's Mark."

Probably, she added, in her head.

"And it's just business," said Emer, in a tone that made it clear that that was *not* what she thought at all.

Juliet took a deep breath. "Well, he has asked me to an exhibition next week . . ."

"Good for you!"

"No, no!" Juliet said. "I was going to say, I don't know. That's just it. I can't work out whether it *is* something, and I'm just rubbish at picking up signals, or it's not and I'm making a fool of myself. He might just be friendly."

"Do you meet him in the same place every time with the dogs?" she asked shrewdly.

"More or less." Juliet thought about it. "He's usually coming down the hill and we're coming up, and we sort of meet by the coffee stand and—"

"Big place, that park," said Emer. "What a coincidence, eh?" She patted Juliet's hand. "It's a date, I reckon. Oh, hang on. He's not married, is he?"

"Divorced. Has a child, though. So I think that's why he doesn't want to rush into anything." Juliet felt her cheeks turning pink. "We haven't really talked about it as such, but we've both joked about how much easier it is meeting new dogs than new people."

"So he knows about your husband?"

Juliet nodded.

"How long is it now, since your husband died?" Emer pushed the biscuits across the table and helped herself. "Forgive me for asking, I know I should know."

"Ten months," said Juliet, without having to think. "On the thirteenth."

"So long enough to be used to it, but not long enough to be healed," said Emer sympathetically. "Had you been together a long time?"

"Since we were fifteen."

"And you're how old now?"

"Thirty-one."

"And you were still together! Wow." Emer sipped her coffee. "If I were still with my boyfriend from school, I'd be either in prison or an institution." She tucked her chin into her neck in outrage. "I certainly wouldn't still be playing tambourine in his fecking hopeless Pink Floyd tribute band. Not for free, anyway."

Juliet smiled. There was something flattering about Emer's honest chattiness, but it wasn't a safe kind of familiarity. She had absolutely no idea what she might say next—but suspected that even Emer's long-standing friends probably felt the same way.

"How did you manage when you went away to college?" Emer went on. "Come on. You can tell me. Didn't you even have a secret university fling or two?"

"We didn't go away—I went to catering college here, and Ben did a year's horticulture course in Birmingham. He commuted—it wasn't that far, and some of it was practical."

"So you've always lived here? You never wanted to move out?

See the world a bit?" Now Emer wasn't even trying to disguise her surprise.

It reminded Juliet of Lorcan's surprise when she'd said they hadn't really gone traveling. It made her want to dig her heels in.

"I had everything I wanted right here," she said. "My family have always been here—my mum and dad have been in the same house since they got married!" But even as she said it, she felt the faintest flicker of an old emotion she'd managed to stamp down so hard it had almost disappeared. There had been a time when she'd quite fancied traveling.

Emer seemed impressed. "Well, fair play to you. You can't put a price on family." She pushed herself away from the table and went over to the fridge to fan herself with the cold air. "It's nice to know that perfect marriages like that really do exist, and not just in cheesy songs."

"I'm not saying it was *perfect* . . ." Juliet began, and now, fanned by Emer's reaction, the emotion was licking around her stomach, catching light on the dryness of many tightly packed thoughts.

"You make it sound pretty perfect," said Emer.

"It was," protested Juliet. "Most of the time. I mean, that's what's so scary about starting again with someone new. Ben knew me inside out. He knew me better than I knew myself. The thought of having to learn everything all over again with someone who can't possibly know me that well and never wi—" She stopped, midword, and clamped her mouth shut. Things were tumbling out that she hadn't actually officially let herself think.

Emer took a Coke out of the crammed fridge, then a bowl of olives, and shut the door. She gave Juliet a long, considered look. With her tumbling brown-and-copper curls and strange caftan tunic over her jeans, she looked like a Celtic fertility goddess, if the gods had started shopping in Monsoon.

"Can I give you a word of advice?" she said.

"So long as it's not 'Time's a great healer' or 'Get a kitten,'" said Juliet. She tried to make it sound light, but she heard her voice harden.

"My mam died when I was fifteen," said Emer. "And overnight, it was like she'd been replaced by the Virgin Mary. My dad claimed they'd never had a cross word, never spent a night apart. She'd certainly never been one for the drink, and she'd definitely never caused the chip-pan fire that nearly wrecked our house. We missed Mammy, 'course we did, but seriously—after a year or two, we were gagging for him to remarry. He couldn't even make a sandwich."

She rolled her eyes. "I gave up the chance to go to Norway in a Transit with the best metal band Cork ever produced, because my daddy couldn't be trusted to feed himself, let alone the dogs."

"Maybe he was still grieving," said Juliet. "You can't put a deadline on grief."

Which was stupid, because she had, hadn't she? A year.

God, I'm as bad as the rest, she thought. Repeating grief catchphrases.

Emer pointed at her. "He wasn't grieving. He was *guilty*. Guilty that he hadn't been better to her when she was alive. It was only the parish priest that kept those two together. And Daddy's way of dealing with it was to make her this perfect woman in his head. No other woman ever got a look in from that day. Everyone was setting him up with the *loveliest* women, but they'd all come back looking shell-shocked, saying, "I had no idea Theresa made her own bread, and looked after Mrs. Flynn while she had the cancer."

"But Ben and I never fought!" said Juliet. "Well, not really. Not about anything that we couldn't make up." Her face felt hot. This wasn't in the script. Emer was meant to be all sad about what a lovely marriage she'd lost. Instead, Juliet was getting distinct flashbacks to that conversation with Louise, when Louise had told her to stop whining about Ben and just get on with it. That if it came to a choice between a man who did budget spreadsheets and finished DIY projects, and a man who made her feel like she was made of sex and flowers, she knew which one she'd go for.

The conversation had headed into very dangerous waters after that. *Very* dangerous.

Emer was looking at her, taking in her flushed cheeks.

"Never? Ever? Oh, come on. Not even about leaving the toilet seat up? Or shelves that never got fixed?"

"No." Juliet felt stubborn. If *she* stopped believing in the life belt of the Perfect Marriage, then she was in real trouble.

"Then he must have had you drugged," concluded Emer. "The better the love, the bigger the fights. And the longer the making up. If you never fight, then aren't you just flatmates?"

Emer's gray eyes were kind, but they were also perceptive. The effect of her gaze, and also her undivided, unbiased attention, started to unpick Juliet's defenses.

"Well, it wasn't always sweetness and light," she admitted. "We'd been hoping to start a family and things weren't happening, which was a bit . . ." She hunted for the right word. The looks. The doubts. The silences, where there never used to be any. ". . . depressing. And we were both self-employed, and things were tight with the new mortgage, and the recession." Good. The recession was much safer ground. That was nobody's fault.

Emer said nothing, and Juliet heard herself filling in the silence with more honesty. "I sometimes get a bit uptight about money, and Ben was always more *que sera sera* than me, which is fine when you're in your twenties." She looked away, at the collages on the pinboard, at the huge Rolling Stones posters on the walls, anything except Emer's face.

They had *had* rows. Just in that last year, though, little skirmishes where once they'd have agreed to disagree. Small rows about big things, then big rows about small, stupid things.

Two days before Ben died, they'd had their first, truly bitter row, sparked by something really silly—him not telling her about renewing the van tax, so she'd bought it too and gone overdrawn. It had turned nuclear, though—after an initial round of "Why don't you ever tell me things?" on both sides, Ben had yelled that he didn't want to sign up for IVF, even though Juliet hadn't even mentioned it, and she'd yelled at him, through her stress headache brought on by dealing with the bank, that maybe it was better if they didn't have kids, if he was going to behave like one for the rest of his life.

The ferocity of the argument had scared Juliet, because as they were yelling at each other, her anger brought all kinds of unwelcome thoughts floating to the surface in its wake. Had she suddenly grown up into a boring adult, or had Ben *never* wanted to travel anywhere you couldn't get a McDonald's? Was he really going to do the work on the house, or was she going to have to arrange it and pay for it all? And could you actually start to dislike someone you loved deep down?

Stupidly she'd decided to confide in Louise, going over there in the hope that she'd tell her that all married couples had rows, that she and Peter had tried for months before Toby was conceived and had squabbled badly in the months before.

She hadn't. Louise had just looked shocked, and that had made her feel even worse.

Oh God, thought Juliet now with searing clarity. *Why can't I go back and take a Nurofen before he walked into the room that night? Why can't I just rewind the clock and not say some of those things? Would that change what happened? I'd give anything. Half my own life to share another half of his.*

Emer was speaking, wandering round her family kitchen as she went, probably not even noticing the lovely homeliness of it.

"I'm not saying you were being kept together by the parish priest," she went on, "but don't do what Daddy did. Don't make it all so perfect in your head that no one else'll ever be able to come close. It's not what he'd want. Ben would want you to be happy now. And your man's a dog owner! It's like Minton's brought you together—now doesn't that sound like interference from a higher place to you?"

Juliet said nothing, but her shoulders were shaking with the effort of keeping in the tension bursting up through her chest. It was as if someone had a remote control that could turn her emotions up to ten, without her even being asked.

Before she could do anything else, Emer was by her side, her arm around her, and her ample bosom pressing into her face like a pillow.

"Jeez, I'm sorry. I wasn't meaning any disrespect to your marriage, honestly."

"It's not that," hiccuped Juliet.

"What is it, then?"

"I just feel so . . ." Juliet probed around the dark feeling, trying to identify it. ". . . guilty."

"Why?"

"Because everyone always used to think Ben and I were perfect, and I let them because it was our *thing*. We were the childhood sweetheart story, like my mum and dad. Then the one time I even mentioned to Louise that things weren't right . . ." She struggled to keep herself together.

"Is this your sister who's the hotshot lawyer with the perfect baby and the husband with his own business?"

Juliet nodded.

"Well? What happened? Did she confess she'd been having an affair with him?"

"No! He died the next day. And the last thing she remembers

about Ben is me saying he wouldn't listen to me about starting a family, and her telling me I didn't know what I had, and that I should go to counseling before our marriage hit the rocks."

Emer squeezed her. "Juliet, you know it's daft to think he died because you said that, don't you? I mean, I don't have to tell you that?"

In her bleakest, most irrational hours, that was exactly what Juliet thought—that her confession had broken some kind of cosmic luck spell—but she didn't want to admit it to Emer.

"I feel like every time someone says what a great marriage we had in front of Louise, she's remembering what I said and thinking what a hypocrite I am."

"No one will be . . . Listen, Juliet, you're *entitled* to have everyone say how wonderful your man was." Emer turned her shoulder so she was looking into her face. "That's fair enough. What I'm saying is that you don't have to stop loving the past to enjoy the rest of your life. The universe has got more in store for you yet. Who knows what?"

Juliet made a noise that wasn't agreement or disagreement. That was what the books said.

"It's like I said to Lorcan, the Foo Fighters are a great band, but if Dave Grohl had said, 'Nope, no more for me. I'm going to grieve for Nirvana for the rest of my life,' we'd never have had the enjoyment of them, right?"

"Um . . ."

Had Lorcan lost someone? Juliet frowned, but Emer was carrying on.

"Are you telling me that you've never talked to your sister about this since Ben died? In all these months? Juliet, that's crazy. What do your family *talk* about?"

"My nephew's babysitting rota, mainly. It's not that simple," said Juliet. "It was a really awkward conversation."

"Awkward how? Did she have a gun out?"

"No! She . . ." How come it was so easy to tell Emer this? Still, if it made her look less crazy . . . "Louise more or less told *me* that she had something going on with some other man. I don't think she meant to say so much, but she was all twinkly and girly, like she had to tell someone."

"Really?" Emer leaned forward, agog. "Who?"

Roisin clattered in from the garden. "Muuuuum, Spike is all red."

"Get his hat. And take his inhaler." Emer flapped a hand in her general direction. "We're talking."

"Can I get some—"

"Get whatever you want. But not the red Coke—that's for Lorcan."

Roisin gave Juliet a particularly penetrating stare and lingered by the open door of the fridge, taking her time over the drinks selection, her ears practically swiveling like satellite dishes.

"Roisin! You've five seconds before the bar closes," commanded Emer. "One, two, three, four . . ."

"Aren't you meant to leave gaps between the numbers?" asked Juliet.

". . . five!"

Roisin grabbed the cans and half a bag of fun-size Twixes and ran out.

"Louise didn't say—" Juliet began, but Emer was holding up a finger.

Wait, she mouthed, then spun round and clapped.

There was a clunk as Roisin, concealed behind the vegetable rack, dropped two of the cans, and a muffled "Feck!"

Emer got up, shooed her out, and closed the back door. "That girl is going to grow up to be a spy or a gossip columnist," she said, not disapprovingly. "So what you're saying," she said, settling herself back down at the table, her chin in her hands as if she were watching the telly, "is that every time you see your sister, she thinks about spilling the beans about her affair, and you think about slagging off your late husband. Well. You should have said."

"I know," said Juliet. "It's been horrible."

Emer gave her a sympathetic smile. "Juliet, I bet she barely remembers it. Don't you think your husband *dying* would kind of take priority in most people's memories?"

"Not in Louise's," sighed Juliet. "She's the kind of person who remembers what you got her for Christmas in 1998. She's the perfectionist in our family."

"Doesn't sound so perfect to me. Is she still seeing this guy?"

"No idea. She's gone back to work and seems to spend every second when she's not there with Toby." Juliet tried to dredge up what details she could remember. "To be honest, I was so annoyed that she'd been telling me to go to counseling when her own marriage was obviously not all it was cracked up to be that I left quite soon after that. I didn't want to know any more."

"You didn't even ask where they met?"

"At some group or other, I think. I was a bit stunned. She went on about how he made her feel like a new person, not just a mum, like Peter did. Peter's an IT designer, bit of a geek. Quite a rich geek now, though. He likes those online games where you're a wizard." Juliet tried to think of some other facts about Peter that didn't make him sound dull. She couldn't. "This other bloke was a bit more . . ." She tried to remember exactly what Louise had said. "More in touch with himself. More physical."

As she spoke, she saw Emer's eyes gleam with intrigue.

"What?" Juliet asked.

"Definitely not an unrequited crush on your husband?"

"She'd hardly be telling me, would she?" snorted Juliet.

Emer widened her eyes so much that Juliet could see white all around them. "Stranger things have happened."

Suddenly, Juliet felt defensive and annoyed. "Well, not in my family. Ben and Louise . . . were friendly, but they didn't have anything in common."

"Okay," said Emer. "Forget I said anything. I'm an awful gossip. Back to the man in hand. This guy Mark. Do you like him?"

"I think so," said Juliet. "Yes, I do."

"Then there you are!" She clapped her hands. "Call it a date. What harm can it do?"

Juliet felt a fizz in her chest. Hearing that from Emer's mouth, rather than her mother or Louise, somehow made her more inclined to agree.

Chapter 17

The days began to move more quickly now that Juliet was busier and the exercise made her sleep through the night, and before she knew it, the day of the private view that Mark had talked about was upon her—the date that had seemed so far in the distance.

Juliet stood in front of her bedroom mirror, trying to work out what to wear while the pile of "wrong" clothes on the bed got bigger and bigger. Nothing looked right, and she was running out of time and options. *That* was what was making her feel sixteen again, not the going-on-a-date part.

It's not a date, she reminded herself. *It's just an evening out.*

But it still felt weird. Juliet didn't quite know the effect she was going for—she didn't want to look like she was trying too hard, but at the same time there was a tingle of something in her stomach that made her reach for something a bit more stylish than her usual jeans.

Minton sat on the bed and watched her, which wasn't doing

much for her churning emotional state either. He seemed confused. Juliet in a skirt wasn't something he'd seen a lot of recently.

"What do you think?" she asked him lightly, twisting so she could see the back. "Black skirt and the gypsy top that maybe isn't very fashionable anymore, or denim mini and the black V-neck top that Louise said washed me out unless I wore twice as much lipstick as normal?"

Minton wagged his tail, uncertainly.

"Okay," said Louise. "Denim mini and the black top and the lipstick it is. And the big boots that your daddy never liked me wearing because he said I looked like I was about to kick over a motorbike."

In for a penny, she thought. *Might as well go out looking nothing like myself.*

As she was zipping up the boots, the doorbell rang and Minton launched himself off the bed and skittered down the stairs to investigate.

Juliet followed more slowly. The boots meant she had to clump down each bare tread sideways and then moonwalk across the hall using entirely different muscles from normal. But it was liberating to have no one tell her she was an idiot for having bought boots she couldn't stand up in.

"Sorry to keep you," she said, when she eventually got to the front door. "Oh, hi!"

It was Lorcan, holding a couple of tins of paint.

"Whoa!" he said, looking up dramatically. "Are stilts back in?"

"Shut up," said Juliet. "It's fashion. And I'm going out somewhere. I might need to look over people's heads."

"You could just pay more and get tickets for the front," he pointed out.

"It's not a gig. I'm going to a private photography viewing, actually."

"Are you now? Who knew such things happened in Longhampton?" Lorcan raised his eyebrows, pretending to be dazzled. "Bit out of my social milieu, private views . . . Anyway, how are you fixed for a bit of bathroom painting tomorrow? I can teach you the mysteries of bathroom gloss."

He lifted the cans so she could read the color: Indian Tea. It was exactly the old-fashioned green she'd wanted, to pick out the swimming-pool tiles around the shower, even though she didn't remember telling him that.

"Won't bother fetching my ladder," he added. "I'll let you do the high bits."

Juliet couldn't help noticing he was barely suppressing a giggle, and she gave him a light shove.

"Stop laughing at my boots, Lorcan. They're fashionable." She paused, suddenly struck with doubt. "Do I look ridiculous?"

"Noo," said Lorcan. "You look great. Really . . . great."

"Really?"

He nodded.

"Not too . . . dressed up?"

"But not too dressed down either? Sounds like a date." He raised his eyebrows. "Ah, lookit, you're blushing—it is a date."

"Not really. It's just . . . a client of mine. His friend's the organizer. I'll probably only stay for half an hour, just for his sake—you know what it's like at these things; they just need bodies there at the start so the artist doesn't look like Billy No-Mates."

Juliet knew she was talking too fast, and probably blushing, but Lorcan didn't seem to be bothered by her apparent brazen hussyness. In fact, he was nodding encouragingly. Like Emer had done.

"Fair play to you," said Lorcan. "You can't go wrong meeting new people. That's what the guys in the band always said, anyway. As they cruised the backstage looking for new people to meet."

"Do you miss being out with the band, Lorcan?" said Juliet, in a pretend sad tone. "Do you wish you got the same kind of groupie on the building circuit? Farrow and Ball–addicted MILFs, begging for your grouting?"

"I do not. I was *terrified* of the groupies," he said. "Emer used to have to scare them off for me with her pinking shears." He sighed. "Hurricane Emer, we used to call her. Went through whole cities, left them flat in her wake. Don't ever do cherry brandy shots with her. Anyway"—he raised the paint cans—"can I leave these till tomorrow?"

"Feel free."

He put them down in the porch, then wagged his finger at her. "Don't you come rolling in with a sore head tonight, either. I don't teach hungover students."

"There'll be no . . ." Juliet began, then saw the twinkle in his eye. "I'll be home by ten, Mum. What you should really be worrying about is me buying some awful picture you'll have to hang."

"I'll bring my hammer," said Lorcan. "Ah." He looked down and saw Minton standing behind her. "Do you want us to pet-sit for *you* tonight?"

"Minton?" she asked. "Do you want to spend the evening playing ticks and fleas with Florrie?"

Minton turned, quite deliberately, and jumped onto the sofa, where he curled himself into a tight, tiny ball.

"I'll take that as a no," said Lorcan.

The Memorial Hall in Longhampton was an unexpected thing of Arts and Crafts beauty, hidden in the middle of a lot of gray flats behind the equally unlovely concrete precinct. Its solid buttressed walls and jam-tart stained glass made it look as if a tornado had swirled it up from the middle of Chelsea and deposited it, like the Tardis, smack-bang in the middle of Longhampton's unambitious town center.

Juliet had only been in once, for the dancing lessons Louise had insisted her bridesmaids and ushers attend before her wedding, so they wouldn't show her up on the dance floor. She and Ben had had one giggling, awkward foxtrot lesson, during which the stroppy teacher had loudly marked them all out of ten and given her and Ben two for skill, nine for effort.

The streetlights were coming on along the road, bathing the hall in an early-evening glow, and as Juliet approached the steps, she couldn't help seeing that evening in a rosier glow too. It had been lovely, once they'd got the hang of it. They'd picked it up quicker than the other couples, because she only needed to glance at Ben to know what he was thinking. He'd steered her round the floor with a mere flick of his blond eyebrows, and she'd let him know all about her mangled toes with hers.

Mark looked like the kind of grown-up man who knew how to dance properly. She bet he had some black tie in his wardrobe that he brought out for smart charity events. Juliet could see him swinging round the floor with that confident smile, making it easy for his partner to follow, dancing with everyone, knowing the right thing to say . . .

She took a deep breath to stop the flock of butterflies that had swarmed into her throat, jostling with the guilty memories.

This isn't about grabbing another man, Juliet reminded herself. *It's just a trial run. With a good-looking, intelligent bloke who has an interesting job, lots of books in his house, who's kind to his dog. That's enough to be going on with.*

It was just a shame she was meeting him in a place with so many memories; but then there wasn't a corner of Longhampton that didn't have some cobweb of her and Ben's shared past clinging to it, so she'd just have to learn to live with it, or do all her dating online from now on.

Juliet steeled herself and headed for the door, where an easel was displaying a big poster of a tree with three dogs and a sheep underneath.

"Hello! Sorry I'm late!"

She spun round and saw Mark hurrying up the steps toward her.

Her stomach fluttered: He looked crisp and handsome, in a stone-colored linen jacket over a white shirt, with navy trousers and a blue checked scarf thrown over the top. It would have looked a bit foppish on someone else, but Mark carried it off. More than carried it off. The admiring look he gave her was the final touch.

"Have you been waiting long?" he asked.

"No, I've just got here." Juliet was glad she'd bothered with the boots. Without them, she'd have been a bit underdressed. With them, she reached nearly up to Mark's ear. He seemed happy to see her, anyway.

"I've been out with farmers all day, so I had to nip home and change. Didn't think anyone here'd appreciate what I've had to wade through today." He leaned forward and kissed her on the cheek, once. "Fresh air's one thing, but what goes with it isn't always so lovely."

He talked through the kiss, so Juliet didn't have time to react. When he leaned back, he was smiling, and she smiled too, feeling a little flutter of relief.

First social kiss from strange man. Tick.

"Shall we go in?" he suggested, sweeping his arm toward the door.

As the man at the desk crossed their names off a list, Mark reached out to collect a couple of glasses of sparkling wine from a passing tray and handed one to her. "Where's Minton this evening?"

"At home. Next door's keeping an eye on him. It feels a bit weird being here without him."

"You two go everywhere together?"

"We do." They were walking through the foyer now, Mark nodding and smiling at people he recognized. He seemed to know quite a few people. "That's the great thing—he's quite portable. Not like Damson."

"Damson likes to think she's portable," he said. "I found her trying to get into my rucksack once, when we were on a long hike together. Although she might have just been trying to cadge a lift. She's not daft."

Juliet laughed. *This is easy*, she thought. *We're talking about the dogs again. And now we can talk about the photographs.*

She and Mark settled into a relaxed conversation as they moved from one picture to the next, taking in the big blow-ups of Longhampton's various landmarks, with added dogs and clouds. Mark had the auctioneer's knack of keeping conversation going; he smoothed over her occasional pauses and panics with simple questions—did she like that one? Did she know where that church was?—and slowly the social party questions started to come back to her. Not too bland, not too personal, just enough to oil the wheels of conversation.

The glass of wine helped, as did not having to maintain eye contact. Once they'd had a look at the main wall and established how Mark knew Christopher, the event organizer, and that Juliet thought Chris might have gone to school with her brother, Ian, a warm, bubbling feeling was buoying Juliet's mood.

I'm having a good time, she thought, with surprise and relief. *At an arts event! Even if my feet are killing me.*

The space had filled up with more guests while they'd been talking, and the side of the exhibition they hadn't managed to see was crammed with guests, nearly blocking the view. Juliet was surprised to see what a varied crowd it was.

"Chris works for the local paper and that glossy *Hamptons Life* magazine you get in dentists," Mark muttered in her ear. "Which is why you see before you the cream of Longhampton's media inner circle. And quite a lot of the outer circle as well."

"Ooh," said Juliet, impressed. Louise would be impressed too. And her mother. Diane sent her brother Ian a subscription to *Hamptons Life* as a way of "keeping him in touch with his roots." Privately, all Louise and Juliet thought it kept him in touch with was Longhampton's obsession with hog-roast-themed fund-raisers and the many faces of the council.

"Did you . . ." she began, turning her head. Mark had been jostled nearer by someone moving through the crowd with drinks, and, elevated by her boots, she accidentally brushed his cheek with the side of her nose.

She froze, and he turned round to see what had touched him and did the same. Their eyes met in an awkward panic, and then Mark laughed and stepped back.

"Sorry! Bit soon in the evening for that sort of thing!"

"Ha!" said Juliet, not sure what she felt about the unsettling smell of his aftershave and clean skin.

There was a buzz from the microphone, and the man who'd ticked their names off the guest list got up on the stage, waving his hands for quiet. "Ladies and gentlemen," he began.

"Oh, here we go," said Juliet, but Mark was looking up at the stage.

Juliet tried to calm her nerves by concentrating on the welcome, the speech, the halting thanks from the photographer, and then the exhortations to buy, buy, buy from the organizer.

"Do you want to step outside?" Mark asked, when the music was put on again. "We can see the rest later. I don't think Chris was expecting so many people to come! Must be the free wine."

He gestured to the yard outside. Someone had put out tables and chairs, and set tea lights in fishbowls. As the sun set, leaving trails of red in the evening sky, they were starting to glimmer.

"Yes," said Juliet. "I could do with a sit-down! My feet are sending *More wine* signals to my brain on behalf of my toes."

Mark glanced down at her feet and made a gasp of surprise at her boots. "I thought you seemed taller tonight. Wow. Those are amazing," he said. "I have no idea how you're standing up in them, but they are . . . amazing."

Juliet liked that response. No sensible observations about her arches, or whether she'd break her ankle, just open admiration. It made her feel unusually glamorous. Unusually . . . flirtable.

She laughed and tottered over to the table, where relief flooded up her hips as she sat down. Mark took another couple of glasses from the tray going round and took the seat next to her.

"So," he said. "This has turned out to be a much more enjoyable evening than I thought it would be, when I got the invite. How's your week been so far?"

The relaxation abruptly stopped. *This is the hard part*, thought Juliet, racking her brains for conversation. *This is where we have to stop talking about the photographs and the dogs and have to start talking about each other. The date part.*

"Have you had a busy day, or did you get a chance to enjoy this lovely weather?" he went on, stretching out his long legs. He wore deck shoes, Juliet noted. Nice deck shoes. Could she ask about his shoes? Was that conversation? "Although I suppose the busier you are, the more you *are* outside, right?"

"Well, we're well into summer holidays now, so it's cats and houseplants, as well as the dogs. So far this week, six dogs, six cats, one lot of tomatoes, and waiting in for a delivery from John Lewis," she said. "Who knew some families needed three washing machines? Makes you wonder what they're washing."

"Sounds better than valuing three herds of dairy cattle for auction in this weather."

"It's definitely better than catering," said Juliet, with a twinge of remorse that she still hadn't got back to Kim with a return date. "August's barbecue season for caterers—my boss'll be singed up to her eyebrows."

"So you're a dog walker by day, caterer by night?" Mark arched an eyebrow. "Is there a hot-dog joke in there I'm missing?"

Juliet told him about Kim's Kitchen, and her famous croquembouches, and some of the funny things that had happened with bridezillas. Mark didn't know the supporting cast of Juliet's working life, as Ben had, but he did know some of the clients Kim and Juliet had catered for. His social circle was "quite varied" because of his work, he explained modestly, and he got to hear all the gossip. He made her laugh with the real story of why the bride at the Hanleigh Court wedding had vanished in a taxi, and where the Labradors at the Williamson wedding had taken all the meat for the barbecue.

"But don't tell your boss!" His eyes flashed in the darkness. "I promised I'd keep it secret!"

"Believe me, she won't want to know," said Juliet.

The night darkened around them, but the outdoor heaters kept the chill away, and the candles in the bowls threw flickering shadows on their faces. Occasionally, Juliet glanced over at Mark and noticed the fall of his fringe into his eyes, and the cute way he pushed his glasses up his long nose as he talked. He was easy to talk to, but there was a flutter of something else too. The frisson of the unknown, as the end of the evening got nearer.

The dusk and the hum of conversation from inside the hall made it less awkward to ask personal questions, and Juliet found herself telling Mark an edited version of Ben's heart attack, and how weird and disorienting the past few months had been, blundering around her new life.

"Nights like tonight really help," she finished. "I mean, going out. And doing new things. I'm a bit out of practice."

"To be honest, this is the first event I've been to in ages myself," admitted Mark. "Got fed up with people asking where my ex was, having to do the whole story . . . Well, you know what it's like."

"I do," said Juliet. "But it gets better. People who need to know hear anyway. And you realize you don't have to tell everyone." She risked a personal question. "Has it been a long time?"

"Long enough," he said with a wry huff. "I moved out in March, but we'd been separated unofficially for a few months before that. I'm just waiting for solicitors' letters now."

"I'm sorry to hear that," said Juliet. "How long had you been married?"

"Not that long. Two years? It was a bit of a whirlwind romance, always very up and down. The ups were great, but the downs . . . weren't. We made that fatal error of thinking that a baby would give us something to talk about, which of course is the most stupid thing in the world, I realize now."

"So I hear. Don't they use sleep deprivation and Barney the Dinosaur as illegal torture?"

Mark laughed, then looked sad again. "Yeah, it's tough. If there are any cracks at all, a few weeks of no sleep soon blows them up.

And it makes you realize what your real priorities are in life. Neither of us behaved very well. We made a real mess of things, to be honest." He shook his head, clearly seeing things in his mind's eye that he didn't want to relive, then squeezed his nose and carried on.

"Anna went to counseling and made me go too, but they basically said what we both knew already—we'd be better off parenting separately. And we are. I mean, the one good thing to come out of this is Tasha. I'd go through all that again a hundred times for her."

Juliet's heart gave a little thud at the besotted expression that came over Mark's face. She could see him glowing, even in the dark. There was something really attractive about a man who loved his children. She'd often pictured Ben with a toddler on his hip, just to admire the handsomeness of it.

"How old is she?" she asked.

"Eighteen months. You want to see?" He got the photo out of his wallet; Juliet pretended she hadn't seen it before, and cooed over it.

"She's gorgeous," said Juliet, thinking of Toby and his chubby hands reaching out for her. Her knowledge of children was pretty limited; she didn't want to say the wrong thing. "So, walking, talking . . . ?"

"Yeah." Mark's unconscious smile broadened. "She's pretty smart for her age. Although I would say that, I suppose. Doting dad. That was the great thing about flexible working hours around auctions—I got to spend proper time with her when she was little. You might have seen us in the park? Me and the pushchair and Damson?"

Juliet shook her head, although she was smiling inside at the image. "I never used to walk Minton, except on weekends. Ben used to take him to work. Daily walks are very much a new thing for him. For both of us, actually."

"Well, you're obviously very good at it. To go from nothing to semiprofessional in a couple of months."

Juliet dropped her head into her hands jokily. "Oh God. So my life has come to this—compliments on my dog-walking abilities!"

Mark hesitated, unsure about whether she was really offended, but she lifted her face to reassure him she wasn't. *He doesn't know me well enough to read my ironic voice,* she thought. What if he doesn't have a sense of humor?

"Minton's probably saved my sanity," she said. "There was a time about six months back when my mum was virtually faking fire alarms just to make sure I could still leave the house in daylight hours. Now I'm walking about six miles a day . . ." She pulled an amazed face. "I don't like to tell her she was right, but yes, dogs do sometimes give you a reason to get up when you don't want to."

Mark nodded. "Well, not just dogs. Tonight, for instance. I don't think I'd have bothered coming if I hadn't asked you."

"Why, thanks," said Juliet. "I think."

He caught her ironic expression this time. "That came out wrong." He laughed. "But I meant it in a good way. I've had a great evening, and I wouldn't have had it if you hadn't been here."

The conversation petered out as they gazed at each other across the table, and the look in Mark's eyes made something flip in Juliet's stomach. It wasn't quite lust, more like nerves, but it was a start. She wasn't running screaming from the yard; she was smiling back.

Fielding definite flirty look from man who isn't Ben. Tick.

Enjoying flirty look back from under eyelashes. Tick.

A shape appeared in the doorway. "Um, excuse me, but we need to clear the hall now . . ."

It was one of the girls who'd been running the bar, holding a tray with empty glasses.

"What time is it?" Juliet pushed her chair back. The lights were on in the hall and people were moving around, stacking chairs and clearing tables. She knew the signs they were sending out from personal experience. If they'd flashed *Please go home* in red lights, it couldn't have been clearer.

"Gone ten. That went quickly." Mark paused. "Do you want to grab something to eat?"

The possibility hung in the air, but Juliet couldn't quite take it. *Leave while it's all going okay*, she thought.

"I should get back. Minton waits up for me. And I can't let you leave Damson longer than four hours on her own."

Mark grinned. "Always on duty, eh?"

They stood up and made their way back into the hall. Juliet blinked in the bright light and tried not to notice the pinch in her toes now that the numbing effects of the wine had worn off.

"Hey, where've you been hiding?" It was Chris, the organizer, standing by a big landscape of the railway station from an angle Juliet hadn't seen before. A quirky blond woman had her arm round his waist and was chatting with another man. As Chris spoke, she turned her head and took in the pair of them. Juliet's pulse sped up with new-person overload.

"Do I see a sticker of yours on any of the photos," the woman demanded of Mark, then smiled at Juliet, "or have you spent the whole night chatting?"

"This is Juliet Falconer," said Mark quickly, introducing her to Chris, and Lisa, who was his girlfriend ("and agent!"), and Juliet tried to fix the names in her rusty social memory.

"Can I call you in the morning?" apologized Mark, as Chris started to ask about something. "I need to get back for the dog. As does Juliet."

"Next time, book a joint babysitter," suggested Lisa. "Double-date the dogs too!"

Mark laughed politely, as did Juliet. The word *date* flashed in the air, and then he was steering her out.

"Sorry," he said, as they walked carefully down the steps. "You must get it too—the *date* thing all the time."

"Mmm," said Juliet. Was that a nice way of saying it *wasn't* a date? The swoop in her stomach took her by surprise.

"Although," he added, with a winning smile, "I wonder if I can persuade you to try this again—maybe not with murky photos of gas towers? Maybe dinner?"

Juliet felt pleasantly swept off her feet. No one had ever taken charge like this before. Even Ben's first move had been the result of a *lot* of background work on her part.

"Yes," she heard herself say. "I'd like that."

It was just a date. That was what grown women did. They dated, tried out a selection of men, of venues. Of personalities.

Be careful, said a voice in her head. *What happens next?*

Before she had time to worry about that, Fate sent Juliet a taxi with its light on. *A sign*, she thought, sticking out her arm to stop it. "I'm not really going in your direction," she started, but Mark didn't let her finish.

"You take it. I'll walk back."

The taxi was slowing down. *What am I meant to say?* Juliet thought.

"Thanks for a lovely evening," she said.

"Pleasure's all mine. Thank *you*." He put a hand on her arm and leaned forward to kiss her cheek. Juliet felt relieved and disappointed at the same time.

"Night."

Mark's face was close to hers and she didn't pull away. Instead, she leaned in and kissed his cheek, more as an experiment. It was soft, with a little roughness where his five o'clock shadow began. Different.

Their eyes locked together as she pulled back, and then Mark leaned forward again, a fraction of a second before she did; then somehow their noses bumped and his lips were pressed against hers. Warm and strong, but firmly closed.

It was the most chaste kiss Juliet had had since she was fifteen. It was also the only kiss she'd had from someone who wasn't Ben.

She braced herself for rockets and clouds of guilt and shame, but there was no molten feeling in the pit of her stomach. Just leftover nerves, and something else she couldn't quite put her finger on.

The taxi honked and she pulled back.

"I'll call you," he said.

Juliet gave him a crooked smile as she got into the cab and gave the driver her address.

Handsome man, kissed. Tick.

"Look forward to it," she said, and waved as the taxi set off toward Rosehill.

Chapter 18

"Louise, tell me if I'm being ridiculous, but do you think the end of August is too early to start thinking about Christmas?" asked Diane.

Louise stopped checking her laptop for the next installment of mystery building supplies for Juliet (this time: the downstairs loo, complete with the perfect corner basin Louise coveted herself) and looked over to where her mother was packing up Toby's day things, ready to go home. Even if it hadn't been one of those questions that came with a ready-supplied answer, Diane was wearing a *Please agree with me* expression.

Privately, Louise did think August was a little early, but that was because she could only see as far as the end of her desk diary at the moment. In the old days, she used to start making her own Christmas cards about now. Christmas cake in mid-September, wrapping July-sales-bought gifts by October . . .

She made a mental note to dig her manic Christmas planner out again, just so she could feel less busy in comparison.

"Not really," she said. "I went into M&S today for lunch and it was full of jumpers and boots. Give them another few weeks and there'll be snowmen and tinsel."

"Good," said Diane, clearly relieved. "I just thought I'd ask, so we could make plans. I want this year to be really special."

Louise made *mwah, mwah, mwah* kisses on Toby's soft head. "Well, it could hardly be worse than last year, could it?"

They both fell silent for a second, just thinking about it.

Last Christmas had been more like an emotional assault course to be struggled through than a celebration, every tradition a challenge. Two months on, the anesthetic shock of Ben's death had worn off for Juliet, and she'd been deep in her angry phase, when even seeing happy couples on television could trigger a furious rant against the bloody unfairness of the universe, followed by tears.

It broke Louise's heart to see Juliet like that, and to watch her parents suffering too. She wasn't drinking as much as Louise would have been in her situation, but Juliet had a drunk's unpredictability, and once or twice Louise caught her looking at her and Peter in his holiday socks with a terrible resentment in her eyes, and she knew it was because their little family looked so golden, compared with the broken bits of Juliet's life.

They weren't golden, of course. She was on a rack of guilt about Michael, and Peter was stuck being the only other man in the house and so having to spend double the time listening to her dad asking for peanuts in Portuguese. Toby had diarrhea, and none of them had had more than four hours' sleep a night, but it seemed churlish to complain, when Juliet kept storming out during the Christmas Day *Coronation Street* because she couldn't bear to see the inevitable proposal.

Louise blamed herself. If she and Juliet had been speaking, they might have got through it. As it was, she just didn't know how to put things right without making it all worse.

Diane heaved the bag onto the table and made googly eyes at Toby, clapping his hands together. "I know a little man who can't wait for Christmas! Eh? We'll have to write a letter to Father Christmas soon, won't we? Let him know what you'd like to find in your stocking?"

"Mum, please don't go mad again. He got far too much last year, it was embarrassing." And wildly out of proportion with everyone else's to make up for the adults' lack of gaiety. Even Juliet had turned up with an armful of Mothercare trains, which Louise later found her crying over. "You know he just likes the boxes," she said.

"Aw. Then let's make sure he has lots of boxes. It's only fair to spoil him before he has a little brother or sister to share with." Diane cast a meaningful look up at her daughter. "Have you and Peter thought . . ."

"No," said Louise firmly. "So—plans. You want to have it here?"

"Yes, I think so. Then we can do the linkup with Ian and Vanda on the Skype." Skype had changed Diane's life, especially at Christmas. The sitting room was tidier for the annual Christmas Day Australia broadcast than the Queen's. "Will Peter's parents mind you being here again this year? Isn't it their turn?"

"Nope, they're going to Vienna for the whole Christmas/New Year holiday." Louise removed the saltcellar from Toby's fingers and replaced it with a toy mobile phone. "It's been booked for months. Pam's already got her outfits picked out."

"The whole holiday? Won't they miss their grandson?" Diane seemed horrified at the thought.

"Not really." Louise had given up trying to explain Peter's parents to her mother. "They're not really baby people. They're giving us some money toward the nursery, though, which really helps."

"Are you struggling? Would you tell us if you were? Because we could . . ."

"No. We're fine." She reached out and squeezed her mother's hand. "Your time means much more to me, Mum. I don't know what we'd do without you. Me and Juliet. You've been so amazing to us this last year. We're lucky girls."

Diane smiled quickly and looked away. The deep lines round her eyes were wet with tears, and suddenly she seemed more fragile than she had earlier, when Louise had found her and Toby playing in the back garden.

"Mum? Are you all right?" Louise put Toby down in his high chair and reached for her arm. She patted it, and it felt thin under the cotton jersey. "Mum?"

"I'm fine," said Diane, wiping her eyes with the tissue she kept up her sleeve. "I just . . . It makes me sad. None of us know what's round the corner, do we?" She blinked and smiled a watery smile, then blew her nose. "We've really got to make the most of everything, you know."

"I do know. Let's make this Christmas a really good one," said Louise, with the same gung ho determination that she was applying to her own life to-do list. So far, apart from the Baby 2 issue, it seemed to be working. "We'll bring the wine, now that Peter's officially in love with the sommelier bloke at the White Hart. You know we went back, for another tasting evening? I haven't seen him so drunk since we first met."

Not that she'd minded. With some encouragement he'd made his way through the list, snogged her in the taxi, and then fallen into a deep sleep until ten the next morning, not even troubling her Spanx this time.

"Do you think Juliet would like to cook Christmas lunch?" asked Diane. "Would that give her something to occupy her, or would she think it's a cheek of me to ask? She could make whatever she liked—I'd even get her all the organic poultry to make that chicken-in-a-duck-in-a-goose-in-a-turkey thing that was on *River Cottage*." When Louise looked dubious, Diane added, "I thought it might be more of a challenge, get her enthusiasm back."

Louise looked askance. "That's what Kim thought about those cupcakes. And we ended up being the ones covered in self-raising flour at three in the morning."

Diane looked constipated, as she always did when she was betraying a confidence. She was a terrible liar, like Juliet. "Between you and me, Kim did ring me, wondering when Juliet was going to be ready to come back. I said I didn't know. But she seems to be much better about leaving the house—she's always back and forth with people's dogs and cats. I don't want Kim to see her around town and think she's taking her for a ride."

"It's a different thing, though, isn't it?" Louise pointed out. "Dealing with cats and dogs, and dealing with people. You can see why she wouldn't want to be around weddings and christenings just yet."

She looked more closely at her mother. Diane seemed to be opening and closing her mouth, as if she couldn't decide whether to say something. She'd also, Louise noticed, got new glasses. More modern ones, with thinner lenses.

Hadn't Juliet said something about new clothes too? Maybe it was this carpe diem thing, but there was definitely something . . . *fresher* . . . about her mother. It reminded Louise eerily of the sheen she'd had about her when she was seeing Michael each week, polishing herself up in readiness for his attention.

Surely not. No, surely not.

"Mum, just spit it out," she said wearily. "I've had a really long day."

Diane looked beyond the kitchen door into the sitting room, where Eric was watching the local news with Coco, his bald head nodding in disbelief. Coco's eyes were fixed on the precariously balanced bowl of crisps on his knee.

Diane dropped her voice. "Did Juliet tell you about her date?"

"Her *date*?" Louise stopped playing with Toby and gave Diane her full attention. She kicked the kitchen door closed, for good measure. "Juliet's been on a *date*?"

"Maybe *date*'s the wrong word. Maybe we shouldn't get ahead of ourselves," Diane added, but her eyes were sparkling. "*But* she went to some do at the Memorial Hall last week with a chap. One of the book club ladies saw her, Edith, you know, with the alopecia. Apparently they were talking away outside for ages. Juliet was wearing those awful boots that made her tower over Ben—do you remember them? Bound to break her ankle in them."

"Mum, forget the boots, who is *he*?" Louise felt a strange mixture of emotions swirl in her stomach. Happiness that Juliet was finally getting some light in her gloomy existence, but tinged with a darker emotion—envy that Jools had a fresh start, a fresh romance ahead of her, with all the familiar falling-in-love euphoria she'd had to turn her back on because of her responsibilities.

She pushed the thought away, ashamed of it, and of herself.

"Oh, she wouldn't say. Just that he was one of her dog-walking clients who'd asked her along to make up the numbers." Diane made a *Well, I don't believe that* face. "Edith didn't know who he was either, just that he seemed very nice. Juliet went all tight-lipped, you know how she does, so I didn't press her. But she should know by now that you can't keep a secret in this town!" Diane wagged her finger. "It all comes out eventually!"

Louise swallowed. That depended on how hard you tried.

"Wasn't she going to tell you?" she asked, instead. "It's a bit off that she didn't tell us. Was it last week? I'm trying to think whether we were invited to that . . ."

Diane immediately started to backtrack, sensing tension

between her daughters. "I can understand why she'd keep it to herself. She knows how fond your father and I were of Ben. And we were, of course, but I'd still like to see her with someone who'll make her happy."

"We all would," said Louise, automatically. Toby was banging a spoon on the table and she took it off him, before it started to annoy her.

"Speaking of Christmas coming," she said, "what's Dad's college course going to be this year? Once he's fully fluent in Welsh?"

The September courses were the big one for Eric. He liked to get the prospectus in July and study it properly, adding to his portfolio of qualifications. He had more GCSEs than Juliet and Louise now.

"Oh, he hasn't decided yet." Diane seemed a bit shifty. "He might not do one this year. It's a big time commitment."

"What?" That seemed strange. "Does he want to spend more time in the garden or something?"

"No, he just doesn't want to tie himself down to a whole year. That Welsh took it out of him." Diane was tidying up the table as she spoke, but it was very tidy already. She heaped the junk mail into a smaller pile, then moved some fruit in the fruit bowl. "He's going to leave his options open."

Louise regarded her mother curiously. There was something fishy about her too: the highlights, the new glasses, starting Christmas before they'd even got the deck chairs in from the back garden. "Mum, is there something you're not telling me?"

"No!" Diane looked up, her eyes bright. "Would I try to keep anything from Longhampton's senior prosecutor?"

Louise said nothing. For a family that could read its members like a book on some occasions, there were a lot of secrets building up.

Chapter 19

"Where do you want these? Sorry, am I interrupting?"

Louise hastily shut the Internet browser window as Tanya, the new office manager, bustled into the office with an armful of manila wallets and bulging case notes.

"No," she said, then, seeing Tanya's *Yeah, right* face, she added, "Okay, busted. I was checking the Tesco order. I always forget something when I do it last thing. Sorry. Pop them on the end there."

"Secret's safe with me." Tanya winked. "You're talking to the woman who came in an hour early to check out the Next sale before anyone else."

Louise laughed conspiratorially and cleared a space on her desk for the files. Her "easing in gently" period was long over; Douglas had loaded her with more court work than anyone else to clear the backlog before they had their productivity assessment by the council.

At least once a day, he managed to remind everyone that they were still under threat of merger with the main county courts in the next district, which only made Louise more panicky about getting back up to speed and into full indispensability mode.

If only being frantically busy took her mind off all the other stuff going on in her head. It didn't. One rogue raiding party of worries just galloped in to distract her from whatever she was meant to be doing at the time. In court, she worried about Peter and her marriage; at home, she worried about what would happen if she got pregnant just before the council announced the merger.

Although that was one worry she could realistically strike off her list. She should be more worried about poor Peter filing for divorce, on grounds of terminal chilliness.

"Louise?"

Louise realized she was staring at the top file, a repeat licensing application. "Sorry. I was just . . . just wondering when the Red Lion's license would be back up for review. And here it is."

Tanya looked unconvinced, but wisely said nothing.

When the door had closed behind her, Louise reopened the Safari window and carried on reading.

Has it really come to this? she thought, her eyes skimming the page for key words. *Affair. Guilt. Loss of desire.* Consulting Mumsnet for advice on rebuilding your life after an affair—instead of asking your mother? Or a friend? Or your sister?

Louise's legal mind pointed out that those were exactly the people you could never ask, and that she should stop asking stupid questions and start filleting for helpful recovery strategy.

It wasn't as if she had any option—she didn't have time to go to Relate on her own. Peter would want to know where she was going, and she valued every moment she had with Toby even more now that she was back in the office. Her NCT friends were all tucked up in their happy mum worlds, and anyway, she didn't want to go back there. She didn't trust herself not to ask about Michael, to find out where he was, how he was doing. It pained her, but she didn't trust that Louise not to weaken again.

The only thing she was sure about these days was that she adored her son and she was incredibly lonely. She didn't even have a Minton to dump it all on. At least Juliet had access to unlimited sympathy and advice, and everyone telling her how perfect her marriage had been, even if she knew different.

Louise felt sick at her own meanness, then opened her desk drawer. The emergency Dairy Milk bar had lasted only thirty-six hours. A record. She ripped it open, broke it in half, and gave herself four minutes' Internet time to consider her options before cracking on with her caseload.

The consensus seemed pretty evenly split on affairs. Either she could carry the burden of her guilt and shame around with her for the rest of her life, as the punishment she deserved, or she could confess all to Peter, be honest about what she'd done and why, and try to start again.

Group A seemed to think punishing Peter with the details wasn't fair, and Louise tended to agree; it was her mess, not his. Group B insisted that she wasn't going to be able to rebuild anything unless it was all out in the open, and much as Louise shrank from even thinking how to begin that conversation, she wasn't stupid. She hadn't moved on at all in the past ten months. Her guilt was the third person on all the agonizing Friday dates with Peter; it wasn't Michael sitting opposite them, so much as her own shame and remorse.

It's me I really need to confront, she thought, breaking the second half of the bar into squares to stop it following the first so quickly. *I'm the one who needs to draw a line under this.*

It hadn't ended in a very dignified manner, after all. One panicky, tactlessly worded text message, one curt reply; then she'd deleted all his e-mails, his phone numbers, every scrap of contact she'd ever had, to stop herself from sliding back.

Not, Louise corrected herself, that there was any sliding back to be done, not physically. It had been the friendship, the sense of being listened to, that felt like a gaping hole in her life. Yes, she'd fancied Michael, but that had come from the time they'd spent together, enjoying their mental connection more and more each week. It had been after Ben's death and that crazy few days when nothing seemed real that she'd allowed things to break out of their natural boundaries. If Ben hadn't died, maybe she could have held things as they were. Let no one down.

Right, said the voice in her head.

As she was reading, an e-mail popped into her in-box. It was from Peter, and the header was *Date-Night Friday*.

Louise felt sick, and not from the chocolate.

Maybe if I saw Michael, and accepted that it was just a friendship that boiled over, not some crashing indictment of my marriage, then I can move on, she thought.

Louise had a sudden flashback to his surprised, handsome face, the moment she'd lost her head and kissed him by the bridge. She hadn't slept for two days, sitting up with a hysterical, bereaved Juliet, then with Toby, but she'd never felt more awake, determined to take every single minute. It had been an incredible kiss. She'd felt light-headed, yet utterly aware.

What if you see him and don't find the right words? argued the voice in her head. *It's not like court. There won't be witnesses called. You're on your own.*

I'll write a letter, she reasoned. She couldn't call or e-mail, having deleted his details, but she could write. Words wouldn't let her down.

She swung round in her leather office chair, pleased with her plan, and watched a pair of pigeons land on the air-conditioning unit outside.

If I don't get my head sorted and my life back on track, I'm going to be stuck in an office with a view of the air-conditioning unit for a long time, thought Louise.

And then, because nothing else seemed important, she pulled a stack of paper out of her printer drawer and started writing.

Juliet's mornings were so busy with other people's households that she'd listened to the entire Jane Austen back catalog on audiobook and had started on Charles Dickens.

Although August was nearly over and the summer holiday season was drawing to a close, her phone didn't stop ringing; no sooner did one family come back from Florida than their next-door neighbors rang and asked if she could pop in and feed their cats and play with their guinea pigs. And bring in their post, check on their son's goldfish, check that their Sky+ was recording all the right stuff, and so on.

Some work she had to turn down because there just wasn't enough time to get round to everyone. Juliet liked to give each cat a proper half hour of tummy tickling and general company, if they wanted it—some, of course, barely bothered to put their heads through the cat flap when she put the fresh bowls down. Others, though, raced up to her and wound themselves round her legs, grateful for the ear scratches and conversations.

It made Juliet feel wanted, and useful. Sorting out the post and doing the little odd jobs for the owners made her feel useful too, but not quite in the same warming way. Maybe spending more time with animals than humans was starting to affect her mind, but giving the pets a bit of company gave her a glow; they were obviously lonely without their humans, and unsure of where they'd gone. Juliet liked to think she was bridging their faith that the humans would come back.

And it was nice to play with cats for an hour or two without the responsibility of owning them. Juliet had always quite fancied a nice big tortoiseshell moggy, but Ben—and Minton—were never keen. Now she had a whole lending library of pets, and most of them loved her. Emer begged her to take Florrie round with her, so she wouldn't have to deal with the menagerie at their own house.

While she was locking up at the Kellys' (two hamsters, three cats, fourteen different types of breakfast cereal arranged on the counter), Lorcan texted her to see if she was around to start grouting the shower tiling at long last. He was willing to give her a grouting lesson if she'd cook him a load of oysters that had fallen that morning off the same lorry that most of her bathroom had already fallen off.

"So long as they're fresher than your jokes," she texted back. "Time?"

"After lunch?"

Juliet checked her watch. She had to take Hector, Minton, and Damson for a lunchtime walk, which would take until two, then nothing until her cat rota at six. Lorcan could mind Minton while she dashed round; then they could eat at seven. And that was nearly a whole day filled up.

She remembered with mild regret that there was a back-to-back showing of some St. Trinian's films that she'd miss now, but Juliet's ritualistic ringing of the *Radio Times* was more of a habit now than a burning desire to see the programs.

"Cool," she texted back. "Bring Guinness."

Damson was thrilled to see Juliet, as usual, but Juliet was even more thrilled to hear that the barking only started when she turned the key in the back door.

The radio was on, as was the television in the sitting room.

Mark liked to give Damson a choice. Under the walking money on the kitchen table, he'd also left a brand-new Kong, with a can of squeezy Kong cheese, and a note.

Dear Juliet,

I've found a great pub for dogs in Hanleigh that lets humans in the bar area! Would you and Minton like to come out for lunch on Sunday? It's called the Pig and Whistle. We'll be there from 1-ish. We could go for a walk after, if Food Boy hasn't overdone it on the lunch, as usual.

Love,
Damson

P.S. Here's a new Kong to replace Minton's spare one. I have destroyed it, sorry. Got bored.

Juliet smiled. It was easier accepting a lunch date from Damson, on behalf of Minton. No pressure in any direction.

Smart of Food Boy, she thought. And thoughtful. No pressure, with their canine chaperones. The more she got to know Mark, the less like a TV auctioneer she thought he was, and more like a real, warm person that she could imagine, maybe, one day . . .

Juliet's stomach lurched, but she made herself go through with the thought. Mark was someone she could definitely imagine . . . cooking in this kitchen with.

She felt something brush her leg and looked down.

Damson was sitting at her feet, with her lead dangling from her mouth. It only took a few biscuits to teach Damson tricks: She could give paw, lie down, and turn round already . . .

"Thanks, Damson," she said, taking the lead and fastening it to her tartan collar. "I'd *love* to join you for lunch. Now, let's go and wear you out."

Louise was supposed to be in a case meeting at three o'clock, but the Probation Service canceled at the last minute while she was on her way across town.

The letter was in her bag, sealed to stop her chickening out and changing anything. It was a good letter, getting everything off her chest, with no need for a reply. Louise felt better for writing it. She'd been honest about how much their friendship had meant to her and had apologized for ending it as she had, without a backward glance. Now that she was no longer carrying those thoughts around with her, she reasoned, maybe it would be easier to fix things with Peter.

Louise wondered if Michael was stuck too. Whether he'd patched things up, or met someone new. It had taken considerable self-control not to ask those questions.

I could drop it in now, she thought, realizing she wasn't far from his house. He might even be in, if he was working from home.

She ignored the suspicious frisson that rippled through her. This was about closing things off. Moving on.

Louise walked briskly off the High Street and headed down Duke Street, past the shops that had started to be refurbished before the recession, and which were now creeping back to their old, neglected state. Louise's court shoes weren't really made for walking—she'd forgotten to put her flats in her big bag in her rush to leave the house—but something about knowing that by five o'clock she'd have tackled the looming problem in her life made her stride out purposefully.

She turned away from the shops and headed along the Victorian terraces behind. She was getting nearer now, only two more streets away, and her heart was racing as hard as it did before Crown Court trials.

Did she want him to be there or not?

At first the letter had been a backup plan, but now that the prospect of actually seeing Michael's friendly face again was getting real, Louise wondered if it might not be better just to drop it in a postbox and save herself the temptation. She could feel herself getting excited, wondering if her hair was all right. What would she say if he opened the door?

Whether it was right or wrong, she felt more energized than she had for months. Her blood seemed to be hotter in her veins.

Louise turned a corner, and suddenly she was outside his house. There was no one around in the houses opposite, and his Land Rover wasn't parked outside. Louise's stomach fluttered; was that good or bad? It didn't mean he wasn't in, necessarily.

She pressed the doorbell and waited. It wasn't one you could hear from outside. There was no sound of footsteps or signs of movement through the frosted-glass panes of the door.

Louise hopped from one foot to the other, then rang again. Then she rapped on the glass, just in case.

Nothing. Obviously no one in.

She pushed aside the disappointment that crept up on her and reached into her bag. Taking out the envelope, Louise eyed the postbox on the side of the house. Despite the buildings' being styled as townhouses, their front doors were too modern to bother with such anachronisms as letterboxes; instead, each house had an American-style box, complete with dinky flag.

You're doing the right thing, Louise. You're dealing with the problem.

Slowly, she took the letter out and dropped it into the box. The lid clicked shut, and Louise turned on her heel and marched away, her heart heavier than she'd expected.

She got as far as the litterbin on the corner before it dawned on her what she'd just done—and why. This was all about seeing Michael. Finding an excuse to see him again. Like some delusional teenager, she'd manufactured her own nonsense reason to do the wrong thing while pretending it was for the greater good. She realized she'd been half expecting Michael to come to the door, his face brightening with pleasure at seeing her again. And he hadn't, because all that had been in her head.

Oh, Louise, you idiot, she cursed herself, horrified at her own lack of awareness.

She speed-walked back to Michael's house on wobbling legs. It was exactly the same, but now there was a bomb in the letterbox, waiting to go off.

Where had all her legal training vanished? What if someone else read it? Anna? What if they were back together? She'd been careful but maybe not careful enough; she knew divorce lawyers who could make a meal out of the few crumbs she'd mentioned.

Clumsily, Louise tried to slide her fingers inside, but the box was designed to stop people from doing exactly that. Her armpits prickled with panic and sweat. She knew it was irrational, but she banged on the door anyway, just in case someone was there.

Her throat went dry. Someone *was* coming down the hall, but the shape didn't look big enough to be Michael. Louise's court-trained mind flipped rapidly through the possibilities, scrabbling for appropriate responses—had he moved? Was this his cleaner? Was this his wife?

The door opened, but she wasn't prepared for the person who faced her.

"Juliet?" she stammered.

It was a small consolation that Juliet looked almost as surprised as she did.

Chapter 20

Louise?"

Juliet had never seen Louise look so shaken. Even though she was wearing her work suit and full makeup, all the color seemed to have drained from her and she looked about to keel over.

"What are you doing here?" Louise asked her, through dry lips.

"What are you doing here, more like?" Juliet replied. Damson and Minton rushed through from the utility room, where she'd shut them in with their muddy paws. "Mind these two—they're filthy."

Louise seemed not to notice. "I came to see Michael."

"Michael?" Juliet felt the rare glow of being in a position to correct the detail queen. "There's no Michael here. You've got the wrong house."

Louise gazed trancily down the hall, but then seemed to recognize something—the modern-art clock on the wall, maybe. It couldn't be the photos, thought Juliet: There weren't any. She'd looked.

She shook her head. "Michael. Mike Ogilvy. He definitely lives here."

"Louise, he's not . . ." Juliet stopped, her mouth dropping as her brain caught up with itself. "Mark. Mike. Oh God!" She clapped a hand over her mouth. "I've been calling him Mark! Well, Food Boy mostly. Thanks for telling me—that could have been really embarrassing . . ."

But Louise wasn't responding with a smile. She looked as if she were about to cry.

"Lou, are you okay?" asked Juliet. "Do you want to come in? Mark . . . sorry, *Mike*, won't be back until six-ish. He's got a herd to value up in . . . Hey!"

Louise was swaying. She reached out and grabbed her arm. "What is *wrong* with you?"

"I need to get something out of there," said Louise faintly, pointing to the mailbox.

"What?" asked Juliet. "Have you sent your anonymous letter to the wrong place? Is he being summonsed for something? I thought that was the police's job."

"Stop taking the piss!" wailed Louise. Properly wailed too. "Just tell me, can you open that bloody letterbox?"

"Yes, probably . . ."

"Then do it. Please. For me."

"Okay. But you've got to tell me why." Juliet wasn't sure there wasn't a trust issue at stake. She never opened the mailbox; the flag was always down when she arrived. Hence no clues that she'd been calling him totally the wrong name for months. Dur.

"I will. Anything. Just . . . get it out."

Juliet looked on the back of the door where Mark—Mike—kept his spare keys. There was a little key that she assumed fitted the mailbox, and with Louise's eyes burning holes in her back, she unlocked it.

"This is a bit unethical," she started, removing a couple of solicitors' letters on thick notepaper, a gas bill, some pizza leaflets, a *You Were Out* notification (shame, she could have collected that, if he'd said) and a thin envelope addressed in Louise's handwriting.

"What's this, then?" Juliet looked at the envelope, as if she were about to open it. "A love letter?" She looked back up at her sister and saw that Louise's eyes were glassy.

Slowly, the cogs started to turn, grinding a vague thought nearer and nearer in her mind. Louise's strange confession about an outdoorsy man—that was *Mark*. And then him and his divorce. The little baby, the same age as Toby.

"Oh my God," Juliet breathed. "It's *him*. Mark's the man you had a crush on before Ben died."

Mike, said a voice in her head. *He's not even called what you thought he was. That's how well you knew him. You* idiot. *How could you even have* thought *this was anything like a new relationship?*

Juliet felt dizzy, as if the walls were moving around her. Louise was talking, but the words faded in and out as her brain tried to deal with the roaring in her ears. She barely knew the man, so how could this be hurting so much?

"It's over, Juliet, honestly. I mean, there was really nothing there to start with. It wasn't . . . it wasn't even a proper affair, really. It was a flirtation that went a bit too far, when I was in shock after Ben died. I mean, Ben dying just made me wonder what was going to happen next, and—"

"Don't bring *Ben* into this, you hypocrite!" spat Juliet. "Don't try to use my husband as an excuse for your own tacky affair!"

Louise's mouth dropped, and then her eyes narrowed. "In

what way have I been hypocritical? I'm not the one going round pretending I had the most perfect marriage in the world, am I? Or have you conveniently forgotten you told me you were having doubts yourself?"

That was too much for Juliet. The outrage that had been simmering away in her for months burst out.

"Have you forgotten what you told *me*? Sitting there with that sanctimonious look on your face?" Juliet adopted a lecturing tone. "'All marriages go through bad patches'? 'It's worth trying harder'? And all the time you were carrying on with Mark. Mike."

"I was talking about your marriage," yelled Louise. "*Your* marriage was worth saving! You and Ben were a great couple; you were meant to be together. I didn't want to see you break up because you were going through some rough patch! It was barely even a rough patch! Ben being a bit irresponsible about money? Well, when wasn't he? I mean, compared with the *real*, miserable rough patch Peter and I were in at the time . . ."

"That's right, you always have to have the definitive version, don't you?"

Louise shot her a bitter glare. "You try coping on three hours' sleep and your husband never helping because he's playing computer games for research and feeling like everyone just sees you as a brain-dead mum. *That* is a rough patch. I knew I was doing the wrong thing with Michael. I didn't want you to get yourself into the same nightmare."

"It didn't look like that from where I was sitting," snapped Juliet. "You looked like someone who was really enjoying having a bit on the side."

"Oh God." Louise put her face in her hands for a second. When it emerged, she looked wretched. "Okay, so for a while it was amazing. That didn't mean to say I didn't feel shit about it too! I felt terrible and . . ."

A car pulled up outside the house opposite, and the pair of them froze. A woman got out and gave them a curious look before starting to unload her shopping. There was a bootful. She'd be there a while.

"I don't want to have a shouting match on the doorstep," hissed Juliet. "And no, I don't think it'd be a good idea to go inside either," she added, seeing Louise's eyes flick toward the hall. She wondered how many times Louise had been in this house. More times than her? Upstairs? She felt cold.

It was bad enough realizing she barely knew "Mark;" having her own sister turn out to be someone she didn't know either was too much for her to stand.

She realized she was still holding Louise's letter.

"Can I have that, please?" asked Louise.

Juliet considered saying no, to punish her. The anger was ebbing and flowing. She tucked it in her back pocket and pulled her keys out of her jeans.

"Here." She thrust her van keys roughly at Louise. Lucky that she'd driven, to fit in all the cat visiting. "Go and sit in the van with Minton. I'll be out in a minute."

Louise looked at the keys, and Juliet regarded her sister curiously. It was so weird to see Louise out of control, nearly hyperventilating. She'd always been the one who could stay calm when the lights went off, or when someone had a nosebleed.

"Okay," she said, and turned to go.

"You might want to brush the passenger seat first," added Juliet, out of habit. "Minton rides in the front. It's a bit . . . hairy."

Mike. Mike. Michael.

Juliet made herself say it over and over again as she sped through Damson's routine in the utility room, filling up her bowl, putting on the radio, fluffing up her bed.

He didn't look like a Mike. He looked like a Mark. How could you *kiss* someone and have his name wrong? It made her feel dirty. And convincing herself that the fact he reminded her of an auctioneer and—wow!—he was one, was a sign? She cringed. She'd had more mature thoughts when she was at school.

The bereavement books were right this time. She'd obviously moved on far too quickly. If anything was a sign, it was this—that she should stay out of the messy world of new relationships. Stay out of everything.

Damson curled up in her basket, easily satisfied now that she'd had her walk. Juliet envied her contented snoozing. The universal *Do not disturb* sign that was sleep was very tempting now, and if she hadn't had her sister and her dog waiting in the car, she'd have gone straight home and done that.

Louise had taken the five minutes on her own to refresh her makeup, and now she was looking a little bit more like the Louise Juliet knew.

"Jools," she said, before she'd even slid into the front seat. "I don't want you to think Mum and I have been gossiping about you, but before you say anything else, is Michael the client you went on the date with? To the private view?"

"Yes," said Juliet stonily.

"Oh." Louise took a deep breath. "What are the chances of that, eh? All the men in Longhampton . . ."

"And you've already had the one I liked," Juliet finished for her. "I don't think it's funny. I think it's pretty par for the course."

"Meaning?"

"Meaning . . ." Juliet gave up any pretense of being mature. She was angry with herself, but Louise was a much easier target. Widow Rage, plus the moral high ground, suddenly released a barrage of resentments she'd squashed down for years. They flew out of her like angry bats. "You always get things first. Exams. Weddings. Men." She paused. "Grandchildren. Mum running around after you. Dad lending you money for your house deposit. It's always you, *achieving*."

"Oh, Jools . . ."

"I never had anything that was just *mine*!"

"You had Ben! You had the soul mate!"

"Don't—" Juliet began, but Louise talked over her.

"You did. No matter what you thought you were going through, it was just a hiccup. You lucked out with Ben. He lucked out with you. You'd have got through it. You'd have been fine. I always looked at your marriage and thought, 'Wow. They're like Mum and Dad. They are *happy* people. They know how to be happy with each other.' "

"Is that meant to make me feel better?" demanded Juliet. "Now that I've *lost* that?"

Louise's face fell. "I don't know. You're a hard woman to make feel better right now. I'm just telling you what I think."

Juliet threw her head back against the headrest and Minton turned round and round, trying to make himself comfortable. He finally settled, halfway up the steering wheel, and looked sullenly at Louise, taking up his seat.

"Were you the woman who broke up his marriage?" asked Juliet, without opening her eyes.

"No. His marriage was breaking up when we met him at the antenatal classes, and then it finally finished when Natasha was born. I had nothing to do with it."

"Really."

"Yes, really." Louise sounded offended. "I might have been a shoulder to cry on, but it wasn't like that. It was about . . ."

"It never is, is it? How it looks."

"Don't be like that. Do you want to know what happened?"

Juliet wasn't sure she did, but Louise seemed determined to get it off her chest, and short of throwing her out of the van, she didn't have much choice.

"Peter doesn't listen to anything I say," began Louise. "He used to, but now he doesn't. He just comes home, demands a breakdown of the day's events, and thinks that's parenting. He didn't listen when I said I was worried about taking time out. He's not listening when I tell him . . . when I tell him I'm not sure about having another baby yet. It's killing our relationship. Michael and I had actual, adult conversations. He made me laugh, he told me about stuff I didn't know. I was going *mad* on maternity leave, Jools. No one ever wanted to talk to me about anything other than Toby."

"That might be because the one time I tried to invite you round for lunch on your own, you bit my head off and said I wouldn't understand how totally impossible it was to go out for lunch until I had children of my own."

"Yes, because just getting him out of the house is such a production, and then finding a sitter, or somewhere to take him where it's safe for . . ." Louise paused, as the implication of what Juliet had said sank in. "I'm sorry if you felt pushed out," she said, sounding genuinely ashamed. "To be honest, I've been so exhausted I barely know what I'm saying half the time."

It was so rare to hear Louise apologize that Juliet had to stop herself from commenting on it. "It's okay," she said. "So it was just talking, was it?"

"To begin with. I mean, don't you find he's the easiest person to . . ." She caught herself. "Sorry. Michael just made me feel like I was actually connected to the outside world again. He knew interesting things. He knew interesting people. Like Peter used to, before he started this company and turned into a workaholic computer nerd."

Even though Juliet couldn't see Louise's face, she could sense the frustration seeping out of her. Louise had always itched to move in more glamorous circles than she did. Her university friend Esther worked on *Ready Steady Cook*, and Louise was always banging on about her "friend at the BBC," as if she produced *Question Time*.

"It's all right for you," said Louise. "Ben had interesting friends. He had *friends*, for God's sake. Peter plays online wizard games. With fat truckers in Tucson who call themselves Glwedyr the Good Witch."

Juliet managed a reluctant smile. Ben's sunny lack of pretension had been one of the qualities she'd loved most about him. He knew everyone, from the jobbing teenager lawn mowers right up to Longhampton's sole old-school posh family whose Gothic folly he'd landscaped. And he could chat happily with them all, in the supermarket or in the pub or in their garden.

"It's a good thing in a man, being able to talk," she said.

Was that what she'd responded to in Michael—having someone to talk to? It couldn't just have been that. She talked more to Lorcan, and he made her laugh, and there was nothing there.

Louise was off again, letting the words spill out as if she'd never had a chance to tell anyone. "We tried not to talk about our home lives too much, but it was pretty obvious neither of us was really happy. I tried to tell you that time, hoping you'd say, 'Absolutely, Peter's taking you for granted,' but you went off on me. And then Ben died. I just thought, 'Oh my God, we could all die tomorrow, so why am I the one being good . . . ?' " She shook her head in disbelief.

Like she's the first person who's ever had that *little revelation*, thought Juliet. She turned to look at her sister, who was staring straight ahead as if the scene were playing in front of her on the windscreen.

"I saw you in the hospital, sitting outside the room where they'd put Ben, and it made me wonder who I was living for," Louise continued. "Me, or everyone else? I've always done the right thing. Always. And where's it got me? So I took Toby round to Mum's, said I had a dental appointment, called Michael, and we . . ." She stopped.

Silence filled the van like poison gas.

"You what?" said Juliet.

"What do you think?"

Oh, come on, own it, thought Juliet. *I'm not going to let you off the hook that easily.* "Here?"

"No."

"Where, then?"

"Coneygreen Woods," said Louise, after a long pause.

Juliet swiveled to face her sister. "But it was October! And that place is full of dog walkers!"

"I didn't know that! I don't have a dog, do I? I wasn't thinking of romantic locations; I just wanted to grab Michael and do all the things I'd been trying not to think about doing for months. It wasn't a rational thought process. I just didn't want it to be my house, or his house, or some hotel."

Juliet sank back in her seat. She wouldn't be able to see the woods in the same way now. Not that she could imagine Louise overcome with animal passion, half naked up against one of the oaks, but she could sort of see him, his shirt tugged out of his cords, his strong arms against the bark. She blinked away the image before it could take root and upset her.

"And then what?" she asked.

"And then it wore off. I saw how devastated you were without Ben, and I had one of those blinding flashes about what would happen if Peter found out. I didn't want to break up Toby's family.

I still love Peter, deep down. I didn't want to be . . . the person I thought I was turning into. I wanted the old me back again."

"Is that why you went back into career mode?"

"Yes." Louise studied her fingernails. "I'd have gone back the next day if I could, but it took quite a few months to talk to Douglas and persuade him to juggle the department around to fit me in. I'd more or less said I wasn't coming back until Toby was at school, so he was a bit surprised when I changed my mind. I know, I know," she added. "Don't remind me what I said about formative years and all that crap. I said a lot of things I now know to be categorically wrong."

"But you could have just stayed at home and kept your knickers on," suggested Juliet, mercilessly. "You could have joined a different baby group. Taken up knitting."

Louise let out a groan. "It wasn't like that. It was about *me*."

Why am I so angry? Juliet wondered. *Why do I want to punish her? Is it because she's betrayed Peter, risked her marriage, and still thinks she's some kind of victim? I'm the one whose marriage is over, and I had no choice in the matter.*

"I take it you didn't tell Peter?"

Louise looked sick. "No. It'd be selfish. That's my punishment, not his."

"But if you're so unhappy about living with Peter that you're looking around for random men to *listen* to you, don't you think he has the right to know? In case there's something he can do about it?"

When she didn't reply, Juliet persisted, annoyed. "You can't just wind the clock back and be the person you were before all this happened. God, if there's one thing I've learned this year it's that. Stop being such a martyr and take this as a wake-up call. Change *changes* you. You've had a baby. And we've all had a bereavement. Only a raging egomaniac wouldn't need to stop and have a think about their life after that."

Louise didn't look at her. "That's what I'm trying to do."

"By getting back in touch with your fling?" she snorted. "Interesting tactic. Did you get it from the Internet?"

"That honestly wasn't what I thought I was doing. I thought . . ." Louise bit her lip. "I don't know what I thought. It was a crap idea. I never used to have crap ideas."

Juliet didn't dignify that with a response, and they sat in silence, staring at the hanging baskets of wilting geraniums clinging to life outside Michael's brand-new townhouse.

We must look like we're staking the place out, thought Juliet. *The two of us, in a gardening van, parked outside his front door—and we're not even here on behalf of his ex.* If it hadn't been happening to her, she'd have found it funny.

Louise cleared her throat, embarrassed. "Can I . . . have the letter back?"

Juliet had almost forgotten she had it in her pocket. She withdrew it slowly. It was crumpled, and thin. "What did you actually say in this letter?"

"It doesn't matter now. I promise I'll talk to Peter," said Louise.

Juliet hesitated, then handed it over. Louise ripped it in half, then ripped the halves in half, then shoved it in her bag. Her hands were trembling as she did up the magnetic fastener.

"Just like that?" said Juliet. "You came here to talk to him, but now . . . you don't need to?"

Louise clutched her bag like a child hugging a teddy bear, her eyes staring fiercely out of the car. "No," she said. "I'm the one who needs talking to."

She rubbed her fingers under her eyes to catch the smeared mascara, and belatedly, as her own anger subsided, Juliet saw how distressed her sister was. She reached over to comfort her, dislodging Minton from his perch. Juliet was still furious—with herself, with Louise, with Mike—but she could tell something was very wrong in Louise's home, and it made her sad that she hadn't known the half of it.

"I'm so sorry, Jools," Louise sobbed into her shoulder. "It's bad enough me doing this in the first place, but now I've spoiled it for you too. I'm such a bitch! I deserve this, but you don't."

"Don't be stupid." Juliet stroked her hair. "It was one date. Well, it wasn't even a date. It was just a night out."

"Michael's a really lovely guy. And I guess he's definitely single now." Louise raised her head and tried to smile. "Are you seeing him again?"

Can't deal with this now, thought Juliet. *Got to get home. Sofa.* Time Team. *Minton. Tea. Maybe even a sneaky Nytol and the duvet.*

"Let me take you back to work." She sighed. "Before the neighbors report us for stalking."

The radio was on upstairs when Juliet opened the front door—she'd totally forgotten about Lorcan and his grouting lesson. Her heart sank. She needed to be alone to unpick the messy knots of what she'd just discovered. Right now, Juliet genuinely had no idea what she thought. It was all too weird.

Quietly, she started backing out. *I'll do a few more laps round the park*, she thought, *see if Hector wants an extra walk. Pretend I got an emergency call from someone with a bored Alsatian.*

But Minton was halfway up the stairs before she could stop him, and about two seconds later she heard Lorcan yelling, "Not in the grouting! Not in the—Oh, you dim dog!"

She closed her eyes.

"Hey, Juliet! School started forty-five minutes ago! Are you looking for a detention or what?"

His accent—funny, familiar, friendly—gave her the same sinking-into-the-sofa feeling as the opening credits of *Come Dine with Me*.

Maybe she didn't need to go out. Maybe it was better to distract herself with DIY. She didn't have to discuss Louise's weird secret life.

"Sorry I'm late," she said, climbing the stairs. "Bit of a detour."

Lorcan was sitting in the bath, in a Cream T-shirt covered in speckles of grouting. His arms were speckled too. As was his hair, which had curled and poufed out in the humid air. He grinned when he saw her and pointed at Minton, who'd jumped into the sink. "Your man there's put his mark on the bathroom."

There was a perfect small paw print in the corner of one tile, where it joined the neat line along the bottom.

"I can go over it later," he said.

"No, leave it," said Juliet. "Like a signature. Okay, where do I start?"

Lorcan seemed surprised at her determined attitude but showed her how to pipe the grouting between the shiny tiles, talking and explaining in his easy way as she grappled with the applicator.

"Hey, you're good at this," he said, approvingly. "Can I get you to come and do next door?"

"It's just icing." Juliet finished the line. It was perfectly straight. It gave her a buzz to think that'd be there for years now. "Piece of cake. Literally. Now what?"

"Start again up here. Gently . . . So did Spaniel Man keep you chatting in the park?" Lorcan asked. He sounded a bit too casual. "Where's he taking you next? A recital? The ballet?"

"No. I didn't see him today." Juliet put the nozzle against the next tile. "Anyway, it's not a date . . . situation."

"No?"

"No." She squeezed and pulled, focusing on the squelch of the paste. The whole point of grouting was to fill her mind with something other than Michael and Louise, but Lorcan's easy company was making it hard not to spill the lot.

"He's just a friend." Michael was a nice guy, but Juliet couldn't get past the fact that even if he'd been separated, he'd known Louise was married. He'd probably even met Peter over a breast pump.

She shook her head to get rid of the image. "He's a *client*. I'm not ready for dates yet. The books say you're supposed to wait until you're not comparing people with your dead husband anymore."

"Ah, the books," said Lorcan wisely. "And were you? Comparing him?"

Juliet considered. "It was more that he was very *unlike* Ben than like him. Cerebral. In a suit. Maybe that's just as bad. Going for the polar opposite."

"I'm no expert"—Lorcan busied himself with cleaning a smear of grouting off the last tile—"but I don't think you ever stop comparing, when someone's made that sort of impact on your life. It'd be more weird if you could just wipe your mind clean, if they've meant something to you."

Juliet glanced over. Lorcan seemed rather guarded. "Are you speaking from experience there?"

He shrugged. "Maybe."

"Anyone special?"

He looked across and gave her a quick flash of his bright smile, but his eyes were sad. "Life's great tapestry. If you want the sunshine, you have to have the rain, as some great philosopher probably once said."

Emer, thought Juliet. Maybe he held a torch for Emer. His first girlfriend, maybe, from home? She held his gaze for a moment, and they could both probably have said something funny, but Lorcan seemed as mired in gloomy thoughts as she was.

Juliet turned back to the grouting and sighed. "Well, the books say it's meant to be easier after a year."

"Isn't that coming up?"

"Six weeks."

It took her by surprise, even as she said the words. Six weeks didn't seem very long to turn the last warm days of August into proper rain-whipped autumn. In six weeks the walk through the woods would turn from lush green and red berries to crisp dying foliage and conkers, and this time she'd notice for herself, instead of having Ben point it out.

"Do you feel up to cooking tonight?" Lorcan asked. "I stuck the oysters in your fridge, but if you can't be bothered, I can get Emer to do—"

"No, no." Juliet put the grouting syringe down. "I haven't prepared oysters for ages." She pulled a long face. "Not since we were all in hospital for bank holiday Monday, anyway."

She let Lorcan look horrified for a couple of seconds and then said, "Joke."

He laughed, and the sound of it made her feel better, at least temporarily.

"I love oysters," he confided. "Takes me back to the west coast. Soda bread, pint of Guinness, roaring fire, attractive female company. Food of love, you know . . ."

Juliet was nodding, but she was actually thinking that she really *hadn't* handled oysters for ages, not since a very posh wedding she and Kim had catered in Hanleigh. They weren't the easiest thing to get right, and if she could screw up cookies and cupcakes, the sky was the limit for crustaceans.

Her confidence wobbled, and a terrible image of poor Lorcan with his head down the loo blazed across her mind. It was hardly a fair reward for bringing her gourmet foodstuffs. And if she was being totally honest, a little bit of her didn't want him to stop thinking she was a gourmet chef. It was quite flattering, the way he'd raved about her flat biscuits as if they were Nigella Lawson's.

"Maybe we *should* let Emer do them," she said. "She's the expert, and I'd hate to waste them. Why don't I get some Guinness instead and take them next door? Is there enough for us all?"

Lorcan looked at her. "There's enough for two. Or one greedy Irishwoman. Listen, I'll tell you what. Why don't I go and get us some Guinness, and you call out for pizza? I fancy escaping the madhouse tonight. I'm sure there's something on telly we can take the mick out of."

"But it's such a mess," she started, and then heard herself. Always saying no, making excuses.

Guinness and a pizza, and a night's telly with someone cracking jokes on the sofa—it sounded like a five-star version of her usual solitary viewing habits. Minton would just have to move up on the sofa.

"I'll find the leaflets," she said.

"Good girl." Lorcan grinned and began packing up his kit with methodical speed.

The best thing about Lorcan, Juliet thought, as she sank into the soft sofa cushion, clutching her can of Guinness a few hours later, was that he and Minton seemed to have reached an understanding.

The terrier was wedged between them, snoozing with his head territorially on Juliet's leg, but his paws pressed up against Lorcan's skinny thigh. No growling, no suspicious wagging.

It was a bridge crossed. A sign that he was a real friend. Two and a half pints of Guinness made Juliet feel quite emotional about that, and she turned to point it out to Lorcan himself.

Or she would have, if his head hadn't been tipped back against the big cushion, his curls squashed in a dark halo, his mouth open as he breathed the heavy breaths of the pre-snorer. His neck was thrown back, making his Adam's apple stick out in his neck, and speckles of five o'clock shadow outlined where a beard would probably spring up, given three or four days off.

Apart from the socks, Lorcan looked quite rock-'n'-roll, and Juliet could imagine him backstage, as a roadie. Maybe even passed out just like this.

Juliet considered waking him up, but she was too comfortable herself. This was what her cozy back sitting room had been designed for. Snoozing in companionable silence with friends, after a decent pizza.

Here's to many more, she said to herself, taking one last sip of Guinness before letting her own eyes droop shut too.

Chapter 21

The next morning, however, Juliet knew she had to talk to Michael, about their relationship (such as it was) as well as about Damson, ideally before Louise changed her mind and went back. This whole affair business was so out of character for Louise that Juliet genuinely had no idea what she might do next. She had a very real fear that Louise might tell Michael that he owed it to both of them to date her tragic widowed sister—and that he might do it.

She sat, going round in circles in her mind. Asking Diane's advice was out, obviously, and her closest confidants had always been Ben and Louise. Juliet didn't have many close female friends these days, and this wasn't something she'd know how to bring up over cupcakes with Kim.

I suppose I could always do nothing, she thought, helplessly. *I don't have to see him during the week; I could avoid the park on the days when he's around. I could leave him a note: Damson thinks it might be better if we didn't let our personal lives get in the way of her walking arrangements.*

Doing nothing didn't feel right anymore. She couldn't get away with doing nothing about fuses, or council tax. In her new life, alone, Juliet had to do something, even if it was wrong.

I'll go and ask Emer, she thought. *She's bound to know what to do when your new date's secretly been shagging your married sister.*

Emer could smell a scandal a mile off and promptly dispatched a wide-eared Roisin and Florrie upstairs with Spike to "play David Bowie" with her makeup bag. It was the ultimate distraction, and the twins didn't wait for their mother to change her mind.

Emer sat Juliet down at her messy kitchen table, sweeping away various newspapers and plonking a tiny liqueur glass down in front of her. It was just them, she said: Alec was in Geneva, Salvador was at "band practice," and Lorcan "the semipro pool hustler" was down at the pub in town, playing pool for the Fox and Hound's B-team.

"He pretends to miss a shot or two," Emer confided, opening a bottle of sloe gin. "Doesn't want the hassle of playing on the A-team. Now, what's up? You've got that sad-dog look on you."

Haltingly, Juliet explained as simply as she could, and Emer nodded, and topped up her glass when it got low. For a bottle that came with a homemade label, it was powerful stuff. Emer claimed she made it herself from a recipe that was "probably illegal in the EU now."

"So what should I do?" Juliet finished up.

"You can stop calling your sister a cheating cow, for a start."

"But she is!"

"Maybe she is, but it's not helping either of you," said Emer. "It was well over before you met this Michael, right? You never know what's going on inside people's marriages, and you go a bit tonto when you have a baby. I've had four. Ask Alec. Actually, don't."

"Not so tonto that you end up sneaking off with some bloke from your NCT class," snorted Juliet.

"Well . . ." Emer looked shifty. "I had my moments. You just feel as if your life's under someone else's control and if you've always been . . ."

"A Stepford wife, like Louise."

". . . in *charge* of yourself. It can make you do really stupid things, simply to prove you're not just a milking machine. Hormones are powerful drugs," she said, widening her gray eyes. "Then add in the lack of sleep, and any other upset—like your sister's husband dying, for example—and you find yourself acting like a loon. It's like being drunk. You regret it in the morning, but you can't help it at the time."

"You sound like Louise," said Juliet. "She likes to tell me how I won't understand until I have kids of my own."

"Well, that's kind of smug but not totally wrong." Emer sighed. "Did you ask her why it happened?"

Juliet fiddled with the stem of her glass. An hour ago, this had all been about her. Now it was about Louise. She felt a familiar irritation that everything in their family eventually swung that way.

Juliet shook her head. "Can we get this back to what *I* should do, please?" she said, conscious that she sounded bit whiny. "I'm supposed to be seeing him, Michael, tomorrow in the park. What do I say?"

Emer didn't answer at once. She gazed at Juliet in a way that Juliet found unnerving, then said, "Well, it's easy enough. Do you like him? Do you want to see him again?"

"I don't know," said Juliet.

"Then I'd leave it. The guy's a free agent, so if you fancied him, and you felt ready for a relationship, I'd say go for it, but if you're not that bothered . . ." She shrugged. "I'd be more inclined to find out what's going on with my sister."

"That's not really answering my question, Emer."

Emer made an impatient noise. "Juliet, I know you've been through some tough times lately, but your sister's playing with fire here . . . She could probably use some sympathy!" She knotted her forehead, trying to control her emotions. "Okay, what should you do? Well, be honest. Tell him you've found out about him and Louise, and that it might be easier all round if you just cool things. You've only had one date. You spend more time with his dog than him. Tell him that. Tell him you want to concentrate on his fecking dog."

Emer pushed herself away from the table and went to open and close cupboard doors loudly. "Do you want some crisps?"

Juliet stared into her tiny glass, feeling quite disoriented, and not just because of the sloe gin. That was the thing about Emer and Lorcan: They had no fear about saying exactly what they thought, instead of just thinking it, like her family. Without batting an eyelid, Emer had upended all the messy, resentful feelings she had collected about her big sister over the years, and they now lay in front of her like bits of broken plate.

But how was she supposed to ask Louise what was wrong when Louise had spent the last six years telling her just how perfect her life was? That wasn't how it worked. "Louise doesn't need anyone's advice, let alone mine."

Juliet was aware of Emer slipping into the chair next to her, but she didn't look up.

"People change," said Emer softly. "And sometimes they do stupid things. You have to forgive them and move on. It's what love is. A great, big, stretchy blindfold. And not in a kinky way, more's the pity."

Juliet's mouth twitched in a reluctant smile, and Emer squeezed her shoulders.

"I don't mean to lecture you, but I had to watch all this going on, and it's so frustrating to see it happen again."

"With . . . you and Alec?" asked Juliet.

"No." Emer shook her head. "With . . . Well, I don't want to break confidences, but it's someone we both know well. Someone who didn't talk to his lady while she was going through tough times and buried himself in work instead. Went off on tours with Alec rather than asking himself whether . . ." She narrowed her eyes in thought, searching for a way of blurring the details, and gave up. ". . . whether it was normal for a woman to lose a baby and never refer to it again, to herself, to her man, to anyone. Men aren't great talkers, so this . . . *friend* pretended it never happened either. It put a gap between them, and it's human nature to fill that gap with someone else who doesn't know the miserable person you've become. So she did."

"Oh," said Juliet, seeing Lorcan in a new light. "And did this friend split up with his . . . lady?"

Lady. It sounded daft coming out of her mouth, yet entirely right in Emer's. And Lorcan would treat his girlfriend like a lady. It was better than *woman*.

"Eventually he did, yes. It was a big old mess, and he said he'd never go through that again with anyone else. Which is why he's bunking up with his old friend from school and her insane gang of brats, and acting like a human pet-sitter for them while her husband's away on tour." Emer clapped a hand over her mouth. "Oh, no," she said, her eyes wide. "I think I may have said too much."

"No, you haven't," said Juliet. "Perhaps it explains why this friend and I get on so well. We're both recovering."

Emer nodded sadly. "I wouldn't trust him with anyone else, but I think you understand."

"I do," said Juliet. "It's harder to find a friend than a boyfriend. At our age."

"Talk to your sister. Try to understand what must be going on. She must feel pretty lonely, if she's on the family pedestal."

"I will," said Juliet. "Thanks."

Hector's owner, Barbara Taylor, had long since stopped visiting her sister in hospital, but she'd found the regular breaks from Hector so invigorating that his outings with Minton and Coco had carried on.

In fact, she confided, when Juliet went to collect him on Friday morning, that Hector's dog walking had transformed her life. Not only had she met some lovely people at the Visitors' Support Center, but she and a very nice widower called Albert Barnes had started going to Pensioners' Lunch Club together twice a week while Hector was strutting his way around the park, oblivious to his mistress's new love interest.

"I don't want to introduce Albert to Hector just yet," she said, tucking Hector into his warm autumn-wear coat. "It's too early days. Isn't it, my love! Want to be sure he's Mr. Right!"

"Well, congratulations," said Juliet. "Glad to be of service."

"I think they'll get on." Mrs. Taylor gazed fondly at Hector, as he gave Coco a rather intimate sniff. "They have so much in common."

Juliet didn't want to know any more, and hurried off, leaving Mrs. Taylor spritzing herself liberally with Rive Gauche.

She'd made some effort with her appearance herself that morning too, although she'd tried not to make it too obvious. It was more for her own confidence than anything else. Still, she'd bothered with lip gloss and put on her new royal-blue coat, not the scruffy old parka of Ben's, and was striding across the park feeling positive. Thick tights, boots, and a nip in the air always did that for Juliet.

As she and the dogs headed into the park, Juliet stuck her iPod earphones in without turning on Lorcan's Irish folk-rock playlist, so she could rehearse what she was going to say to Michael. But she'd barely started up the hill toward Coneygreen Woods when a familiar figure in a Barbour jacket appeared from the depths of the wood and headed down the path, a pretty spaniel trotting at his side.

Hector made a lunge forward, stepping up his pace, and Minton followed.

Nerves tightened her chest and she fought the temptation to turn on her heel and avoid the whole embarrassing conversation.

Michael waved at her from a distance, the usual too-far-to-speak dog-walker wave, and she forced herself to smile and wave back.

It wasn't hard to smile at him. He was still the same handsome, unthreatening antiques-expert chap—only now, of course, Juliet couldn't help imagining him in a clinch with Louise.

Why does everything have to be so complicated? she thought.

Then he was near enough to speak, and she dragged her face back into neutral and racked her brains for something dignified to say.

"Hi!" said Juliet, staying far enough back for a kiss hello not to be an option. He seemed to notice.

"Hello! How are you?" he said. "Saw there wasn't a note from Damson the other day—everything okay?" His eyes were wary behind the dark-rimmed glasses. "I wasn't sure if . . . Did I say something wrong about going out for lunch?"

Juliet took a deep breath. "No, but . . ."

"But . . . ?" Michael raised his eyebrows. "Oh, no. Were the photographs that bad?" He was trying to be light, but his usual confidence seemed more stretched than usual.

"Oh, this is really awkward," said Juliet, "so I'll just say it. I know about you and my sister. Louise. Louise Davies, from your baby group," she added, then realized she was probably adding too much information.

Michael's cheery smile faded, to be replaced with horror, then embarrassment. "Louise is your sister?"

Juliet nodded. "We don't look very alike. We're not very alike. But she is my sister, yes."

He closed his eyes, mortified—or wondering how much she knew—then opened them and looked at her directly. "I'm sorry," he said. "I can see how you'd find it hard to know where to start."

Juliet respected him for not denying everything straight away, at least.

"Before you quite rightly have a go at me, is it rude to ask how you know?" He frowned. "I mean, did she tell you, or has there been . . . ?" His voice trailed off and he seemed genuinely worried.

"Do you mean, has there been a gigantic bust-up with her and Peter and now your affair's common knowledge all over Longhampton?"

"That wasn't quite how I was going to put it. And I wouldn't call it an affair either."

"No. No one else knows. She told me herself." Juliet walked over to a bench and sat down with a thump. This wasn't going quite as she'd planned. Suddenly, it felt like a very personal conversation to be having with someone she didn't really know that well at all.

Michael sat down beside her, and Damson sat next to him. Reluctantly, Minton and Hector trailed over too, unwilling group participants in the counseling circle.

"So, go on," he said, his usual confident tone somewhat muted. "I'm sure you've got a lot you want to say."

"I don't know if I have," Juliet admitted. "I'm not sure I want to know much more than I already do."

"Which is what?"

"That you and Louise met at NCT classes, and you enjoyed some long conversations which erupted into woodland passion when my husband's death conveniently reminded her about the fickle finger of Fate. And that it ended when she got her head together and realized what she stood to lose."

"Is that what she said?" Michael sounded wounded by her brutal summary.

In her mind's eye, Juliet saw Louise's glow when she'd confessed about her "crush" before Ben had died, and the real distress in her eyes outside the house the previous day. It *had* meant something to her, and from the strain on Michael's face, it had meant something to him too. She was being harsh. It wasn't a nice feeling.

"I'm sorry. She said you listened to her, and made her feel interesting. It's just that . . ." She struggled to put her thoughts in order. "It's so not Louise. Her marriage is everything to her, and I never had her down for a sneaking-around sort of person. Look, this is none of my business, really. You don't have to tell me anything."

Michael stretched out his legs in front of him. "How is she?"

"She's okay," said Juliet cautiously. Last week, she'd have said that confidently. Today, she wasn't so sure.

"I haven't heard from her since she . . . since the start of November last year. It wasn't her fault, by the way, that my marriage broke up. Don't blame her for that. And I don't normally make a habit of chatting up married mothers. But Louise said she really wanted to try harder with Peter, so we decided it was best to cut all contact."

He shot her a sideways glance, and Juliet knew he was dying to ask her whether Louise and Peter were still together.

"We really did spend a lot of time talking," he said. "I wish we could have met differently—Louise is great company. Did she ever sign up for the art classes at the college?"

"Louise? No."

"Why do you say it like that?"

"Because she . . ." Juliet was about to say, *Because she has no interest whatsoever in art*, but then realized that opinion was based on Louise dropping art at GSCE instead of geography in 1993, whereas Juliet had taken art *and* home economics *and* music. She was the arty one; Louise was the academic.

She heard Emer saying, *People change*. Maybe that was the point. Louise obviously had a secret inner life that no one knew about, and it had escaped.

"Because she's really busy with Toby, and she's gone back to work," Juliet said, suddenly feeling sad for the way Louise had ruthlessly shoved that chatty, art-studying woman back into her suit and sent her back to her desk, as if she'd never existed.

"She went back to work," repeated Michael. Obviously it had been something they'd discussed, by the heavy way he said it. "Right."

There was a brief silence, and Juliet wondered what else Louise had been planning that they didn't know about. Maybe she should ask her.

"Sorry if this is a leading question . . ." he started.

"Go on."

"Is she happy?"

"I think so. It's been a tough year for us all."

Michael didn't reply immediately. He seemed to be weighing his response, and because she'd run out of questions herself, with no clear idea of where to take the next, even more awkward, stage of the conversation, Juliet had no intention of rushing him.

Instead she reached into her pocket and found some treats for the dogs. She didn't have to tell Damson anything before the spaniel had dropped into an obedient sit at her feet.

An awkward pause filled the air between them as a walker they both recognized passed by with her border terrier. Everyone chirped hello in cheery voices, and Hector had a cursory letch at the dog.

"I . . . Oh dear." Michael shook his head. "I can't find a good way to say this either."

"Go on," said Juliet. "You're really a woman."

He laughed. "No. I'm not." He turned on the bench, and his hazel eyes searched her face. "I really like you, Juliet. I had a great time at that exhibition. I don't want to rush you into anything you're not ready for, and I really, really don't want to hurt anyone's feelings, but does this mean we can't have that pub lunch? And just take things as they come?"

The question hung in the air, like a spinning penny. Juliet felt as if she were at a significant moment in her life, where she could start choosing directions instead of letting the momentum take her wherever. There was no one else to check with now, except herself. Well, and Minton.

Yes? No? Her instinct failed her, but Louise's face floated up in front of her mind.

No. It would be too hard.

"Michael, don't take this the wrong way, but I think it's probably better if we don't," she said. "I enjoyed the other evening too, but I don't think I'm ready to date just yet."

"And when you do, you want something more straightforward?"

"I'm starting to think nothing is ever that straightforward. Not at our age." Juliet leaned forward and stroked Damson's feathery ears.

"At our age." Michael made a snorty noise. "Still, I guess a bit of complication means you haven't led a boring life."

Is that so bad? Juliet wondered. *Ben with no nasty surprises on his laptop. Me with no stamps in my passport. Are we just nice, straightforward people, or have I been missing out on something all these years?*

"Will you carry on walking Damson?" he asked. "I'd hate for her to miss out because of human complications."

Juliet smiled up at him. Michael was a nice guy, the sort her dad had always been on at her to bring home. If she got to know him, they might have their own in-jokes, or discover they liked the same cider. But something was missing at the moment. There was something a bit "researchy" about it, as if she were edging out into new water.

That could be her, not him. The year still wasn't up.

"I'd be happy to," she said. "I hate breaking up with dogs."

The trouble was, Louise thought, as she watched Toby splashing around in the bath, Peter sitting on the edge, her husband was a really nice guy.

Compared with the lying, cheating, drinking, fighting, abusive louses who came across her desk like an army of scabby rats, she had married a man who didn't even *exist* in their world. So why had she been sleeping on the floor of Toby's room rather than share a bed with Peter and his enraging snore that ended in a sort of choking whistle?

Her stomach clenched. After she'd come in from work still reeling from her horrible experience outside Michael's, she'd found Peter already in the kitchen, up to his arms in Waitrose ready-meal packaging. He'd dished up a proper three-course meal again, with candles and Classic FM, and revealed over pudding that he'd booked them into a country hotel in a fortnight's time for a "romantic getaway break." He'd expected an "Ooh" of delight, but Louise's first thought had been one of horror, and she'd come out with something about babysitters.

She didn't want to think about the crestfallen expression on his face. It made her feel nauseated with guilt and shame.

What is wrong *with me?* Louise screamed inside her head, as Peter squirted water into a delighted Toby's mouth.

"Mind the water, it's got bubble bath in," she heard herself say, in her mother's voice.

"I know, it's fine," Peter replied mildly. "It was just a splash, eh, Toby?"

It was Michael, she thought. Letting Michael back into her head just reminded her that she wasn't the perfect wife she'd hoped she was, and at the same time, she'd never get to be the free spirit who ran off to do art classes either.

The phone rang and Louise jumped.

"I'll get it," she said, unnecessarily, since her son and husband had eyes only for each other.

She picked up the extension in their bedroom and noted irritably that Peter hadn't put his underpants properly in the laundry basket. They hung off the edge as if they were trying to escape.

"Hello?"

"Lou, it's Juliet. Are you on your own?"

Louise sank onto the bed and kicked the door shut. Her heart had started to bang in her chest. "Yes, I am."

"I saw Michael today. I met him and—"

"What did you say?" Louise demanded.

"Nothing." Juliet went quiet. "Well, not nothing, obviously, but he did most of the talking." Pause. "He's still separated from his wife." Pause. "He said you were fantastic." Longer pause. "He hopes you're happy."

Louise tried to ignore the reluctance in Juliet's voice and let the words sink into her head. Michael had actually done it. He'd broken free, and moved on too, by the sound of it, if he was asking Juliet out.

She closed her eyes and leaned her head against the metal frame of their big double bed. What was causing this ache in her chest? That Michael had moved on from her, or that he'd done what she couldn't and got a grip on his life?

"Louise?"

Louise forced her eyes open, and the first thing she saw was the photograph of her post-birth, exhausted and triumphant, with Toby on her chest.

"So, are you going to see him again?" she asked, amazed at the bright voice she managed to drag up from somewhere.

"No," said Juliet. "Only his dog. Are you?"

"No!"

"Don't sound so aggrieved. It's a genuine question."

"No," repeated Louise. "I'm not. I promised myself I'd make things work here with Peter. For Toby. And I'm going to do that."

"That's what he said you'd said."

"Do I get extra points for that?"

Juliet laughed at the other end, and then turned serious. "Lou, you've got so much that's good in your life. I don't think you realize just how good it is. Please don't screw it up. I don't think Mum could handle a divorcée on top of a widow."

"I do realize," insisted Louise. "I know exactly how lucky I am. I'm just . . ."

Desperate for someone to let her be someone other than boring Louise? Not sure Peter was ever going to ask her opinion about anything other than pasta Bolognese versus lasagne? Her world felt secure again, and she thanked God that her stupidity hadn't led to her losing it, but it wasn't ever going to get any bigger.

Juliet made a tsking sound. "Well, you know best. As always. Anyway, I've got to go."

"Are you off out?" Louise felt a swift burst of envy. Juliet's social life seemed to have picked up lately, between the pet-sitting and the Kelly family inviting her round for meals.

"No, I'm babysitting next door. Emer and Lorcan are off out to a pool tournament."

"And you're babysitting? Sorry, I didn't mean that to sound so shocked."

"They're not *babies*. We're just going to watch a DVD and then they'll bugger off to bed, I hope. Anyway, I just wanted you to know I'd spoken to Michael. In case you were wondering."

"Thanks. But I'm not wondering," said Louise firmly.

I'm not wondering, she repeated to herself, as she put the phone down.

"Mummy!" yelled Peter from the bathroom. "Can we have a nice warm towel, please?"

I'm not wondering, she repeated, and headed for the airing cupboard.

Chapter 22

The anniversary of Ben's death arrived like a dental appointment; Juliet lay in bed, waiting for the numbers to tick over to midnight on her clock radio, then lay there staring at the minutes as the day began to eat itself away.

His mother, Ruth, called at eight o'clock. She sounded as if she'd been up all night waiting for the polite telephone-calling hour to come round.

"I can't believe it's a year," she began, and immediately burst into tears. Juliet could barely make out the words.

"I know," she said, moving around the room, getting Minton's breakfast ready before Coco arrived.

She listened as Ruth remembered what she'd been doing when the phone call came—from Juliet's dad, who'd silently taken the burden of phoning people from her. She murmured sympathetically while Ruth speculated about what Ben would probably be doing now, whether she'd be a grandmother, whether Ben would have expanded the business and moved nearer them.

Juliet didn't want to stop Ruth, today of all days, but the wistful fantasies scraped away at her own wobbly self-control. She wanted to point out that Ben *hadn't* been the most dynamic businessman, and maybe *she* felt devastated that there would be no mini Ben gurgling out from a pram, walking round the park with Minton.

She bit her lip. Juliet didn't feel like a weight had been lifted from her shoulders today; in fact, a leaden realization had settled in her stomach that life was going to go on, but with no one to share her jokes or warm her toes in bed when the rain was lashing against the windows.

And even if she did find someone—terrifying though that thought was—they'd never know the teenage her, or the twenty-something with the peachy skin. Her best years had gone, and Ben had taken all the memories with him, leaving her, tired and secondhand, to face the rest of her life.

"So, you don't mind if it's just me and Ray on the bench plaque, do you?"

Juliet had been filling Minton's water bowl, but now she stood up and concentrated on Ruth's voice. "I'm sorry?"

"The plaque on the bench. There were only so many characters, and it's going to say, *In Memory of Benjamin Raymond Falconer, 1979–2011.* New line, *The son who lit up our lives.* New line, *Donated by Ruth and Raymond Falconer.*"

Minton lapped noisily from the bowl and Juliet ignored the splashes of water he was getting everywhere.

"I thought it was going to be from his friends and family? Wasn't it bought with the collection money at his funeral? Half for charity, half for a memorial?"

Ruth made a half-tutting, half-sighing noise. "I know, Juliet, but Ray and I have organized it, and we've put in quite a bit extra ourselves, you know, to get a really good oak bench, so we thought . . ." She let her voice trail off so she didn't have to add,

We'd be in charge. Ben hadn't moved out of home into a flat with Juliet at nineteen for no reason. Juliet wondered if Ruth had ever forgiven her for that. Whether she thought he'd still be around now if he was in his room in their duplex, watching *Top Gear* with his dad and mowing their lawn.

"He was my husband," said Juliet. Her voice was tight with the effort of containing her hurt. "He wasn't *just* a son. He was a friend, and a lover, and . . . and a dog owner."

"Juliet, you can marry again," Ruth replied dramatically, and Juliet knew she'd been looking forward to saying it for months. "I will never have another son. Ever." She started crying again, angry, gusting sobs that seemed to chide Juliet for her apparent lack of feeling.

But Juliet didn't want to cry; she was more concerned about Ben's stuffy bench not even remembering their relationship.

"I might not marry again," Juliet protested. "I won't find another man like Ben, I know that."

"But you can try. My life is over! Juliet, I can't talk any more now. I'll be in touch." Ruth hung up, and Juliet was relieved.

She stood looking out the window at the garden, her eyes not seeing the bare branches of the trees, or the ferns turning bronze against the far brick wall.

All she could hear was Ben's voice in her head, telling her to ignore his mother, the drama queen. That his memorial was all around her, in the garden, in his dog, in their love.

So why am I decorating the house? Juliet asked herself. *Why is my life moving on? Is that wrong?*

The doorbell rang, and her mother's voice called through the house. "Are you there? Everyone up? We're here!"

She sounded too cheerful, as if she had to double her efforts today.

Juliet looked down at Minton and nudged him with her foot. He hadn't run through to greet the door, as he always did.

"Go on," she said to him. "I'm fine."

She went through her day's routine on autopilot, constantly aware of the time sweeping her nearer and nearer to the hour when Ben died.

Juliet wanted to do something to mark the moment, but she didn't know what. She was scrabbling to hold on to the last remaining minutes of the year, as if tipping over that threshold would break some kind of final bond she had with him.

She walked the dogs, then came home to an empty house and read the cards from a few friends who'd remembered. It didn't feel right to prop them on the mantelpiece, or throw them away, so they stayed on the shelf by the door, awkward reminders of awkward emotions. She made supper, fed Minton, and talked listlessly to her mother when she came to collect Coco, bearing a huge box of chocolates, all the time feeling as if she had an appointment to go to at a quarter past eight.

As the light was fading, Juliet went into the back garden and looked around the leafy confusion springing out from each side of the lawn. It was embarrassing how little she'd done to it, and she apologized to Ben in her head for the shaggy hedges and overgrown borders.

There were signs, though, of what he'd started. The rosebushes that her dad had pruned by the back door offered up some velveteen yellow and red flowers, and the herbs had thrived with no attention. As Juliet swept her hand through the mint and lavender and rosemary bushes, the air filled with scent, and for the first time in ages, she felt her nose twitch at the combination of medicinal, sweet fragrances. It had all carried on growing without him, just as she'd managed to keep going. A bit wild, but still growing.

Slowly, thinking of Ben with each plant, Juliet began to make a bouquet of stems, as he'd done for her wedding bouquet.

Rosemary, because she hadn't forgotten how much he loved her, and never would.

Dead seed heads from her untrimmed lavender, for the lavender bags she'd talked about making for the wardrobes they never bought. *Ben, you were right*, she thought, sadly: *I* didn't *find time. But maybe I will.*

Mint, for the deep-green tiles in the bathroom that was now finished, and was just how he'd have liked it.

Tiger-yellow chrysanthemums for the front sitting room, which was going to be the next project, once she got past today.

The Kellys were all out, and there was an unusual calm hanging over the dusk-shaded garden. It made Juliet feel as if she'd stepped into some sort of time bubble, where she could turn her head and see the house's original occupant, tending the roses in a crinoline. She wondered if Ben had slipped into that half-lit world now. Maybe one day in the future someone would be picking flowers in the dark and see a handsome blond man trimming the hedge, his long muscles glowing too healthily for a ghost.

Didn't they say that people with the most passion for life were the ones who imprinted themselves on their surroundings forever? That would be Ben. In his garden.

Juliet braced herself for the backwash of sadness, but it didn't come. Instead she felt a sort of peace in herself too, that Ben could choose to wander somewhere he'd been really happy, and maybe it would be here. She wanted him to be happy, wherever he was, because she was finally starting to grasp the fact that he *wasn't* going to walk through her door again, telling her it had been a mistake. He'd gone.

She reached the end of the lawn, where they'd pointed to the old brick wall and talked about the sweet peas and raspberry canes, and sat down on the damp grass, looking up at the squat white façade, with its sash windows and the date plaque she'd fallen in love with on the first viewing. Someone, in 1845, had sat where she was and thought, *Finished.*

That's my house, she thought, and corrected herself immediately. *Our house.*

The words hung in her head. *No, my house,* she decided, quietly. *My grouting. My fuse box. We didn't start any of the plans we made.* I *have. On my own. The house it's turning into is mine. And if I think of it as ours, it means there's always going to be someone missing.*

Besides, those magnificent plans, and the lack of movement on them, had been the tiny thorn that had started the bad feeling between her and Ben, the little resentments that had festered into something bigger under the skin of their happiness, and then finally erupted into the only serious argument they'd ever had.

Now the wash of sadness came, but instead of pushing away the memories of those final words she'd said to the love of her life, Juliet faced it. If she couldn't face it today, when was she going to?

She felt something warm pressing against her leg, and she saw that Minton had woken up and run out looking for her. His eyes were worried and he licked at her hand.

"I'm sorry," she said, fondling his ears. "Today of all days. How mean of me to make you think I'd abandoned you too."

Minton rubbed his head against her leg and rolled over, his tail tucked between his back legs. The submission broke Juliet's heart and she tickled his tummy, trying to cheer him up.

Then she picked up her bunch of stems and got to her feet. The wet grass had soaked through her jeans, and now a fine mist of rain had started to fall. She registered that it was cold, but a sudden determination had gripped her and she barely noticed.

"Come on, Minton," she said. "We're going out for a walk."

Juliet put Minton's lead on and stepped out of the porch into the fresh evening air.

It was still raining lightly, and she pulled up the hood of her jacket, setting off down their little residential street. At the end, she took a deep breath and turned the opposite way to her normal route, down the road that had once had the blacksmith, and the bakery, now the Old Forge, and the Old Bakery (flats A, B, and C). For the last year, she'd avoided walking this way, unable to see any of the landmarks without seeing Ben too.

I don't know where I'm going, she thought, masochistically. *I don't know exactly where Ben died, because* I wasn't there.

The still image of Ben collapsing in the empty street, surrounded by blank windows and silence, went through Juliet's heart like a knife, as it always did. It hurt even more now, because after a year of being properly alone herself, she knew what panic he must have felt, flailing like a drowning man for attention and finding nothing.

Although he hadn't been entirely alone. He'd had Minton with him.

Juliet's stomach lurched and she glanced down at the little terrier, trotting along at her heel as if they were just out for a bonus nighttime walk. The streetlights were making his creamy coat yellow, like unsalted butter, and she had a flashback to the nights they'd spent in Tesco's car park, Minton chasing his light-up ball under the twenty-four-hour security lights while she threw it robotically and cried at the same time. That seemed a different lifetime now too.

They passed the big detached villa, and the painted terrace of cottages, and each time she looked to see if Minton was reacting.

It was irrational, she knew, but part of her hoped he'd understand, and show her where she should direct her grief. How far down the street Ben had stormed, still stinging with anger after their row, before he'd suffered his massive, unexpected heart attack.

The ambulance man told her later that Minton had waited with Ben, barking and barking and barking, until eventually someone had come out of their house to see what the hell was going on with the bloody dog. With extraordinary bad luck, Ben had collapsed outside one of the few houses in Rosehill that belonged to someone he didn't know, and because he'd stormed out of the house in just his football kit, with no ID, no phone, nothing, they had no way of knowing who he was.

If only Ben had put Minton's collar on, as she was always nagging him to do, they could have phoned her immediately. She could have got there in time. Instead, she had to wait until . . .

Juliet stopped and closed her eyes to stop the image forming, but it formed anyway.

Minton, on her doorstep, alone, his tail wagging side to side in that scared, submissive fashion that told her something was wrong. She thought he'd been kicked, to begin with, he looked in so much pain.

Oh God, her first reaction had been crossness; the last dregs of her anger at Ben had been directed at poor little faithful Minton. She'd shouted at him for running off without his collar.

And then the knock on the door, the out-of-breath paramedic who'd run after Minton as he'd hared off up the road, trying to keep the white dog in sight. His expression, when she'd opened the door with her scared, exhausted dog under one arm, her face still tense and tear-streaked from the argument.

Juliet sank onto a nearby low wall and pressed the lock on Minton's extendable lead to stop him from going farther. He returned to her side at once, leaning into her leg and sniffing her hand for a treat. She reached automatically into the pocket that always had a Ziploc of kibble in it now for Coco and rewarded him, but her brain had gone on to the dot-to-dot analysis and she couldn't stop it.

If Ben hadn't stormed out like that, his heart wouldn't have had that sudden spasm all alone somewhere on Longhampton Road.

If they hadn't had a row, he wouldn't have stormed out, pumped full of adrenaline, his mind reeling with hurt and resentment and shock that his soul mate wasn't actually sure if she wanted to have children with him, after fifteen years.

And if she hadn't yelled at him that if he couldn't even get the bathroom started, when would he get round to potty training, or paying for nursery, or any of the other boring tasks that she found herself having to do, then maybe he wouldn't have yelled back, or stormed out, or died . . .

Juliet stuffed her hand into her mouth as a sob broke out of her.

Ben had died because they'd had a massive row about his not facing up to adult life the way she was.

She'd been tiptoeing around it for months, but that was the tough truth. The house wasn't ready to have a baby in. It wasn't even safe for their dog. Left to Ben, it never would be, and he hadn't seemed to care that it was driving her mad. If she were really honest—the sort of honest she'd been with Louise, out of sheer desperation—Juliet had started to wonder whether maybe they were growing at different rates, like an unbalanced tree: Ben the eternal teenager, happy to do favors for other people and worry about tomorrow later, and Juliet the reluctant adult, paying the bills, worrying for two.

It was the thought that maybe they weren't the perfectly matched couple that had made her sick and sad and angry—not him. Not Ben himself.

She was vaguely aware of a car slowing down, then stopping.

"Hey, Juliet! Do you two want a lift? It's raining."

Juliet looked over and saw Lorcan leaning out of his van. Emer was in the passenger seat with Roisin squeezed between them, and from the banging in the back, she guessed the rest of the Kellys were traveling with the tool kit and using it to play steel drums.

She shook her head and tried to look normal. "No, you're okay."

"Ah, go on," yelled Emer. "We're going via the chipper—we're celebrating Sal getting his first gig! Oi! Shut up in the back!"

Juliet managed a weak smile. "Tell him congratulations, but I'm fine, honestly."

Lorcan leaned out a bit farther, peering at her strained face. Then his door swung open, with the engine still running, and his jeans-clad leg appeared. "Emer, you'll have to drive home," he said, jumping down. "I'm going for a walk."

"You're not . . . Ah, Lorcan. Will I get you two some chips?" Emer twigged that something was up and slid across the seat to get behind the wheel. She didn't look entirely confident about taking over, and the expression on Roisin's face wasn't too positive either.

"Dunno. I'll ring you," said Lorcan, not looking back. His gaze was fixed on Juliet, and his dark eyebrows were creased with concern.

Juliet started to protest that he really didn't need to, but something about his solid presence made her feel better and awkward at the same time. She waved as Emer ground the gears and lurched off, to shrieks of protest from the passengers.

"Are you going somewhere in particular?" he asked, spotting the bouquet in her hand, as well as the dog lead. "Ah. Okay."

Juliet didn't say anything.

"Want some company? You can tell me to get lost if you'd rather be alone."

Juliet pressed her lips together, trying to keep her emotions in check. "I'm . . . I don't know. I was just going to walk around where Ben died and leave these somewhere. It's a silly idea."

"No, it's not." Lorcan didn't say anything else, and Juliet realized that was one of the things she liked most about him. He just said what he thought, and left it at that, unlike so many other people around her, always telling her how she should feel, how they'd feel in her situation, and on and on until she wanted to scream.

He inclined his head toward the road, and without speaking, they set off, Minton trotting ahead of them.

Images of Ben's last night pushed through Juliet's head, as she saw the walls and trees along the road through his eyes. Most of the darker thoughts she'd managed to pack into the back of her mind over the last year, "saving" them until she was strong enough to give them proper space, but now she made herself face them. Because if not now, when?

Had Ben been thinking of her—angrily—when he'd had his cardiac arrest? It tormented her more than anything that his last thought of her had been pain at the hurtful things she'd said. She hoped, had bargained with God, that he'd seen some happy memory of the two of them together, before he died.

Was it really selfish to wonder that?

Juliet realized Minton had stopped and was sniffing around a lamppost. For a mad second she wondered if this was it, if this was the place Ben had collapsed, outside . . . She peered to make out the curly iron sign. Outside the Gables.

It could well be. By the time the paramedic had banged on her door, Ben was in the ambulance on the way to the hospital, even though it was already too late, and she wasn't in a state to ask the man exactly where it had all happened. He'd taken pity on her hysteria and removed the keys from her shaking hands, driving the van to the emergency room, even though, he told her, he wasn't really supposed to.

She stopped. Lorcan had stopped as well, and she knew he'd

twigged to what she was doing. *Maybe it would have been better to be alone*, she thought. *I could have said a poem or something. Recited lyrics from* X&Y.

But as she thought it, she knew there was no point. This was more about her than Ben. She celebrated him every day in little ways, not just Grief Hour, which had shortened recently. Coldplay was wearing off. No, this was more about her, making it through a whole year without him for the first time since she was fifteen. Battered, and stunned, but still breathing.

"I could go," Lorcan offered, reading her face. "If you want some privacy."

Juliet slowly shook her head. Ben wasn't here. He wasn't going to materialize like Banquo's ghost, and in any case, hadn't she preferred him haunting her own garden, not some random portion of Rosehill's residential area?

"No. I'd only stand out here talking to myself until the owners come out. At least we look like two normal human beings having a chat."

"Fair enough." He peered at the hedge next to them, trimmed into a fat oblong. "This is a good-looking hedge. What'd you call this?"

"Box," said Juliet. "Can you smell it? Always reminds me of National Trust houses, and Olde England." She rubbed the leaves between her fingers and inhaled the dark-green scent. "Ben loved box. He talked about growing some in the garden and cutting them into topiary shapes. It would have taken years."

"Better get some soon, then. Add it to the list. For the house," he added, as if she had some other list.

Juliet twisted the leaves in her fingers. He'd have stopped at this hedge to admire it. Ben always stopped to smell the flowers and plants. Maybe his last thoughts had been about dark-green hedges and shears and her in a summer dress in their garden full of box-cockerels.

Slowly she took her bunch of herbs and flowers and pushed it into the dry center of the thick box hedge, until it vanished from sight in the scratchy twigs.

"Good-bye, Ben," she whispered. "I'm sorry. I love you."

She closed her eyes as the tears pushed up her chest, and then they sank down again. Juliet had become skilled at taking the temperature of her grief, monitoring tiny fluctuations like a nurse, and now she felt a strange calm relief at the edges of it, like glimmers of light around the curtain on a winter morning.

"Okay," she said, in a voice higher than her normal one. "Let's go home."

"Are you sure?" She felt Lorcan's hand on her shoulder, comforting. "You can stay here as long as you like. I can take Minton home, fend off passersby, whatever."

Juliet let out a long sigh. "No. I don't know what I thought would happen. I thought it would all be different today. But I'm just the same."

"What did you want to be?"

"I don't know. My old self? A new, stronger self?"

She had a sudden mental picture of herself as a superhero butterfly, bursting out of her old body, shiny and strong. Ready for a new life.

But I don't want a new life, she thought, automatically, then wondered if that was absolutely true.

The thought shook her.

"You're a strong woman," said Lorcan. His hand turned her gently into his shoulder, where she laid her head. It was comforting, brotherly, and she let herself stay like that for a moment before raising her head.

"Right," she said. "Take me somewhere very noisy and distracting. But not a pub. Or to play pool."

"I know just the place." Lorcan sighed. "Unfortunately. How do you feel about recorder practice?"

"Perfect," said Juliet.

Chapter 23

Louise stared at the pink gloop in her cocktail glass and wondered what on earth had made her think that Ferrari's had suddenly acquired a London cocktail maker. This wasn't a cosmopolitan. Not unless you now made them with . . .

She tried to work out what the tastes were on her tongue.

Ribena and surgical spirit.

"Can I get you another?" asked Peter, cheerfully finishing off his small glass of white wine.

"Are you trying to get me drunk?" she replied, only half joking.

"Yes!"

Louise thought he probably was too—a few cocktails had led to some outrageous behavior in the old days. But knowing that he knew that wasn't helping; her body was clinging to sobriety like a determined Victorian spinster, no matter how much alcohol she forced into it.

"Come on, let your hair down," said Peter, mistaking her hesitation for maternal concern about Toby, dropped off at Diane's for the evening. "Your mum's happy to have Toby till the morning. Here, have a look at the cocktail menu. What's the Ferrari's house special?"

"Antifreeze and cider?" Louise dragged up a smile and was rewarded with a real look of pleasure on his face.

She reminded herself that many women would love to be bought drinks by a good-looking company director with all his own hair. Peter was making a real effort, and so was she. Fresh shirt for him, full makeup for her, proper grown-up conversation about nonbaby themes. What the Internet advice people called "you time," designed to recharge a flatlining relationship.

I have got to try, thought Louise. *Even if it feels like I'm acting in front of a big green screen and none of this has anything to do with me.*

Maybe another cocktail would do it.

"Okay," she said, pushing her glass away and reaching for the laminated cocktail menu. "Why don't I try a martini? They can't get that wrong—it's just gin, vermouth, and an olive."

"Perfect. One more drink each and we'll move on." Peter's smile broadened. "To venue two."

They were sitting in the bar area of the restaurant, but they weren't there to eat, apparently. That was venue three.

"And where *are* we going?"

"Surprise."

"I'm not sure Longhampton has that many surprise venues." The waitress hovered and Peter ordered another glass of wine for himself, and a dirty martini for Louise. She handed back the cocktail menu. "Are we going to bingo?"

"No!" Peter sounded aghast, then realized she was joking. "Not bingo. This is a *date*." He reached across the table and took her hand, linking his fingers between hers, and smiled. "It has been pointed out to me that maybe the wine tasting was a bit selfish. This is more of a *date* date."

"Pointed out by whom?"

Peter shook his head. "Doesn't matter. I tried to remember what sort of stuff we did when we first met—you know, the things we'd do because you liked them—and . . . here we are. Cocktails, surprise venue, dinner."

Louise started to take umbrage at the implication that she'd forced him into a load of tedious dates, but she pushed that aside and focused on the sweet underlying message—that Peter had dragged himself along to things because he wanted to be with her, all those years ago.

Not *all* those years ago, she reminded herself. Eight years ago. She still had jeans from then in her wardrobe.

"Like what?" she asked, a smile creeping into her voice. "Don't tell me that when I was *hauling* you to the Wolseley, you'd rather have been at home with your needlework?"

"I would. Given a choice between that and the stand-up comedians. To be honest, I never got half the jokes." Peter grinned, and there was a flicker of warmth that reminded her of the old days.

"If I'd known that—" she started, but the drinks came, suspiciously quickly, and she stopped.

"Cheers," said Peter, and she raised her glass to his.

The martini tasted of dishwasher fluid, but she still smiled as she took the first revolting sip.

Louise found that she got used to the taste of Ferrari's martini, and the second cocktail fanned the little spark of goodwill into a warm glow. By the time Peter helped her into her jacket, they'd reminisced about some mad nights out she'd totally forgotten about, and she was feeling much more positive about the whole evening.

"Where are we *going*?" she asked him again as they set off down the deserted High Street.

"Patience," he said, with pretend despair. "Were you this bad at Christmas?"

"No, I never even shook a parcel. Juliet was the tape peeler." Louise tucked her arm into Peter's and leaned into him as they walked. The thought of Christmas made her feel glowy too: Toby's first Christmas he'd stand a chance of remembering, everyone round at Mum's. They could make it especially nice for Juliet this year. Make her feel part of *their* family. Because she was. Auntie Jools.

"I like this surprise element," she said, and realized she meant it.

They walked through the empty streets, their feet echoing on the pavement. All the shops closed on the dot of five thirty, and Ferrari's was the only upmarket restaurant on the High Street. Longhampton was a ghost town after six, apart from the crime-hotspot area around the two nightclubs, Duke's and the Player, both located conveniently close to the police station.

The first chill of winter hung in the evening air, and Louise was glad she'd brought her coat, despite its not quite going with her outfit. The cocktails were warming her from the inside, and she enjoyed the sensation of cold air on her face.

"Now, *this* is reminding me of our first dates," she said nostalgically. "Going out for drinks in town, after work. Do you remember how cold it was that winter? And we had to choose between a last drink and a cab home . . ."

It seemed like someone else's glamorous life now. Staying out late talking, missing the Tube, walking through the rushing London streets at midnight, wobbling on her heels but not wanting to say good night, finally finding a cab with its light on, then jumping in together and kissing so hard they forgot to give directions . . .

The thing is, said a voice in her head, *you once had times like that. There was once passion and flirtation and sexiness there. You can get that back.*

It doesn't have to be with Michael. Peter was once interesting too. He could still be like that.

The thought ran through her with such electricity that she shivered.

"Cold?" he asked, putting his arm around her. "Do you want my jacket?"

"No, I'm fine." She was touched by his automatic gallantry; Peter was, she reminded herself, and always had been, thoughtful. He'd never gone home without making sure she was safely on her way.

Peter steered her off the High Street and down North Road.

"Aha!" said Louise. "The plot thickens! We're not going to bingo . . ."

"I can't help thinking I've built this up too much," he replied dryly.

"No, I *like* not knowing where we're going." As Louise said it, a penny dropped in her head, and she realized that was why she was feeling so much more flirty toward him. "I mean, we've got into such a routine, haven't we? It's nice, not having that predictability."

Peter pulled a rueful face at her, but he didn't disagree.

They turned a corner, and Louise let out a laugh when she saw where he'd brought her.

"Oh my God, the Memorial Hall! Dancing lessons! You've brought me dancing?" She turned to him and gave Peter a little push. "You pig! If I'd known we'd be facing scary Angelica and her bloody social foxtrot, I'd have stuck to just the one cocktail! And put on some flatter shoes!"

Peter put up his hands in self-defense. "It's not dancing lessons. What do you take me for, a masochist?"

"So why are we here? It's too late for soft play."

"There's an exhibition on. Final week." He looked pleased with himself. "You used to drag me to the Photographers' Gallery when—"

"Once."

"Well, once was enough. I thought you'd like an evening of culture, and this is a photographic exhibition of the town, and it's late opening tonight." Peter checked his watch. "Until eight. Which is thirty minutes—that enough culture for you?"

"Plenty," said Louise. She smiled, flattered that he still remembered. "Thanks."

"And if you really like something, we could buy it," he added manfully.

She knew he was thinking about the abstract photo, *Pebble in Oil*, he'd ended up buying for her at some awful gallery, because she'd pretended to like it. Peter really had put himself out over the years.

"We don't have to go that far," she said.

Several other couples were browsing around the exhibition when they went in, drifting slowly around the polished wood floor of the hall, admiring the big black-and-white framed images on the walls.

Louise took a leaflet with the photographer's biography on it, as well as the details of where the various landscapes had been taken. *It'd be nice*, she thought, to get something for Mum and Dad—it was their ruby wedding anniversary coming up, and they'd lived in Longhampton all their lives.

It occurred to her that this must have been the exhibition

Juliet had been to with Michael—there couldn't be two exhibitions of Longhampton photography. Her heart gave a faint tug, but she concentrated hard on the lovely evening she was having.

Peter came up behind her, and she took a long breath, smelling his aftershave without turning round.

"Is that the bus terminal?" he murmured in her ear. "Very moody."

"It is." Louise had always dismissed that treat-your-husband-as-a-stranger-on-a-date role play as impossible—how could you forget years of toothpaste irritation and nose picking just like that?—but two cocktails down, she was beginning to see the possibilities.

"I prefer the landscapes," she murmured back, pointing at a dramatic shot of a tree backlit against a winter sky, its clawlike branches reaching upward. "I think that's near Rosehill, by Juliet's."

"He's a landscape kind of guy, isn't he?" Peter observed. "I suppose they're easier. Not so much movement."

"No, look, there's some people." Louise took a step sideways into a corner of the room, pointing at an intimate portrait of a couple almost silhouetted on a park bench. The man's arm was stretched out behind the woman and their heads were tilted close together, as if they were sharing secrets or about to kiss—it wasn't clear which, but the mood was Hollywood romantic. "That's gorgeous! Has someone bought this? We should see if . . ." She trailed off, her eyes suddenly focusing properly on the image.

"Am I going mad, or is that you?" said Peter, in a joking tone. He started to say something else, but then stopped, his tone not joking anymore.

Louise stared at the photograph. It *was* her. Her and Michael. His face was more hidden than hers, but even if his glasses and her distinctive long nose weren't enough of a giveaway, she'd have known it from the eager way they were leaning into one another.

That fierce hunger to talk and talk, to learn more about each other, gobbling up the minutes—it was captured in that tiny slice of sky between their half-open mouths.

"That *is* you, isn't it?" he repeated. His voice was slightly metallic. "That's that winter coat you had, with the toggles."

Louise didn't want to look at him, but she couldn't stop her head turning. When she did, any words she did have froze in her throat. Peter had transformed from the gentle IT geek she knew. His face was tense and older, and he was very still, as if all his energy were going into being calm.

She swallowed. Now that the moment had come to confess it all, her brain spun into total denial mode. For the first time in her whole career as a Crown prosecutor, Louise understood the insane stories gabbled out in the witness box: *It couldn't be me; I wasn't there. I don't know him. I've never seen him before in my life.*

I will never look at those desperate liars with scorn again, she thought. It wasn't so much telling the lie; it was that her brain didn't want to *be* the person who'd be left standing there, once she'd owned up.

"I don't . . ." Her mouth had gone dry and her tongue clicked. Louise knew her reaction had given him his answer already; what he wanted now was for her to deny it.

A woman passed by behind them and gave her a curious look.

I want to save my marriage, she thought clearly. *If I really wanted out, I'd admit it and go. It's a good sign that I want to lie, but if I don't tell the truth now, it's over anyway.*

"Yes," she said, in a tiny voice. "It's me."

"And who are you with? If you don't mind my asking." Peter sounded very calm. "Or is it an old photograph?"

She knew he was giving her a chance to wriggle out, but there was no way this photo could be over eight years old. They both knew that.

"No," she said, summoning all her courage. "It's not an old photograph. That's Michael Ogilvy. From the NCT class."

"And are you . . . ?"

It hung in the air between them.

"We're just talking," said Louise.

Peter said nothing, but stared at the image. Louise couldn't tear her eyes away, her heart breaking inside her chest, spreading hot tar through her, spoiling everything.

It wasn't the near-kiss that was so betraying; it was the intimacy of his arm along the bench, the inclination of her head. The hungry closeness that had vanished from their own relationship.

"This isn't you, Louise," he said, very quietly, then turned on his heel and walked out.

Louise listened to each footstep like a gunshot on the sprung floor. She could hear Angelica, their dance teacher, stamping out the steps for their wedding dance and she felt a childish panic to drag the clock back, to make all this go away so she could start again and do it properly this time.

"Peter!" She spun round, but he was at the door already. Then he was gone, without turning back.

The couples left in the exhibition couldn't disguise their stares, as she stood motionless, the warmth draining from her veins as the cheery cocktail exuberance evaporated in a flash.

Louise felt as if she'd never be warm again.

Juliet put her fresh mug of tea on the windowsill and curled up in her red armchair, with Minton tucked into the crook of her legs and Coco curled up in her basket by the window. She looked at the two dogs, one snoring, one preparing to snore, and decided that she didn't need to do the Grief Hour thing anymore.

"From now on, we miss Daddy to our own timetable," she told

Minton, cupping his velvety ears. "Now, what do you fancy on telly?"

This was the first night that week that she'd properly settled down to lose herself in some good viewing. There'd been some emergency babysitting next door one night when Lorcan had to work late while Emer needed to take Salvador to a bowling party; then, on Tuesday, postwork painting of the front room had gone on until midnight with pizza and Guinness. Diane had dragged her out to some fund-raiser for the dog rescue center on Wednesday, where she'd finally managed to put names to three embarrassingly familiar dog-walking faces and avoided her mother's clumsy attempts to introduce her to "a lovely man" called Dennis who'd conveniently just adopted a border terrier.

Or maybe the border terrier was called Dennis. Juliet still hadn't got the hang of asking the owner's name first.

"It's a relief to have some time on our own, isn't it?" she said, flipping through the *Radio Times*. "Never thought you'd hear me say that, eh?"

The phone rang by her side and she considered ignoring it. Ruth, Ben's mum, had been on again about the memorial bench, and the more Juliet thought about it, the more it wound her up. Ruth had recently announced she wanted to put it in the crematorium where "everyone would see it," not in the park or near something that Ben would have sat to look at, like a particularly well-planned garden.

But if she ignored it, she'd have to listen to Ruth's message, and that was worse. They went on for ages and usually ended in tears.

Juliet sighed and picked up the phone. "Hello?"

"Juliet, it's Emer," wailed a familiar voice. "Help me. I've to go to one of these awful kitchenware parties and I need someone to stop me spending a fortune on whisks. Come with me. Hold my purse."

It was nice to feel wanted, but Juliet knew if she got up, she'd be reeled into the warm chaos of next door. Grief Hour might be off, but she still needed some solitude to keep her emotions from bubbling over like an unattended pan of milk.

"I can't," said Juliet firmly. "I'm looking after Coco for the evening and I've promised Mum I'll give her a bath."

"Bathe her tomorrow; buy stacking bowls tonight!"

Minton's ears pricked at some sound outside, and he slid off her knee.

"Look, I've got to go," said Juliet, to howls of protest from Emer. "I think someone's at the door. I hope it's not you. Ring me if you need shouting at."

She clicked the phone back into the charger, and as she did, the doorbell rang, right on cue.

"Some guard dog you are," she observed to Coco, who hadn't even looked up. "No, really, I'll go . . ."

Juliet padded through the sitting room, now soft sage on two walls, and opened the porch door, shivering at the change in temperature. It was nearly time to put the heating on properly.

The doorbell pealed again. "Hang on," she protested, fiddling with the bolts. Lorcan had put in an extra one "for security" and it was stiff.

The door swung back to reveal Louise on the doorstep, looking haggard with shock.

Juliet had a flashback to the glimpse she'd caught of herself in the hospital window the night Ben died. Gray drawn face, hunted eyes, wild hair—like something you dreaded glimpsing in a mirror on Hallowe'en. The scary thing was, she'd had no idea she looked like that.

"Louise!" she said, shocked. "What's happened?"

Louise's eyes burned, drilling straight through Juliet. "Why didn't you tell me?" she croaked.

"Tell you what?"

"The exhibition. Why didn't you *tell* me?" She wobbled on the step. "Did you do it on purpose? Was that it? Is this your idea of a *punishment*?"

"Lou, I honestly don't know what you're on about. Come on in."

Louise didn't move, so Juliet grabbed her arm and pulled her inside, before Emer heard her talking and came round to investigate.

She's told Peter about her affair, she thought. *It must be that. That or she's had some kind of breakdown. Or has Michael been in touch?*

Juliet cringed at the possibilities—Michael calling while Peter was in, maybe? Or e-mails? Did Louise delete e-mails? Or was it something else? She wasn't making any sense.

"Mind the paint cans," she said, steering Louise through the dropcloths and boxes toward the cozier back room. "Now, sit there and tell me what's going on." Juliet pushed her sister into the big red armchair and perched herself on the footstool.

Then she got up again, unable to settle when Louise was radiating such distress. "Do you need a drink? Brandy? Sweet tea?"

Coco stirred in her basket, saw Louise, and curled up again, afraid of being ejected.

"Just tell me whether you knew."

"I swear to God," she said slowly, "I have no idea what you're talking about. Now, please, tell me."

Louise seemed to believe her, because she put her head in her hands and groaned like an animal. "There's a photograph in that exhibition Michael took you to—of us. Me and him, on a park bench."

"You're kidding." Juliet's mouth dropped open. How had she missed that? "Are you sure it's you?"

"Yes, it's us. You *honestly* didn't see it when you went?"

"No. There were loads of people there, and my feet were killing me—we didn't go round the whole thing." Juliet didn't add, *We skipped half of it so we could go outside and flirt and drink wine.*

She felt a sick wave of responsibility. This was her fault. She could have stopped this, bought the photo, anything.

If she hadn't been distracted by her "date." If she hadn't worn those boots. If she'd bothered to look at the photographs properly, not just ticking off the landmarks she already knew . . .

"When did you find out?" asked Juliet. "Did someone tell you?"

"No. Peter took me there as part of our date tonight. We saw it at the same time."

Juliet hissed with horror and racked her brain for comforting thoughts. "But it's been up for ages now. Surely if it's *obviously* you, someone would have seen . . ."

"It's a silhouette, but it's definitely me. You can tell. Peter saw straight away; there was no point denying it." Louise started to cry, big gulping sobs that shook her shoulders. "What am I going to do, Jools? He just looked at it, and looked at me, and he walked off. He didn't even shout."

"But what are you doing in this photo? Are you . . . kissing?"

"We're *talking*." Louise wiped her nose, bitterly. "Just talking."

Just talking? How bad could that be? Juliet wondered if Louise's guilty reaction had told Peter more than he'd have guessed on his own.

"But did he actually say . . . ?"

"Juliet, Peter knows. He's not stupid. I could tell—he looked at me as if I were something he'd trodden in."

"I . . ." Juliet started, then realized she had no more comforting things to say, other than that at least she didn't have to worry about telling him.

Still, that was it, pointed out a voice in her head. The worst was over: Peter knew.

It was like the moment when the doctor appeared at the side of Ben's cubicle, pulling the curtain aside with that solemn expression clouding his bloodhound face. *This is the worst moment, and it's over,* she'd thought then, as if she were hovering serenely over her shell-shocked body, slumped in the orange plastic chair. *Nothing can ever happen to me that'll hurt more than this does now.*

Juliet crouched at her sister's feet and took her hands in hers. They were smooth and long, compared with her DIY-scuffed hands. Louise's rings glittered in the lamplight: engagement solitaire, wedding band, the eternity ring Peter had bought her when Toby was born.

"Is Toby still at Mum's?" she asked.

"Yes." Louise looked up, despair etching lines around her mascara-smeared eyes. "Oh God, should I go and get him? Can *you* go and get him, bring him here?"

Juliet was about to add, *What, with Coco and Minton on the loose?* but for once she bit down on it. Not the right time.

"Tell Mum I've asked you to fetch him," Louise added. "Please? Before Peter goes round."

Juliet could imagine the hysterical panic that would trigger in her mother, Juliet pitching up in her van to collect Toby for no apparent reason. "Lou, I don't have the right car seat," she said gently. "And anyway, he's fine there with Mum. She won't be expecting you to collect him till tomorrow."

"What if Peter's phoned her?" Louise looked horrified. "I don't want Mum and Dad to know. Not yet. Not till we've . . ."

"I'll phone Peter too," said Juliet, before she could think what a teeth-clenching conversation that would be. "Don't worry. I'll sort it out."

"Thanks, Jools." Louise managed a half smile and then looked as if she were about to burst into tears again, this time with gratitude and bewilderment that Juliet was the one taking charge.

"I'll make some tea," said Juliet. It sounded a bit weird, coming out of her mouth instead of someone else's. She understood now why she'd been offered pot after pot of the stuff; it was an automatic reaction, to do something, however small, that might help. "You need a cup of hot sweet tea."

Then, when she'd forced a mug on Louise, she picked up the phone and steeled herself to call Peter and then Diane.

As the dial tone sounded in her ear, Juliet made a note to thank her dad, for making all the calls she hadn't been able to. She hadn't even been aware of him taking the phone off her. She just remembered her father's broad back, turning away from the bedside with his shoulders set, heading out to make the calls.

Juliet's heart expanded, realizing just how lucky she'd been to have her family around her. How much she loved them for filling in gaps in her grief that she'd never noticed, for slowly nudging her back to life when she'd wanted to die too.

"Hello?"

Juliet swallowed. "Peter," she said, "Louise is here with me . . ."

Chapter 24

I thought we agreed, no rubbish paintings. You're going to cover up my immaculate handiwork."

Lorcan made his "outraged camp interior designer" face as Juliet unbuckled Minton from his harness and held him over the mat to towel his paws, wet from their morning walk. It had rained again, and he loved a puddle.

"*My* handiwork, you mean," she replied, unfastening her own thick jacket. "I'm just letting you tidy it up."

The front sitting room was nearly finished now. The walls had all been painted the soothing sage green, with creamy skirting boards and pine bookshelves fitted into the recesses alongside the chimney breast. One of her pet-sitting clients, Mina Garnett, had offered her some heavy silk curtains that she was getting rid of, following her revamp of her beautiful garden flat.

Juliet took them gratefully and didn't let on she'd noticed that the revamp coincided with a sudden absence of Mina's boyfriend's clothes in the laundry basket.

"So what's that, just delivered about an hour ago?" Lorcan demanded. "And is that the kettle I hear going on? I'm gasping for a cup of tea."

"I have no idea, and no." Juliet spotted what he was talking about: a huge bubble-wrapped parcel propped up against the far wall. Her excitement flickered for a second, but then it dawned on her. *I bet I know what this is*, she thought, and went into the kitchen for a pair of scissors.

As an afterthought, she flicked on the kettle. They'd both need a strong cup if this was what she thought it was.

"Present?" asked Lorcan. "From an admirer?"

"You've been spending too long around Emer." Juliet hacked away. "My admirers send me complimentary poo bags."

The first layer of plastic came away to reveal the silver edge of a framed photograph. From the bit she could see, it was of two people on a park bench.

Juliet bit her lip. Michael hadn't wasted any time. She'd only spoken to him an hour and a half ago; she'd called as soon as it was polite, well out of earshot of Louise, who was finally asleep in her bed. His reaction had been about the same as Juliet's—panic, mingled with abject guilt for not spotting it sooner—and he'd promised to "sort things out."

Juliet hadn't expected results this fast, but then again, he seemed like the kind of man who made calls and got things done. If the situation hadn't been so miserable, she'd have been impressed.

"What is it? Don't tell me it's that nudie one of your man with the baby," asked Lorcan cheerfully.

"Give me credit. Go and make the tea, there's a good builder," she replied, grinning, but when Lorcan was safely in the kitchen, she pulled off the rest of the wrapping and studied the romantic image in front of her.

Oh, Louise, she thought, aghast. It was a heart-stopping

photograph—it captured a moment between two people who'd clearly forgotten anyone else existed. Even though the faces were nearly in shadow, their attraction shimmered out from the frame. But it was a *private* moment. Juliet suddenly understood Louise's strange half-scared, half-delirious expression when she'd nearly confessed that night before Ben died. She even understood her weird lurking around Michael's house.

With that tiny tilt of Michael's head, and the laugh in Louise's mouth, the photographer had captured the shared-breath intimacy of a flirtation teetering on the brink of something more so perfectly that Juliet felt like a peeping Tom. This was what Louise had been trying to explain—the listening. The friendship. The excitement. It wasn't just a tacky bunk-up in the woods; it was a real connection.

Juliet couldn't help feeling a tremor of jealousy, but she pushed it away. God, she'd rather be single for the rest of her life than have to deal with what Louise did now.

"What a mess," Juliet breathed to herself.

"Blimey," said Lorcan, over her shoulder. "I take it back—that's a great photo. Hang that wherever you want."

"I'm not hanging it anywhere," said Juliet, pulling the bubble wrap back over it like a shield. "I'm going to get rid of it."

"Why?"

Juliet had gone beyond the point of filtering things to Lorcan. She might edit a bit for Emer, but Lorcan had a way of relaxing her into full confession, whether she was aware of it or not.

"It's Louise. And Spaniel Man." Juliet explained as quickly as she could, and Lorcan's eyes widened briefly, then turned sympathetic.

"Not great," he said succinctly. "But it happens."

"Not in our family," sighed Juliet. "We've only had one divorce in the last thirty years, and there was cross-dressing involved. Mum's going to be beside herself."

"Your mum doesn't know?"

Juliet shook her head. "Nope. Louise wants me to go with her to tell her. She hasn't needed me to do that since she broke Mum's Carmen rollers in 1988."

The loo flushed upstairs.

"Hey, hey? Who've you got upstairs, then? You dark horse." Lorcan started to pantomime shock, but then realized that she might *have* someone staying and struggled to look disinterested.

Juliet batted him. "It's Louise. I gave her one of the emergency sleeping pills Ben's mother forced on me. She probably didn't hear you let yourself in." She gripped her hair and pulled a face. "Once I've taken her to get Toby from Mum's, I've got to take her home. Peter's not there, thank God. I don't think I'm up to refereeing that one."

The phone call to Peter had been the biggest favor she'd ever done Louise. He'd sounded as if he were talking to her from inside a well, answering only in half-sentences. He was, he said, going to stay with his friend Hugh for a few nights. To think.

"Do you want me to make myself scarce?" asked Lorcan, gesturing to the paint. "I mean, this can wait. We can do it another time."

Juliet shook her head emphatically. "Please don't. It's only the thought of having a fully decorated sitting room for Christmas that's keeping me going."

Lorcan grinned. "I'll make that tea for when you're back. And I'll stick this in the shed, right?"

"Would you?" said Juliet. "Right at the back. Cheers."

Louise tried to get her thoughts in order as Juliet drove toward her house but had to give up after ten silent minutes. Her thoughts refused to go into list form. Instead, horrible images pushed past the practicalities: Peter's stricken face, Toby shuttling between divorced parents, her mum and dad blaming themselves, having to tell people . . .

All her fault. Despair compressed her head, crunching down on her shoulders. No to-do list was going to sort this out. Where were you even meant to start?

"Did you enjoy the shower?" Juliet asked, randomly.

"What?"

"The shower. It's good, isn't it?"

Louise vaguely remembered standing under Juliet's shower this morning. In her dopey state, she'd forgotten to admire the magnificent bathroom she'd spent months secretly supplying.

It *had* been a nice shower, now that she thought about it. Powerful.

"It makes me so happy," Juliet went on, "to have a proper shower in the mornings. I'd forgotten how nice it is not to have to juggle spray attachments. Emer told me that. Take time to enjoy the little things. A good, strong shower. Cherry blossoms. Green traffic lights—"

Louise stopped her before she started listing things indefinitely. "Is that meant to be some kind of comment on my current situation?"

"Not at all." Juliet indicated and turned left onto the one-way system, lurching into a gap Louise would have held back from. Coco protested in the back of the van; Minton, wedged in by her feet, braced himself. "I just find it helps, when everything else seems to be going totally wrong. Little things."

Louise bit her lip, not wanting to snap at Juliet. What was the point of little things right now? When her marriage had collapsed, and her family was imploding, and she wasn't even the person she thought she was? And, more to the point, everyone in Longhampton who'd been to that exhibition knew that too?

Juliet pulled up outside the house. The Picasso was still there;

Peter obviously hadn't taken it. Or maybe he was still there. Bile rose up in Louise's throat.

Juliet turned in her seat. She scanned her face with concern and spoke quickly, as if she were wary about giving advice.

"Listen, two things. One, only people who know you very, very well would know that's you in the photograph, okay? And let's face it, they're not the sort of people who go to photographic exhibitions. So stop thinking the whole town's talking about you, because they're not."

"How do you—"

"I've got it in the shed. Michael had it biked round. Forget the photo—it's gone."

Louise felt a featherweight of stress lift off her shoulders.

"And two," Juliet went on, "I don't want to tell you that I know how you feel because that's one of the least helpful comments ever. But I know what it's like to feel as if you're all on your own. I know that . . . that rooted-to-the-spot-with-fear feeling. But your marriage *isn't* over. You can save this. If you're honest, and if you want to."

"Can I?"

"Peter loves you," insisted Juliet. "And you love him. If you didn't, you'd have left him for dust the instant I told you Michael was divorced. Right?"

Louise clutched her keys until they cut into her hand.

She did want to save it. That was why she felt so sick—it was fear that she couldn't.

"Come on," said Juliet, in her new role as the organized one. "Let's get going."

Juliet knew her mum had detected drama as soon as she walked through the door with Louise behind her, Coco and Minton following at a safe distance.

"Both of my girls here at once and it's not even Christmas," she said, pretending to look baffled, but not quite hiding her delight. She had her chef's apron on, and Toby on her hip, hands splayed out like starfish at the sight of his mother. A spicy waft of freshly baked Christmas cake floated through from the kitchen. "Eric! Turn off that television—we've got two visitors!"

"Hello, Toby," said Juliet, in her squeaky baby voice. Probably better to use him as a distraction. "Have you been making Christmas cake with Granny? Bit early for that, isn't it?"

"We're getting organized this year," said Diane, looking flustered. "Did some wrapping last night, didn't we, Toby? Look, here's Mummy! Have you two had elevenses yet? I'll put the kettle on . . ."

Louise held her arms out and Toby leaped into them. Her brave face crumpled, and she had to press his head into her shoulder so he didn't see her well up. Luckily, Diane didn't notice, already on the way to the kitchen to slaughter the fatted fruitcake.

"Do you want me to tell her?" Juliet murmured, and Louise shook her head. She looked determined, if tired.

"No, I will. It's my screwup."

She took a deep breath and headed toward the kitchen. "Mum," Juliet heard her say, "can I have a word?"

The kitchen door closed behind them.

Juliet went into the sitting room with Toby and the dogs, where her dad was watching an old episode of *Antiques Roadshow*.

"Hello, love," he said, when she sat down on the sofa next to him. Coco leaped up between them, and he patted her head absentmindedly. "Don't tell your mother Coco's on the sofa."

"I won't," said Juliet. "I won't tell her you've hidden your fudge in that Snack a Jacks bag either," she added, helping herself.

They sat in companionable silence, Toby playing with some boxes on the floor, oblivious to the dogs. Juliet forced herself to listen to the television, instead of straining her ears to hear what was going on in the kitchen. Was that a cry of horror? Sobs?

"Now that's a nice bit of pottery," said Eric, as an old lady pretended not to know that her commemorative Wedgwood bowl was worth "upward of a hundred pounds."

"Mrs. Cox has got three of those," said Juliet. "She lets her cat drink out of one of them."

"Really?"

"Really."

This is the whole point of family, she thought. *The security of a good dull conversation about* Antiques Roadshow. *Whatever's going on in the kitchen, Louise has got us. We'll close around her, the way they did for me.*

Juliet reached across Coco's solid back and put her arm around her father, pressing her head against his checked shirt.

"I love you, Dad," she said. "I'm glad you're here."

Eric made an embarrassed grunting noise and pushed the Snack a Jacks packet toward her. Juliet helped herself to an extra-large bit with chocolate on it.

Chapter 25

Juliet lowered the baking tray onto the kitchen table and inspected the contents for scorches, spreading, cracks, or weird floury bits where something hadn't mixed right.

There weren't any of the above. Just four lines of perfect butter cookies, golden brown, and neatly edged.

"Blimey," she said to Minton. "That's three in a row. Do you think I might be getting the old mojo back?"

Minton wagged his tail halfheartedly, but it was past midnight, and Juliet wasn't really expecting excitement from a dog that was usually in bed several hours earlier these days. Minton's late-night forays to Tesco were behind him.

She broke one of the hot biscuits in half, wafted it around, and then nibbled at it, burning her tongue. It tasted delicious, so delicious that she nearly cried with relief.

Juliet had been seized by a sudden need to bake at ten that night, after watching a program about some banker who'd given up her job to make gluten-free cupcakes that looked, to Juliet, as if they tasted of knitting wool. It was the first time since Ben died that she'd actually *wanted* to bake something; she didn't count the fruitless sessions she'd forced herself through. Scared of failing—because then she'd know she'd really lost it—she'd chosen a recipe she could make with her eyes closed, put on the late-night radio phone-in, and let her hands go through the motions.

The results sat before her on her stackable cooling racks: three stories of crisp butter cookies made with the cutters "Minton" had given her the Christmas he arrived—bones, Scottie dogs, kennels.

Juliet had churned out thousands of butter cookies over the years, cut and iced into booties, footballs, golf bags, wedding bells. But none of them tasted as good as these did, hot from the oven in the middle of the night, cooked with some dubiously out-of-date ingredients.

The rain spattered cozily against the kitchen window while the radio caller burbled on about the state of the bus station. Juliet leaned back against her unfinished kitchen cabinets and surveyed the mess of scales, bowls, and spoons around her. If it hadn't been the middle of the night, she'd have called Lorcan to give her a second opinion. He liked cookies. He'd eaten enough ropy ones over the past few months—he deserved some that had turned out right.

In fact, maybe that should be her next project: brownies. A lightbulb went on over Juliet's head. She should see if she could make better brownies than Lorcan's famous recipe, and get the Kellys to judge.

A smile spread over her face as she scribbled the shopping list on the chalkboard—more eggs, cocoa, flour, sugar. She contemplated pulling on her boots and going out now, to the all-night Tesco, her old haunt, but decided against it. Juliet didn't mind shopping during the day so much now.

And Louise. Louise could probably do with some biscuits too.

She pulled out her scales again, to make another batch while she was on a roll. It felt nice to be helping her family for a change, supporting them instead of being the one who needed propping up. She was still a widow, but some days Juliet was too busy being a sister or an auntie for it to be her first thought.

"You know what, Minton? I think I'm safe to go back to work," she said aloud, but as she said it, she immediately wondered if that was what she really wanted.

On the other side of town, Louise was curled up on her sofa, listening to the rain drumming on the roof of her conservatory. It was way past her bedtime too, but she was so far off falling asleep that she couldn't be bothered going through the bedtime motions.

She desperately needed a good night's sleep. She had to go in to work in the morning; three days off was about as far as she could stretch a mystery stomach bug when she was famous in the office for taking a case in court even when she was in the first stages of labor.

Should have made it a broken leg, thought Louise wryly. Susie from the NCT group was married to a doctor; she could have pulled in the sick note as a favor she was owed for that parking-fine advice.

As the thought wriggled across her mind, Louise blanched at the lie. She was on a truth purge now; not even white lies felt acceptable. But all she seemed to do these days was trot out little white lies, to keep everyone else happy.

The person she hated lying to most was Toby. Toby had asked for Daddy every night since Peter had stormed out, and she'd told him Daddy was away on a special business trip and that he'd be back soon. She wasn't sure how much he'd understood, but the anxious look in his baby-owl eyes made her feel horrible. Being with Mummy at home instead of being at the nursery wasn't much fun when Mummy was on the brink of tears the whole time and didn't want to leave the house.

Juliet had called every day, "to check that you're okay," and Louise had finally understood how frustrated Juliet must have been when everyone was doing that to her, forcing her to say, "I'm fine," when she obviously wasn't. Juliet had even dropped round to see if she wanted to join her and her collection of mutts on a head-clearing march around town, but Louise wasn't so sure the disaster she'd created could be sorted out by hauling a Labrador up a hill.

Her mum had called—more white lies about being fine; even Michael had called, late the previous night, after Toby was in bed.

Michael. Louise's stomach turned over. When she'd heard his voice, she'd felt an almost physical sadness, and all the smart things she'd been going to say in her letter slid out of her brain. He'd been apologetic, and sad, but he hadn't expressed any regrets, and he hadn't suggested meeting again.

She'd been sad too. Hearing his voice made her realize how much she missed his observations, his questions. In a different time, or a different place, they could have been best friends, maybe more. In some parallel existence, spiraling off in another dimension, maybe they *had* both decided to leave and she'd become that different person she'd always secretly wanted to be—funkier clothes, interesting parties, a husband who knew about land and history, not obscure programming codes she didn't understand.

As they'd spoken, Louise had wandered around the house and had found herself in front of her wall of wedding photographs. She and Peter, the new Mr. and Mrs. Davies, dancing at their reception, Juliet and Ben hand in hand at their own wedding, their parents beaming with pride at Toby's christening. Happy. Happy families.

I still want to be that woman, she'd thought, with a yearning that took her by surprise. The intensity of the feeling had burned away the last traces of longing for her parallel reality life, and as Michael had told her about Anna applying for full custody of Tasha, she'd realized she was listening, not fighting back jealousy.

Parallel Louise had drifted off into the realms of fantasy, trailing her fancy scarves and amusing friends, and real-life Louise had let the certainty of her decision settle inside her, anchoring her to the wooden floor of her home.

When Michael had rung off, Louise had sunk onto the sofa and cried for half an hour, from relief as much as anything else. Then she'd washed her hair and blow-dried it back into the smooth bob she used to be able to do in under five minutes.

That was last night. Tonight, no phone calls. Still no call from Peter.

The rain intensified on the conservatory roof and Louise considered the little bottle of American sleeping pills Juliet had given her, themselves an offering from her jet-lag-expert neighbors. She shook the bottle. Four in there. Not enough to "do anything silly," as her mother would put it. It was tempting to take one to help her get through the night, but if Juliet had resisted them with a dead husband, surely she ought to be up to coping with just a missing one? And then Toby was upstairs. She couldn't knock herself out with a baby in the house.

Louise's body was heavy with weariness, while her brain raced. She *needed* some rest. She had to face her mother in the morning when she dropped Toby off, and she'd want to know what was going on. Louise hated not knowing what to say. It made her feel so powerless, and this exhaustion was making her say stupid things.

Half a tablet. What harm would that do? It was no worse than a glass of—

A key turned in the door and Louise sprang to her feet, rushing through to the hall.

Peter was standing in the doorway, his hair plastered to his head, the shoulders of his mac soaked. He looked ten years older, tired and drawn. He hadn't shaved for a few days, and he had a loose sort of anger about him that she didn't recognize. He was carrying the squash bag he'd taken with him the night he'd left the house, and a suitcase she assumed he'd borrowed from his friend Hugh, with whom he'd been staying. Both bags looked empty.

As soon as Louise saw him, her lovely, quiet man, standing there in the house again, where he belonged, the carefully prepared list of points she'd made broke down under the tidal wave of words spilling out of her mouth.

"Peter, we need to have a proper talk," Louise gabbled. "I want to explain. I need you to understand how much you mean to me, how much our marriage means."

"Do you?" he said.

"Yes! I still love you. I *always* loved you. It's just that the last year and a half has been so hard for me, with Toby and maternity leave and everything. We're both always so *tired*. But it's normal for couples to go through rough patches. You read about it all the time; it's the hardest part of any marriage, the first few years with children. We have to readjust . . ."

Peter hadn't moved from the door, and when she took a step toward him, her hands outstretched, he shrank, and that hurt Louise more than a slap would have.

"Is that what you were doing?" he asked sarcastically. "Readjusting? On a park bench with some married man from the NCT group?"

"Yes," said Louise, riled out of her pleading by the steel in his tone. It hadn't *all* been her fault. "I was trying to work out if I was still a person or if I only actually existed as the mother of your child."

"What's that supposed to mean?"

"That you stopped talking to me like an adult, once you were back at work and I was stuck at home all day! All we ever talked about was Toby's routine, or what you'd been doing at work. I was going mad with boredom, but you didn't want to see. I didn't just turn into a different person when Toby was born, Peter. I'm still me!"

It was Peter's turn to look as if he'd been slapped. "So it was *my* fault you had an affair? Is that what you're saying?"

"No! But Michael listened to me. He made me feel I had something to say other than, 'Where are the baby wipes?' "

Peter flinched at the mention of Michael's name, and his face hardened, as if he too had gone off track with his prepared questions. "How many times did you sleep with him?"

The effort of controlling himself showed in the twitching muscle near his eye. He was hurt. Louise knew she'd hurt him, and her bravado slipped.

"It doesn't matter."

"Of course it matters!" Peter's eyes flashed. "How many times? And don't lie to me, Louise."

Louise's jaw tightened. She had a sudden flashback to the diving board she and Juliet had had to dive off at swimming club. Juliet had gone first, jumped off straight away. Even taken a run-up off the board, whereas Louise had counted the steps on the way up, picturing the drop increasing with each one.

There was no way back from this. It was going to hurt, but she had to be honest.

"Once," she said. "Once, and I knew I'd made a mistake."

As she spoke, Peter's shoulders dropped and his whole body

seemed to deflate. Louise realized he'd been hoping she'd say, *Never. We never slept together. It was just talking.*

"I'm telling you the truth so we can start again," she wailed. "I made a mistake! I made one stupid mistake, but now I know what a mistake it was, and I want to get some help so we can rebuild our marriage, because it means *everything* to me. Our family's all I've ever wanted . . ."

Peter pushed past her, heading for the stairs with his empty bags.

"Where are you going?" she yelled after him, then remembered Toby was sleeping in his nursery. "Don't wake Toby."

"I'm going to get some more of my things," he said, in a furious whisper.

"Don't," begged Louise. "Come home. We can talk about this and sort it out. I've found a counselor. We can get some . . ."

Peter spun round and glared at her. Even in the darkness he looked livid. "I can't bear to be here. The whole town has seen my wife gazing into the eyes of some other man, and you want me to be here playing Happy Families? Louise, you can organize most things in your life, but you *cannot* organize my feelings."

Louise recoiled, and Peter went into the bedroom and began shoving socks and pants into his squash bag, socks that she'd rolled up and filed into neat honeycomb segments.

"I'll come round tomorrow night after work to see Toby," he continued. "I don't want him to suffer. If you want to go out, that's fine."

"I don't," she said. "I want us to talk."

"Well, I don't. Not until I know what I think." He went over to the wardrobe and shoved in an armful of shirts, still on the hangers. The hangers were Louise's concession to her reduced ironing time. Before Toby, they'd been neatly folded and laid in the chest of drawers like tiles.

"Are you still staying with Hugh? Does he know? What did you tell him?"

"Seriously, Louise?" Peter turned and looked at her disparagingly. "Is that all you care about? What people will think about our marriage? Don't you think it's a bit late for that, now that everyone in town's had a good look at it?"

"No one will know it's me," she pleaded. "If it were so obvious, someone would have said something . . ." But she didn't believe it herself, and he knew it.

There was a grumble from Toby's room, the preliminaries to a full-on scream.

"Don't go in," said Louise. "It'll unsettle him to see you. I'll do it."

For a second, she thought Peter was about to go in, just to defy her, but he seemed to think better of it.

"I'll see you tomorrow, maybe," he said, and turned back to his packing.

With her heart aching, Louise went in to settle their son.

Chapter 26

As the days got shorter, Juliet's timetable got tighter, as she aimed to squeeze all her dog-walking commitments into the diminishing window of daylight hours between the misty mornings and the dark afternoons.

People were already talking about it being a white winter. She had to wrap up more every day, heading out across the frost-rimmed fields in her woolly hat and big coat, with socks inside her boots to keep her toes warm when it rained. And there was no choice about going out, whatever the weather; the gloomier it got, the more calls she had from fair-weather owners, but Juliet was so busy with the clients she had that she only took on new walkers if her regulars said yes.

Minton, Hector, Coco, and Damson didn't care about the drizzle or the chilly November air, barking at the plumes of white breath that billowed out of their mouths on cold mornings after their frantic ball chasing. Juliet soon found she was less bothered about weather conditions too. If it weren't for the dogs, Juliet wouldn't have noticed the rusty autumn color palette of the woodland ferns or enjoyed the crackling echo of dead twigs in the woods when she was the only person there.

She reckoned she probably *would* have been made to notice the extra effort the groundsmen had made in the park to keep the beds bright with flowers when the trees around the edge were losing their leaves—and she thought of Ben every time she checked in the *Spotter's Guide to Nature* she kept in her jacket. It didn't hurt quite so much to think of him now, or at least when she wished he were around to share a particularly gorgeous sunset, the pang was gentle and didn't make her turn away from it herself.

Juliet reckoned this was progress.

Shorter park hours meant longer DIY hours at home, and when she wasn't dog walking, she was sanding down doors or washing walls with Lorcan, who dropped in several times a week, around his other jobs.

Slowly the house was starting to look like a proper home, albeit without a lot of furniture. As Juliet pointed out to her dad when he came to trim the mountain rowan bushes, there were several places you could stand downstairs where it was fresh paint as far as the eye could see. A spare room upstairs was done, as well as most of the downstairs, barring the kitchen; that was a whole project, Juliet knew. Finishing the kitchen also meant finally she had some time to do a few shifts for Kim but only if they fitted in around her dog walking. Kim seemed fine with that, and Juliet was too, for the time being.

They hadn't decorated much upstairs because Juliet had been struck by a sudden squeamishness about the bedroom. Changing it would mean painting over the last traces of Ben, and decorating it to *her* tastes, not theirs. And it'd also mean spending time in there with Lorcan, with the great big elephant-bed in the room, lurking there as a reminder of both their complicated pasts.

It wasn't just her. Lorcan seemed loath to discuss colors or any building work upstairs, apart from sending a mate to inspect the ominous crack. Juliet dreaded hearing that there was some kind of major defect—a few months ago, it was the symbolism of a crack in her bedroom wall that haunted her, but now she was more worried about the actual state of her house.

"Plaster work" had been the verdict. "Just don't get a cowboy plasterer in this time."

It would have been nice to have her bedroom done for Christmas, but Juliet didn't push it, because frankly, things were busy enough as they were. Her afternoons felt like going back to school; the sky darkening outside as they worked, Lorcan teaching her new skills, and then the tea breaks they had, when they could sit back and admire the improvements, and he could eat her biscuits. So long as there were no burned bits, Lorcan would dunk it, and eat it, and compliment it. Their friendship had blossomed into a jokey, sometimes flirty, sometimes brotherly-sisterly one, and there were times when it almost tipped into something else, only for both of them to back off so fast it was hard to say who'd backed off first.

Still, she thought, on the bright side, the house was finally coming to life around her. Even if her dad was doing the garden and her next-door neighbor was doing the DIY, Myrtle Villa was starting to feel like her home.

Louise had always declined Diane's invitations to join her merry band of volunteer dog walkers on the weekends, on account of having better things to do with her precious time off than be hauled across the park by a pack of stir-crazy rescue dogs. She included cleaning, ironing, and watching Peter wash the car in that list. Frankly, anything above dental surgery would have been preferable to getting her jeans muddy and her coat hairy.

She'd also dismissed Juliet's claims that walking Minton had kick-started her brain after months of fuggy grief. Nice, but then surely anything was better than sitting around at home crying?

So it was with some reluctance—and disbelief—that Louise found herself steering Minton and Hector around the park with Juliet one nippy Saturday morning in early December. Juliet had Coco and a rescue shih tzu called Gnasher, and Diane was a good ten minutes behind them, thanks to a misbehaving pair of golden Labs.

If Peter hadn't taken Toby out for the day, leaving her at home with her claustrophobic thoughts, she'd never have agreed to it, but now that she was out, and the blood was pounding through her veins (Juliet kept up a professional's pace), Louise had to admit it was filling in the hours quite well.

Without pausing for breath, Juliet had been telling her all about her new downstairs loo, the one kitted out with a beautiful miniature washbasin that Lorcan had got for a song off a mate doing a warehouse conversion.

It hadn't been near a warehouse conversion, of course. Louise had found it, Diane had paid for it, and VictorianPlumbing.com had delivered it to the Kellys' house the previous week, ready for installation. At least Juliet was doing that bit herself, with Lorcan's help.

"I even got the wrench out and did the U-bend," she was saying, proudly. "Lorcan said he'd take me on as a plumber's mate, if I want another job to add to my portfolio. I've got good, strong wrists, apparently. You'd love what we've done, Lou. It's perfect, right down to the brass taps. I keep nipping in there, just to look at the mirror!"

Louise thought about telling Juliet where all the mysteriously convenient building supplies were coming from, but she looked so animated when she talked about her home improvement lessons that Louise didn't have the heart to spoil any part of it. The fact that Lorcan seemed to have magical access to everything she really wanted but couldn't quite afford normally was part of that.

"So are you and Lorcan . . . ?" she began, with a leading nudge, but the clouds reappeared in Juliet's face at once.

"No," said Juliet. "We're friends. I feel lucky to have made friends like Lorcan and Emer—I don't want to spoil it." She kept her eyes fixed on the ball she'd thrown for Minton. "Anyway, I'm not ready. I think it'd be really unfair to the other person. I'm not in a position to deal with anyone else's complications as well as my own."

"Is this about Michael?" Louise asked shrewdly.

"Michael's a nice guy, but I don't want to date him," said Juliet. "It's too weird. For you, for me, for him—nightmare. I'm walking Damson still, because she needs me, but . . . No."

Louise could see her casting about for a change of subject.

"So where's Peter taken Toby today?" Juliet asked.

"The petting zoo in Hanleigh." Louise yanked Hector's nose away from Gnasher's rear end for the tenth time since they'd left. "He's going to be there till three, so I've got to be back to change over."

"Change over?"

"He's going out again. With Hugh. He said he'd be back late—he might even stay over." Louise didn't add that she'd actually prefer that; it was better than putting up with the angry silence that hung between them whenever Toby wasn't around to witness his parents ignoring each other.

Peter had moved back in, moodily and for Toby's sake only, but the atmosphere in the house was glacial at best, hostile at worst. It was like living with a flatmate again.

Juliet turned to her and looked sympathetic. "How long's this going to go on, Lou?"

"This what?"

"Stop pretending. Mum's not here; she can't hear you. You and Peter—not talking to each other."

Louise stared straight ahead. The fur trim on her hood prevented Juliet from seeing the pain in her eyes, which was a good thing. In the end she'd weaseled out of telling Diane, and instead managed to convince her mother that the tension was just down to a tiff about her working hours and Peter's snoring, but Juliet was harder to fool. She had antennae for sadness now, and asked questions with a fearless directness that Louise was lacking herself these days in court.

"How long's he been home?"

"Three weeks."

"And you're still living like total strangers? With that . . . that *rota* he drew up for childcare? I don't know how you're coping. I'd be going mad. Wouldn't it be better if he just moved out properly for a while, to give you a chance to clear the air?"

"No! I don't want him to move out." Louise bit her lip. She hadn't told anyone else this. "He was going to rent one of those new-build flats by the hospital, just a studio, but it seemed so final. I went mad and told him to put the money into Toby's trust fund, not chuck it away. I don't want people knowing our business—you know what this place is like for gossip."

She sensed Juliet was looking at her, and she knew what she was going to say.

"Does it *matter* what other people think?"

"Yes," said Louise. "It does to me. People know me and Peter. I don't want them talking about us."

"You worry too much about what people think," said Juliet. "Look at me. My husband dropped down dead in the street at thirty-one. Front page of the paper one week and forgotten the next. You wouldn't be the first solicitor to be separated. Look at Mina Garnett. Her boyfriend moved out a while ago now . . ."

"Has he?" asked Louise, intrigued.

Juliet flushed. "Um, maybe I shouldn't have told you that. Anyway, how long can you keep this up? If you can't talk to each other, you should go to counseling and let someone else referee," she went on. "If you don't clear the air and work out what was wrong to begin with, you might as well stay locked up together in silence for the next fifty years."

Louise turned her head, surprised by the shift in Juliet's attitude and the supportive impatience in her voice. Impatience with Peter, not her. When they'd talked in the car outside Michael's house, she'd felt the disapproval coming off her sister in waves, despite the hug she'd doled out. She'd felt more chided then by Juliet's revulsion than by her own shame, and that was saying something. "You really think that?"

"Yes," said Juliet. "I've been thinking about it, and I think you were stupid, but . . ." She unclipped Coco's lead now that they'd reached the open part of the park where dogs could run around. One or two other walkers had already unleashed their hounds, and Hector was straining at the collar with excitement. "It has been pointed out to me that we don't know what goes on in people's marriages. And it's true. We don't."

"I didn't mean to hurt him," said Louise. "I never wanted that. But things weren't right. They hadn't been right for a while."

"So fix them."

"It's not that *easy*," she said, thinking of Peter's pride, his hurt silences. "He bottles things up. He's an only child, like Ben, you know. Hates talking. Won't come with me to Relate."

"Go on your own. He'll soon get himself along if he thinks you're getting a head start on the bitching."

Louise laughed. She'd forgotten how dry Juliet could be.

"Seriously, Lou," she said, and her voice was urgent, as if Diane might catch up with them at any moment, "don't let this go on any longer. I know you love him, deep down. I know he adores you. And you both adore Toby."

"Don't . . ."

"This'll make me sound like the mad auld widow of the West Midlands, and I don't care, but I can't let you dither around like this anymore. You know what the biggest regret of my life is? That the last proper conversation Ben and I had was a row. About something so silly and trivial I can't really remember what it was. And we weren't even rowing about that—we were really rowing about both of us wanting a baby, but me not being sure we could manage! So it wasn't even a proper row. It was a waste."

"I wish you'd told me that." Louise stopped walking and took her sister's arm. She could see Juliet's awful strained expression at the funeral in her mind's eye, and now it took on a different shade in her head. "Why didn't you tell me that?"

"Because I worried about what people thought." She raised her eyebrow. "And you know what? It didn't matter." Juliet's face was wretched, but she wasn't crying. "I felt guilty for so long, thinking you were judging me for moaning about him the night before he died, and really . . ."

"I never thought that," said Louise. "I was too busy worrying that I'd told you too much about Michael. I never doubted how much you loved Ben for one second. No one did."

Minton and Hector were straining at the lead, trying to follow Coco as she meandered around the fallen leaves, her gray muzzle twitching at the occasional smell. Juliet bent down to let them off, and they disappeared in a flurry of short legs. She didn't let the rescue dog off but patted his head and let him sniff her hand, rewarding his patience with a biscuit.

When Juliet stood up again, she pushed her fringe out of her eyes so Louise could see her properly. Her cheeks were pink with the cold air, and her brown eyes were very bright in her pale face. Louise couldn't help noticing she was wearing makeup for the first time in ages, a pretty dusting of green over her eyelids, the old Juliet flickering behind the sad exterior of the new one.

"What if Peter doesn't come home tonight? What if he's run over, or chokes on something at the petting zoo? What are you going to remember—the years of happiness you and he had, or this stupid silence? Talk to him. For God's sake." She paused. "On the surface, you've still got it all for everyone to admire. Nice house, nice husband, lovely baby. But what have you really got in the end, if you're not talking to each other? It's a shell. It's a *prison*."

Louise had never seen her sister like this: grown-up and cross and wise. "I will talk to him," she said, touched. "It's his birthday next weekend. He's thirty-nine."

"Well, make it one to remember," said Juliet, and offered her the manky plastic ball-thrower contraption. "Here, have a go with this."

"What do you do?" She took it gingerly, glad she was wearing gloves.

"You throw the ball and watch the dogs love you forever. Go on. It's life-enhancing for everyone. Forget the slobber."

Louise wasn't sure she could, but she aimed at the middle of the park and flung. The tennis ball catapulted out of the head with a gratifying flick and looped across the grass, sending the dogs into a volley of delighted barking as they raced to get it first. Hector's stumpy little legs flew, all paws off the ground at once, and their ears all bounced like puppies', even Coco's. Their simple delight of the chase was infectious, and Louise felt her mouth widening in a smile as Minton leaped several feet in the air to grab the ball as it bounced up high over Hector's head.

"See?" said Juliet, and Louise nodded in agreement.

Louise already had Peter's present in the spare-room wardrobe: a cashmere jumper, bought in the New Year sales and wrapped in green tissue paper.

She looked at it, parceled and labeled by her in January, then stowed away with a cedar ball tied to the ribbon to protect it from moths in the intervening eleven months.

I don't even remember doing that, she thought, amazed. But she could remember the compulsion to wrap and twirl the ribbons, to have her present drawer topped up, to have drawer liners in, in case her mum came round and her cupboards didn't look adult enough for a married mother of one.

What kind of a mad perfect housewife was I? she wondered. *How could I act as if the world were ending after Michael on one hand, and be buying birthday presents nearly a year ahead for my husband on the other? Maybe Juliet's only half right; maybe it's me who needs the counselor.*

She put her bag of new presents on the dressing table and began to wrap them in the same tissue paper from the present drawer. There was a lot of it, with matching ribbons, rosettes, and glitter.

It was Friday night. Toby had been dropped off at her mother's to keep up their pretense of Date Night, even though the last three had seen Peter go off to a film with his mates, leaving Louise lying in the bath, pretending to read a novel. Tonight, though, was going to be different.

Louise had gone into work—something she'd found herself

doing more and more, in order to keep up—but left early and come home via Waitrose for a selection of really nice food. She wasn't a great cook, but she was determined to make an effort, even if most of it was carefully reheated. There was a good bottle of wine chilling in the fridge, one of the ones he'd liked at the wine tasting at the White Hart, and she'd cleaned the kitchen and put fresh flowers on the table.

Her fingers moved deftly, parceling up the little gifts and dropping them into a bag, as she rehearsed what she was going to say as he opened them. She hadn't let herself consider what might happen if he just dumped his bag and went straight out.

Peter, if I could turn back the clock, I'd . . .

Peter, can't we just . . .

"Peter, I love you," she said aloud, and shivered, but the sound of the front door opening stopped her in her tracks.

Louise panicked. He was at least an hour early. She hadn't had time to shower or change or wash her hair or anything. And—she glanced anxiously at herself in the wardrobe mirror—she looked stressed and a bit creased.

For once she shoved aside her own appearance in favor of the bigger picture. She grabbed the bag of presents, ran a hand through her flat hair, and dashed down the stairs to find Peter hovering in the hall, flicking through the post. He hadn't taken his jacket off. Good sign, or bad?

"You're not going out tonight, are you?" she blurted.

"I might be going out for drinks with some guys from work," he said mildly. "Why? Did you have any plans?"

"Yes! I mean, I've cooked dinner. It's your birthday," she added, unnecessarily. "I've got you a present."

"You shouldn't have," he said. He sounded like meant it.

"Glass of wine?" asked Louise. "Go on! Go mad, it's that oaky Chardonnay you liked, from that vineyard that only employs female wine treaders for their dainty feet." She knew she sounded a bit demented, but she didn't care. If she got him into the kitchen, she was halfway there. Even if she ended up jamming a chair under the door handle, she was going to cook her husband dinner and apologize.

Peter smiled quickly, but it didn't reach his eyes. "A quick one."

"Great!" Louise ushered him into the kitchen and sat him down at the table. "Have a crisp. Or an olive?"

"Flowers?" he said, in a pretend surprised voice. "The good napkins?"

Louise flinched. She knew he was taking the mickey out of her reluctant reaction to his efforts at dates at home. It made her cringe, thinking of the obvious way she'd rebuffed his advances.

She struggled to hide her reaction. No point getting into a row.

"Of course! It's your birthday, isn't it? There you go," she said, putting the wine in front of him and pouring one for herself. "I've got you a few little things," she added, taking each present out of the bag and laying them in front of him, in order.

"What's this?" Peter took a big slug of wine and viewed the little pile suspiciously.

"Presents. For you."

"You *really* shouldn't have," he said. His face tightened. "I don't think presents are going to change what's happened. Do you?"

"It's not like that. I wanted to give you something from me," said Louise simply. "They're not expensive. Do you remember how we used to get each other really sweet presents, when we didn't have much money? This is . . . that sort of thing. Go on. Open the first one."

He started to say something, then changed his mind. Quickly, as if he were humoring her just to get it over with, Peter slipped the ribbon off the first long, flat parcel and unfolded the tissue paper.

Louise held her breath.

"Oh, it's lovely . . ." His face changed and he looked up at her, to show her he meant it. "It *is* lovely."

It was a framed photograph of the three of them, not one of the expensive studio portraits they'd had done above the optician's, but a snap Juliet had taken at their parents' house on her phone. Toby was on Peter's shoulders, laughing gleefully at Louise peeking round Peter's back. They were a little triangle of love, their eyes only on each other.

"Thanks," he said. "I'll take that to work. Put it on my desk."

Louise's smile wavered. "You know you and Toby are my whole world, don't you?"

"Toby, maybe." He wasn't looking at her.

"You too. I mean it, Peter. We just need some time together as a couple, to connect again. I've talked to Mum about taking Toby if you can get some time off to go away together, maybe Venice? Or just—"

"Is that another present?" he said, pointing at a small package.

She pushed it over, and he pulled off the ribbon, then the tissue.

Inside was a box of Pregnacare vitamins, tied to a box of Wellman supplements.

Peter looked sardonically at her. "Nice idea, but I think you need more than just the tablets to make a baby."

"I know." Louise swallowed, conscious of the nights she'd pushed him away, out of guilt. "It's to show you that I do want us to have another child. But I want to plan for it, and talk about it, so we don't end up driving each other mad like we did when Toby came along."

"We drove each other mad?"

"Yes, we did. We didn't talk about anything other than him; we let being parents take over our lives; I lost sight of who I was, and what you meant to me." Her mouth was dry and she had to lick her lips. "I don't want to make excuses, but I don't know what I turned into. It was as if I were two totally separate people—Louise at home with Toby, being a mum, and this other Louise, who just wanted some attention that didn't involve nappies. That's one of the reasons I was so desperate to go back to work, to make everything the way it was before. But now I know you can't do that."

"Oh, I know that now," said Peter, his voice tense and metallic. "I've tried, these last weeks. I've tried to pretend it didn't happen. I tried to blot it out of my mind, that photograph, knowing you wanted another man more than me, but I can't. It's changed everything."

"Not everything," said Louise. "It hasn't changed me loving you, or Toby being the most wonderful thing in our lives." She paused. This wasn't going right. He was supposed to be more thrilled about the baby idea.

Maybe I should just go, she thought, but Juliet's face floated up in her mind, urging her on.

She put the next present in front of him; this was the "proper" one. The one that she thought was really boring but that gadget-loving Peter had had on his wish list for ages.

"What's this?" Peter asked, unwrapping more crossly. "Oh great, sat nav."

He didn't sound that thrilled.

"You said yours was getting a bit out of date. Look, I've programmed it so this is home. So you'll always know where to come. Where we are." Louise knew she sounded desperate now.

"Thanks," said Peter. He checked his watch.

"One more." The final throw. Louise passed him a little box, wrapped up in a wonton knot of tissue.

He unfolded it; it was the ring box their wedding rings had come in.

"Oh God, Louise, not . . ."

"Open it."

He met her eye and sighed, wearily. Then, because he really had no option, he opened it.

Inside were tiny rolls of paper, jammed into the gaps where the rings had been.

"What's this?"

"Unroll them."

Slowly, Peter unrolled the scraps of paper and read the numbers and letters. "I don't get it."

"They're passwords," said Louise bravely. "To my e-mail, to my mobile, to my Internet banking, to my computer. Everything. I know I've broken your trust in me, and it's going to take a lot for you to trust me again, but I swear to you, I've got absolutely nothing to hide. You can check up on me anytime of the day or night—I don't mind."

"I don't want to police you . . ." Peter looked horrified.

"It's not about that. It's about me saying to you that you will never, ever have a reason to doubt me again." Louise stretched out her hands across the table, her eyes brimming with tears. She knew this was her last chance; their marriage, their lives together would turn left or right after this moment. "I've been so stupid, but I've never been more sure of how much I love you, Peter. You are the man I want to grow old with. If I lose you, I'll regret it for the rest of my life. Please, can you try to forgive me?"

Peter pushed his chair back, and for a sickening moment, Louise thought he was about to storm out. He stared at her across the table, almost unrecognizable as the awkward but quirky man she'd known in the early days, and her heart flickered with a nearly forgotten desire for his long, rangy body. She never wanted to see him so distracted and angry again, but part of her thrilled at the newness of a side she hadn't seen before.

Maybe she didn't know him inside out. Maybe there was hidden terrain to explore over the next forty years.

"You're not the only one who's been stupid," he said gruffly. "I didn't realize you were struggling. I thought just because you'd got everything under control you didn't need my help. I felt like I was in the way."

"How could you feel that?" Louise nearly yelped. "The more stressed I am, the more organized I get! Haven't you realized that? In all these years?"

"I stopped looking," he said. "I stopped asking."

He stood up, and Louise held her breath, terrified he was about to walk out. It sounded like an exit line.

But it wasn't. Peter reached over to where she sat and pulled her to her feet, wrapping his arms around her so their faces were close.

"I don't want to lose you," he said with a fierceness that surprised her. "And I never want to see you beg like that again."

Louise had no good line. She hadn't dared plan that far. Instead she kissed him with a hunger that neither of them had felt since their very early days, and the good dinner burned to a crisp, unattended, in the oven.

Chapter 27

Juliet didn't subscribe to the popular whine that Christmas started earlier and earlier every year, because for her, Christmas generally began in September, when she and Kim made their first round of corporate mini Christmas cakes.

But this year, without the cake reminder, Christmas had ambushed her as far back as October. The requests for holiday pet-sitting started to come in thick and fast, but she turned them all down, bar Hector—Mrs. Taylor was off on a cruise with Albert, her fancy man—and some feeding of Boris and Bianca for Mrs. Cox. Mrs. Cox was off on holiday too, to visit one set of grandchildren in Florida for Christmas, then on to another set in Tuscany for New Year.

"That's the joy of three husbands, my dear," she said, pressing "a little something" into Juliet's hand as a seasonal tip. "One lot of children of my own, then two sets of stepchildren make a nice clutch of grandchildren to take care of their old granny's holiday requirements."

"Three!" Juliet couldn't stop herself. She'd noticed the plethora of family photos, but not three wedding ones.

"All before I was sixty too." Mrs. Cox sighed and put her hand on her chest, her wedding-ring hand with the single diamond solitaire. "Bob died on active service when I was just twenty-seven, God bless him, then Lionel was in a car crash, and poor Walter had a blood clot. Life's not one long poem, Juliet. It's a book with a series of chapters. You're sad for a while; then you turn the page and see what happens next."

Juliet smiled and made a mental note to tell Louise. She'd never believe that nice, white-haired Mrs. Cox was a thrice-married siren. How had she never asked about that? The things you learned when you looked after people's pets.

She did wonder, as she was strolling back down the road with Minton, whether Mrs. Cox had been offering her some gentle advice, but the idea of her old piano teacher advising her about love was slightly harder to get her head around than Mrs. Cox's wedding-ring collection.

Juliet spent whatever spare time she had in the afternoons listening to cheesy Christmas albums and making enormous pans of chocolate fudge, marshmallows, and honeycomb. Now that her baking magic was back, she couldn't stop, and she had got her jam thermometer out to tackle her Christmas-present list.

Her dad always asked for fudge at Christmas, and both sets of aunties loved Juliet's shortbread, which she baked and packed in pretty tins. Louise pretended she didn't eat refined sugar, but she could go through a pan of marshmallow in the course of one *Mary Poppins* or two festive episodes of *Coronation Street*. Juliet didn't have a lot of spare money to spend on gifts, but she wanted to do something to make up for the gloom she'd cast over everyone's day the previous year. *This year,* she thought, *I can sweeten it up.*

A Willy Wonka gift box solved the problem of what to give the Kellys for Christmas. They weren't exactly a hard family for Emer to buy for—Roisin had made her need for a saxophone very clear for a while, and Spike wanted "a black-and-white pig"—but Juliet wasn't sure where their friendship had reached, in present terms. She also got the feeling that Emer's modest house (chosen, she now knew, for its proximity to Alec's parents, who had promptly moved to Dundee two months after the Kellys moved in) belied a sizable income, if the constant deliveries from Net-à-Porter were anything to go by. On her current tight budget, she didn't want to embarrass herself by handing over a Body Shop gift set only to unwrap a Mulberry handbag or similar.

The good thing about being a cook was knowing that generous jars of sweets always went down well, and it answered the other dilemma: what to give Lorcan. Juliet planned to make him an extra tin of biscuits, with different layers of the favorites he'd eaten over the last few weeks. She thought about putting a little note in saying, *Each "mmm" from you was a step on the road to kitchen recovery for me*, but though it was true, she couldn't find a way of putting it that didn't make it sound horrendously cheesy.

She was whisking rosewater and lilac food coloring into her third batch of marshmallows, listening to *Now That's What I Call Xmas*, when there was a knock at the back door, and Roisin and Florrie trooped in, closely followed by Lorcan.

"Are you cooking?" asked Roisin, her eyes widening at the sight of Juliet's pink K-Mix.

"I am confecting. Florrie, please can you keep any livestock in your pockets," Juliet instructed. "This is a nuclear sugar area."

"We've just come to deliver this," said Lorcan. "We're not stopping."

He nudged Roisin, who swept an envelope out of her pocket and presented it to her with a deep bow.

"What's this?" Juliet turned over the envelope and saw that it was from Florrie & Roisin Kelly, Laburnum Villa, the Grange, Rosehill, Near Longhampton, Worcestershire, the World, the Universe.

"It's a special invitation," said Florrie, solemnly.

"To my debut," said Roisin, with a dramatic flourish. "I'm the angel!"

Lorcan rolled his eyes. "Remember what we talked about, Roisin. You're *an* angel. Not *the* angel. And it's bad form to sing louder than the Virgin Mary just because you can."

"Salvador's in it too," said Florrie. "He's playing his bass in the band."

"The baby Jesus has a rock band now? That's very modern," said Juliet. "Are the Three Wise Men his backing group?"

"It's the school Christmas event," Lorcan explained as she opened the flap and pulled out the card. "Emer's allowed two parent places, plus a grandparent place—obviously we're a bit short on grannies next door, so she wondered if you'd like to come with us."

"You can hold the video camera," said Roisin graciously. "And be in the *entourage*."

"I'd be honored!" Juliet wanted to laugh, but she felt a lump in her throat as she read the painstakingly printed card, inviting "Dear Juliet and Minton" to a "night of Christmas cheer at St. Winifred's School." Roisin and Florrie had drawn angels in glitter, and, incongruously, giant plum puddings, plus a dog that looked like Minton with reindeer antlers.

"I don't think Minton can make it, though," she apologized to Florrie. "He has a very full social calendar this time of year."

"Say if you have too," Lorcan added. "It's not compulsory."

"What do you think I'd be doing?" she asked, amused by the idea that she'd be anywhere other than in her armchair.

"I dunno. But I don't want you to think *we* think you're short of dates coming up to Christmas." Lorcan stumbled over his words, trying to sound casual. "You might want to be out at parties, not hanging around schools with these attention-seeking eejits. And me."

"Lorcan, I'd only be hanging out with you anyway—here, with a paintbrush and the skirting boards. I might as well be at the school, listening to DJ Jesus and his angelz." Juliet pulled an excited face at the girls, who were waiting for her reaction. "It's years since I've been to a nativity play. I can't wait. It's going to be *mega*!" she added, in a bad impersonation of Roisin.

"I don't sound like that," howled Roisin, delighted.

Lorcan stopped fidgeting with his tape measure and grinned up at her from under his dark lashes. He had quite a shy smile, for a man who wore jeans as tight as he did, and Juliet felt a flipping sensation in her chest that reminded her so clearly of being at school that she could almost feel the braces on her teeth.

Immediately, she felt herself pull back as if she'd touched the sugar pan. Hadn't she learned her lesson with Michael? It was too soon. And now she knew it wasn't just her with issues to get over; there was even more reason to keep their friendship as it was—a lovely, supportive warmth in her life.

Paint fumes, she told herself. It was paint fumes and the holly-and-mistletoe effect of winter messing with her head.

"Well, prepare to be blown away," he said. "Emer's done the costumes. And she's had Alec send all the spare material from Spiderweb's last tours so they're not short of spangles in Bethlehem this year. Oh, no. The shepherds just have to follow the crackle of Lurex to the stable. I just hope the shepherds don't have candles."

"I have a light-up halo," said Roisin proudly. "Although Mrs. Barker doesn't know that yet!"

At four o'clock on the day of the nativity play, it started to snow.

It snowed so thickly that Juliet had to wonder if Alec had hired some stage-effects company to arrange it for the kids as part of their Christmas present. She'd got back from walking Damson in the park, where the bandstand was festooned with colored lights just beginning to glow in the dark, when the first flakes began to flurry around in the air, settling first on car roofs and postboxes, and the edges of the curbs, quickly turning the pavements dusty white, then more dense white and, within an hour, a matte blanket of crunchy softness over the whole street.

Lorcan knocked for her at six, while she was still deciding what to wear.

"You're not meant to be here for another half hour!" she yelled down the stairs as he let himself in with a "Hello?"

"I had to come. Emer's driving me mad, trying to decide what to wear. I mean, how hard it is to get dressed for a nativity play in a blizzard? You just wear everything you've got, right?"

Juliet thought it was quite endearing how little Lorcan understood about women, despite living surrounded by them.

She took a final look at her reflection and decided that she'd better go in the outfit she had on: a denim skirt, thick tights, and a soft green cashmere jumper Louise had given her, for no apparent reason. She thought it might have been a man's jumper by the way it fell off her shoulder, and it made her feel both small and warm, which was no mean feat.

It was nice to have her generous sister back, she thought. The big sister who'd tell you what suited you, but then buy it for you too.

"Pleeeease, are you ready to go?" Lorcan yelled up the stairs. "We've got a car coming in ten minutes. Emer wants the kids to arrive in style."

"Ooh, a limo?" Juliet ran down the stairs. "Rock-'n'-roll!"

"We'll be arriving on a snowplow if she doesn't get a move on. Oh!" Lorcan turned round from inspecting the last coat of paint on the radiator and did a double take. "You look nice."

"In this?" Juliet wasn't expecting compliments, not in that outfit, but she took them happily. "Thanks."

She grinned; Lorcan grinned.

Juliet felt her face redden and wondered if he was getting a bit of the old butterflies too. He was certainly looking at her in an appreciative way. He didn't look so bad himself, in a beaten-up leather jacket with a hoodie underneath.

Then Minton and Hector bustled up for a fuss and the moment was broken.

"I was going to take them to my mum's tonight, but I guess they'll be fine here," she said, pulling on her snow boots. "Minton's not a chewer, and I've got everything out of Hector's reach." She gave the dachshund the beady eye. "I hope."

"We thought we'd head out for a pizza afterward," said Lorcan. "Are you up for that?"

"Yes, please," said Juliet. "Lead on!"

It was strange how a night out at the primary school with next door was giving her more butterflies than an actual date.

The car that arrived to take the Kellys to the school wasn't the standard-issue Longhampton taxi. It was a huge black limo, with blacked-out windows, snow chains, and a driver in shades.

Emer was also in shades, and the most outrageously rock-chick outfit Juliet had ever seen her in. She teetered confidently out of the house in high-heeled Vivienne Westwood boots, a tight bandage dress, lots of scarves, and a full-length shearling coat that swept around the snow like something from Narnia.

Juliet's warm glow dimmed somewhat. She stared mortified at her worn snow boots, until Emer leaned across the seat and said, in a nervous undertone Juliet hadn't heard before, "Do I look okay?"

"You? You look amazing," said Juliet. "If I didn't already know you, I'd want to make friends with you at once."

"Oh, cheers. It's just that I never know what to wear, and I don't want to let the girls down." She sighed and took off her shades. Emer looked endearingly nervous, despite the fact that she was wearing emerald glitter on her eyelids. "The mums here have this cool uniform going on, sort of what you're wearing. Well, more or less. *This* is what the mums at their last place wore and I'm used to it, but"—she peered at Juliet's skirt—"flat shoes, knee-length denim . . . why can't I do that?"

"Really?"

"Really."

"I'll show you," said Juliet, patting Emer's knee. "Don't worry. You just need a padded vest. The rest'll follow."

"And they're all so *well behaved*," Emer went on, chewing her nail.

"We're here!" screeched Spike. He was the only Kelly in the car with them; Salvador, Roisin, and Florrie were backstage already.

Inside the school hall, the four of them took their places in the family row. The audience was already packed, and Juliet could feel all eyes on them as they inched their way past knees and handbags. It tickled her the way Emer swung between shyness toward the other mums and their obedient offspring, and habitual head tossing. It also tickled her the way everyone gazed at Lorcan with undisguised admiration, and then at her, with envy.

The lights went down, there was an expectant hush, and the angels started singing, and one voice carried through the mainly in-tune chorus. Only one angel was giving it the full Mariah Carey vibrato. And when the curtain rose to reveal three clouds' worth of baby-faced angels in tinsel halos and startling holographic tunics, only one of them was doing full jazz-hands interpretation of the song, much to the furious head shaking of the teacher on piano.

Emer beamed and zoomed right in with the video recorder, ignoring the mutterings of "*X Factor* . . . television today . . ." from the other parents.

"If that angel doesn't watch herself, she's going to get kicked off of that cloud," murmured Lorcan right into her ear, and Juliet's whole body tingled.

Juliet knew she hadn't had nearly enough exposure to nativity plays, because tears were running down her face from the moment the angel Gabriel appeared in the garden. Lorcan had to pass her a tissue from the mammoth supply in Emer's bag.

When Florrie appeared as the shepherd, carefully leading a pair of lambs, ably played by two white West Highland terriers that Juliet recognized as Jock and Aggie from the park, Lorcan himself was in tears and they sniffed in unison right through to the grand finale, in which Sal's bass guitar was in direct competition with his sister's improvised soprano wailing over the rest of "Little Donkey."

As Mary and Joseph took their bow, Emer, Lorcan, and Juliet leaped to their feet as if they were at the Royal Albert Hall. Emer let out a piercing wolf whistle, while Lorcan made a sort of rock howl that caused everyone to turn round to look at them. Juliet didn't care. She was bursting with pride at Florrie, and Roisin, and Sal, and the rest of her adopted family. It was only when Roisin started making heavy-metal devil horns from the back of the angel chorus that she decided it might be better to whisk them out, rather than let Roisin milk the encore.

The limo driver had waited in the car park, still in his shades, and he swept the seven of them out of the car park to the clear envy of the dads trying to reverse out of the snow.

Half an hour later, they were installed in the best booth table at the Pizza Parlor on the High Street, covered in garlic butter and watching fresh snow swirl against the windows as the Christmas lights glowed outside, looping electric paper chains across the road, back and forth, red and yellow and green.

"So, where are you having the big day?" asked Emer, as the pizzas came.

"My mum's. I'm cooking."

"*You're* cooking?" said Lorcan. He raised an eyebrow, the only person who really knew about her struggles to get her enthusiasm for the kitchen back.

Juliet nodded. "I've been practicing. In fact, you might find Santa has a sweet tooth this year."

"Good for you," he said quietly, and gave her a gentle kick under the table. Juliet blushed, unaware his leg was so close.

"So when were you thinking Santa might drop round?" Emer asked, picking daintily at a salad. "Only we need to get you over for a Christmas drink before we go."

"Go?" Juliet's fork froze, halfway to her mouth. It hadn't even crossed her mind that the Kellys wouldn't be next door for Christmas.

"We're going to Ireland to spend time with the family," Roisin informed her. "And then Mum and Dad are going off to New York for some *special bonding*." She made an *Ooooh* face, which Spike copied, to Florrie's mortification.

"We always get New Year to ourselves somewhere special," said Emer. "I look forward to it from about January ninth. Alec uses it to earn credits for the first half of the year, so it's amazing. This lot get to stay with their cousins out in the west. And if you think they're bad . . ." She rolled her eyes.

Juliet couldn't imagine.

"And are you going out there?" she asked Lorcan, as casually as she could manage.

"Haven't decided yet," he said. He sliced up his pizza, then rolled it into thick chunks for easy dispatch. "I'm keeping my options open. There's a gig I could go to in Dublin, or an all-nighter in Cork that's always good *craic*. And I've a mate runs a bar in Edinburgh, so I might head up that way."

Juliet felt sad that he hadn't even considered staying in Longhampton, but then why would he? she argued. New Year was a time for being on your own and thinking, as she would be, or being with your mates and getting hosed, like Lorcan. And if you were going out on the lash, there were a lot better places to do it than here, especially if you had contacts in roadie gangs all over the country.

"Or there's always here," said Emer, cutting her a sideways glance.

"No, Longhampton's shocking at New Year," said Juliet quickly. "Once you've seen the mayor doing 'Auld Lang Syne' wrong on the town-hall balcony, you've seen it all. I bet New Year's a lot more fun in Ireland than it is here."

"That depends on the—" Lorcan started, but a wail from Florrie cut him off.

"Salvador's put ice in my hoooooood!" she wailed.

"And you wonder why I try to get a whole week at New Year?" Emer asked Juliet, her eyebrows raised right up into her hairline.

Roisin banged her spoon on the table. "Ice cream. Roisin Kelly wants ice cream!"

As they left, Roisin and Salvador bundled along with Emer, shrieking and chucking snowballs into the air. Florrie slipped her small hand into Juliet's to walk down to where the limo was parked, and Juliet felt a tug of affection for the quiet little girl.

She looked down and smiled. Florrie smiled back and didn't say anything.

Juliet felt another hand take hers, a bigger hand this time.

It was Lorcan. He held it up, and held up his other, which was holding on to Spike.

"Break dance!" Juliet said, doing an old-school swoop along the line.

The children laughed and made the ripple go back and forth, but when they saw the limo's lights ahead, they broke free and ran toward it.

Lorcan didn't let go of Juliet's hand. "Better keep hold of you," he said. "Slippy pavements and all that."

Juliet didn't contradict him. And she didn't let go of his until they were safely at the van.

It was going to be a very long week without the Kellys.

The snow lingered, thickening itself each night, ready to defy the forecasters the next day. It looked like it was going to stick around until Christmas, much to the delight of the Kelly children, who already had all of Led Zeppelin and Queen recreated in snowman form in the back garden.

Juliet dropped her jars and ribbon-tied parcels of sweets round one morning before her walks. When she got back, there was a small box on the doorstep, cocooned against the snow in a plastic Waitrose bag.

Juliet stamped the snow off her boots and took the whole thing through to the kitchen to unpack it. It was very heavy, and she realized to her disappointment that the Kellys had gone off, en masse, going by the scribbled list of "please, please, please favors," including the feeding and care of Smokey the cat and Florrie's menagerie of small pets, along with a roll of notes to pay for it all.

The card inside the bag was a proper American-style Christmas portrait of the whole family dressed up in costumes. Salvador was a drummer drumming, Florrie was a swan a-swimming, Roisin was a maid a-dancing, Spike was a French hen, Emer was five gold rings, and a baffled Alec was a partridge in a pear tree.

Inside it read, *To our lovely neighbor and pet-sitter. Thanks for putting up with the madness. Rock-'n'-roll, the Kellys*. Everyone had signed it.

There was a bottle of Emer's sloe gin, a bag of ludicrous handmade organic dog biscuits from Harvey Nichols, and a fabulous Pucci scarf "so you can put some wow into bow-wow walking."

Juliet had never worn a scarf, but she decided this was the year she'd start.

The box, though, was separate, and unwrapped. It was also very heavy.

Juliet took it out carefully and slit the Sellotape holding the top edges together. She pulled it open and took out the folded note on the top of the shredded paper.

It read:

Found this for you and the house. Have been hunting for the right size and shape for ages. You should be really proud of what you've done this year. I've never worked with such a talented builder.

May next year be full of openings and opportunities knocking on your door (get it?!).

Love from Lorcan

His handwriting, though messy, was bold, half printed, half cursive; somehow reminiscent of Lorcan himself. She smiled at the compliments, although she wasn't sure she deserved them; he'd been the one who'd done most of the work.

She put her fingers into the shredded paper and felt something cold and metallic. Slowly, she lifted out a beautiful brass door knocker, polished and restored to a burnished sheen.

It was a beautiful thing, made of liquid curves and dappled with age. It was even nicer for being so personal. Lorcan must have spent ages cleaning it up, back into the condition in which the original buyers must have found it. Juliet felt her chest tighten with emotion as it warmed in her hands, releasing a sweet, musty smell of polish.

Ben would have loved this, she thought, already seeing it on the front door, shining against the new red paint. It had a *something old, something new* quality to it that summed up the slow reawakening of Myrtle Villa.

It's time to welcome people into my house, she thought. *All I need on New Year's Eve is a tall, dark handsome man with a lump of coal and some whiskey.*

It was a shame that the man who fit that description was so far away.

Chapter 28

Christmas Day followed the pattern of all Christmas Days at Diane's house, barring the previous year's subdued gathering. When Juliet arrived at nine A.M., she was comforted to see that the Buck's Fizz was already separating in the glass jugs, and *Carols from King's* was soaring magnificently in the background. Despite the early hour, the tin of Quality Street chocolates sat open on the sideboard, with seven green triangles probably removed and in Diane's secret drawer for later.

Juliet had come with a full vanload: The trays of foil-covered food she'd prepared the night before were in the back, along with the bags of presents, all safely packed away from Minton and Hector. Both of them were sporting festive collars and had been walked around the block before breakfast to avoid any "giddiness" in the face of wrapping paper.

Diane already seemed slightly tipsy on Buck's Fizz when she opened the door, and Juliet took a step back as the blast of warm air hit her. For some reason, lost in the mists of time, her mother always turned the heating up a couple of notches on Christmas Day, which wasn't helping her flushed cheeks.

"Merry Christmas!" she cooed, weaving a little bit. "Oh, you are a good girl," she added, seeing the trays. "Your father's been looking forward to this for weeks!"

"Well, I hope it's worth it," said Juliet. "I feel like I've been in an episode of *Animal Hospital.*"

Eric appeared behind his wife, also glowing in his Christmas shirt. It was red, with reindeer on the collar—a gift from Ian in Australia. Normally Eric only had to wear it for ten minutes, for the family photo, but now that they were doing videoconferencing, he was stuck in it all day.

"Merry Christmas, Dad!" said Juliet. "Or should I say, Santa?"

"Ho, ho," he said, deadpan. "Merry Christmas. Shall I take those off you?"

As Juliet and Eric ferried her cargo of food, presents, and dog stuff, Juliet felt a strange mixture of emotions. It was nice to be drawn back into the familiar rituals of their family Christmas—the terrible jokes, the way her mother would try to force a salmon roulade down her at any moment, despite its being before breakfast—but there were gaps where Ben should be. He was the one who laughed at Dad's jokes and always choked down a couple of awful prawn appetizers.

Instead it was just her. *I need to make my own rituals,* she told herself, filling in the ache with some positive thinking. Like the lovely prebreakfast walk with Minton and the croissant she'd savored this morning. That could be a start. Other people could join in if they wanted.

And Boxing Day. She could do a Boxing Day tradition—was there some tradition she could borrow? What did they do in Ireland? Lorcan would have some Guinness-based suggestion, no doubt.

The thought of Lorcan's cheery company made her miss Emer too. It would have been nice to escape round there afterward, to pick at their enormous spread and loosen her buttons on their big leather sofa.

Juliet's mental slideshow abruptly shifted to the chaos that would be created by four Kelly kids, plus unlimited sugar, plus a visit from Santa, plus Emer, all her family, and the drinks cabinet, and she changed her mind. Maybe her real Christmas treat was her tranquil, finished sitting room.

"Where's Lorcan gone for Christmas?" Diane asked, as she decanted the potatoes into the pan, ready for roasting. "He could have come here."

"They've all gone to Ireland, to Emer's mum in Galway," said Juliet. "Then Alec and Emer are flying to New York for New Year, and I think Lorcan's going to some gig or other in Dublin."

"Ah. Is Lorcan not seeing the new year in with a friend?" Diane raised her eyebrow meaningfully.

"He's seeing it in with several friends." Juliet didn't look up. "It's a reunion of his old road crew. He'll probably turn up here on January second with a new tattoo and a weeklong hangover."

"He's a nice man . . ." Diane began, and Juliet knew where this was going.

"He's a lovely man, but he's got a lot of baggage," she said firmly.

"Really? What sort?"

"Enough," said Juliet. "Meaning that together we have enough to restock Left Luggage at Heathrow. I don't think it would help either of us."

"You mean you've discussed—"

"Hello! Hello!" The sound of Louise arriving was drowned out by Diane's squeals of excitement as Toby thundered into the kitchen, dressed in a plum-pudding outfit, his chunky little legs sticking out of the bottom in white tights.

Louise herself appeared moments later, in dark jeans and a long cashmere cardigan the color of holly leaves. Peter followed behind, freshly shaved and carrying a couple of bottles of champagne. The overall effect was very "magazine Christmas special."

"Hello, all!" he said, raising one of them in salute. Juliet noted that the wedding ring was back on. So was Louise's. Also back in place was Louise's glowy family smile, though without the touch of manic Stepfordness that had crept in lately.

She just looks happy, thought Juliet. And that was something she didn't take for granted anymore.

The morning sped past in a blizzard of presents and wrapping paper, chocolates and glasses of Buck's Fizz, and Juliet was glad to escape into the kitchen for most of it, her nerves steadied by her countdown list and every single one of her mother's pans.

It wasn't the most complicated meal she'd catered—a crown-turkey roast for five adults, a toddler, and three dogs—but it was the most satisfying to dish up, even if the potatoes were a bit overcrisp and the carrots wouldn't have passed Kim's al dente test.

"That is the best. Christmas. Dinner. Ever," said Peter, pushing his chair away from the table after the final helping of trifle. He patted his flat stomach appreciatively.

"To the chef," said Louise, raising her glass.

"And absent friends," added Diane quickly, and Juliet raised her glass too. She was drinking apple juice. She didn't really want to get weepy today, and having to drive the van back was a convenient excuse.

"Time for a nap, I think," said Eric, putting his napkin on the table.

"Oh, no, you don't," said Diane. "We've got to call Ian! In Australia!"

"So we have," Eric said heavily. "In that case, I'll just go next door and start tidying the living room." As he squeezed past Juliet, he gave her a friendly wink, which she pretended not to see, in return for his not drawing attention to the roast potato she was feeding Minton under the table.

While Juliet and Diane had been clearing the remains of the meal, and Louise coaxed Toby to have a nap in his travel cot, Peter had brought Diane's laptop down from her study (previously the spare room) upstairs and had set it up on the television, for the full-screen effect. It had taken him a suspiciously long time—nearly the entire time that Diane, Louise, and Juliet had been locked in a tedious discussion of various relatives—but now the laptop was ready for the ceremonial Christmas message from Ian.

Juliet heard the Skype tone ringing first, because she'd been standing shivering in the garden, supervising a three-dog loo break, and was sneaking into the sitting room for a rifle through the Quality Street.

"Mum! Louise!" she yelled. "Ian's ringing!"

She clicked on the green pickup button and Ian's face appeared on the television. He was even more tanned and had lost some more hair since last time, but his polo shirt was virtually bulging with antipodean good health. Juliet couldn't help noticing that he'd set up the Skype so there was a magnificent view of the beach in the background. Was it too late to turn their camera away from their lopsided Christmas tree? she wondered.

"Hey, Juliet! How's it going?" he asked, in a ridiculous Aussie twang.

"Give over, Ian, you're not in *Neighbors*," she said cheerfully.

"And a merry Christmas to you too," he replied, more Englishly. "Hey, Louise! How're you doing?"

"Good, thanks," said Louise, bouncing an emphatically not-sleepy Toby in her arms. "Look, Toby, it's Uncle Ian! Look at his lovely plasma-screen television!"

Juliet shot her a sideways look. The trouble with Skype was that you couldn't roll your eyes while you talked, and a bit of eye-rolling was mandatory with most family conversations.

"Is that Dad?" Ian asked, as Eric tried unsuccessfully to sidle past the camera. "Hey, Dad! How's it going?"

Juliet pulled Louise to one side and put Toby's high chair firmly in front of the camera.

"Isn't he looking like Dad?" Louise muttered under her breath to Juliet as she installed her son in it.

"Does that mean we've started looking like Mum?" Juliet muttered back.

"No," said Louise. "Mum! Stop washing up! Ian's on."

"What? You didn't tell me!" There was the sound of a baking tray clattering onto the stove, and Diane appeared at the door, pulling off her rubber gloves and fluffing up her hair. One year, Juliet decided, Mum would actually engage a hair and makeup artist for this Christmas Day broadcast.

"Dad, come on." Louise marshaled everyone in front of the computer, and they stood awkwardly around behind Toby, who wriggled vainly in search of escape.

"Hello, Ian!" Eric yelled, as if the satellite were voice-activated. "Can you hear us?"

"Yeah! Totally! Hi!" he said, and the image pixilated as he waved. "Vanda! Vanda, come on, get the girls . . ."

Vanda, Ian's wife, and Bethan and Taya, their little girls, appeared in front of the screen. Bethan and Taya were thirteen months and four respectively; they were miniature versions of Vanda, with blond mops of hair and brilliant smiles.

"Hi!" they chorused, waving at the screen. They were all wearing reindeer antlers.

"Hi!" everyone chorused back.

"So, what's been happening?" Ian asked.

Louise took that as her cue to start reeling off Toby's latest achievements at nursery, interspersed with some proud nods toward Peter, and Juliet started to zone out a bit. She didn't mind not talking about herself; it was nice not to be the center of attention for once. Ian could see her, could see that she was fine; she didn't really want to discuss her ongoing struggle with widowhood on Christmas Day.

She glanced down at her feet, where Minton was lurking, never far from her side. He looked ready to escape for his walk; his internal walk timer seemed to know there weren't many hours of daylight left.

Not long now, mate, she mouthed at him. That was the joy of dogs: You never needed an exit strategy when you had a poo bag.

Her dad nudged her in the ribs. "I'll come with you," he muttered. "You can't manage three dogs on your own. And, er, there's something your mother and I need to tell you . . ."

Juliet was about to point out that she managed at least three, usually four, every day when her attention was dragged back to the laptop by Vanda's excited voice, chipping in over Ian.

"So, we can't wait to see you here!" said Vanda.

The trouble with these group Internet conversations was that you were never quite sure who was talking to whom, thought Juliet. Vanda seemed to be staring right at her, and it would be rude to pretend otherwise.

"Who? Me?" Juliet pointed to herself. "Vanda, I'm not coming. We didn't book the tickets in the end."

"No, not you, Jools. Your mum and dad!" Vanda's friendly face nearly split in half with her dazzling smile. She had lovely teeth, almost as lovely as her butterscotch tan. "We've got the taxi already to get you, Diane—neat way of missing out on the New Year's Day hangover, eh?"

Juliet wished there were an option to look at the screen Ian and Vanda were seeing, because she had a strong sense that it was a classic. She wouldn't have been surprised if Louise had keeled over backward like a felled tree.

Behind her, Diane was making spluttering noises, then snapped, "Eric!" presumably to stop her dad slinking off.

"Mum!" Louise, again, behind her, managed to sound outraged and hurt simultaneously. "You're going to Australia? Since when?"

"Since they decided to come out on holiday . . . then offered to stay for when daughter number three arrives!" Ian looked ecstatic. "Oh wow! Quick, Vanda, do a screen capture! Quick! Ah, fantastic, that's one for the wall, all right!"

"Congratulations," said Juliet, since nobody else was saying anything. Nothing properly audible anyway.

"We're so thrilled your mum and dad'll be here," said Vanda, and this time Juliet knew she was being directly addressed, since Diane, Louise, Peter, and Eric were locked in a babbling competition with each other, slightly to the side of the laptop. "It's just so much for me to cope with, two little ones and the business and everything. I've had a few complications, and with my own mum and dad not being around anymore, God bless them, I was really at my wits' end."

"So how long are they staying?" Juliet tried to do some math in her head, but she had no idea how pregnant Vanda could be.

She was a personal trainer; she'd power-walked herself to the labor unit last time.

"Well, for a few months after the baby comes, but your dad's booked open-ended tickets, so we'll see, won't we, hon?" said Vanda, blithely unaware of the fresh round of gasps this set off behind Juliet. "It's not like we'll be on top of each other now that the granny flat's finished in the garden."

Juliet heard Louise repeat, "Granny flat," and didn't want to look round to see what expression accompanied it.

"As soon as they ring off, let's take the dogs out," muttered Eric, and Juliet fixed her grin and nodded.

Longhampton's main streets were already grimy with slush where Christmas-morning family pilgrimages to Granny's had churned up the fresh snow, but the municipal gardens were relatively untrodden. When Eric pushed the gates open for Juliet to let Minton, Coco, and Hector in, it looked like a winter wonderland.

Thick snow lay over the low hedges and flower beds like plump pillows, with the ornate bandstand, frost sparkling on its wrought-iron finials, rising up in the middle of the park like a musical box that might open up to reveal a sugarplum ballerina spinning on its roof. One or two brave robins hopped on the bare branches of the snow-heavy trees, and the sun glittered over the whole magical scene. It just needed a giant Santa on a sledge parked across the bowling green, thought Juliet, and it would be like one of Mum's Christmas cakes.

She paused for a moment to let the picture-postcard view sink into her memory, taking its place alongside her older memories of the town. *You couldn't take a photo of this*, thought Juliet. *You couldn't capture the tang of the chilly air, or the stillness, or the intense whiteness of the snow, but when I look at the bandstand now, I'll think of this. Because I was here, in this second now.*

"Would you look at that," said Eric, with affectionate surprise. "Who'd have thought this scruffy old town could look so magnificent?"

Juliet smiled. Her dad thought Longhampton was so "scruffy" he'd lived there his whole adult life, brought up his family, and never moved away from its modest charms.

"I've been here every day for nearly six months now, and I don't think I've ever seen it looking so gorgeous," she said, then added, "Ben'd go mad if he could hear me saying that. I mean, look—no plants! No trees!"

"He'd love to hear that you'd been here every day for six months," said Eric. Juliet loved the way her dad could put his finger on things, without any of the hushed mawkishness that crept over some of her mother's observations about Ben. She felt closer to Ben in this park than she did in their unfinished house sometimes.

"Shall we . . . ?" she said, not wanting to bring the mood down, and felt better immediately as they set off again.

Out of habit, she and Minton turned clockwise, working their way around to where the coffee stand usually sat at the foot of the hill. A few brave souls had been out already, and Juliet noted the selection of big and small Wellington-boot prints, as well as the variety of paws pressed into the snow.

"How long have you and Mum been thinking about this trip?" she asked, since they were on their own. "Why didn't you say? Why leave it until a few days before you left?"

"Because we hadn't actually made up our minds. We wanted to see how you were this Christmas." His shoulders hunched; big emotional conversations weren't really his field. "The books said some widows have a relapse around now, and we didn't want to leave if you were in a low way. And all this business with Louise . . ."

Juliet shot him a sideways look. "What business?"

"Oh, I know all about it. I'm not daft. Or deaf. We didn't want to go away with her and Peter not speaking."

"But that seems okay now."

"It does. Thank God." He eyed her cautiously. "And are you . . . ?"

"Fine. I'm fine," said Juliet. "But how long have you been planning it? You can't just head off to Australia for six months on a whim."

"We've been talking about going away for quite a while now." Eric looked rather shame-faced. "When Ian came back for the funeral, he was saying how much he and Vanda hoped we'd go over and spend some time with his girls. We're getting on a bit now, and he doesn't want them to miss out on the chance to get to know us. And for us to get to know them, of course. And"—his eyes twinkled under his hat—"don't take this the wrong way, but it'd be nice for your mother to have a bit of a holiday too. She needs a break, what with all she's had to cope with this year."

"So *you're* having a second honeymoon."

"Well, it's our first. We only got a couple of nights in the New Forest, first time round." Eric sighed nostalgically and offered her some fudge from his pocket. "Have some of this excellent handmade fudge. It's very exclusive."

"Thanks, I will," said Juliet. She knew it was excellent; she'd made it herself. "None for you, Coco," she added, as the dog looked up at the rustle of the packet. "That's why you had to have your teeth scraped. *Dad*."

He stuffed the bag within easy reach and carried on. "To be honest with you, love, your mother's been wanting to go since Bethan was born," he said. "But then Ben died, and you needed her, and when you started to rally round, Louise wanted to go back to work and then Toby needed her."

"You're making me feel awful," said Juliet. "Like we've been stopping you from doing what you want."

"Don't be daft," he said. "It's what parents are for, looking after their young 'uns."

He touched his hat and Juliet smiled as they passed Wild Dog Café owner Natalie and her basset hound, Bertie, walking in the other direction. She was arm in arm with a tall, good-looking man—her husband, Juliet presumed; that was a new bit of information to discover for the new year.

"Anyway," her father went on, "we've saved up a bit since then, and we'll be able to make a decent holiday of it. Between you and me, I've always fancied seeing Australia properly. We're not going to spend all the time there with Ian. Well, I'm not. We're going to get a camper van and do some traveling."

"So *that* was why you didn't sign up for a course this year."

"Rumbled." He sighed. "Nothing gets past you."

It was all falling into place now, thought Juliet, much like an episode of *Murder, She Wrote*. "And why Mum's had her hair done and got new glasses and generally looks like she's having a new lease on life, despite looking after Toby during the week."

"What did you think she was up to?"

"I guess I didn't . . ."

"It's nice to have a project," interrupted Eric. "It's given us both something to talk about. Something to plan." He looked over at his daughter, his nose red with cold beneath the tweed cap. Juliet tried to imagine that nose on Bondi Beach, smeared with zinc cream, and failed. "We don't just spend our days walking the dog and watching television, you know. We have a life."

"*I* walk your dog," Juliet pointed out. She tucked her arm into his, to show she didn't mind. "And I suppose she'll be coming to live with me, will she? So you two can go off gallivanting. It's okay. I understand. It's like going to boarding school, isn't it, Coco?"

Eric patted her hand, and they walked on, enjoying the crunch of the snow beneath their boots. When he spoke again, there was the slight catch in his voice that Juliet heard only when he'd had an extra glass of whiskey at Christmas.

"You two girls are the most important thing in our lives. And Ian, of course. But we've got to the stage where we're thinking about doing things for the last time. We want to make the most of these years, your mother and me, before we're too incontinent to get on the plane."

"You're not *old*," Juliet started, but she knew what he meant. "Anyway," she said, "you don't have to be old to worry about doing things for the last time, do you? It's my New Year's resolution—to *do* things, and not wait."

"Sounds interesting," he said. "What are you going to do? See the world? Change jobs?"

"Well, I haven't decided yet," admitted Juliet. "But I'm not going to say no to things. That's my main resolution. Not saying no."

"It's a good place to start," her father agreed. He paused. "Although I still say no boys with motorbikes."

"Okay, Dad," said Juliet.

There were one or two other escapees from the Christmas table, using their dogs as an excuse to have a crafty cigarette, in the case of the Man with the Airedale, and sneaky phone conversation, in the case of Teenager with Scottie Dog. Juliet smiled and wished the owners a happy Christmas, as Hector, Coco, and Minton sniffed around the dogs and let them pass.

"I'm guessing that dog belongs to his granny," Juliet muttered to her dad, as the teen shuffled past, the phone disappearing into his hood and the sooty Scottie nearly disappearing into a drift.

"He's called Hamish, and she has a tartan shopping trolley to match his coat—he sometimes rides in it. Minton thinks he's a bit soft."

"Sounds like you and Minton have made some new friends," said Eric.

"I suppose we have," said Juliet.

They walked round the perimeter path in easy silence as the sun faded and the dark pallor of winter afternoon began to shade the white banks of snow. When they reached the wrought-iron gates that led back into the main street, the colored Christmas lights had started to glow against the leaden sky. Red and yellow starbursts, suspended above the road.

Eric stopped, and Juliet knew from the anxious knit of his forehead that he was about to deliver whatever it was he'd actually come out with her to say.

"Juliet, love, please tell me the truth. If you think you're going to struggle, we won't—" he began, but she stopped him.

"No," she said. "I want you to go. I want you and Mum to fly out there and travel and stay out for as long as you like." Tears were forming in the back of her throat, thinking about her parents and their well-worn, comfortable love having its final glorious fling under the Australian sun. She could see them holding hands in a camper van, discovering new things together after so many years.

They'd been together since they were just fresh-faced, inexperienced kids at school too, like her and Ben. Would she and Ben have been setting off on an adventure at their age, after grandchildren, jobs, all the wear and tear of a life together? Would their love have struggled through the rough patches? Juliet wanted to believe it would, even if she knew, now, that that door had closed forever.

"I wouldn't have got through this last year if it hadn't been for you," she said. "Mum making me eat and forcing me to get outside.

You dealing with all that paperwork, keeping the garden under control. But I'm going to be fine. Louise is going to be fine. You brought us up to face our problems and we will. It's time for you to put Mum first. You and Mum."

"Juliet . . ."

"Haven't finished." She gulped, trying to keep her voice steady. "And if you fall in love with the place when you're out there, stay. Have an adventure together. Don't come back for us. This is time for you two now. You've earned it."

She looked up and saw that her father's pale-blue eyes were swimming, his face twisted to try to hold in the tears.

"Cold," he managed. "Making my eyes run."

"Daddy, don't cry," she said, flinging her arms around his neck, and they stood in the middle of the park and hugged and hugged until Juliet felt the snow start to fall on her face again.

Chapter 29

The dull days between Christmas and New Year were always Juliet's least favorite part of the holiday season, and this year each day seemed to drag on twice as long as normal.

The hours were unmarked by comforting chunks of weekday television, just floundering among *What time is it now?* Harry Potter films that merged into one wizardy mass, and the weather neither warmed up nor snowed again. It felt like Sunday afternoon for hours and hours at a stretch, with New Year looming up at the end, and she really wasn't looking forward to that.

New Year had been her and Ben's special night. They'd never gone in for Christmas as much as New Year; as teenagers, New Year's Eve had been the night everyone planned for, making sneaky phone calls to arrange rendezvous during the queen's speech and buying glittery party outfits at the sales. After their friends went off to university or to jobs in the city, the old gang had met up again in the town center for quite a few years, doing the same lap of the pubs and bars, ending up on the bandstand in the park for the bells.

Since they'd been married, Ben and Juliet had saved New Year's Eve for themselves as a reward for shuttling back and forth between his parents, her parents, and various relatives and social events. Juliet cooked something really special, and then they wrapped themselves up to sit outside to drink the bottle of champagne that Ben always got from the nice couple with the complicated lawn that only Ben could get to go into stripes.

This year, Juliet knew she'd have to face it on her own, and it filled her with dread and determination in equal measure.

Louise and Peter invited her round for dinner, of course, but she turned them down as politely as she could. They were in some strange second-honeymoon phase, with lots of private smiling that Juliet was pleased to see but still didn't really want to partake in, as a bystander. The only place she'd have considered going for New Year was next door, to whatever out-of-control hooley the Kellys would have thrown, but they were still away, as proved by the reluctant presence of Smokey in her kitchen every night.

Other people's pets were what got Juliet through the drab days to New Year's Eve, as she trudged round the slushy paths with Hector, Minton, Coco, and a couple of other regulars, temporarily ejected from their houses on account of allergic relatives. They were always pleased to see her, always happy to flail madly across the park in pursuit of a ball, and always happy to collapse in a heap when she got home.

Juliet let all three of them join her on the sofa for an afternoon doze. When she woke up, disoriented by the heavy breathing around her, Minton's head was jammed up against her ear and Coco—now less tubby but still regrettably flatulent—had broken wind. Even so, Juliet felt a low-level happiness that she hadn't felt in a very long time. Her first thought wasn't sadness; it was an unambitious sort of contentment.

To ward off any last-minute invitations from Louise on New Year's Eve itself, Juliet volunteered to drive her parents to Birmingham Airport to catch their afternoon flight.

"You're *sure* you don't mind?" Diane asked for the twelfth time, leaning forward from the backseat of their car. She was wearing her sunny Australia clothes underneath her snowbound Longhampton zip-up padded coat, ready to emerge like a sequined Per Una butterfly on the plane. She'd never been one for color before, but when Juliet had taken her shopping for holiday outfits, she'd picked up floral after head-spinning floral, and looked so happy while she tried them on that Juliet had to wipe away a tear when she wasn't looking.

"It's a bit late now, Mum," said Juliet, glancing in the mirror. "We're on the motorway, in case you hadn't noticed."

"No, I mean about taking Coco. And looking after the house. You will check the electricity? They were saying at the book group that even if you turn everything off, there's still a risk." The words were old-school Diane, but she wasn't putting her whole back into the worry. Juliet noted that she hadn't even mentioned the possibility of floods or squatters.

"Stop it, Diane," said Eric, calmly. "Louise is going to do her bit. And if the house burns down, Juliet, we'll bring our camper van back and live on your back lawn."

"We will do . . . Oh, Eric. Don't." She sat back down, then leaned forward again. "You've got Coco's folder? With the vet's details in? And you'll carry on taking her to weigh-ins, won't you? I don't want her to miss out on her gold lead when George says she's done so well . . ."

"*Yes*, Mum."

"Good girl. Oh dear, I'll miss my Coco." Juliet saw her mother's lip wobbling in the rearview mirror. "Will you do Skype? So she can see me?"

"And we'll ring you too, love," said Eric, patting her knee.

Juliet grinned. It was sweet, the excitement buzzing from the pair of them. Even her dad had put his new "traveling trousers" on, with pockets for all his bits and pieces. Yes, they were starting to look a bit old, with their gray hair and thicker glasses, but at the same time, Juliet had never seen them looking so young either.

She didn't think she'd ever loved them with such intensity as when she waved them off from their boarding gate.

By the time she got home, it was too late to wander around the shops and too early to start making herself some supper.

After some desultory tidying up, Juliet found herself staring at the bedroom walls, with Lorcan's paint chips in her hands and Minton watching her from the doorway.

Now both the front and back sitting rooms, the hall, and the bathroom were done, and the kitchen was a project all on its own; the bedroom was the next obvious room to tackle, but they'd managed to avoid it, because even mentioning the word *bed* felt weird. *Bed* space. *Waking up* to different colors. Silly, when they were so easy about everything else, but it had made Juliet feel awkward, and Lorcan had seemed a bit uncomfortable too.

Standing in the dying light of the year, though, Juliet was seized with a fizzing desire to get on with it. New Year, new start. She couldn't do much about the wall with the crack, but she could take down the curtains and clear the surfaces ready for action. If half of it was done already, it would cut down the time they'd have to spend in here.

Lorcan had drilled her well in the importance of preparation in quality decorating, and she worked methodically through his list, carefully taking down her wall of photographs, cleaning the room, and shrouding her bedroom furniture in dropcloths while the sun set outside and the radio moved from afternoon show to drive time to preparty buildup.

It felt good to be doing something physical, wearing herself out like Minton racing after his ball. Juliet wanted to go to sleep tonight, to sleep and sleep, and then wake up in the New Year, all the midnight regrets and agonizing over while she dreamed. Whenever her brain slid sideways to her parents, napping on each other's shoulders in premium economy, or loved-up Louise and Peter, getting dressed up to go out for a grown-up dinner, Juliet scrubbed harder and focused on cleaning all the cobwebs out of her room.

After a while, Juliet's arms started to ache pleasantly. The bedroom wasn't big, but it was dominated by a lovely window, looking out onto the garden. The daylight seemed to linger longer, reflected in a ghostly sheen from the unbroken blanket of snow outside.

Juliet gave herself a break when it started to get dark. She felt she'd earned it.

All her daily things were now in the newly decorated spare room, and what she didn't need she'd put in the wardrobe, out of the way. The room was clean, a blank canvas for the new year.

Good, she thought, and went downstairs to make herself a pot of tea.

Juliet was engrossed in a star-studded Poirot murder mystery and halfway through her second brownie when she realized that Minton wasn't in his usual spot on the sofa.

Cozy television viewing wasn't the same without him, so she

put her plate down, out of Coco's reach, and got up. "Minton? Minton!"

After a brief pause, she heard a guilty scuttle of claws on bare wood from the landing upstairs. Juliet knew that scuttle. It was the Scuttle of Stealthy Stealing.

"Minton, what have you got?" she called out, prepared to forgive whatever he'd nicked. It was so long since he'd chewed anything, and it was Christmas, after all.

"So long as it's not poisonous," she added, jogging up the stairs to find him. "I'm not taking you to the vet's on New Year's Eve. I can't afford you to be *that* ill. Where are you?"

She heard movements in her bedroom and pounced inside. But when she saw what was hanging from his mouth, her good mood evaporated.

"What have you done?" Juliet stared at the remnants of cloth hanging out of Minton's mouth.

It was Ben's green checked shirt. His favorite one, the one she'd kept hidden in the wardrobe, so precious that she didn't even use it for Grief Hour because, masochistically, she never wanted to get used to it. The green shirt was the one thing that she imagined still smelled, very faintly, of Ben; he'd worn it the day before he died, then thrown it in the laundry basket, too late for Juliet's weekly wash. She'd slept with it for weeks, inhaling his familiar scent and crying into its overwashed softness. This was the last piece of clothing that had traces of Ben on it. And now it was ripped and covered in slobber and hanging from Minton's jaws.

"Oh, no," she breathed, and then, as she took in the room properly, the full impact of what Minton had done hit her.

She must have left the wardrobe door ajar when she put her stuff in, because he'd got the box of Ben's belongings open and worked his way through like a crazed sales shopper, high on the smell of his master. He'd chewed the shaving brush she'd given Ben for Christmas. He'd had a go at his last pair of socks. Ben's wallet was now perforated with teeth marks. But the shirt was the worst loss.

I'll never be able to curl up in that again when I want to be near him, thought Juliet, and she felt sick.

Minton gazed up at her from the bed. His eyes were guilty, but he didn't drop the shirt from his mouth.

"Drop!" Juliet commanded shrilly.

Minton didn't respond. It was as if he couldn't bring himself to let go of Ben's smell now that he'd found it after so long. He backed away slowly on the bed, shirt between his teeth, keeping his gaze fixed on her as his tail swept from side to side. The wag of shame.

There were shreds of shirt scattered over the dropcloth already. One button was lying on the floor, where it had been chewed and spat out.

"Minton! Drop! Drop it now! Now!" repeated Juliet. Her voice was metallic, scary. It sounded harsh even to her own ears, and Minton looked terrified.

"Give that to me!" Juliet barely knew what she was doing, so powerful was the rage boiling inside her. She grabbed for the shirt and yanked so hard that the little terrier went flying off the bed. The force of her effort made her stumble backward herself, and she crashed against the chest of drawers, cracking her skull against the side.

Tears sprang to her eyes as the first sharp wave of physical pain hit her, closely followed by the duller pain of Ben's ruined possessions. Juliet shoved her hands into her hair, praying she wouldn't feel blood.

She closed her eyes and heard the rattle of claws as Minton scrabbled his way out of the room and down the stairs as fast as he could. Faster than was safe for him.

He's running away from me, she thought, sick with shame. *I've hurt Minton.*

But then she looked down at the precious shirt, shredded and ruined beyond repair, and couldn't stop herself from crying. *Again*, she thought. *When am I ever going to stop bloody weeping?*

The tears poured out of her, and at some point in the sobs, Juliet became vaguely aware that this was crying in the same vein as throwing up, or passing out—it was her body reacting, not her. These tears were more about hurting her dog, and missing her mum and dad, and generally feeling flat after Christmas, and being alone for New Year, just when she'd got used to having mates next door. It was about more than some stupid shirt of Ben's. There was room in her life to get upset about more than just Ben. Which was almost a good thing.

You've got other shirts, said the voice in her head. *This one isn't more important than poor* Minton.

Juliet sobbed almost happily until there were no tears left and the light had gone completely from the room. She felt quite calm and cleansed, but sadness still hung around her. It was New Year, and she was on her own.

Minton hadn't come up to find her. Neither had the other two.

They were probably hiding in a cupboard, she thought guiltily. Hiding from the evil dog-sitter and her inexplicable rage.

She turned the alarm clock round on the chest of drawers; it was a quarter to nine.

This time last year . . . Juliet started to think, then stopped herself.

Actually, she could barely remember last year. She'd been in a Xanax-and-sherry haze. *Don't turn into one of those women like Ben's mum*, she reminded herself. Wallowing up retrospective misery.

Still, a drink wasn't a bad idea. And a peace offering for Minton.

Juliet stumbled downstairs in the dark and went into the

kitchen. "Minton?" she called out, in her most conciliatory tone. "I'm sorry. Minton?"

There was no sign of Minton, but Coco and Hector were curled up on the kitchen sofa, his bushy beard tucked protectively over her solid haunch. They looked at her anxiously, as if she might fly at them too.

"It's okay," sighed Juliet. "Drama's over for tonight."

She got a tumbler out of the cupboard and poured herself a big glass of the jewel-like sloe gin Emer had given her for Christmas. It smelled like medicine, and Juliet took a big sip.

"Ahh," she said, automatically. The sweet liqueur burned down her throat and spread out through her veins like purple velvet. "That is very good stuff. I should probably have something to eat," she went on, opening the fridge and inspecting the uninspiring contents. There were still cling-filmed dishes from Boxing Day, the remnants of various pies and trifles her mother had forced on her.

"But to be honest with you, dogs," she finished, "I can't be bothered."

Juliet swung the fridge door shut and topped up her glass. Maybe Minton could have the leftover pie, as a treat. Now that she'd calmed down, Juliet was haunted by the pathetic image of him going so mad with delight at finding his master's long-lost smell, wanting to chew and lick and roll around in everything, that he simply forgot himself.

Minton was always so well behaved, so grateful for the second chance she and Ben had given him, that he was very careful not to do anything naughty. He'd never done anything wrong, for fear they'd tie him up and walk away from him too.

Juliet blinked hard. *Stop it*, she told herself. *Getting maudlin at New Year's for old people, not thirty-somethings. He'll come out when he's ready.*

She turned on the kitchen radio and curled up on the sofa next to Coco's comforting warmth, her glass and her phone within reach, but after half an hour, there was still no sign of the terrier.

"What are we going to do?" she asked Coco and Hector, ruffling their ears. "Cluedo? Charades? *Jools Holland's Hootenanny*?"

Hector licked her hand and Coco slumped her head against her knee in answer. Juliet reached for her phone. No messages.

I could text Lorcan, she thought. *Just to wish him Happy New Year before the networks get clogged up at midnight.* Her fingers hovered over the buttons.

She wondered where he was now. In a bar in Dublin, probably, laughing his easy dark laugh, sinking pints of Guinness in his jeans and some 1970s-band T-shirt. Surrounded by other curly-haired, sexy, Irish builder types. Probably playing pool, and winking at pretty girls . . .

Juliet frowned. Wasn't that just a Thin Lizzy video she was imagining? Anyway, Lorcan was at a gig, so chances were he'd be all sweaty and euphoric, bouncing up and down at the front playing air guitar.

I'll text Emer instead, she thought, and spent twenty minutes composing a message that didn't sound as if she were sitting on her own in an empty house with three dogs.

As soon as she pressed send, Juliet wondered if it had been a good idea to write, *Love from Minton, Hector, and Coco.* Or to refer to the sloe gin.

She rolled her eyes at herself. This wasn't going according to plan. But at least she wasn't sobbing in a corner over her wedding album. Scaring the dogs, getting tipsy, and starting to decorate the bedroom was a definite step up from that.

Juliet watched the *Glee* DVD Louise had given her for Christmas and grazed her way slowly through one of the boxes of chocolates she'd been given by grateful clients.

An hour later, Minton slunk in, his tail between his legs, and crawled under the sofa. He only ever went under there during thunderstorms, when he was scared. Juliet patted the space between her and Coco and coaxed him to join them, but when she reached down to pick him up, he growled at her.

Chastened, Juliet pulled her hand away and left him alone.

She was in the kitchen making some porridge for herself to soak up the gin when she heard a noise. What was that?

Juliet turned off the radio to hear better, and froze.

A scary retching, hacking sound. Then Coco's anxious bark.

She turned the hob off and hurried back into the sitting room.

Minton was on the floor, retching, his back arched in effort. There were four big pools of vomit on the rug, watery and full of partially digested shaving brush, dog food, and, oh no, buttons. His lips were pulled back from his jaws in a horrible rictus, and Juliet saw to her horror that his gums were pale. Coco and Hector looked on anxiously.

"Minton! Are you okay?" She couldn't stop herself. "Of course you're not okay. Oh God. Oh God."

She knelt down beside him and shoved her fingers into his mouth, trying to dislodge whatever was in there, but she couldn't feel anything apart from his slippery tongue. Minton looked up at her, his eyes white and rolling. It looked as though he'd been trying for some time.

"I'm sorry!" she wailed. "I can't get it!"

Juliet probed around some more, but all she succeeded in doing was temporarily cutting off Minton's air.

She sat up. Her head felt thick and stupid with the sloe gin, and she struggled to clear it.

What were you meant to do with choking dogs? The book.

Where was that book she'd got, the dog encyclopedia that was meant to have first aid?

Juliet ran through to the sitting room, searching the boxes marked *Books*. Her hands were trembling as she yanked at the parcel tape, one eye still on Minton in the kitchen. He didn't seem to be choking, just desperately trying to sick something up, but he looked weak, and every effort seemed more feeble.

She opened box after box until she came to the right one. Her fingers wouldn't flip through the pages properly, and she had to keep herself from dropping it.

"Hang on, Minton," she called out desperately, as she searched the index for *Choking*. "Hang on. I'm going to sort it out."

Finally, she found the page on retching. Her eyes scanned the possible causes—there were lots—but the advice was in bold. *Call the vet if your dog is vomiting repeatedly*, it said in bold. *Internal blockages can be fatal, and dogs will quickly dehydrate trying to rid themselves of the obstruction.*

Juliet dialed the surgery number with wobbling fingers. In all the time she'd had Minton, she'd only ever been to the vet for routine boosters and checks. He was hardy, like Ben. Never needed the doctor. She didn't even know whether there would be anyone there on New Year's Eve at—she checked her watch—a quarter to eleven.

Please pick up, please pick up, she prayed, chewing the hangnail on her spare hand until it stung. *Please, please, please . . .*

After ten agonizing rings, someone answered. "Hello, Longhampton vet emergency line."

Juliet recognized the voice—it was Megan, the Australian veterinary nurse. She worked at the rescue where Diane volunteered and was the only person Diane knew who could make Coco roll over for a biscuit.

"Please help me," she blurted out. "I think my dog's eaten

something. He's retching, but I can't feel anything blocking his throat. I don't know what to do!"

"Okay, step one, calm down," said Megan. She was always very calm. "You're not the first person to ring up with a dog who's helped himself to the Christmas tree this week, and we haven't lost any of them. So far. Step two, do you know what he's eaten?"

"No." Juliet glanced over at Minton. His eyes were shut and he was panting. Then he pulled back his lips and tried to vomit, but couldn't. "He was chewing a load of stuff earlier—it could be a button; it could be a bit of shaving brush."

She pushed away lurid images of what shards of plastic might be tearing Minton's insides.

"How long's he been trying to throw up? Is there any vomit?"

"Yes, there's a lot. He . . . he went and hid when I shouted at him for chewing Ben's things, and that was several hours ago . . ." Juliet's voice cracked, but she forced herself not to cry. She owed it to Minton now not to lose it.

"Is that Juliet?" asked Megan. "And Minton?"

"Yes."

"Oh, *no*." Megan sounded more concerned for her than Minton. "This is just what you don't need on New Year's Eve. Listen, Juliet, the best thing you can do is to bring him in right away. I'll tell George you're coming and he can check Minton over. He might be dehydrated, and that's not good for a little guy his size." Megan sounded concerned. "And are *you* all right? I know it's upsetting, but he'll be fine."

"My dog's choking to death!"

"Not yet, Juliet," said Megan firmly. Juliet wiped her nose and hung up. "It's going to be okay," she said to Minton. He was shaking, the tremors clearly visible through his thin skin. "We're going to go and see Dr. George in the van . . ."

She wobbled as she went to kneel down, and the realization

hit her—she was way over the limit to drive. She'd had at least three shots of gin. Big home shots too, and on an empty stomach.

It's okay, she thought automatically. *Ben can drive and I'll—*

Juliet's hand flew to her mouth as panic swept through her. There was no Ben. Just her. Minton was seriously ill and she'd trapped them both in the house, with half a bottle of sloe gin.

The panic was followed by a secondary wave of self-loathing. How could she be so stupid? So selfish?

She gripped the kitchen table and stood up. *Think logically. Can't drive the van. No buses. Taxis—need to get a taxi.*

Juliet crouched next to Minton, stroking his ear as she dialed. She couldn't get through to the first two firms in the book, the third was booked up all night, and the fourth had an hour's wait for the next cab.

Minton was gasping now, but still pathetically licking her hand, trying to apologize for what he'd done. Juliet could barely stop the tears running down her face as she flicked through her phone, trying to find someone who'd be in, someone sober. Someone who wouldn't mind being rung on New Year's Eve by a recent widow probably wanting to howl at them about being alone.

Mum and Dad—she didn't even know which country they'd be flying over now.

Emer—no, she'd be in New York now too.

Louise. Juliet speed-dialed Louise, but the phone went straight to voice mail. So did Peter's. Oh, no. They'd be in the restaurant by now, holding hands and talking about The Future.

"Oh God!" wailed Juliet. Minton pawed ineffectually at his belly and let out a long, painful sigh. "Not you, darling, sorry . . ."

Kim's phone was off—as it always was when she wasn't working.

Michael.

Juliet looked at the number in her phone address book, and Michael's capable face rose in her mind's eye. She hadn't seen

Michael in person since that last awkward meeting with Damson, but there'd been a couple of notes recently, left with the walking money, and she'd scribbled a chatty reply.

He'd got that photograph out of the exhibition and round to her house in about ninety minutes. Michael was exactly the sort of gallant chap who'd gallop to her rescue now. If he wasn't with his baby daughter. Or some new, less complicated girlfriend.

Juliet's stomach twisted. She had promised Louise that she would leave that can of worms well alone; it was business only. If she called Michael, begging for his help, it might just tip them back into friendly contact. He might think it was an excuse. She might be so grateful she'd accept his offer of a drink.

Who was more important to her? Minton, or Louise?

Why do I always have to decide these things when I'm on my own? she howled to herself.

The phone vibrated in her hand, as if it were impatient with her.

Juliet pressed the pickup button without thinking. "Hello?"

"Hey, Juliet! How're you doing on this final night of the year?"

The voice was familiar, soothing. Relief spread through Juliet like a balloon expanding in her chest, and thoughts of Michael, Louise, and anyone else were shoved aside. "Lorcan!" she nearly cried. "I so wish you were here right now!"

"Why? Is there a party round at yours, or have your fuses blown again?"

Juliet sobbed and laughed at the same time, and it turned into a painful cough. "No, I'm having a disaster."

"Worse than the fuses? Have Louise and Peter landed you with the babysitting?"

"No, I'm serious. Minton's choking on something, he's been sick, I need to get him to the vet's, and I can't drive the van because I've been on Emer's sloe gin all night. And there are no taxis, and everyone's out." She paused for breath, because her voice was getting higher and higher. "Do you know anyone who could come and get me? Has Alec got a magic car service or something?"

"Leave it with me," said Lorcan, his voice suddenly serious. "You stay right there, and don't panic. Make yourself a cup of coffee. Keep an eye on the little fella. I'll call you back."

There was some noise in the background, but Juliet couldn't make out whether it was a bar or the gig or what.

"But, Lorcan, aren't you in . . ." she began, but he'd rung off.

She sank back onto her heels, cradling Minton in her arms.

"It's going to be okay," she said. "Hang on."

Because she didn't know what else to do, Juliet turned the radio back on in the kitchen. It was playing "The Boys Are Back in Town," and she felt a strange sense that the house itself was trying to make her feel as if she weren't so alone.

Hurry up, Lorcan, she thought fiercely, as Minton's breathing became even more labored. *Hurry up.*

Chapter 30

Five minutes later, her phone rang again, and it was Lorcan.

"Are you ready to go?" he asked, without any preamble. "Coat on? Minton ready?"

"Yes!" Juliet started to hunt for her shoes and her coat, and Hector leaped off the sofa, thinking they were off for a last walk. "No, you stay there," she snapped, tugging on a trainer. Coco didn't move.

"Got your keys? Your purse?"

"Yes." Juliet had wrapped Minton up in a throw from the sofa and picked him up gently now, her phone clamped against her shoulder. "You two have a nap and listen to the radio," she commanded, closing the kitchen door on them. "What's happening?"

The doorbell rang and she hurried down the hall with Minton in her arms. "Don't tell me you've flown here," she said, only half joking. "What was it? Floo powder? Or a Tardis?"

"Neither," said Lorcan, as she opened the door to find an enormous bearded man on the step. "It's my mate Sean, from the DIY superstore. He's going to take you to the vet's."

It was the most ludicrous reaction in the circumstances, Juliet knew, but she felt a tug of disappointment that it wasn't Lorcan himself standing there.

Sean smiled, revealing several missing teeth. The remaining ones gleamed out of his beard. He looked like a Hell's Angel Santa. Terrifying but kindly at the same time.

"He runs a homeless soup kitchen at New Year," Lorcan explained. "Sean's the only guy I know who'll be sober by now. Say hello, he won't bite."

"Hi, Sean," said Juliet, then shook herself. "Listen, we don't have time for chitchat," she said to Lorcan.

"Good, because you won't get a lot of chitchat out of him at the best of times. Call me when you get there and let me know what's going on," he said. "And give Minton a scratch from his uncle Lorcan, won't you?"

"I will." Juliet felt herself being bundled, gently, toward yet another builder's van. "Lorcan, if I've left it too late, I'll never . . ."

"He's a survivor, is Minton," said Lorcan. "So are you. You just hang in there, both of you, right?"

Juliet started to thank him again, but Sean fired up the Transit and she couldn't hear anything above the roar of its ancient engine. Then they were lurching off down her road, past the box hedge where she'd secreted Ben's memorial bouquet just a couple of months ago, onto the deserted main road and through the night toward the vet's, Minton's fragile head laid on her chest like a baby's, and she forced herself to listen to his ragged breath.

George the vet was outside waiting for her, his broad frame silhouetted in the doorway, when Sean pulled up in a swirl of gravel.

"He's very weak," she said, as he marched up to the van and took the little dog from her arms.

"Bloody terriers," said George briskly. "Second only to Labradors for hoovering up the most unholy rubbish. How is Ten-Ton Tessie, by the way?"

"Do you mean Coco?" Diane had warned her that George was on the brutal side of brusque, but she'd always said it with an adoring sigh. Juliet could sort of see why: Despite his tetchy air, George was already feeling around Minton's mouth and throat with a mixture of tenderness and expertise.

"I do. Lovely girl. Awful plaque. Naughty owner. Right, I think we're going to have to get this chap in for an x-ray, I'm afraid. Can you come with me, please?"

Juliet turned to wave a grateful good-bye to Sean, then had to jog to keep up with George's long strides as he hurried back into the brightly lit reception area.

Megan was sitting at the desk, ready in her scrubs, and she gave Juliet a smile as George steamed past, barking instructions to her as he went.

"Wait here and we'll be with you as soon as we can," she said, and followed him out.

Juliet sank onto the nearest chair and stared at a poster about Drontal wormers.

Please don't let this New Year be as bad as last year, she thought. *I don't have many loved ones to lose at this rate.*

Juliet had never felt time pass so slowly as the ninety-five minutes that elapsed while Minton was in surgery.

George's wife came in after an hour to offer her some coffee, which she accepted gladly, and Megan popped her head round the door to let her know that they'd removed a selection of buttons and partly digested plastic shards, but George was having a bit of trouble rehydrating Minton and wasn't sure if he'd given himself a bit of poisoning. If she wanted to go home for the night, George's wife would give her a lift.

Juliet said no, as politely as she could, and insisted on staying until Minton was safely in the recovery unit.

She was dozing off when, at a quarter to two, bright lights dazzled the waiting room, and she blinked, startled. A car had pulled up right outside the window, and when the headlights went off, Juliet was left with dancing dark spots in front of her eyes.

Must be someone with an emergency, she thought, as the door was shoved open and a figure in a leather jacket appeared.

"Juliet? How's it going?" It was Lorcan. Anxious, stubbly, a bit whiffy, but there.

Juliet sprang to her feet, but the coffee, the tiredness, and the bright light made her wobble, and he reached out to stop her from knocking over a display of prescription cat food.

"Steady on," he said, tightening his arms around her as she buried her head in his shoulder. "What's happened? Is he out yet?"

Juliet couldn't speak. The relief of being held was too much for her. That, and the smell of Lorcan's leather jacket, and his other smell, the smell of him, so familiar from their hours of painting, and his showing her where to grout and file and plane. *He smells like home*, thought Juliet, out of nowhere, and it made her want to cry, from a bittersweet mingle of emotions.

She pulled herself away before the tears could come. Juliet was done with crying. Her eyes were already aching from this afternoon. She rubbed her nose with the back of her hand and tried not to let Lorcan see how overcome she was.

"He's on a drip," she said. "They're trying to rehydrate him. If he gets through the next hour, he'll be okay. If it weren't for you, sending Sean round, George says Minton . . . Well. The next hour's the important one."

Lorcan examined her face. He didn't need to ask, *What if he doesn't?*

"Right, then," he said, sitting himself down on a chair. "We'll be needing this while we wait." He offered her one of his earphones and withdrew a carton of orange juice and a Kit Kat from his jacket pocket. He patted the seat next to him. "You'll have to budge up a bit. And it's Free's *Greatest Hits*. I was listening to it on the way up. Makes me drive fast."

Juliet settled herself next to him, so close that his jacket squeaked. "You drove up? From Dublin?"

"Didn't go to Dublin in the end, went down to London instead." He pushed the earphone gently into her ear. "Wasn't drinking, because of having the car and being out with a mate who's just out of rehab, so I set off when I got your call, and the roads were pretty empty. And like I say, Paul Rodgers is da man for motorway driving."

"You drove back? And missed Big Ben? For me? Um, for Minton?"

"For both of you," said Lorcan. "Knew the little fella would need bringing home, and thought you'd need some company. Anyway, let the music take your mind off it."

Their heads were very close and Juliet was finding it hard to concentrate on the tinny sound of 1970s rock fizzing in her left ear, when she could smell Lorcan's skin. He smelled of old leather and soap.

Her mouth went dry as she noticed the soft skin around his Adam's apple, and the dark hairs that started in the hollow of his throat. The earphones were forcing her to look, while he stared straight ahead, drumming his fingers on his tight-jeaned leg.

"Lorcan, I know you said that—" she began, but he held up a finger to stop her.

"Ultimate guitar solo," he said, and closed his eyes to appreciate it.

This is weird, thought Juliet. *Chained by the ear to a man I—yes, okay—I think I really fancy, but with whom I get on better than any friend I've made since . . . well, Ben.* She knew it would be really easy to kiss Lorcan now, if she wanted to, but part of her held back. Did he want to? He was sitting very close to her and hadn't made a move. And she was scared of losing the friendship she'd started to rely on in her new life. How often did friends like that come along? Friends who'd drive up from London and organize taxis for your dog.

And the thought of kissing made her feel nervous, in a way she hadn't felt since school. The kiss she'd had with Michael didn't really count; it was just a gesture, an action she was almost looking at from outside. If she kissed Lorcan, it would be a messy, real mingling of lips and tongue and taste, and it made her shiver with fear and longing.

"I really missed you this week," she said, a bit too loud, on account of the earphone. "You and the Kellys, I mean. It was too quiet next door."

"Did you?" Lorcan turned and grinned. Even closer now, close enough to see the scratchy beginnings of his beard. He'd gone a few days without shaving for the holidays and it suited him. "I missed you."

"Did you?"

"Yeah. You and the dogs."

They gazed awkwardly at each other, noses almost touching. Then Lorcan's phone buzzed in his pocket.

"Ignore it," he said. "So, this week, was it very—"

The phone buzzed again and he tutted.

"Answer it," said Juliet, inches from his mouth. "It might be someone else with a sick animal who needs transport."

"Get out of here. I'm not Rolf Harris. I only do dog rescue for special cases."

It buzzed a third time, and then Juliet's phone pinged with a message too.

They both went to check them and the earphones yanked out of their ears and clattered against Lorcan's jacket.

"Ow," said Juliet, rubbing her ear. "And it was just Louise, wishing me Happy New Year. And Mum."

"Snap," said Lorcan. "Only mine was from Bono."

"Really?"

She looked up and Lorcan was grinning at her. "No. Only if Emer's sending out New Year's greetings on his behalf. Which I wouldn't put past her."

Juliet's smile hovered at half-mast as an unfamiliar longing swept through her. Lorcan was extraordinarily good-looking, even in the harsh strip lights of the waiting room. She really, really wanted to put her lips against those strong cheekbones and feel the roughness of his beard.

"You know what this means?" he said, arching an eyebrow.

"No, what?" said Juliet. She felt awkward, and teenage.

"It means . . . It's a new year! Happy New Year!" Lorcan crossed his arms in "Auld Lang Syne" and grabbed her hands. "May this year be full of happiness and new experiences and quality decoration. And friendship and new beginnings."

Juliet let him bounce her hands up and down. "And which are you hoping for?" she asked. "Friendship . . . or new beginnings?"

Lorcan stopped bouncing her hands and looked her straight in the eye. His own eyes were dark and a little wary, and for the first time that night, he seemed unsure of himself.

Juliet held her breath.

"Is it greedy . . . to hope for both?" he asked. "If we're both very careful about it?"

She shook her head, then nodded, unsure which was the right response for *Yes, please*, and the wariness left his face, to be replaced by a nervous pleasure.

Still holding Lorcan's hands in hers, for the first proper time since she was fifteen, Juliet leaned forward, closed her eyes, and deliberately kissed a man for the first time, right on the mouth.

Lorcan's lips moved slowly under hers and then parted, and his arms went over her head and around her waist, pulling her to him as he kissed her.

It didn't feel like kissing Ben. It was different. Not better or worse, but different. And Juliet knew that it was different because *she* was too: older, tougher, sadder, but her own self. A grown woman who could deal with sick dogs and wallpaper and relationships that might not be perfect.

Lorcan pulled back and rested his forehead on hers. He let out a long, low breath, as if he'd been holding it in for ages.

"Is this okay?" he whispered.

Juliet nearly laughed. "Okay? In what way? Are you looking for marks out of ten?"

"No! I mean, I know you don't feel ready for anything new, and I totally understand that, but . . ." He looked up, and Juliet melted at the intense look in his blue eyes. "I thought I needed to wait too. But I've wanted to do that for quite a long time."

"It's definitely okay," said Juliet. "More than okay." And she leaned in to kiss him again, reaching for his prickly jaw to pull him closer.

"Juliet, I've got some— Can you break that up, please? I don't care if it is New Year; this is a surgery, not a nightclub."

They sprang apart, like guilty teenagers. George was standing by the door in his blue surgical scrubs, pulling the latex gloves off.

"Thank you," he said. "Now, Minton's all stitched and stabilized and tucked up in the recovery ward, so there's really nothing more that we can do tonight. He should be fine by tomorrow afternoon, so if you want to drop by then to collect him . . ."

"Tomorrow?" said Lorcan. "New Year's Day?"

"Dogs don't do bank holidays or hangovers, do they?" George winked at Juliet. "As I'm sure you'll find out soon enough."

"That's fine," said Juliet. Sloe gin hangover or not, she could already see herself striding through the snow in the park, Lorcan's hand in hers, and her little pack of dogs running ahead, huffing their white breath in the crisp air. In her head, they were all heading up the hill toward the woods where the trees were covered in snow now, but where the fresh buds were already planning their spring escape.

Epilogue

The best time to plant cherry trees, according to Ben's battered old gardening manuals, was early spring, after a cold winter.

Juliet stood in the garden, watching Lorcan digging the hole, and felt warm inside, even though it was still chilly enough for hats. They were all watching Lorcan digging—her, Louise, Peter, and Toby. Emer was supposed to be making them coffee with her flashy cappuccino machine, but she'd been gone for a while.

"Shouldn't I be using one of those commemorative shovels?" he asked, between gasps. The ground was still quite hard. "Aren't they compulsory for memorial plantings?"

"Is a new shovel not good enough?" demanded Louise. "Come on. We polished it and everything."

"It's perfect," said Juliet. "And so are these."

She was still admiring the cherry tree saplings, now little trees in their black containers. It was hard to imagine that one day they'd be big enough to spill blossoms over the road like Ben's favorite tree on the hill, but they would. Eventually. Given time.

"I still can't believe you grew them, Lou," she said.

"I didn't grow them, Ben did. He set them up, and grafted them. I just helped them along."

"Same difference." She squeezed her sister's arm. "Why didn't you tell me? I can't believe you kept it so quiet!"

Louise glanced sideways and made a rueful face. "I didn't want to jinx it," she admitted. "I wanted to make sure they were going to make it first."

"But they have," said Peter. He was sitting on a bench with Toby, helping him throw a ball for Minton, who was humoring them by bringing it back. Coco was watching, in a grandmotherly fashion. "Let's not get morbid here. It's a lovely idea, this memorial route thing. Where are the others going?"

"First one here, then the next down by the canal, one in the park, and then one on the way up to Coneygreen Woods."

"And I'm not digging all the holes," gasped Lorcan. "Before you even suggest it."

When Louise had told Juliet about the saplings waiting in her greenhouse, Juliet's first thought was to make a little orchard of cherry trees along her back garden. Louise had pointed out, practical as ever, that it wouldn't leave a lot of room for grass, but she couldn't bear the thought of getting rid of the spares.

It had been Louise's idea to plant them along her dog-walking route, so she'd be able to follow a path of blossoms with Minton once a year, and then it had been Louise who'd generously offered to twist some arms in the council planning department to have them planted in the spots that Juliet chose.

Louise had done some really kind things, thought Juliet. Kindness that she'd managed to ignore, out of childishness.

She gave her another squeeze.

"What was that for?" asked Louise.

"For sorting out the bathroom. Buying all that stuff and getting Lorcan to fit it." She raised her inquiring expression to include him. He was as much behind it as them. "Why didn't you tell me about that either?" she asked. "Or was I just being dumb?"

"You were . . . in a difficult place," said Louise, diplomatically. "You kept going on about wanting to do everything yourself, and Mum didn't want to make you feel we were crowding you any more than we already were."

Juliet knew she was being tactful from the guarded look on Peter's face. It was only now that she was emerging into something approaching normality that she could see how hard she'd made it for her family. And yet they'd stuck it out, hovering protectively on the periphery of her life—Dad mowing the lawn, Mum dropping Coco off, Louise ordering ceramic tiles.

Lorcan painting away in silence, while she went on and on as if she were the only one with a broken heart.

Thank God he'd had the patience to stick with her.

"You were being a little bit dumb." Lorcan smiled. "I'd like to find this magic lorry that manages to lose an entire bathroom suite with matching tiles. Maybe it's got gold and silver on it too. There!" He stuck his shovel into the ground. "Done."

"Are we ready?" asked Peter. "Do you want to call Emer?"

"She might need a hand with the coffees," said Juliet. "Can you pop next door and help her?"

"No problem. Don't plant without me!"

"Come!" said Toby, holding out his hand, and Peter reached down to take it. They walked up the garden together, the picture of father-and-son cuteness.

"That's so adorable," said Juliet. "It's good to see you two getting on."

"We're getting there," said Louise. "Peter's working four long days and taking Friday off, so we're sharing the childcare a bit. And we're doing a course together at the college, one night a week. Introduction to pottery. We're both useless. Dad would be so proud."

"And is it . . . helping?" Juliet didn't want to go into details, even if Lorcan was pretending to tug out some weeds.

Louise smiled and nodded. She looked like a totally different woman when she smiled. "It's helping a lot. We've got a lot to talk about."

"Good," said Juliet, feeling warm again.

A distant screech announced the arrival of the Kelly deputation from next door. Roisin and Florrie headed it, playing their recorders like court trumpeters, followed by Spike and Salvador, and Emer bearing a tray of steaming coffee mugs.

Peter was leading Toby a safe distance behind, as far out of harm's way as was polite.

Louise looked horrified. "That's so dangerous!" she started. "They could fall and . . ."

"Seriously, Lou, that's not the half of it. You want to see what they can do if they get hold of that shovel." She waved at Emer, who was wearing a floaty selection of scarves in celebration. "Hello!"

Minton and Coco galloped over to greet them, nearly causing the recorder trumpeters to fall over. Louise had to suppress a yell.

"Hello!" yelled Emer. "Thanks for waiting!"

"Wouldn't do it without you." Juliet had asked Lorcan to dig a hole near the fence, so that the Kellys would have a share of the magnificent foaming blossoms too, come springtime. Not to mention the cherries themselves in the summer.

And that was the whole point. Ben might be gone, and they might not have started a family tree of their own, but he'd left this tree for her to share with her family, her neighbors, the families who came to live in Myrtle Villa long after Juliet had grown old and gone herself. Every year, for a week or so, there'd be that life-affirming explosion of nature fizzing in abundance, ridiculously generous and spectacular. It didn't last long, but it would come again next year. And the year after, and the year after that.

Tears came to Juliet's eyes, but they were happy tears.

Lorcan saw her blinking and stepped over at once, slinging his arm around her shoulder. The gesture was friendly, but she knew he'd been watching her with that protective love that seemed to grow slowly each day, as they each dismantled their barriers.

"Ready?" he said, softly.

Juliet took a deep breath and nodded. As Emer noisily marshaled everyone into some song the kids wanted to sing to give the tree a good start in its new home, Juliet picked up the first sapling, shook the earth off its roots, and began to plant it in the soil, bedding it in with her hands. She pulled the freshly turned soil in over it, and Minton sniffed around, tasting the strange new smells churned up by Lorcan's spade.

This cherry tree has only just started to grow, she thought, as she pulled her little dog in to her side. *Like me.*